MW00615873

BATMAN

RESURRECTION

BATMAN
RESURRECTION

JOHN JACKSON MILLER

BATMAN CREATED BY
BOB KANE WITH BILL FINGER

RANDOM HOUSE WORLDS
NEW YORK

Copyright © 2024 DC & WBEI.

 BATMAN and all related characters and elements
© & ™ DC and Warner Bros. Entertainment Inc.
WB SHIELD: © & ™ WBEI. (s24)

Published in the United States by Random House Worlds,
an imprint of Random House, a division of
Penguin Random House LLC, New York.

RANDOM HOUSE is a registered trademark, and RANDOM HOUSE WORLDS
and colophon are trademarks of Penguin Random House LLC.

Library of Congress Cataloging-in-Publication Data
Names: Miller, John Jackson, author.
Title: Batman: resurrection / John Jackson Miller.
Description: First edition. |
New York: Random House Worlds, 2024. | Series: Batman ; 1
Identifiers: LCCN 2024023177 (print) | LCCN 2024023178 (ebook) |
ISBN 9780593871904 (hardcover ; acid-free paper) |
ISBN 9780593871911 (ebook)
Subjects: LCSH: Batman (Fictitious character)—Fiction. |
LCGFT: Superhero fiction. | Detective and mystery fiction. | Novels.
Classification: LCC PS3613.I53858 B38 2024 (print) |
LCC PS3613.I53858 (ebook) | DDC 813/.6—dc23/eng/20240531
LC record available at https://lccn.loc.gov/2024023177
LC ebook record available at https://lccn.loc.gov/2024023178

Printed in the United States of America on acid-free paper

randomhousebooks.com

2 4 6 8 9 7 5 3 1

First Edition

Book design by Edwin A. Vazquez

To Tim Burton,
Michael Keaton, Jack Nicholson, Kim Basinger,

Michael Gough, Robert Wuhl, Pat Hingle,

Billy Dee Williams, Sam Hamm, Warren Skaaren,

Benjamin Melniker, Michael Uslan, Danny Elfman,
and all those who inspired me in 1989—
and 2 the memory of Prince

PROLOGUE

SO MUCH TO DO . . .
AND SO LITTLE TIME

*T*HERE'S GOT TO BE *a better way to read a map!*

Karlo Babić lowered his map and squinted up at the street sign, barely visible. Someone had knocked out the streetlight—or shot it out. In this neighborhood, there was no telling. The sun was about to set, but nobody in this part of Gotham City ever laid eyes on it after three anyway. The buildings were too tall. Karlo had moved to the city years ago and still had never gotten his bearings. It was worse when he was in a hurry—like now.

Culver and Klebbs. But which way on Klebbs is Culver?

A beer truck whisked past, splashing through water puddled by the afternoon rain. It soaked Karlo and map alike.

"Thanks, pal!" Angrily, he shook the crumpled sheet. *There's got to be a better way to find an address!*

He glimpsed at his watch. *Two hours to showtime.* He'd have to ask someone. Preferably a cop—but the last time one of those had been in this neighborhood, he was probably riding a horse. And Karlo didn't think it was smart to ask one when he was headed to make a deal with what could be a—

There! Karlo spotted what he was looking for ahead and threw the map to the ground. One more piece of litter wasn't going to make a difference here, and time was wasting. He dashed toward the corner.

Culver was barely an alley, in either direction. Another choice—

but a simple one. He picked the more dangerous-looking one and hurried down it.

A curly-haired man emerged from a doorway without a door. "Where's the fire?"

Karlo stopped cold, and without thinking, took a step back. Someone else might not have. The punk wore a dirty cap and a single earring—was it a tooth, a claw, a white banana? He didn't appear to be armed. Karlo was taller and bulkier, but he wasn't wired for violence—not the real kind, anyway. And around here, it was safe to assume this character wasn't alone.

He wasn't, though the individual who emerged next from the doorway was even less imposing. A scrawny guy in a neck brace, carrying a gym bag. He saw Karlo and turned immediately to go back inside.

The first punk barked at him. "Get back here, Eddie!"

"Oh!" Hearing the name, Karlo reached into his pocket and produced a crumpled sheet of paper. "I'm looking for Eddie and—are you Nick?"

"Guilty," the earring guy said. Once the mawkish Eddie reappeared, Nick sized Karlo up. "You don't look like you're in the market for what we've got. You a cop?"

"What?" Karlo looked around, flustered. "No!"

"Then who sent you?"

"I called the number." Karlo opened the sheet. "There was a flyer—"

Nick smiled at Eddie. "Y'see? Advertising works."

His injured partner stammered a response. "Yeah. *Ad-ad-advertising.*"

It was the first peep that Karlo had heard from Eddie—and it was drowned out by a loud mechanical clang from somewhere up the street. Eddie nearly jumped out of his shoes in response. His bloodshot eyes darted in one direction, and then another.

Karlo was befuddled. The person he'd spoken to on the phone had specified this meeting place, but Eddie seemed more frightened of the area than he was. "Is he all right?"

Nick shrugged. "Don't mind him. Somebody put him in the hospital."

"*Ba-ba-ba—*" Eddie stammered, almost involuntarily.

Nick spun and clapped his hand over Eddie's mouth. "Don't say it! We don't say that word!"

"Don't say what?" Karlo asked.

"Don't mind him. He hallucinates." Nick gripped Eddie's scratchy face more tightly. "Now shut up. *Shut. Up.*"

The smaller man squirmed but went silent. But as soon as Nick released him and faced Karlo, Eddie blurted out, "*Batman!*"

"Where?" Nick said, just as jumpy. Realizing no one was about, he let out a deep breath.

Karlo looked from one punk to the other. "What, you met Batman? For real?"

Nick calmed down. "Yeah. Attacked us both—cops tried to get us on armed robbery, but they couldn't hold us."

Karlo found that hard to believe. He'd assumed Batman was just another stunt to sell newspapers. Nobody had ever taken a picture of him. But it didn't matter. Karlo looked down at the gym bag. He reached toward it. "Is that it? I need it bad!"

Nick waved him off. "Hold on. Gonna need to see some cash here."

Karlo started to go for his wallet—only to flinch. "I'm . . . not sure."

"Relax," Nick said. "We ain't gonna steal your money. We don't do that no more."

"No, no more," Eddie said. "We're honest bus—" He spent another ten seconds on the word *businessmen,* long enough to drive Nick to distraction.

"Give me that," Nick said, yanking the gym bag away from his partner. He pivoted toward a garbage can that still had its lid. That served as a makeshift counter as he unzipped the bag. "Take a look at the merch. But if you say no, we've got a dozen other buyers."

Karlo stepped over and looked inside. He couldn't believe it. "This is the good stuff?"

"You bet."

Karlo reached inside and pulled out one container after another, squinting at them in the waning light. Lipstick tubes. Boxes of mustache and hair dye. Blusher compacts. "This is amazing. What did you do, clean out a perfume counter?"

Eddie squeaked a response. "No!" He moved forward, trying to appeal to Karlo. "We didn't take nothin'."

"Quiet!" Nick shoved Eddie away before looking back at Karlo and the goods. "What's it to you how we got it? What's important is *where* we got it. Every bit of it is imported."

From out of state is good, Karlo thought. *Out of the country is better.*

One week ago, a crazed character called The Joker had started tainting consumer products with something bad—Smylex, he'd called it—and it *did things* to people. Karlo didn't understand how it worked; he was years past his last science class and he did lousy in those anyway. Whatever it was caused seizures accompanied by uncontrollable laughter, before freezing facial muscles into a smiling rictus at the moment of death.

Karlo hadn't been watching when a broadcaster had died on air from exposure, but neither good taste nor respect for their lost colleague had prevented Action News from rerunning the footage again and again. It had sent Gothamites into a full-fledged panic. But where others were searching for answers during "Gotham's shopping nightmare," to use the term a beleaguered newscaster had used just an hour ago, Karlo was simply searching for cosmetics that could be trusted.

And he wasn't sure about these. He looked at one item after another. A lot of it was unlabeled. "Safe stuff's impossible to get. How did you—?"

"We got it from a guy who knows a guy," Nick replied. "Dude said he had a truck in from Central City."

That was reasonably far away, Karlo thought. "Selling makeup isn't illegal. Why did you ask if I was a cop?"

"Again with the questions!" Nick yanked the bag back and closed it.

Eddie piped up. "It's not *sto-sto-stolen*. Don't tell the Bat!"

Nick whipped off his cap and struck Eddie with it. "I told you to stop saying that!" He put his hat back on and glared at Karlo. "We're on the straight and narrow now. Do you want any of this stuff or not?"

Karlo looked at his watch. Time was running out—and he decided it didn't much matter whether the goods were stolen. He reached into his jacket pocket and brought out his wallet. "How much for all of it?"

Nick sneered. "All of it? You can't afford—" He stopped when Karlo opened the wallet, revealing a lot of cash. Nick brightened. "And you thought *we* robbed somebody!"

"It's not mine. I'm buying for someone else. How much?"

Nick smiled at a quivering Eddie before looking back. "Let me see." He reached unthreateningly for Karlo's wallet and counted. "Yeah, all this should cover it."

"That's crazy!"

"It's a seller's market, pal."

Karlo thought for a moment—and looked at the darkening shadows in the street. "Leave me a twenty."

Nick thought about it—and plucked a twenty out to put in Karlo's hand. As Karlo eagerly leaned over to grab for the bag, Nick chucked an empty wallet into it. "Guess the wife needs her eyeshadow," he said. "But you ain't gonna take her someplace nice on a twenty."

"I'm not married," Karlo said, rising. "I need it to get a cab—if I can find one." He turned and ran for the street. There was still time.

NIGHT HAD FALLEN WHEN Karlo's cab turned onto Theatre Row. He'd first seen the broad avenue with its colorful lights back in an old movie, one where everyone that set foot on it burst into song. *On Theatre Row, it's the place to go . . .*

And go he had. Karlo had harbored the acting bug forever, and he knew he had the chops. He'd quit a good job driving an airport shuttle bus to pursue his calling. But Theatre Row had not been kind to his dreams. Not being able to sing or dance wasn't fatal. His face was. He didn't have the right look, or so the casting directors always said. "We don't have a Frankenstein's monster role," as one had uncharitably put it.

At the same time, his general good nature kept him out of playing the heavies. Oh, he knew he *could*—he was broad-shouldered, with a prominent brow that gave him a scowl that could scare children. But didn't Gotham City have enough bad guys in real life?

Instead, he'd survived by being malleable—by fitting himself into whatever role the troupe needed him for. He ran lines with other actors, mended costumes, did makeup, built sets, handed out playbills, cleaned toilets—anything, just to appear in crowd scenes. He would learn the lines of the more difficult actors, on the mere chance he might get asked to understudy. He never went on, but he liked the feeling of being close to the stage.

He watched all the famous venues approach—and then recede as the cab passed them by. Their lights were still on, but many of the shows were dark, having paused in response to The Joker's poisoning wave. Half of going to live theatre was being seen going to live theatre, and that meant getting dolled up. The hardy few seeking entertainment now had to visit Theatre Row's side street, which housed venues too defiant—or too desperate—to close.

Like the Capra.

There was no better name for a movie theatre—except that wasn't what it was. The dilapidated venue hosted stage productions, and Karlo had heard it wasn't named for the film director at all. The cabbie glanced out the window at it as the taxi came to a stop. "You're early for the show. Or there just ain't nobody here."

"Actually, I'm late." Karlo paid the driver and fought his usual impulse to wait for change. "Thanks. Gotta go!"

He hurried past the marquee that he'd gotten to know too well. He'd stood on a rickety ladder the day before to put up the movable letters. They read:

THE GOAT'S TOWN PLAYERS PRESENT
TOLLIVER KINGSTON IN
TH3 T3MP3ST

The Capra and its repertory company put on the classics not out of devotion or pretension, but necessity: the Bard didn't charge rights fees. It said something about the star—and the state of the theatre company—that his name got the only spare "E" they had.

That had been one of his many demands. The bag Karlo carried was another. He rounded the corner and made for the stage door. He entered, bag in hand, and looked around. Several of his colleagues milled about, helping each other to get ready. "Tolliver! I've got it! *Tolliver!*"

"Finally!" From the far end of the hall, a man wearing a turquoise cape festooned with golden stars pushed his way through the crowd to face Karlo. "I've been waiting for you all day. And I've told you again and again, it's *Mister Kingston* to you!"

"Yes, Mister Kingston."

Tolliver Kingston wasn't *that* much older than Karlo, but the gulf between them was wide. With his firm jaw and wide, expressive eyes, the man wearing Prospero's magic cloak had the right look, if not much else. He'd been a recurring soap-opera villain, but his most recent onscreen death had come as a surprise to him—and his agent. Karlo surmised that they'd finally had enough of his attitude. It had brought the actor east to Gotham City, where he had found his exile lasting a lot longer than he'd expected.

And Kingston had used every opportunity to take it all out on Karlo.

"You're a dreadful slowpoke! Curtain's in thirty minutes. What else can go wrong?"

"Something else went wrong?" Karlo was afraid to ask. "Did I do it?"

"It's that fool Milford."

Karlo released a breath. "Our Caliban."

"Not tonight. He's at home. He used some breath spray and now he thinks he's been poisoned by Smylex."

"Oh, no!" Karlo liked Milford. "Is he all right?"

"He's delusional. Milford's breath is already a biological weapon." Kingston looked down at the bag. "Is that it?"

"I got everything, just like you asked. It's all imported."

Karlo unzipped the bag, and Kingston looked inside. He eyed Karlo. "You're sure?"

Karlo didn't know what to say. "I paid enough for it."

"No change?"

He shrank. "It cost everything you gave me."

Kingston groaned—and rubbed the bridge of his nose. "I don't have a choice. These lines are back. And have you seen my eyes? I'm not getting good sleep."

"Tolliver—" Karlo stopped, correcting himself. "Mister Kingston, I wouldn't worry. People are here for your performance. They all understand what's going on. We're about the only show open! If you went on without—"

"What are you talking about?" Kingston grabbed Karlo by the shirt and yelled into his face. "They *say* they'll understand—but all they'll remember is Tolliver Kingston looking like something the cat dragged in. And then I'll be doing skits for seniors in the activity room." He released Karlo with a shove. "I might as well go out there naked."

Karlo wanted to say that Gotham City had suffered enough—but decided he'd never get to say anything else.

Kingston looked at the bag again. "People vouched for this?"

"People did." Karlo inhaled. What weight an endorsement from Nick and Eddie was worth, he hesitated to say.

"You swear it's safe?"

Karlo shrugged. "I can't do that. I mean, I haven't tested it, but—"

Kingston grabbed him by the collar again. "Carlin, that's wonderful!"

Karlo was too stunned to correct him. "What?"

"Milford's out. His understudy's that skinny kid—no Caliban. *But you could do it!*"

"Me?" Karlo got excited. He was an actor, after all. "I know the role. I go over it with Milford."

"I've heard you. You'll do it!" He pushed the bag into Karlo's hands. "You'd better get ready."

Karlo looked down at the supplies, not understanding. "For me?"

"You can't be Caliban looking like that."

"But don't you want your stuff out of here? We both appear in the second scene."

"That's why you need to get ready fast. You'll test the makeup first—and then you bring it to me."

Karlo realized what Kingston was asking—and had the nerve to say something. "You want me to be your guinea pig?"

"An *actor*, Caliban." Kingston put his arm around Karlo's shoulder and guided him down the hallway. "Besides, there's nothing to worry about. That ridiculous harlequin on TV—it's all a publicity stunt."

"Then why did you send me to—"

"Do you want to argue or act? Because I'll tell the director to go with the kid. Do we understand each other, Karlo?"

Karlo nodded, as astounded by the opportunity as the sound of his correct name.

"Splendid. Now, I've got a wig to fit. At least nobody's panicking about *those!*" Kingston stormed into his dressing room and slammed the door behind him.

Karlo turned and hurried into the changing room Milford always used. He wanted to think Kingston was doing something nice for him, to make up for months of miserable treatment. But of course, there was a catch. Yet—

—even so, it might work out. Karlo approached the mirrored table and used his arm to sweep all the existing, now-suspect supplies off into a garbage can. He threw the bag onto the table and began unloading its contents.

The first thing he saw was that the wallet in the bag wasn't his. Nick had made a switch. It stung that Karlo's ID was gone, but that was the only damage. If Nick had a thing for credit cards, he was going to be awfully disappointed.

"Fifteen minutes to curtain," came a voice from the corridor. "You don't want to disappoint the brave souls who left the house looking like hell. Fifteen minutes!"

Karlo stopped what he was doing and rushed to the door. Outside, a white-haired stagehand stood clutching a clipboard. "Don't forget to announce me!" Karlo said.

"Announce you? *You?*"

"As Caliban!"

"Oh, yeah. Mister Big Star told me." The old man removed the pencil from behind his ear. "What's your name?"

I've only been here for twelve years! He rolled his eyes. "Karlo Babić!"

"Bah-*beesh?*" The stagehand frowned. "What kind of name is that?"

"Croatian."

"What's it mean?"

Karlo shrank. *"Old woman."* He immediately thought better of it and stopped the stagehand from writing. "Wait! No, don't put that down."

He remembered all the great actors of old, and the names on the posters on his walls at home. A brainstorm struck. "Use my stage name."

A white eyebrow went up. *"You* have a stage name?"

"Just use it. *Basil Karlo.*"

"Basil. Like the leaf?"

"Like the guy who played Sherlock Holmes!"

"Gotcha. First name, a detective. Last name, the fink in *The Godfather.*"

"Karlo with a 'K'!"

"Fine, fine." The stagehand started to write. "You sure you don't want to go for the full 'Karloff'? You've got the look for—"

From down the hall, Kingston bellowed. *"What's keeping that idiot?"*

The stagehand smirked. "I think your co-star is calling for you."

"Just a few minutes, Mister Kingston!" Karlo hurried back into the dressing room and slammed the door shut.

Karlo removed his shirt. He wasn't in the kind of shape he wanted to be, but he knew he could make a better misanthrope than the understudy. Having made Milford up many times, he knew what to do. The large container of foundation he'd bought would serve for skin paint, with shadow and rouge applied to give him a look that was perfectly macabre.

His mind wasn't on the powders and creams he was applying, but rather what would complete the effect: his performance. He went over his lines as he dabbed and rubbed. He hissed, *"This island's mine, by Sycorax, my mother, which thou tak'st from me!"*

How poetic—how *Shakespearean*—life was. Prospero had come to Caliban's island and bound him to his will, and Kingston had done the same to Karlo. But in a strange way, another figure in face paint, The Joker, had given him his big chance to show the world who he was, and what he could do.

"All the charms of Sycorax—toads, beetles . . ."

He found himself breathing hard. He tried to remember the lines.

"Toads, beetles, bats . . ."

Bats. The way the little punk had said "bat" was funny. Karlo hadn't dared laugh at him. Now he felt a smile coming—and a good laugh, well-delayed.

But he didn't laugh. His eyes went wide, and he looked at his face in the mirror. He didn't recognize what he saw. His cheeks, where he'd rubbed the coloring, were misshapen. Arched, angular.

His first thought was that the lights were failing again.

His next was that he'd gotten it, the laughing sickness.

But he wasn't making a sound. And as he pushed at his cheeks, he was able to make his tensed-up muscles relax. Only they didn't stop there. They sagged, becoming jowls. His skin burned—and pawing at it only added to the pain. He grabbed his head in agony, only to find his hair coming out in clumps.

Karlo stood, knocking the chair over behind him. He tried to scream, but all that emerged from his misshapen mouth was a horrid gurgle. The world spun. And as he started to fall, a single confused thought intruded on his agony:

Why didn't it make me laugh?

ACT I

A LIVING WORK OF ART

CHAPTER 1

YOU GOTTA LOVE THE DEAD, Alexander Knox had said many times. *They don't eat much, and they never bug their neighbors.*

No one lasted long on the police beat if they went squirrelly when seeing a dead body. You couldn't cover crime without encountering a victim—or twelve, as once happened to Knox during one of Carl Grissom's infamous wars. The mobster's lieutenant, Jack Napier, had likely done some of the killing that night; both of them were corpses themselves now. Grissom went the usual way for his kind, while Napier had gone crackers and plunged off the tallest cathedral in creation.

Knox had missed his chance to see Napier's body that night, now nearly six months ago. Injured in the rampage, he had instead seen it in the hospital on the front page of his own *Gotham Globe:* The Joker, cracked like an egg, smiling up from the imprint he'd made in the pavement. The publication of the grisly image had provoked surprisingly little controversy. The people of Gotham City needed to see that the one who'd brought them such terror was gone for good.

But for Knox, it'd been all bad. Vicki Vale hadn't taken that picture—she was definitely preoccupied at the time—and someone else had gotten the byline on the story of the century. *His* story, of Gotham City's greed, of The Joker's diabolical plan, of Batman's incredible response. Back on his feet and on the beat, Knox had watched as someone else got nominated for his prize, all his legwork for naught. It wasn't long before he was dealing with dead bodies again.

Only tonight, the corpse was a building.

The Capra was dead, having closed months earlier as another casualty of the Smylex panic. Ambulance lights had heralded *The Tempest*'s opening night, driving away the last remaining customers the ailing theatre had. The last play Shakespeare wrote without a partner turned out to be the final act for the Capra. The members of its company had gone their separate ways, but the corpse remained: a rundown building nobody could determine the ownership of. People had been fighting over the body ever since.

The Stantons, the Wallaces, and the Shrecks had sought the site for development, which brought out the usual people protesting that a piece of Gotham City's history was at risk. Knox doubted that any of the daytime picketers had ever set foot in the firetrap when it was open.

But while the Capra was dead, it wasn't deserted—not tonight.

Tipped off that people had gone inside, Knox had found the back door jimmied open. He entered the theatre, moving cautiously through halls that had been without power for weeks. But someone had some juice, if the hard-pounding music he was hearing was any indication. He followed the sound to where light flickered through a stage access door. *Is the show back on?*

He tested the stairs leading behind the stage. They looked creaky, but with the music blaring he figured no one would notice. Ascending, he saw that wooden scenery from the ill-fated final performance still stood on set, with PROSPERO'S ISLAND stenciled on the back. He found a small seam in the facade and crept up to peek through it.

Somebody's having a clambake. A beach party was raging on the island set. A bonfire burned in a large metal garbage can; next to it was a huge boombox. Wild partiers danced around them while clutching glass bottles. Some they smashed against the stage floor; others, they hurled over the seats in the once-great hall. The great size of the auditorium had so far kept it from filling with smoke; if the Capra ever had fire alarms, they weren't going off.

Knox gently put his hands against the scenery to steady himself as he looked more closely through the opening. There were close to a dozen adults, he figured, several wearing party masks. No—*clown masks*. There had been a run on those at novelty shops since The Joker's demise, and they'd become the disguise of choice for the city's more impressionable lowlifes. But these characters' mischief seemed limited to vandalism, fire code violations, and bad taste in music.

On top of everything else, he noticed a strange gassy smell. Wherever it was coming from, this seemed like a good place not to be. Knox was about to sneak away when a loud voice bellowed through the hall, audible over the music. *"Knock it off!"*

The dancers looked off to stage left. A hulking brute stomped into view, carrying a canvas bag. He tromped up to the boombox and switched it off. That's when Knox saw what was on the bald new-comer's face: black sunglasses, worn in a dark building in the middle of the night—and a giant black mustache that looked like it belonged on a cousin of Yosemite Sam.

Knox silently mouthed his name: *Lawrence!*

As The Joker, Napier had co-opted members of Grissom's gang—as well as varied remnants of the other outfits he'd taken over. He'd also hired out, bringing in a cadre of assassins trained in special weapons and martial arts. Lawrence was just good old-fashioned muscle—and someone who had improbably survived the night of The Joker's parade of terror in spite of his own foolishness. *The Lucky Lunkhead,* Knox had called him.

Based on the damage in the belfry of Gotham Cathedral and where Lawrence had been found, the police had surmised that the bruiser had attempted to jump Batman only to smash through the floor. He was fortunate there was another floor underneath to land on. Gothic architecture hadn't been as kind to one of his cohorts. The rough landing had knocked Lawrence for a loop, and he'd wound up in traction—and then prison. Which is where he'd been, until a botched transfer the week before.

Lawrence's presence at the Capra took this misdemeanor mayhem to another level, Knox thought. He fumbled for his recorder. He'd never heard Lawrence speak—he hadn't said a word in his arraignment. But the bruiser's voice boomed loud and deep as he shouted at the revelers.

"Quit screwing around!" Lawrence dropped the bag he was carrying onto the stage with a thunderous bang. Inebriated hooligans stood motionless as he approached. He loomed over one of them and seized his bottle. "Who brought the hooch?"

The drunken clown-face quivered. "We—we found it!"

"Found it?"

"Behind the concession stand. The opening night that never happened." Clowny shrugged. "Hey, man, no sense letting it go to waste!"

"Idiot!" Lawrence struck the guy hard with the back of his hand. *"You're supposed to waste the building!"*

Why? Knox wanted to ask. And even more than that: *For whom?* Startled into motion, he accidentally pushed against the scenery too hard—only to see the display start to tip forward. He grabbed at nothing, unable to prevent the plywood forest from crashing onto the stage in front of him.

Knox froze as all eyes turned in his direction. The reporter grinned sheepishly. "How ya doin'?"

"Get him!" Lawrence shouted.

Knox turned to run—only to trip over an electrical line. He lost his recorder as he fell. Scrambling to recover it proved a mistake, costing him valuable moments. No sooner did he return it to his overcoat pocket than the vandals were upon him.

Another command from Lawrence. "Into the light!"

The masked partiers dragged Knox to center stage, before the trash-can bonfire. The lone female among the punks shouted into his face. "Come to see a show? It's canceled!"

"He's canceled," said one of the two partiers holding him from behind. "He's a cop!"

"Guys, guys. Relax," Knox said. "I'm not a cop."

"Bull!" The woman yanked at the tie beneath his overcoat. "Dressed like this, what are you?"

"Health department. I thought this was Perluigi's Pizza." Knox strained against his captors. "I'll just be heading there now."

"You're staying!" Lawrence yelled.

Knox shrank. "I'm staying." Wisecracking had been his way out of a jam since his schoolyard days. It usually didn't work then, either.

"Frisk him," Lawrence ordered. If he wasn't in charge before, he was now.

The woman fished through Knox's opened overcoat and found his recorder. She held it up like she'd never seen one before. "Where'd you get this?"

"I can get you a rate on one," Knox said.

"It's mine."

"That's what I meant. It's yours. Happy birthday." He watched as she fiddled with it. "Don't eat the battery."

The sight of the recorder rang a bell for Lawrence. "You're that reporter. Knox."

"And you are Lawrence." There was no sense pretending now, Knox thought; they'd seen each other in a court appearance. "You're looking better. I'm sure it's nice to be out and about. But I thought you'd be anywhere but here. Chicago, Metropolis."

Lawrence got into his face and snarled. "This is *my* town."

"Yeah, I guess you still have library books checked out here."

Lawrence stepped back, and Knox breathed marginally easier. *Woof. Fish for dinner!*

The tough turned and went back for the bag he'd dropped. "Did he see any of you without your masks on?"

"Naw, we kept them on like you said," replied the guy Lawrence had smacked. "I mean, except when we took a drink." His mask was only halfway on.

With a swift move, Lawrence grabbed the guy by the neck. He positioned the mask properly. Knox spoke quickly. "I didn't see any faces, honest."

The woman pointed at Lawrence. "You saw *him!*"

"No, I thought he was Lawrence *Welk*. I forgot my glasses." He glanced at Lawrence. "His are nice, though. Are those designer?"

Lawrence shoved the bag into the hands of the clown he'd chastised. "Pass those out, fool."

If Lawrence thinks someone's an idiot, Knox thought, *the world's in trouble.*

Knox watched as what looked like clubs were distributed. Only when Lawrence approached the fire with one did Knox notice the large knot of fabric wrapped around one end. Lawrence shoved the wrapped end into the fire to light it. Others followed his lead, and soon everyone besides the two goons holding Knox had makeshift torches aflame.

Lawrence pointed toward the rest of the house, more visible in the light. "Tell me you did the job."

"Before you got here," the woman replied. "We doused the seats down here and in the boxes."

That's when Knox noticed them for the first time: empty fuel cans in the aisles. His heart sank. "Waste the building" wasn't about trashing it. *They're gonna burn the theatre down!*

He saw Lawrence staring at him. "Look, I told you, I can't identify anyone. And if anyone asks, I saw you board a flight to Bolivia."

"Shut up. I'm thinking."

"Take your time."

It soon became clear to Knox that Lawrence wasn't used to making decisions any more complicated than "spicy or mild." Maybe the torches would all burn out, and indecision could save his skin. It was best to stay quiet and hope for the best, he concluded—

—until his reporter's curiosity got the better of him. "Listen, I understand the masks—but why clowns? I'd have thought this town had its fill."

The woman pointed to her mask and saluted. "The Joker was our *guru.*"

"He changed the game," said one of the guys holding Knox.

"And he lived to party!" said the other.

"So you knew him," Knox said. "You worked for him?"

"We saw him on TV!" said two at once.

Knox felt like he was missing something. "I get it, you like his style. But you," he said, addressing Lawrence, "he wound up being a heap of trouble for. So why hang out with these guys? The Joker's gone. What's the appeal?"

Lawrence stood unmoving, staring behind his sunglasses. Finally he answered, "He always knew what to do." He tilted his massive head and spoke as if in response to a sudden realization. *"What would The Joker do?"*

A moment's silence. And then the drunkest of the torch-toting clowns muttered, "Roast him."

"Roast him," said another, louder.

"Roast him! *Roast him!*" Like angry medieval villagers, Lawrence's companions advanced on Knox, waving their flaming weapons.

Fire in his face, Knox strained again against the pair holding him. "Wait, don't!"

"Stop!" Lawrence yelled. They did—and Knox breathed with relief. But it only lasted a few seconds. "Save the torches for the job," Lawrence commanded. He gestured to the fire barrel. "Roast him *there.*"

The guys holding Knox spun him once to face the fire—and spun him again as they dragged him, kicking and yelling, toward it. Two others passed off their torches and grabbed his feet.

Knox had been tossed bodily into a big garbage can as a schoolboy; that day, he'd needed a change of clothes. There was no going home after this one, he knew, as the foursome hefted him into the air. He could sense the flames licking at the back of his coat as they brought him over it. Knox thrashed, feeling the heat and seeing nothing above but the darkness of the rafters—

—and something else.

It came down like a foul ball in a baseball game. Something white and round, rocketing in his direction. But before it struck him, it exploded, showering him, the trash can, and everyone holding him with gooey foam.

The startled foursome bearing him fell back, dropping him beside a trash-can fire that was choking and dying. Flat on his back, Knox wiped his eyes clean just in time to see that the void above was no void, but rather the bloom of a darkened cape, opening as its wearer descended.

Batman!

CHAPTER 2

*T*HAT'S RIGHT, BATMAN THOUGHT as he dropped toward the startled goons. *Look at me.*

The expansion of his cape when he descended from a line served a practical purpose. Lightweight skeletal spokes in his cape went rigid, causing the assembly to expand like an umbrella, catching air and slowing his descent. For anyone directly beneath him, it blotted out light from above—and gave anybody below with weapons a lot to shoot at that wasn't his body.

But just as important: *It looked astounding.*

In a situation where he could be seen, the cape made a statement that acted on criminals' natural instincts: *Something bigger than you is coming, and you'd better run.* And theatricality—no pun intended, given the setting—was especially helpful in drawing attention away from a hostage.

Even Alexander Knox. Batman had identified him from the rafters right away; no one else would talk so much when his neck was on the line.

He deactivated the cape, returning it to its usual state seconds before his boots touched the stage. The fire in the trash can was sizzling and dying, and the four toughs who'd held Knox had dropped him. All, the reporter included, were drenched with flame retardant, and some were coughing for breath. Two were still on their feet; two quick punches put them down on the stage on either side of Knox.

Batman glanced down at him. "Don't move."

Others *were* moving. From above, Batman had identified seven possible targets in addition to Knox's captors; Lawrence was one of them. They all held torches, now the only light in the place. That made it easier.

"Get him!" Lawrence shouted.

Batman smiled.

The torchbearers in the aisles rushed the stage like angry medieval villagers. Batman wanted them there, and not in the areas where they'd spread gasoline. He pulled a metal box from his belt. Responding to his grip, it sprouted black wings on either side. He tapped the red button on it, and icons representing enemies appeared on its small monitor. He'd tested the new weapon on motionless dummies, but never against real opponents. *Let's try five,* he thought.

He slung his latest-model Batarang toward the nearest would-be assailant on the stage. It struck the guy on the side of his head, knocking his mask off and causing him to drop his torch. The Batarang pivoted in midair, computing the best angle of approach to the second torchbearer, and continued its journey.

Another strike—and then a third.

It soared toward Lawrence next—only to sail high over him and vanish into the darkness. The titan gave a laugh. The failure surprised Batman, but it *was* a field test—and he was already doing something else.

Earlier, he'd simply dropped a fire-retardant grenade from above, letting gravity do the trick. Now he deployed a projectile launcher, which he pointed toward the first victim of the Batarang. The guy was still on the floor, grasping his jaw and moaning; he wasn't the threat. That was his torch, which had fallen and ignited scenery. Batman pulled the trigger, launching a smaller version of the grenade toward the fire. Another loud *chuff* and the flames vanished in a spray of foam.

He'd just finished dealing with the third accidental blaze when Lawrence lurched toward him, joined by two others. Batman hadn't intended the launcher as a weapon, but gave something a try, firing it just in front of the approaching assailants. Foam erupted from the charges where they struck the floor, showering the would-be attackers' shins and turning the stage into a greasy hazard. The pair flanking Lawrence slipped immediately, catapulting into the air and coming down hard.

Lawrence, meanwhile, slid comically across the floor toward him. Batman stepped aside and shoved as the bruiser went past, redirecting him. He went somersaulting into the orchestra pit and disappeared, landing with a horrific crash.

Batman extinguished more of the dropped torches before dealing with another assault. Each time, the theatre grew darker—until he faced the final torchbearer.

"Whoa," the guy said as Batman advanced toward him. The guy seemed drunk—but that had not impaired his judgment. Instead of offering a fight, he just handed his torch to Batman, turned, and ran.

Batman could hear others following suit, leaving the theatre in all directions. But not all. "'Scuse me," Knox called out. "Little help here!"

The adventurer turned to see what initially looked like an octopus—a multi-armed mass that took a moment to resolve into separate figures. Several of Knox's initial captors were wrestling with him on the floor. A clown-masked woman emerged from the pile-on.

"Back off, Bats. Or we'll wring this guy's neck!"

Batman suppressed a sigh. They always made it difficult. But he had an answer, which he grunted. "Okay."

From amid the scrum, Knox yelled. *"Okay?"*

Batman strode away—only to stop when he reached the stereo boombox. Holding the torch before it, Batman quickly evaluated its capabilities. *This'll do nicely,* he thought.

He took a gadget from his belt: one he used when tapping into electronic networks. He ran the short patch cord into the line-in on the stereo. Then he pitched the torch into a puddle of fire retardant, dousing it and leaving the whole place in the dark.

One goon called out, "I've still got him!"

"You've got *me*, you idiot!"

From the sounds of the scuffling and swearing, they'd turned on one another in the confusion. Triggering his mask to deploy the night-vision lenses over his eyes, he saw that was the case; the threat to Knox was paused for the moment. That was all he needed. He advanced toward the boombox and deployed his ear protection within his mask. He flipped it around in his hands so its enormous speakers faced toward the struggling Knox and his captors.

He couldn't hear what came after he flipped the switch, but he knew what it sounded like. The device was inspired by the phone phreaks of old; technological vandals who used sound. He'd tested sonic weapons but didn't have any on hand; this was the next best thing, a horrific screech boosted to over a hundred decibels. From the stage of an auditorium like the Capra, Batman imagined the sound had to be quite impressive.

Certainly, it got results. He could see them in the infrared: people one by one disengaging from the scrum. Batman didn't know which one was Knox, but nobody could hold him and their ears at the same time. Boombox before him, Batman advanced on the group, who fell over one another trying to get away.

Batman turned around. The clown-faces had scattered in all directions, exiting wherever they could. Down in the orchestra pit, he could see a large shape—probably a recovered Lawrence, waving his arms. *Probably ranting about his stereo being stolen.*

That was fine; the job was done. Batman yanked his electronic device free and disengaged his ear protection. Then, with a firm grip on the stereo's handle, he twirled once like an Olympic hammer hurler. He timed his release precisely, such that it hurtled toward the orchestra pit. The term *boombox* suddenly became more descriptive, as the machine struck Lawrence hard. The henchman howled.

When the silhouette of Lawrence came into view again in Batman's night vision, he was on the move—but not toward the stage. Abandoned in the dark and in pain, Lawrence scrambled out of the pit and past the seats, seeking escape. Batman paused. He wanted to bring the criminal in, and had several tricks at his disposal to bind him—but the darkness made using some of them more difficult. And there was the moaning from behind.

Batman looked back to see a shadowy figure crawling away on hands and knees at the far backstage wall—and in danger of falling down the stairs in the dark.

Knox. "Blind and deaf," the reporter said, apparently to no one. "Deaf and blind."

With a last look in Lawrence's direction, Batman decided capturing the criminals would have to wait. Needing more than his night vision could provide to navigate the mess onstage, he switched the apparatus off and went again for his belt. Picking out the rafter he'd perched on earlier, he fired a dart at it. The projectile embedded itself into the support and ignited, casting a white glow on the whole area.

Batman saw that Knox had stopped moving and was sitting, staring up at the impromptu lighting fixture. The reporter rubbed his temples. "I'm deaf. You've made me deaf."

"You'll live."

Knox cupped his ear like an old man and yelled. *"What's that?"*

"I couldn't catch them all," Batman said, approaching him. "I needed them to leave."

"Asking questions is my whole job," he shouted. "Who's going to read my articles when my only question is '*Hah?*'"

"They'll watch TV." Batman looked Knox over. He looked like hell but didn't appear seriously injured.

Knox shook his head vigorously, flinging foam from his hair. "Thanks," he said, voice at a more normal volume. "I wasn't really enjoying the show." He looked down at his foam-soaked clothes. "You sure know how to ruin a suit!"

Batman ignored him. Lawrence and the others were gone, but his real quarry now was something else. He walked about the stage, searching.

Knox stood up. "Seriously, thanks. I'm lucky you were here." Realization crept across his face in the next moment, and his expression changed. "Wait. Were you following me?"

"Following Lawrence." Batman had been looking for the criminal ever since hearing about his breakout—an escape from a police van carrying him to a medical evaluation. As he walked across the stage making sure the location was secure, he addressed Knox without looking at him. "Why were *you* here?"

"Following a lead."

"Dangerous."

"It's where the money is." Knox paused. "I think someone said that once."

"Willie Sutton. He was a criminal. Robbed banks."

"Yeah, your great-grandbat probably caught him."

Batman didn't respond as he continued investigating. It didn't do to speak much. Alexander Knox had spoken with Bruce Wayne before. The crime fighter altered his voice and mannerisms as Batman, but a reporter was a trained observer. Knox might make a connection.

"Boombox Boy is back in action pretty fast," Knox said, undeterred. He stepped to Batman's side. "Defacing paintings, burning theatres—maybe the *Globe* should hire him as an arts critic."

From what Batman had briefly seen from above, it looked like Lawrence was on a schedule. *He's no vandal.*

Knox joined Batman in searching the stage. "I'm hoping my recorder's here somewhere," the reporter said. "What are you looking for?"

"You'll know it if you see it. Did Lawrence say who he was working for?"

"No, but a bunch of people want this property," Knox said. "And it's not because they want to bring back *Guys and Dolls*. I got a tip that people were entering the place."

"You didn't call the police?"

"They might have been squatters. Homeless. I didn't want them arrested."

So the newsman has a heart, Batman thought.

That impression lasted until Knox added, "I wanted to interview them. Sympathetic Davids against the corporate real estate Goliaths. The kind of soap that used to sell papers until you started flying around."

Batman kept searching. He spied one of the rubber masks, fallen on the floor. He picked it up carefully, as evidence. "Clowns again."

"Garden-variety Joker nuts," Knox said. "It's like he's got a cult. He's their hero."

"He was psychotic."

"In cults, that's a plus. At the paper I've started calling them the Last Laughs."

Batman stopped—and pivoted. Facing Knox for the first time, he glared at him. "Don't give them attention."

Startled, Knox's eyes widened. "Why not?"

"It dignifies their behavior. Popularizes them."

Knox chuckled. "That's funny, coming from you. Without our stories you'd still be a myth."

"I never wanted the people's attention." He held the mask before Knox. "I just want *theirs*."

"Can I quote you?"

"No."

Knox held up a finger. "You never said we were off the record."

"It was while they were trying to kill you." Batman clenched the mask tightly in his fist before throwing it aside.

Seeing that, Knox seemed to let it go. "Eventually Gotham City will run out of clown masks. It's never face paint, do you notice? They aren't committing to the role."

Batman had noticed. He attributed part of it to a general lingering fear in all Gotham City of personal care products; the theatre he was standing in had failed because of what tainted makeup had done to an actor here.

"I don't get why they called this place the Capra," Knox said. "It's not a movie theatre."

Batman surprised him by responding. "*Capra* is Latin for goat."

Knox did a double take. "The Bat speaks Latin?"

He pointed to the boxes, where gold-painted goat horns were part of the design.

Making a connection, Knox snapped his fingers. "Yeah, the troupe's got 'Goat' in the name. But why goats?"

"Look it up."

Before he could come up with a rejoinder, Knox bumped something with his foot. *The Batarang.* He knelt to pick it up—

—and Batman snatched it from his hand. "I'll take that."

"No finders keepers?"

"No." Batman triggered the errant projectile to withdraw its wings. This prototype would need more work. It was likely the presence of the torches had fouled up its detection systems—and he would definitely need some kind of tracker on it for cases like this. *The one thing you want in a boomerang is to get it back.*

Batman heard the approach of sirens outside the building. *Someone must have noticed all the people exiting,* he thought. He'd seen enough. "Have them call the fire department," Batman said, "so the place doesn't go up by accident."

"Sure," Knox said.

Heading offstage, Batman found something on the floor: Knox's recorder. He pitched it to him.

"Thanks," Knox said. He held it up. "Hey, listen, if you've got a minute—"

Batman turned his back to Knox and fired a grapple at the rafters.

The reporter didn't give up. "I'll tell my old partner you said hello."

Batman paused. He spoke without turning. "Vicki Vale?"

"Yeah. I guess now that she's gone you've moved from rescuing her to rescuing me."

Don't expect me to make a habit of it. A swirl of a cape, and he soared into the air.

CHAPTER 3

*H*ELL WAS OTHER PEOPLE'S MUSIC.

As dawn broke hours after the botched Capra job, Lawrence maneuvered Gotham City's streets on foot, serenaded by the peppy stereos of cabs passing by with their windows open. He couldn't respond in kind. He'd thrown his boombox away soon after escaping the theatre; Batman's stunt had blown out its speakers. It was another in a long list of things Batman had destroyed. The good times were over.

A clock on a bank read six.

I'm late. The big guy won't like it. He walked faster.

Lawrence hadn't minded when The Joker was calling the tunes. He'd been the best boss Lawrence had ever worked for. The clown had assembled a small army of toughs capable of just about anything, and while he occasionally killed one of his allies at random, Lawrence hadn't feared him. The Joker was living his own movie; someone had to provide the score. But the music had ended in Gotham Cathedral. The Joker had gone to his grave—and Lawrence to the hospital and then prison. And while he'd recently made it out again thanks to some fool forgetting to lock a van door during a transfer, Lawrence had found there was no going back to what was.

Commissioner Gordon had announced that the cops had rounded up all The Joker's men, and they very nearly had. Those still outside were the dregs. Cowards that had fled the parade or bailed earlier. And then there were the newbies: the kids and assorted weirdos that reporter Knox had so nervily disdained. Knox was a weakling, but he'd been right about that. Lawrence had tried to do something with them anyway and it had blown up in his face.

There was nothing left but the walk of shame.

He entered the seven-story garage and hurried upstairs. A lone limo sat on the third floor, its lights off and motor running. Lawrence exited the stairwell and stood beside the vehicle's darkened windows.

He waited solemnly for three minutes before the rear window finally rolled down with an electric whir. A white-haired man was reading from the stock page of a newspaper. "I hate garages."

"You picked the place, Mister Shreck."

"I hate garages because they're expensive, and always in the wrong place. I never can get locations near my stores. If things had gone well tonight, I'd have had the spot I wanted—and you and I might have met in my office instead of here." Shreck continued to study the newspaper. "I looked out my office window a few hours ago, Lawrence. And do you know what I didn't see?"

"I don't follow."

"Nonsense. Following is *all* you do." Shreck turned the page. "Fire trucks, Lawrence. A steady stream of fire trucks, lights flashing, heading toward the blaze. The poor, dilapidated Capra, a relic from another era, done in at last by Father Time and bad wiring."

"Batman showed up."

"An hour after your people broke in, according to the police scanner. And somehow in all that time nobody could find a match."

Lawrence didn't try to make an excuse. Max Shreck owned department stores and a lot more, but he wasn't born rich, and he gave every indication that he'd run over a few people on his climb to the top. The man spoke crisply, with a mix of erudition and street posturing. Lawrence had heard that even Carl Grissom had avoided crossing him. It was better to let such people talk.

"I trusted you because of what you specialize in. Mayhem. Destruction." Shreck crumpled the newspaper in his hands and faced Lawrence for the first time. His cold eyes narrowed. "Do you know what *I* specialize in?"

"Selling toys?"

"*Power.*" Shreck nearly spat the word. "Power is what I specialize in. The fall of Carl Grissom—and that macabre madman who followed him—has left a power vacuum in your community, if one can call it that." He put his hand on his chest. "It's not *my* community, for sure. But it helps me on occasion to draw on yours—so long as I have partners on whom I can depend."

Somewhere behind Lawrence, a door slammed. He didn't flinch.

"I took your call because you said you intended to reconstitute," Shreck continued. "A new partner, to perform certain . . . *assignments* that become necessary." He frowned. "People who wet themselves at the sound of Batman's name don't have what it takes."

"We all got away."

"You all fled."

"I'm still rounding up talent. It's early."

"Strange, it looks late to me." Shreck checked his watch. "Now there can't be another attempt on the Capra—not without drawing too many uncomfortable questions. And so customers of my store in that location will have to continue walking far to spend their money with me."

Lawrence frowned. He'd sent a bunch of clowns out on an audition, and they had screwed this one up, but good. Now he was broke, unemployed, and without his tunes. He was out—if Shreck let him walk away at all. He heard a noise off to the side again, and the electric window of the limo started to go up.

Then something happened to Lawrence that rarely did.

He had an idea.

"What if we burn a *bunch* of stuff?"

The window stopped rising, then lowered again. Shreck peered out at Lawrence. "Hiding the destruction of the Capra within a series of calamities?"

"Yeah. You said there were more places you wanted hit anyway, in other parts of town. Give me a shot."

Lawrence thought about the sounds he'd heard and wondered for a moment whether he'd used the wrong expression. Shreck amplified that concern when he reached into a compartment in front of him. But what the retail mogul drew out was not a weapon.

"Get your act together, fast. Wait for a call." Shreck pitched something colorful out the window. "Oh, don't ask for any more of these. Our novelty department's out."

The limo lurched forward, its tires squealing. Lawrence reached down to pick up what Shreck had thrown.

A clown mask.

Lawrence let out an aggravated grunt. Some of the punks he'd corralled into helping him had signed up out of nostalgia; others were wannabes and loons hoping for some kind of contact high from someone who'd been around Napier. But they were no good as they were. One more in a mask or a dozen more couldn't have stopped Batman tonight.

Shreck's right. It didn't matter how many targets he was given. None of it mattered. Lawrence knew the truth: he was a follower. He was no boss—and certainly no Joker.

He gripped the clown mask in both mighty hands, intending to rip it in two. To hell with Shreck's plans and running a new crew. He was getting out of town, and that was—

Someone dropped a beat. Drums, pounding, up ahead, followed by a trumpet blare. The music was coming from the stairwell he'd used to enter the garage. Thinking about the noise he'd heard earlier, he approached the door.

Behind it sat a boombox. Brand-new and a better model than the one he'd discarded, making the stairwell sound like a coliseum. Lawrence looked both up and down the stairs to see who'd left it.

Nobody. Someone had pressed the play button and left. He leaned down to shut it off—but before he did so, the music was replaced by something else.

"Hello, Lawrence. It's been a while."

He didn't recognize the voice; the speaker was using some kind of mechanism to disguise it. But whoever recorded the message seemed to know *him*.

"That's right, my immense friend—we used to work together. I was the one who helped you get out of prison."

What? Lawrence didn't know anyone had done that.

"A transfer for evaluation. An unlocked door. Keys, conveniently left in the ignition of the pickup truck you used to escape. It was red. Do you believe me now?"

His eyes narrowed. Whoever made the tape had his full attention.

"I've been watching you in the days since. Getting the old gang back together is a fine idea—and I want you to keep at it. You're no leader, and certainly no brain. But people respect a strongman—and if they think you're taking orders from someone smarter, you can make them do anything."

Lawrence scowled. *Who is this?* He racked his brain, trying to remember anyone from his past. It couldn't be someone from his present. Shreck had just been here, but this didn't sound like him.

The next words seemed to confirm it. *"I don't care who you do jobs for right now—millionaires or mobsters. Take them all. Just stay alive, stay out of prison—and keep building. Organizing. Recruiting."*

A pause, during which Lawrence started to say something. "How the hell should I—"

"You're talking back to a tape, Lawrence. I know you. But I also know you can do this. Do you hear me? Don't give up. When I need you, I'll let you know." Another pause. *"This tape will self-destruct in five seconds."*

Behind his shades, Lawrence's eyes went wide. He turned to run, only to fumble with the handle of the stairwell door. By the time he got it open, five seconds had elapsed—and a chuckle came from the boombox.

"Just a little joke. Destroy the tape—and do try to be less gullible. You're no good to me dead."

```
PROTECTED FILES
FILENAME: DAILYJOURNAL
TUESDAY, 8:01 A.M.
................................................

WEEKEND TESTS YIELDED LITTLE NEW DATA
SO MUCH STOLEN FROM ME
WILL GET IT BACK, WILL NEVER GIVE UP
NEW TOOLS IN DEVELOPMENT
```

CHAPTER 4

THE CATHEDRAL WAS HAUNTED.

The Joker was up here in the belfry—and Vicki with him, as his prisoner. He'd captured her on the street soon after bringing down the Batwing. But they weren't the only ones here. As Batman emerged onto the top floor of the colossal edifice, he discovered others were lying in wait. Threatening him with death, while The Joker and Vicki danced.

First came the Martial Artist, the one he'd faced as part of the museum rescue. He assaulted Batman, screaming the whole time. Batman swiftly silenced his attacker with a well-placed piece of metal.

Then came the Boxer, slinging a heavy chain. With The Joker still dancing with his hostage, the Boxer gave Batman the toughest hand-to-hand fight of his short career. Taking the pummeling, Batman realized that fisticuffs wouldn't be enough—

—and he realized something else. *Something's wrong here.*

But there was no time to think on it. The Boxer knocked him against the great bell, causing him to fall into the shaft. At the last instant, Batman caught himself—and flipped upward, using his legs to grapple his opponent. The Boxer slammed noisily into the bell before plummeting, screaming into the void.

I remember that, Batman thought as he scrambled out of the shaft. But something was still missing. *Or someone.*

When Vicki distracted The Joker, Batman got his chance to approach. But by now he knew he was reliving past events—and he thought he knew why. "Excuse me," he said.

The Joker looked at him—and gave a start. But Batman made no move to attack. "'*Excuse me?*'" The Joker repeated. "That's all you're gonna say? Nothing about devils and moonlight?"

"No. This is a dream."

The Joker rolled his eyes. "'Beautiful Dreamer' is *my* song."

"It's still a dream. This wasn't how things happened."

Batman crossed his arms—and watched as The Joker suddenly began growing in stature. His chalk-colored face grew rubbery, like a novelty-store mask. Horrified, Vicki dashed away to hide.

"You got me," the villain finally said once he reached his new bulky height. He removed his mask and stood revealed as Lawrence, complete with his sunglasses. "How'd you know?"

"Because when this really happened, you fell through the floor before I met the Boxer. And I saw you tonight, which is why you're on my mind now."

Lawrence snorted. "You never gave me a second thought before."

"No." Batman let his guard drop. He hadn't given a second thought to any of it. But seeing Lawrence had jarred something loose. Something was wrong—and it was wrong even then.

And he had just realized what it was.

He peered at Lawrence. "What are you doing here?"

"It's your dream. You just said—"

"I don't mean now. I mean then. You and the other two guys. Nobody saw any of you enter the cathedral after the Batwing crashed." Pacing, Batman gestured to the ramparts, now empty. "The Joker and Vicki entered from the street. I followed. But how'd you get here?"

"Who cares? You're crazier than the boss!"

"I know how it sounds. I just never thought much about—"

Realization struck, and Batman stood frozen.

"Maybe you're here because The Joker knew he was going to enter the cathedral! And if he knew that—"

Batman spun—in time to see the hoodlum's face twist and re-shape into The Joker's. The new massive version of The Joker lunged toward him. "You're getting warm, Batsy!" he said as he seized Batman by the shoulders. "A brisk fall will cool you off!"

Batman pitched backward, his head striking against the great cathedral bell with a clang. It resounded as he fell, snatching helplessly for something on his belt that would save him. But all he found was darkness—and laughter, never stopping . . .

BRUCE WAYNE WOKE UP, SWEATING. Tangled in sheets, he pitched forward—only to bump his head on the underside of a table. For the first time since childhood, he'd fallen out of bed.

A silken voice sounded alarm. "Oh, Good Lord."

Still dazed, Bruce asked, "Vicki?"

Julie Madison stood over him. Red-haired and statuesque in her designer dress—and mad. She kicked him in the ankle. "Gee, thanks. See if I come to your rescue again."

Bruce rubbed the side of his head and tried to return to reality. "Sorry, I was having a dream."

Julie's expression softened. "A bad one?"

"A doozy."

"Serves you right. You were gone half the night." She reached down to help him up.

Standing, he got his bearings and remembered. His date with Julie, the night before, had ended at Wayne Manor. Later, he had slipped out to hunt Lawrence—and save the Capra. "I told you I might have to step out. There was a call from Tokyo."

"And yet nobody came in the room to tell you that there was one."

"I called *them*." Sheets still wrapped around him, Bruce parted the curtains and peeked out. Most of the morning was gone. "I don't control when the markets open."

"Well, I'll forgive you for that—and for running out on me. I didn't even notice when you got back."

There were Gotham City socialites, and then ones who worked for a living—or made a pretense of doing so. His friend and occasional paramour Julie Madison had done more than most. An aspiring actress, she'd found some success—though Bruce knew the popular view was that she'd been aided by nepotism and her other connections.

If that bothered her, she hadn't stopped asking for help—at least not from him. She stood behind him as he dressed. "Are you sure you're going to be able to fill the boxes?"

He stared blankly at her reflection in his mirror. "What boxes?"

She rolled her eyes. "Earth to Bruce. *Pygmalion*, silly."

"Oh, yeah."

"It's like I told you. We've only sold half the premium packages for opening night." She gripped his wrist. "People may finally be ready to come back to theatres, after all the chaos. But we can't leave anything to chance."

Bruce understood. At Julie's prompting, he'd arranged for the first performance to serve as a benefit for a charity he was affiliated with. The Capra may have failed, but the Imperial Theatre was larger and renowned, and there was still time to save it. A sellout might do the trick. "I'll make some more calls."

"Great. Rehearsal's at two. Time for me to get back to the fight!" She kissed the side of his face and slipped out.

By the time Bruce put on a robe and reached the foot of the stairs, Alfred was holding the door for her. "Always a pleasure to see you, Miss Madison. Give my regards to George Bernard Shaw."

"I will. Bye, Alfie!"

Bruce smirked and gave a little wave. "Hi, Alfie."

The old man regarded him icily. "I tolerate quite a bit in my service, sir. But there are boundaries even for me." A gentle smile returned. "How are you, Master Bruce?"

He winced. "I had another nightmare."

"Sleeping at night usually renders more pleasant dreams. You might give it a try."

"I could give an egg or two a try."

Alfred gestured to the kitchen. "Already prepared, sir."

"Of course they are."

Much of the interior of Wayne Manor was under constant surveillance; he and Alfred used the recordings whenever a social occasion might yield some intelligence that would be of interest to his activities as Batman. The bedroom was off-limits, of course. Yet somehow Alfred had an unerring sense of when Bruce arose every day, no matter how erratic his schedule was. The breakfast was always ready in the kitchen, the coffee always poured. And his newspaper was waiting, crisp and folded and leaning against a vase.

He paged through it as he ate. There was nothing about what had happened at the Capra; Knox hadn't had time to file a story before the *Globe* went to press. It was just as well, especially for Julie's play at the Imperial. Bruce doubted it'd be helpful to the metropolitan theatre scene for customers to know a place they used to frequent had become a battleground.

"An article on page six may be of interest," Alfred said.

"Another crime?"

"Another benefit."

"Hmm." Mildly startled to be directed toward something that wasn't a job for Batman, Bruce flipped to the society page. What he saw there made him gawk.

Like theatre, another part of the art scene had suffered during The Joker's reign of terror: this one, more directly. The Flugelheim Museum was the peculiar place that had thrived early in the Smylex panic; its restaurant's patrons were rich enough to have their makeup and hair gel flown in. But it had been invaded by The Joker and his band, who'd gassed the patrons and vandalized the art collection before Batman arrived on the scene.

Bruce had made an anonymous donation to repair the skylight that he'd destroyed during his rescue of Vicki Vale, but that hadn't solved all the museum's woes. "The insurers blame the museum for inadequately protecting its collection," Alfred said. "Not one of the works was under glass. The underwriters may never pay out."

"So they held an auction?" Bruce stared at the photo depicting several paintings, all defaced by paint splotches. "I don't believe this. They sold them?"

"The sale escaped my notice, sir. I seldom pay attention to the world of *pop art*," Alfred said, his distaste over the last two words evident.

Bruce shook the paper as he read. "A million dollars." He looked at Alfred. "They raised a million dollars!"

"One million five hundred sixty thousand, to be precise. A number of bidders from around the world—but also quite a few locals."

The idea baffled Bruce. "What did they want, *souvenirs*?"

"Edward Hopper's *Approaching a City* painting went for ten times its original price," Alfred said. "It was signed 'Joker Was Here.'"

Bruce blanched. "That's disgusting."

"I particularly noted the statement from Miss Van der Orr. She bought Gilbert Stuart's unfinished portrait of George Washington."

Bruce read from the story. "She says, 'This is more than a painting with a dollar sign painted over it . . .'"

"'. . . it's a symbol of Gotham City's resilience in surviving a historic ordeal.'" Having finished the quote from memory, Alfred pursed his lips in disdain. "Some symbol."

"I'm pretty sure Dottie only saw the dollar sign." Bruce squinted. "What happened to the idea of restoring them?"

"Well, sir, it is the Flugelheim. Perhaps they seek the Mona Lisa for the opening of a new *snack bar*." The last two words again dripped with revulsion.

Bruce read down the list of buyers, a who's who of people who would do anything for attention. "Make sure everyone in this story gets a call about the theatre benefit. They can afford it."

"Yes, sir."

And people think I have too much money.

Bruce tried to continue reading—and eating—but what he'd seen had put him off. He pushed the plate away. "Alfred, they're worship-ping him now."

"Who, sir?"

"The Joker. After all that he did—all the people he killed and injured—they're buying the paintings he ruined like religious relics. And people I've been facing are wearing masks to look like him. I don't understand how they can be following him, knowing what he was. It's not—"

"Not right?"

Bruce shook his head. "I was going to say it's not *normal.*"

Alfred took the plate. "Might I suggest that your own outré ap-pearance has changed what 'normal' is for a great many?"

"What, you think I'm causing this?"

"You did select your guise to create a psychological impact."

"On *criminals,* Alfred."

"But you've impacted others, as well—from the good citizens of Gotham City to the bad ones. In different ways, including ones which you could not have predicted."

"I never considered that." Bruce looked off into space. "There's something else I never thought about—until seeing Lawrence brought it up. The police never found out how he got into the cathedral the night of the parade, did they?"

Alfred seemed startled to be asked. "No, sir, he confessed noth-ing. I did record The Joker calling for a helicopter off the radio band, but that vehicle didn't appear until later. There were no other mes-sages."

"I didn't think so." Bruce looked down.

The butler frowned. "The Joker *is* much on your mind. Perhaps you can dispel that by better understanding his power over the masses. And you can draw upon someone who thinks about this very subject." Alfred gestured to the newspaper. "Page seventeen."

"I love how you memorize the morning paper."

"My employer rises rather late."

Bruce smiled and searched for the page. "Professor Auslander is wrapping up his lecture series this afternoon on the behavior of crowds."

Hugh Auslander. Since his arrival in Gotham City months earlier, he had quickly risen to prominence in its intellectual circles. A polymath, he knew as much about psychology as medicine, and one of his many academic pursuits was the study of mob mentality. The term referred to crowds, and not criminals—but Bruce realized he might be able to find out something more about the people he faced.

And Bruce had already given Auslander a very important job.

He nodded. "I can still get to this lecture. I need to talk to him anyway."

"Very good, sir." Alfred picked up a voluminous tome from the counter. "I can finish reading my book while I wait for you."

Bruce looked at him—and tilted his head. "Why don't you come in with me?"

"Sir?"

"This thing I'm doing—Batman—looked one way when I started. I knew what I wanted to do, and what it would take for me to be done. I knew what that world would look like. But after meeting The Joker, that's changed."

Alfred raised an eyebrow—but listened.

"I don't recognize the world I'm seeing." Bruce tapped on his chest. "For me to understand what's going on in here, I need help understanding what's going on out *there*. Help from the smartest people I know." He looked to Alfred. "*All* the smartest people."

Alfred gave the faintest hint of a smile as he put the book on the table. "I'll bring the car."

CHAPTER 5

"**E**VERYTHING IS REFLEX," Hugh Auslander said. "Everything is reaction."

From afar, Bruce Wayne studied the gray-haired man behind the Gotham State University lectern. He looked like he was born to be there. Knowledge and wisdom in a tweed three-piece suit and tiny round spectacles. And he had a voice to match: authority, seasoned with a little gravel. The auditorium was standing-room-only—and his listeners were hanging on his every word.

"Regard Carl Auer von Welsbach," Auslander declared, directing his attention to a giant face being projected in black-and-white on the screen behind him. "I promise he isn't a cousin, though he is from one of those countries the *Globe* mistakenly thinks I'm from."

Indeed, Bruce thought the man in the archival photo looked like a younger version of Auslander himself, right down to the beard and mustache—and the whispers from the audience suggested that others felt the same way.

"In 1903, Carl Auer mixed iron and cerium, which reacted by creating an alloy. When that alloy is struck, it reacts by oxidizing rapidly." Auslander turned and faced the crowd. "And *you* have just reacted with confusion: '*Why is this old fool speaking to us about chemistry?*'"

Chuckles from the audience.

"Or perhaps you reacted with indignance: *That damn newspaper! I thought this talk was about popular culture!*"

Guffaws from the crowd.

"Or maybe even personal embarrassment." His eyes went wide. "*Am I in the wrong room? Are my senses failing? Can I be trusted to pass my genes to a future generation?*"

Raucous laughter. Bruce smiled; beside him, even Alfred grinned.

Auslander tapped his forehead. "Each answer would have created a physical reaction within you. A storm of mental electricity. The production of adrenaline. A flow of blood to your skin, otherwise known as a blush." He reached into his jacket. "But you will react differently to something you recognize."

He took something out of his vest pocket. "It happens that von Welsbach's alloy, which oxidizes when struck, reacts with butane."

Bruce had already guessed what it was. *A lighter.*

Auslander held it so the audience could share in Bruce's sense of recognition. But then several watchers gasped as the aged doctor thrust his hand over the unlit lighter. "Hmm. Another reaction," Auslander said, observing the faces in the crowd. Some expectant, some concerned.

He flicked the lighter. "And another."

The flame licked the bottom of his hand for several seconds, during which even Bruce flinched. "And another," Auslander declared through gritted teeth as he saw people's responses.

"*And another!*" The professor quickly deactivated the lighter and drew his palm to his mouth in an expression of pain. He winced. "I speak nine languages, and I am mentally swearing in *all* of them right now!"

The audience reacted again—in a cascade of emotions that the speaker promptly delineated as he wiped his hand on a handkerchief.

"In ten seconds you experienced surprise, revulsion, relief, sympathy, and amusement. All beginning with a bit of metal, a few drops of fuel, a dead Austrian, and an old man's foolhardiness in trying to prove a point." He folded the handkerchief. "We all believe we are individuals, with free will. But the physical drives the psychological, which again drives the physical—and it does so on a universal scale. We speak of mass traumas because the masses can be traumatized, as one. *But we can also act as one, and that saves us.*"

Applause, for what had become the most famous line from "As Titans Battled," Auslander's series of magazine essays sure to become a bestselling book. The current holder of the Thomas and Martha Wayne Chair at Gotham General Hospital had taken the shaken city by storm, offering ways to make sense out of all that had happened to the collective psyche.

Bruce thought it was good that Alfred had called ahead to reserve their seats. The arrival of a Gotham City socialite—butler in tow—at any public event could be expected to cause a disruption, and he didn't want to take attention due the professor. It turned out not to matter. The audience only cared about Auslander. He'd made a name for himself in several disciplines, mostly through papers he had authored; a year ago, Bruce hadn't seen him in person or on television.

But Auslander was anonymous no more—and *everyone* wanted to know what he thought about one psyche in particular. Bruce and Alfred included.

"I close by returning to The Joker," Auslander said.

Jack Napier's transformed face replaced that of the chemist on the slide behind him, and its sudden appearance caused a ripple of unease that Bruce shared in.

"This image prompts one reaction now, but when you first saw him, you thought something else," Auslander said. "Because what is a clown? It is something which people are presumed to like—predisposed, if you will—because of our cultural conditioning."

Images of other, friendlier clowns replaced The Joker on the screen.

"I would say it goes even further than that. Fewer people today have personal memories of circuses, after all—so how to explain the clown's universal appeal? The answer lies in biology, and how we relate to other beings. From a young age, infants can recognize a smile, and replicate it—finding they can manipulate their facial muscles to express affinity."

The final slide showed only two dots and a curve—the simplest smile of all.

"A clown, of course, is nothing *but* a smile."

"What about sad clowns?" someone in the audience blurted.

The professor chuckled, and others joined in the laughter.

"Sad clowns only prove my point," the lecturer said. "Sad, angry, or happy, the expressions painted on their faces are a form of communication that predates vocabulary. You will find an expressionless accountant, a teacher, a doctor! But you will never see an expressionless clown. They *are* communication, a communication meant to create behavior in others."

He turned to face the image of the simple smile. "It is *this* which Jack Napier, already suffering from maladjustment and probable mental issues, tapped into after his physical alteration. People who saw that face became receptive to suggestion. And he used that to the detriment of others. Thank goodness he is gone."

Amen, Bruce thought, even as other people said it.

Auslander looked at his pocket watch. "I must get to my patients, but there's time for a question."

A woman stood up. "Professor—or is it Doctor?"

"I am both, a doctor of medicine and professor of—well, time is too short for that." He smiled. "Proceed, please."

"What about Batman?"

Auslander paused, seeming startled to be asked. "What about him?"

"Why doesn't he have the same cult of personality as The Joker?"

He smirked. "His signal shines over the city at night. That isn't famous enough for you?"

The audience laughed.

"I don't mean to say that," the woman said. "With all the sketches that have appeared, Batman isn't exactly a faceless figure. But he hasn't inspired the same numbers of people trying to dress and act like him."

"Designer jet planes being out of the range of the common man may have something to do with it," Auslander replied.

More laughs. Bruce resisted the impulse to look at Alfred.

Auslander took off his glasses to polish them, apparently using the pause to give the question some thought. When he finally spoke, he came out from behind the lectern.

"I like that term of yours. I contend the mask means that Batman *is* a 'faceless figure'—and that is why people cannot identify with him. As noted, we are a visual species, dependent upon social cues. Batman flees from cameras, and also hides his face. Millions of people looked into The Joker's eyes—and while they saw madness, the smile was something they recognized, even if they couldn't fathom his real intents."

He paced to the edge of the stage. "Batman is, by contrast, inhuman. Emotionless and inscrutable. Those who see him instead react to their memories of a bat—a harmless creature which nonetheless strikes fear in anyone who is not a zoologist. I suspect that is by design. But people will never identify with Batman himself. You might as well ask people to see something of themselves in a grandfather clock."

Bruce blanched—just in time for him to realize that Auslander had finally laid eyes on him.

"Now, I must get to my patients," the doctor said. "Remember, while this talk may have been of some small benefit to you, those who really need the help are in Gotham General's Smylex Ward. I ask that you support the charity as you can. Thank you."

People were still applauding after he'd claimed his notes from the lectern and stepped offstage. Bruce and Alfred were allowed to pass security to meet him.

The industrialist took the lecturer's hand. "Good talk."

"Thank you, Mister Wayne—and Mister Pennyworth," Auslander said, regarding Alfred.

The butler smiled. "Good of you to remember, sir."

"Eidetic memory," Auslander said, touching his own temple. "My curse, but it helps with etiquette." He looked at Bruce. "I am pleased to see you. If I'd known we had a celebrity in our midst, I might have mentioned you."

"It's not necessary."

"To what do I owe the honor of your attendance?"

"The speech, of course. But since you mentioned it, we should discuss the Smylex Ward."

"Of course." Auslander gestured for the pair to follow him into a back hallway. "I'm headed there now. Walk with me to my car."

The Joker's war on consumer goods had claimed a number of lives before Batman discovered what combinations created Smylex— but there was a larger number of victims who had not died. Some people's exposure to the combined chemicals had been limited. In other cases, the mix of chemicals itself had differed just enough to trigger some harmful effects but not fatal ones. Luckier victims saw less severe symptoms, ranging from mild rashes and facial tics to bouts of giggling.

The worse-off were still hospitalized. Some, comatose.

The Joker's misuse of the Axis Chemicals factory had made Gotham City the epicenter of exposure, but effects had been felt across state lines, along interstates, and wherever the city's residents traveled. Raw chemicals from Axis made it into the products of a hundred companies, which was part of why it had taken so long to determine that the factory was the source. It hadn't initially occurred to Bruce that Napier would return to the place where he was deformed, much less take it for his lair. But it made a twisted kind of sense, and that was the only kind in The Joker's world. Finally making the connection had allowed Batman to put the factory out of commission for good.

"I'm glad you found my little talk edifying," Auslander said as they reached the lobby. "In a small way it allows me to treat the collective harm Joker did to minds—just as at the ward we treat the bodies."

"They're both worth doing," Bruce said.

"Most assuredly," Alfred said as he held the door open.

"Then we all agree." Auslander stepped outside with them and peered at Bruce in the sun. "I have asked for more money. I expect that's why you're here."

Bruce nodded. He'd wondered how best to broach the topic. "Your last report says the number of patients increased, rather than decreased."

"People are detecting later side effects." Auslander began walking toward the reserved parking spot where his modest compact car awaited. "Intake has increased."

"But there are also reports some patients may not even have had real exposures," Bruce said. "You've been taking them in nonetheless."

Auslander halted. He raised an eyebrow. "Someone on staff told you this?"

Bruce didn't deny it. "This is good news, though, isn't it? The real impact is declining." He put up his hands. "I'm not talking about touching the funding for the patients in long-term care. I'm sponsoring a benefit night at the Imperial to help with that. But—"

"You fear the flood." The doctor nodded. "The problem is, every patient must be seen—and as you noted, the numbers have increased." He clasped his hands. "I was just speaking in there of the psychology of crowds. In a mass trauma, survivors desperate to empathize will seek ways to participate in others' ordeals."

"Interesting." That led to the question Bruce really wanted to ask. "Do people ever think that way about—" He paused, not wanting to say The Joker's name. "About the perpetrator?"

Auslander scratched his hairy chin. "A good question. Certainly, criminals copy other criminals all the time—especially if they perceive them to have achieved more success. In The Joker's case, he was, for a time, the most impactful criminal in the history of American law enforcement." He nodded. "Yes, the garden-variety criminal would cling to that. They don't see him as a failure. They see him as a role model."

Bruce looked to Alfred. The butler gave a slight nod. *Understanding sought, understanding received.*

"Thank you, Professor. I've been meaning to visit the ward again sometime."

"Certainly, Mister Wayne. Just alert my office ahead of time. Now, I really must go," Auslander said, opening his car door. "In your business or mine, the costliest problems are the ones that happen when you're not looking."

CHAPTER 6

"... *THE ISLE IS FULL OF NOISES, sounds, and sweet airs, that give delight, and hurt not* ..."

Karlo did not hurt. He drifted painlessly in rich, sweet air, as he had for countless hours. His mind was on a distant island, recycling the words of Caliban, the monstrous man.

"*Sometimes a thousand twangling instruments will hum about mine ears* ..."

As Caliban, he heard the birds and insects, as always—but the other noises were with him again. Beeps, steady and syncopated, alien to the jungle setting. The machine hum, fading in and out. All sounds on the summer breeze wafting through the palm trees.

"... *and sometimes voices, that, if I then had wak'd after long sleep, will make me sleep again* ..."

A woman spoke. "How are we today, Mister Karlo? It's Miss Mindy."

Her voice was light and pleasant, but unwanted. Miranda was the only human woman on Caliban's island—all the others were spirits with fancy names like Ariel, Ceres, and Juno. "Miss Mindy" was certainly not one of them. Whoever she was, she had interrupted his flow. Karlo had memorized the role and the words were all he had, running endlessly through his mind. Interruptions threatened everything.

"Time to change the linens, hon. I'm just going to turn you on your side. Here we go!"

The island quaked. Trees split, and coconuts fell from them. Karlo felt the world going sideways.

"You're not getting any lighter," the woman's voice said. "I guess that's good."

Light ruptured the sky. There was no mistake: something was happening. But Karlo knew it didn't have to be bad. After all, even Caliban had dreams. And in them, he had looked to the heavens for his heart's desire.

". . . the clouds methought would open, and show riches ready to drop upon me . . ."

Riches, yes—but most of all, Caliban sought deliverance from his tormentor. *Freedom.*

"All done with this side," said Miss Mindy. "But I forgot something. I'll be back." A light chuckle. "Don't go anywhere!"

Don't go anywhere?

With the sound of each fading footstep, another part of Caliban's island fell away. When he heard a door close, his paradise vanished—with another world taking its place. And Karlo remembered how reality had disappointed Caliban. Disappointed him enough, such—

"—that when I wak'd," Karlo mumbled, *"I cried to dream again!"*

He opened his tear-soaked eyes—and was blinded. He shut them quickly.

It took several seconds for him to realize he was lying on his side. His muscles were stiff and would not respond. He felt as though he were lying on a giant marshmallow—but as moments passed he realized it was his own flesh, puffy and robbed of blood flow. There was something on his face, helping him breathe—and umbilical cords attached to his body. A tube went up his nose.

Karlo had no recollection of having been born; who did? But he had the distinct sensation that it might have felt like this.

He pushed off the mask and inhaled—and winced as his fresh island air was replaced by the smell of antiseptic. He pulled the tube from his nose and strained to sit up. The cords attached to him were sensors, stuck to the skin beneath the robe he wore. He pawed at them, trying to get them loose.

"I'm back!" Miss Mindy said. "Did you miss me?"

He laid eyes on the middle-aged woman, but no recognition came. She gawked at him. "Oh, my lord!"

In his daze, Karlo spoke with the only words he had, those that had been in his head. The words of Shakespeare's misanthrope. "Art thou afear'd?"

She hustled toward him. "I wouldn't try to get up, hon. You're not even supposed to be able to!" After checking on him for a moment, Miss Mindy stepped over to the door and called into the hall.

Karlo ignored her. He was in another dream, surely—an unhappier one, apparently, in a hospital room. He'd hated the buildings all his life, since his mother entered one and never came out. He wanted to pinch his cheek to end the dream—but something was already gripping him there: the contacts on the side of his face. He felt for one. It wouldn't come loose. Fumbling around, he found the wire and pulled on it.

And pulled. The skin of his cheek went along with the wire, stretching to an angular shape that he could see out of the corner of his eye. When the contact finally popped off his face, it left what looked like a pimple an inch high.

"You've been in a coma," the nurse said as she stepped back into the room. "You—"

Karlo had been sixteen the last time someone called him "Pizza Face." He hadn't been that age in a long time, but he immediately turned away from her, facing the wall. He drew his index finger to his face and pressed on the protuberance, mashing it into his jawline. It smushed down to nothing, which pleased him.

But then he couldn't get his finger free. Trying to pull it loose only resulted in the skin stretching like putty, stuck to the digit. That led to him placing more fingers on his face, first from one of his hands and then the other.

A perverse thought entered his mind: he was Pizza Dough Face.

He heard her step toward him. "What's wrong? Show me."

He winced and yanked his hands away from his face, freeing the adhering skin from his fingers. He turned to the nurse and smiled with satisfaction.

Miss Mindy fainted.

"You're overacting," Karlo wanted to say after she fell to the floor—but he wasn't the director of this dream. He ripped the rest of the contacts free and got out of bed. Imaginary or not, the hospital room was well furnished; there was a mirror outside the bathroom. He staggered to it and took a look—whereupon the actor nearly fainted himself.

Every place a finger had previously adhered to was now a prong of flesh, rising from puffy cheek and forehead skin that no longer mimicked the shape of his skull. *I look like a blowfish!*

Karlo started to reach for his cheeks again, only to think better of it. He snatched a towel from beside the sink and buried his face in it. This time, he didn't have the sensation of his skin adhering. He breathed more easily—

—until he withdrew the towel and looked in the mirror. The protuberances were gone, but so were the familiar contours of his face, flattened by his act. He winced in horror—and tidal waves of skin rippled across Karlo's face, traversing his skull and jaw. They turned back as he changed his expression. Dream or not, it had to stop. *Wake up, Karlo!*

Someone entered through the partially open door. "Mindy! What's wrong?"

It was a young man. Not a doctor, but someone in the white scrubs of an orderly. He saw Miss Mindy on the floor first and hurried toward her. She was starting to revive, but Karlo was the one that really needed assistance.

His face still in macabre motion, Karlo reached out toward the man and begged for help. But all that came out of his misshapen mouth was a grotesque gurgle.

"Yahh!" the startled orderly yelled, putting his hands before him. "Get away!"

Karlo moaned again. *Help me!* he tried to say. But whatever was happening to his face was also acting on the muscles that controlled his voice. He'd spoken before, but now all he could manage was a throaty gurgle.

He grasped at the orderly, who shoved him away in panic. "Stay back!"

The push sent Karlo, who was still shaky on his legs, into a monitor stand. One of its sharp edges caught him in the ribs. Without thinking, Karlo responded to the pain by lashing out, smacking the orderly with such force that he flew backward, tumbling over Mindy and into the far wall.

She screamed. *"Victor!"*

Karlo gawked. He'd been on a wrestling team in high school but had never struck another human being in anger. Yet he was filled with rage and wanted to strike something else. But the orderly was unconscious. Karlo looked at his hand, the one that had delivered the blow. It, too, looked different. His muscles, tensed up, had brought the skin taut and angular, as if covering bones made of metal.

Cowering on her hands and knees as she checked on young Victor, the nurse shrieked. "Stay away from us!"

The door opened again, revealing a gaunt gray-haired man in a white lab coat. His eyes widened as he beheld Karlo. Two more orderlies were behind him, ready to enter. Karlo clenched his fists, looking for somewhere to go.

The newcomer barred the door with his hands. "Remain where you are," he said.

Karlo seethed. There was no way a gaunt man like that could stop him—and the sight of more orderlies out to hurt him just angered him more. It seemed to be his response to everything.

"No one will hurt you. Don't try to leave, and they won't enter."

Karlo struggled to calm down. He'd spoken earlier, but no words had come since his deformity appeared. Somewhere between the shock and anger—

"My name is Hugh Auslander," the man said, lowering his arms. "I run this wing of this facility."

What facility? Karlo wanted to know, but only managed grunts.

"You're in Gotham General Hospital," Auslander said, hands before him. "You're confused right now. You've been through an ordeal. A long ordeal—"

Karlo gestured to his face, animated in anguish. He couldn't get his features to go back the way they were supposed to be—and he couldn't remember how to speak in his own voice, either. He had to let his body speak for him. *What is this?*

Auslander spoke in even tones. "You were exposed to the chemical agent Smylex. It affected your body, which reacted by shutting down, putting you in a comatose state. Do you understand?"

Karlo looked to the mirror again—and saw something worth striking. He smashed it with his fist. Again and again, causing it to shatter. If it cut his hands, he didn't notice. He just had to make that face disappear.

Auslander was having trouble restraining those behind him. He barked something at them and closed the door, shutting them out. Then he faced Karlo again. "Sir, you're overwrought. You must calm down."

Karlo kept striking the mirror. A shard scraped his hand, but it did not draw blood. The red mark vanished after a second. That settled it: he was still in a nightmare. *Send me back to my island. Send me back to the other dream!*

The doctor—if that was what he was—noticed it, too. "Calm yourself, please. I can help you understand what's happening." He reached for something on a nearby table. "We have to study this."

Study?

Karlo saw it, now: Auslander had a syringe. He cast an eye back to the bed. How long had he lain in it? He didn't know. He just knew he couldn't go back there. He still couldn't form words in his own voice, but it occurred to him that Caliban had words that would work. When Auslander took a step toward him, Karlo's face firmed up and he bellowed in a dark baritone, *"I shall be pinch'd to death!"*

His outburst—angry and iambic—caused the doctor to freeze. "That's from *The Tempest*."

Sensing the change to his face, the actor guessed at what had happened. Karlo was a non-entity; "be yourself" was the most useless advice he'd ever gotten at an audition. He simply didn't know how. But somehow, Karlo's dreamworld rehearsals had found their way into his muscle memory—and given him words that he was able to speak.

He couldn't tell Auslander to keep away, but he could say something else. He grabbed the fallen equipment stand and lifted it over his head. *"I am subject to a tyrant, a sorcerer, that by his cunning hath cheated me of the island!"*

The door opened—and to his right, the orderly he'd struck rose. Auslander stepped cautiously forward, now flanked by his employees. "Please, sir, you must allow us to—"

Karlo pictured himself smashing the doctor in the head with the metal stand. *Let Auslander lie in the bed, with tubes and wires coming out of him,* he thought. But the satisfaction he felt just at imagining it gave him pause. Just enough that he turned. He held the stand before him and drove it through the window.

More broken glass. "Sir, stop!"

"Freedom, high-day! High-day, freedom! Freedom, high-day, freedom!"

Climbing the chair meant for visitors, Karlo threw his arms before him and hurled his body through the window. He didn't know what floor he was on—but as he went through, he had a single, jarring thought.

The higher, the better.

DOCTOR AUSLANDER HURRIED TO the window. Barely mindful of the broken glass, he strained to see what had happened to the patient. No one was in sight.

All sorts of possibilities went through his mind. He turned back to the bed and reached for the medical chart, which had fallen to the floor in the commotion.

Patient Thirty-Five—some sort of actor, that made sense—had been comatose since contact with several chemically altered products during the Smylex panic. That was an unusual reaction, if far from unique. Yet there was more to it, as the doctor had noticed before. Instead of atrophying during his paralysis, Thirty-Five maintained his body weight and muscle mass. Intubated at the start, he'd even begun breathing without assistance. The doctor had checked on the case several times in recent weeks.

Fascinating.

He registered the commotion around him. The nurse was at the phone, receiver in her hand. "Switchboard, this is Mindy. Put me through to the police!"

The doctor looked back, startled. "What are you doing?"

"The patient attacked us, Doctor!"

"Let me have that." He reached for the receiver, and she quickly yielded it.

"Gotham City Police," said the voice over the phone.

"This is Doctor Auslander at Gotham General. I'm just testing to see if this line is working."

"It is." A pause. *"You couldn't have called anyone else to test that?"*

"I'm just confident to know we can reach you if necessary. I won't disturb you further. Thank you." He put the receiver on the cradle.

Mindy gawked at him. "Doctor, he's on the loose. He hurt Victor!"

The doctor put up two fingers to correct her. "He is also hurting, Nurse. Confused. We can take care of this ourselves. *We* will find him."

"But—"

"Smylex survivors have enough to contend with without people panicking over something that may be a unique case. Do you want to be responsible for the start of a new prejudice?"

She blanched. "Of course not."

"Very well." He faced the other orderlies. "If you find him, do not harm him. Report directly to me." He lifted the receiver and started to dial. "I'm calling security. We'll handle this on our own!"

CHAPTER 7

I F IN HIS BEWILDERED state Karlo had hoped for a swift end to his torment in leaping out the window, it did not come. The hospital room was only on the second floor. But it might not have mattered if it was higher. He'd felt no pain whatsoever when he landed—and, since then, had run across the campus with an athleticism that he'd never possessed before.

It didn't make sense—but then nothing did anymore. Nothing but running. Caliban had wanted to escape Prospero; Karlo wanted to avoid the hospital and being immobilized in bed. He vaguely remembered wanting to be released from someone's control before that—but try as he might, he couldn't remember that person's name. He'd finally come to accept that he wasn't dreaming, but his memories of life before the island were still clouded.

Nothing was wrong with his feet, though. Dashing barefoot across sidewalk, pavement, a rock garden; all these things should have torn his poor feet to shreds. But as he crouched atop gravel behind a large garbage bin outside the hospital, he stared down in disbelief. The soles of his feet had taken on the appearance of track shoes, only without the rubber: a grid-like network of raised welts had appeared on them.

He stood gingerly, moving from one foot to the other. The gravel wasn't painful. It was as if his flesh had responded to his activity by adapting to protect the bones of his feet—but that wasn't possible, was it?

People ran past on the other side of the bin. They were desperate to catch him—and as his blood surged, Karlo grew more desperate not to be caught. But a man with a melted face in a hospital gown was certain to be seen.

Creeping out from cover, he spied a van parked at the loading dock. When its driver went inside the hospital, Karlo rushed toward the vehicle. Ducking to stay out of sight, he climbed inside. It was a service vehicle of some kind; it only had a driver's seat.

He beheld the happiest sight he'd seen since waking up: the keys sitting in the change cup in a box next to the driver's seat. He took them—and, in his excitement, dropped them to the floor. He had just leaned over to get them when he caught sight of his face in the rear-view mirror.

Papa!

It wasn't, of course. The man was long dead; Karlo's facial features took more after his mother's. But somehow the muscles of the actor's face had moved just enough that they recalled the shape of his father's brow, the arch of his cheekbones. And as he looked, the likeness grew better. But for the eyes, he was looking at his father. His father—

—the car thief.

Karlo flinched. *What am I doing? Stealing a van?*

It was insanity. He wasn't anything like his father. Marta Babić's little boy would never do such a thing. He'd been tempted to steal a bicycle once, only to chicken out after remembering the sight of his father behind bars. He dropped the keys back in the cup. And as his expression changed, the offending features of his face melted away. Not into his own—no such luck. But it gave him pause. Had he somehow willed the new appearance, subconsciously?

Before he could think on it more, security guards passed in front of the van. Two were carrying batons; another, a net. Karlo quickly ducked—and listened.

"—Auslander wants him brought in," said one searcher. "He's got something wrong with him."

"Everybody in that whole wing's got something wrong with them."

"Not like this. Hope this guy likes being strapped down!"

That was all Karlo needed to hear. He hit the floor and crawled on his belly into the back of the van. There were no side windows in the rear, but the little light that came in from the back told him he'd lucked into just what he needed: *I'm in a laundry truck!*

He was rooting around trying to find clothing when he heard movement ahead. He quickly buried himself between the mountains of bags. A balding man climbed inside, found his keys, and started the van without checking his cargo. Karlo let out a breath. He envisioned a clean escape, like in all the prison movies he'd seen. Watching films had paid off.

Searching for clothes in the dark while mashed between laundry bags, on the other hand, wasn't easy—especially when the driver proved to be desperate to get done with his shift. The van lurched through turns, shifting the load on top of Karlo. Then the driver would gun the engine, creating another avalanche. *At least this means we've left the hospital,* Karlo thought.

After finding countless sheets and pillowcases, he discovered a bag that had a different kind of tag from the others. Opening it, he found it was full of hospital scrubs. Shirts and pants would beat his hospital gown, and he'd seen many people wearing them on the bus before. The thought cheered him as he awkwardly changed clothes on the floor of the van, between bags. He could catch the D27 for his apartment and hide until this whatever-it-was passed.

He'd finished dressing when he remembered he didn't have any money. He looked forward at the cup in the console next to the driver: it held change, which any Gotham City motorist needed for tolls. Figuring it was better than stealing a truck, Karlo crept ahead. In between swearing at traffic, the driver—a paunchy, older man—had cranked up a ball game on the radio, all of which offered some cover.

"Get off my ass!" yelled the driver.

Karlo tensed up, thinking the words were for him—but honking from behind told him the driver was responding to something else. The driver adjusted his rearview mirror a little too far, allowing Karlo, frozen in panic and with his hand on the change cup, to look right into his eyes.

"Gah!" The older man slammed on the brakes, throwing Karlo and everything behind him forward. Whoever was tailgating the van slammed into it with full force, sending it into motion. The vehicle careened through traffic, tilting as it did; Karlo tumbled. He barely caught sight of a telephone pole up ahead before the van crashed into it, shattering the windshield.

Noise everywhere, and now glass. Recovering, Karlo saw the driver hunched over the steering wheel. Some cars were getting air bags, but this van didn't have one—and while belted in, the old guy appeared injured. Karlo reached out for him, trying to help; he unbuckled his belt and pushed him back in his seat.

But while bruised, the man wasn't unconscious—and instead he screamed once again in Karlo's face. Or rather, at it. Backing off, Karlo saw why in the mirror: apparently his face had responded to the events by making him look like a shrieking, bug-eyed menace.

"Get back!" the driver said, reaching under his seat. Hand shaking, he produced a handgun.

"No, don't!" Karlo tried to say—but it came out more like something from a sea monster.

The driver fired a shot, just past Karlo's head. Ears ringing, he lashed out, shoving the man back. He pivoted, intending to dart out the passenger door—only to spy the change cup, which miraculously still had something in it. He grabbed it and moved.

"Thief! Bring that back!"

Another shot, zinging past his other ear just as he opened the door. Karlo didn't know whether the accident or the shock had been making the driver miss, but neither was he going to ask. Karlo hit the street.

Rush hour traffic had snarled from the accident; the gunshots had sent emergency services workers and any rubberneckers fleeing. Karlo, who didn't know geography well when he had all his faculties, ran down the street with his cup of change, still barefoot but un-hobbled by the accident. He passed a damaged truck, likely the horn-honker that had struck the van, just as he heard the first police sirens. Wherever he was, he couldn't stick around—not if he didn't want to wind up strapped into a bed.

Several people cried out as he passed. He didn't need to hear what they were saying. *Look at the man, his face messed up from the wreck. Was he shot in the face?* He didn't want to know. He just needed a miracle—

—and found it, far away down a cross street and heading toward him. Not just any bus, but the D27, which took a long and winding route that he knew led home. It would miss all the chaos on the avenue the crash was on, and he spied a sign for a stop just up the street. It would reach him in a little over a minute.

Another horrified look from a passerby reminded him he needed to do something about his face. There was only one thing he could think of. He grabbed a newspaper out of a trash can and opened it. He carried it in front of him as he walked, trying to seem nonchalant as he headed for the stop. Acting was the one thing he was certain he could do.

He seemed like any other self-involved Gothamite when he climbed the steps into the bus and plugged coins into the slot, all without ever looking out from behind the broadsheet. This was a rush hour run, and many seats were filled; he didn't think it was smart to sit with anyone anyway. He stood with the straphangers, bracing his body against a post while shielding his face from view with the paper.

A commuting orderly, that's what he was. Nothing to see here.

As the bus resumed its route, he chanced to look at the paper before him. Bruce Wayne was dating some actress again. The Flugelheim was auctioning off artwork someone had defaced—who would ever do a horrible thing like that? He scanned the headlines and pictures only before chancing to look at the paper's date.

Oh, my God. Events were slowly coming back to him. The auction article had mentioned The Joker. Auslander had mentioned Smylex. He remembered those things, and their association with the last thing he now recalled: preparing the Capra for the debut of *The Tempest,* which had occupied his feverish brain for what he now realized were months.

I was in that bed for months!

He was beginning to process that when a male rider nearby addressed him. "Dude, you're a mess."

Karlo responded by bringing the paper up, and even closer to his face. A child spoke, next. "Ooh! Disgusting!"

What now? Nobody could see his face. Karlo started to move away—only to look down and see his clothes were covered with dark blood.

This time, Karlo yelled out. The accident must have been worse than he thought—or maybe whatever was wrong with him had gotten worse. He threw the newspaper in the air and clutched at his clothes. Screams came from all over the vehicle.

Karlo realized with relief that the blood was dried. There'd been a different tag on the bag he opened; the clothes were destined for a heavy-duty laundry or the trash as medical waste. Some surgeon had worn these. He just hadn't noticed in the dark. Now he could see people were pointing not just at his clothes, but at his face. He looked up into the mirror at the front of the bus and nearly screamed himself. Those mirrors always distorted one's appearance; his needed no help. He looked every bit the blood-soaked gargoyle.

As travelers crowded away from him, he tried again to speak, but he couldn't even hear himself over their yells. People repeatedly pulled the signal cord to get the bus to stop; ahead the bus driver noticed and began to slow down. Karlo shouted in his direction. *Don't stop now—*

"Freeze, freak!"

Karlo looked into the barrel of a gun—and, behind it, the face of a punk with sunglasses and spiky purple hair. This time, Karlo lifted his hands.

"Get back," the young man shouted. "I don't know what you are, but get back!"

The kid was clearly tripping on something, Karlo realized; reality wasn't entirely registering for him. *Welcome to the club.*

But Shakespeare had given Caliban no lines suitable for confrontations on public transportation, and when Karlo tried to speak again, the sounds that came from his mouth only served to amp-up the gunman further. He waved the pistol inches from Karlo's misshapen nose. "I'll kill you, man. I'm tired of demons—"

This time, Karlo's bark was intentionally feral. *I'm tired of people shooting at me!* He seized the punk's wrists—and squeezed hard, pouring out all the anger and confusion of the last hour. The gun falling to the floor of the bus, Karlo yanked the guy forward and slammed his head into one of the metal supports.

Screams, everywhere. Behind him, several wary would-be heroes had stepped forward—while ahead, the driver had pulled to a full stop.

Without thinking, Karlo reached down and grabbed the gun. He fired it once at the ceiling; the bullet pierced it, going through.

More yelling, as the riders backed off at the sound of the shot. Even the would-be heroes stood back. Karlo's face twisting with anger, he advanced toward the driver and called out something in almost-understandable Caveman: *"I have had . . . enough . . . of today. I paid my fare. Keep driving!"*

"Yes, sir!" The bus lurched forward.

Standing beside the driver, Karlo grabbed the metal post atop the stairwell with his free hand and hung on. He watched as the bus nearly clipped a limousine in the intersection. That would have been a shame, Karlo thought; it was a beautiful Rolls-Royce, like a movie star of old might have had. But at least it wasn't a police car. Hijacking a loaded bus was almost certainly worse than taking a van, but he figured any jury would understand his motive.

I've had enough of today. I'm going the hell home!

CHAPTER 8

THE ROLLS-ROYCE REACHED the shadiest part of the deserted garage. "Stop here," Bruce said. "Keep the motor running."

"Yes, sir." Alfred put the car in park. "I'll keep watch."

After his late night, Bruce hadn't expected any action; after seeing Auslander's lecture, he'd gone to a Chamber of Commerce meeting like a good citizen. At one time, he'd considered cultivating a madcap playboy persona to better hide his double life as Batman, but that simply wasn't him. He was well aware of all the good things he could do as Bruce Wayne and was willing to do them as an active part of the community.

Batman was for the problems that Bruce Wayne couldn't solve. A runaway bus qualified—especially after spotters on the police band reported seeing a figure with a gun. It had nearly clipped their vehicle; now, the radio said it was making chaotic circuits downtown. Accidents and roadblocks had barred it from leaving the area. That meant Batman still had a chance to get there—if Bruce could get changed in time.

The classic auto enthusiasts who admired his Rolls-Royce would have been appalled by the secret modifications he'd made to the black luxury car. The back seat of the 1956 Silver Wraith had been removed and replaced with a replica version of his own design. Its cushions flipped up to reveal a compartment containing a special version of his Batman armor: more portable, of course—but also much different in function.

He'd been tempted to apply the car model's name to the capeless outfit, because when he was not in motion, it looked a drab silvery-gray. Its monotony was offset only by the yellow emblem on his chest-plate, which was intended, as always, to divert shooters' aims away from his head. But Bruce expected that Batman during the day would *always* be in motion. Any threat serious enough to bring him into full view would probably require that anyway.

That was when the Dynamic Camo uniform really went to work. For it, he'd drawn animal-kingdom inspiration not from bats, but rather bioluminescent squid that generated light to match the levels in their surroundings. As the suit's chain mail–like network of tiny composite-material tiles protected his body, emitting diodes nested between certain cells projected varying amounts of light.

It was by no means a chameleon suit; even *his* technology hadn't advanced that far. Yet the more he moved—and the faster he did it—the more difficult he was for the eye to track. It wouldn't prevent him from being photographed, and it wouldn't evade a solenoid sensor. But his regular suit appeared less threatening in daylight, and it made sense to use gear that offered other compensations. "Deploying." Batman emerged from the car in the gray suit. Alfred pulled away immediately.

Entering the stairwell, Batman found an open area between the flights of stairs leading up. He fired a grapple at the faraway ceiling. Its motor brought him to the top floor faster than any elevator. They'd been lucky to find a tall garage; he needed to start high for what he had in mind.

Soon he was running across the rooftop—and heading toward the one next door, confident that any chance observer would have to look twice to identify what they were seeing.

He reached a cornice. "Third and Conway," he said into his mic.

"The bus is at Sixth and Hathaway, heading north."

"Check."

Batman's daytime kit was significantly lighter, especially given the absence of a cape. It came in handy now, as he had a lot of ground to cover, part of it obstructed. Decades earlier, Georges Hébert, a French naval officer, had developed the *parcours du combattant* as a fitness regimen; Batman doubted that any of his obstacle courses involved vaulting air-conditioning units and sliding down fire escapes. But he was glad he'd incorporated such training into his workouts. Had he arrived by Batmobile at this time of day, he likely wouldn't get near the errant bus without doing more vehicular damage himself. Going on foot was faster—and crossing busy streets was less of a problem when one had the ability to zip-line across.

He'd traversed four blocks—and descended four floors—by the time Alfred reported next. *"The bus is now at Seventh and Walcott."*

"Getting closer." He could hear the sirens—and a distant blat. It gave him an idea. "Where's the fire engine coming from?"

"The dispatcher has not said. But in this area, it's sure to be Oak Plaza Station."

Batman had already surmised that—and guessed that it would serve him.

Breathing hard, he rounded the side of a ledge and looked onto a long boulevard: Atlantic. A mile to the left was Oak Plaza; to the right, he saw a trail of damaged vehicles, some of them smoking. The bus was just visible at the end of all of that, farther ahead than any line could carry him.

He had other plans. Hearing the emergency vehicle approaching, Batman reached for the longest cable spool on his Utility Belt. Figuring that he was on the fourth floor, he sought a sturdy surface more than twenty feet down across Atlantic. He fired a dart attached to a line—and then tested its stability. It would provide a much faster ride than the ones he'd used before, and it would be more difficult to stop, especially as there was no place to light on the other side.

That didn't matter. He wasn't going to ride all the way. Hearing the siren growing louder, he spied the fire truck out of the mass of police vehicles to the left and did some fast mental calculations.

Then, as the hooting vehicle screamed closer, he snapped a carabiner onto the line and leapt toward the street.

He slid down and across—but mostly down. The world whisked past, and part of his brain initially asked him what the hell he was doing. It still did that in moments like these. But with the truck hurtling toward his location, he was back to calculating. Leaping on the vehicle without falling off would require him to release the line at the right time; landing somewhere relatively flat with something to grab onto required even more precision. He found the moment and let go.

"Ooof!" Even with boots designed to absorb impacts, the hard landing hurt—but he couldn't think about that. Grabbing hold of something was the first order of business. Once he did, he began slowly making his way forward.

It wasn't a ladder truck, but an urban rescue vehicle; that made sense, given the kinds of damage the bus was doing—and which might be done to it. He found a perch on the cab and looked ahead. Police cars in all three lanes of the boulevard formed a chevron, with the fire truck behind. The bus was just ahead of them, clipping parked cars as it charged ahead with abandon.

Alfred spoke. *"It's at Atlantic and Tenth."*

"I'm looking at it."

"Then you should know the police are placing spike strips at Twelfth. They have the area beyond surrounded."

Batman frowned. He figured this was coming, but it raised the chances of a tragic end. It posed dangers, and not just for the speeding bus; two Gotham City officers had been killed laying spikes for The Joker's sedans months earlier. And if it turned out that the gunman on board was another copycat, then bringing it to a stop surrounded by cops might be the worst thing for the passengers.

It would be so much easier if he could just talk to the police, not manipulate them—but even with his new working relationship with Commissioner Gordon, that seemed like a step too far. It could lead to his detection, and also jeopardize any cases against people Batman caught. That was a problem as it was.

No, he had to get to the bus first—away from the police trap.

Standing against the wind, he spotted what he needed ahead. He drew the bulkiest trick from his Utility Belt: a handheld launcher loaded with two bat-shaped projectiles. The targeting system was similar to his Batarangs but resided on the launcher itself. He slapped the underside of the weapon against the top of his left wrist, where it adhered to a mount-point on his gauntlet. Internal gyros held the launcher steady while he worked the targeting with his right hand.

Firing solution resolved, he pumped the trigger twice. The bat-winged projectiles launched moments apart, their releases timed precisely. Each soared ahead, over the row of police cars—and then past the bus itself.

He hadn't missed. They found their targets at nearly the same time: opposite ends of the cable suspending three traffic signals over the Eleventh Avenue intersection.

Each of the signal units weighed fifty pounds, and when the sparking contraptions struck the street, they sent colorful shards flying directly in front of the path of the wayward bus. Whoever was driving the vehicle braked violently.

With the bus screeching to an unexpected stop, the police cars veered off on either side to avoid striking it. Passing the bus, they sped through the intersection, bumping harmlessly over the fallen cable and remnants of the traffic signals. The spike strips beyond them were another matter. The police cruisers struck the impediments and spun out of control. Chaos ensued, with the squad cars finishing in a pileup that blocked the police approaching from Twelfth.

It all transpired in mere seconds, with no apparent harm to the drivers—and exactly as Batman intended. He figured it would be better if the police were kept at a safe distance while he did his work.

When the fire truck beneath him skidded to its own stop, he was ready. He leapt from the rooftop, allowing the momentum to send him toward the bus. He landed atop it, chest-plate first, and hung on, fully expecting that the vehicle's reckless odyssey could begin again at any second.

Instead, the bus sat for several moments. The rear door opened, disgorging a stream of terrified commuters. As they hurried toward the sidewalk, Batman moved to the edge of the roof near the door.

He wasn't surprised that the last person off was in uniform; the Army had its arsenal not far from here. Batman called down to her. "Who's left?"

His voice caused her to stop in her tracks. She gawked when she saw him—but she answered. "Just the driver—and the guy with the gun."

That meant the hijacker had apparently not stopped everyone from exiting. *Interesting.* He wondered if it was another of Lawrence's masked reprobates—someone who'd lost his nerve. "The guy—is he a clown?"

"He's a *monster!*"

Batman didn't know what to say to that. "Get these civilians out of here."

Reflexively, the soldier raised her hand to salute—before stopping halfway. She hustled to help the others.

The motor still running, Batman decided not to take any chances that it was over. He leapt to the street, grabbed a pellet from his belt, and hurled it inside the door. As smoke quickly filled the bus, he donned a face mask from his Utility Belt to cover his mouth and bounded up the steps inside.

Through the billowing cloud, he heard excited chatter up the aisle. It sounded like words being exchanged between the driver and someone—only the other half of the conversation was unintelligible, more like guttural grunts. He felt a jolt through the floor under his feet, as the bus went back into gear. The vehicle rocked as the driver forced it over part of a median divider as the vehicle cut across the lane, avoiding the disabled police cars beyond the intersection as it made for a side street.

No, we're done driving. Batman strode through the smoke and drew a weapon from his belt. Ahead, a tall figure in the cloud held a gun on the driver. The hijacker had the brawny physique of a wrestler—but his attire was something else. He wore what looked like pajamas, spattered with blood. *And no shoes.*

An Arkham Asylum escapee, if Batman had ever seen one. It was time to end this. He uttered a single command: "Stop."

Not looking back, the culprit spoke over his shoulder. It was the choked, gurgling voice the hero had heard before—but this time, the words began to sound like something familiar: "Go away."

"I told you to stop." Batman hurled the bolo he was holding through the smoke. The cable wrapped around the hijacker's chest, pinning his arms such that the gun was pointed at the floor. Batman advanced and grabbed the subject's shoulder to spin him about. "Drop the gun!"

The hijacker looked back at him. He wasn't wearing a clown mask—but neither did he have a human face. The skin bubbled and shifted, like lava on a volcanic bed. But there was a man in there somewhere, baring normal teeth through a misshapen mouth. He flexed his chest, and Batman's cable expanded—and fell to the floor as he exhaled. Then, like lightning, he reached out with his free hand and grabbed Batman by the neck.

Batman stared. "What *are* you?"

The hijacker leaned in close, face to hideous, growling face, and shouted in a barely intelligible snarl, *"I've had a really bad day!"*

CHAPTER 9

KARLO'S DAY HAD STARTED off weird and gotten worse. It was all fantasy now, a series of moments he was living through, a passenger propelled by terror and rage. And the latter had found a focus in the gray-clad masked man whose neck he held.

Next to Karlo, the harried driver looked back, astonished. "Batman!"

Batman? Karlo remembered the name from before his incapacitation. Some urban legend, a vigilante that came out only at night. The person at the end of his arm didn't look like a dark avenger. But he had appeared out of nowhere, from sudden smoke. One more part of his nightmare-by-day. Karlo knew he wasn't real—

—until he felt the nightmare's fist.

Batman's punch was prodigious, a right uppercut directly into Karlo's jaw that sent half the flesh on his face hurrying for the other side. He glanced at the bus's overhead mirror; he looked almost like a cartoon character. But this sort of thing didn't surprise him anymore—nor did the fact that he otherwise didn't feel the punch. He shook off the hit. As he did, his cheeks and chin reappeared.

"I said to leave me alone," Karlo growled. His voice was coming back, at least, if distorted. If the secret to speech was trying to sound like whatever his face resembled, shouting in angry-monster mode was working.

His neck still clutched, Batman delivered jabs to Karlo's midsection, one after another. It didn't faze the actor.

"I just want to go home!" Karlo turned his head to the driver and made what he thought was his most commanding face. "Drive!"

"Yes, sir!" The driver floored the accelerator at the exact moment that Karlo gave Batman a mighty shove. The costumed character tumbled backward into the smoke, out of sight.

That was better. Karlo looked out the front of the bus. There weren't any police cars in this direction. Maybe he'd solved whatever dream puzzle was necessary to allow him to wake—

From the cloud, Batman launched himself through the smoke, arms outstretched. He had something in his hand, sparking—some kind of electrical weapon. Without thinking, Karlo brought the gun before him and fired. The shot struck the yellow symbol on Batman's chest, causing him to fall back with a jolt.

Oh, no!

Nightmare or not, Karlo hadn't set out to hurt anyone. He'd even told the passengers to get off the bus. It wasn't that he thought this scenario was real, because he didn't. But while he'd often suffered cruelty, he'd only ever dealt it out in his own head—and his newfound capacity for that frightened him. He'd let his anger get out of control in the hospital and with the earlier gunman—and now he'd shot someone? Karlo took a step forward to check on the masked man.

He got a kick in the chin for the crime of caring.

As Karlo tumbled backward, Batman bounded from the floor, somehow having survived the gunshot. He grabbed Karlo's gun-holding wrist with his left hand and punched him squarely in the nose, again and again.

That, Karlo felt. Enraged, he started forward, intending to bowl Batman over. But his opponent was set. Batman put his whole weight against Karlo, pinning him and his gun arm against a seat. "Drop it!"

"I'll drop you!" Karlo struggled, attempting to bring the gun into contact with Batman's body. He unloaded, firing again and again—

but each shot just missed the gray-clad character's body, tearing into seats that once had been full of people, until the shots gave way to clicks.

He looked at the gun and growled. "Empty!"

Still pinning Karlo, Batman called out. "Driver, you hear that?"

"You better believe it!" The beleaguered bus driver slammed on the brakes, sending both combatants tumbling. Batman took the worst of it, going headfirst into another support.

Karlo rose first. The front door was open; the driver had left through it, trailing an exiting cloud of smoke behind him. Meanwhile, the bus was still in gear—and sirens were audible again outside.

Seeing Batman struggling to get up, Karlo stomped on his chest, forcing him down with more of the strength that he shouldn't have. "Stay there!"

Then he turned. Remembering his shuttle-driving experience, he settled into the seat—and glanced into the large mirror above. Not to see his own face; he'd had enough of that. But half of his earlier job was keeping an eye on the kids. Keeping track of an urban legend shouldn't be too much different.

Batman was trying to stand when Karlo slammed on the accelerator. He upshifted—and then did so again. Up ahead, the street terminated before a row of businesses, all darkened because of the after-five hour. If there was any jolt that could awaken him from a dream, this was it.

Behind him, Batman reached his feet. "Stop!"

"Nothing doing, Nightmare!" Smiling as he gripped the steering wheel, he gunned the bus across the intersection and held on. He closed his eyes as the great machine sped toward an unscheduled retirement.

BATMAN STUMBLED BACKWARD, helpless to stop the bus. He knew where they were—and where the hijacker was heading. There was no tool left on his Utility Belt, no acrobatic move that could change its path.

There was only the rearward of the two side doors, still jammed open from earlier. Ignoring the world flashing past outside, he knelt, ready to leap out—only to remember at the last second that he wasn't wearing his usual gear, but a lighter armor.

This is going to hurt.

He leapt, tucking his body as he did so. He struck the pavement hard, going into a roll. The sudden flash of pain was complemented a second later by a horrific screech—followed by a colossal boom.

Out of his roll and on his side, he saw the bus had smashed head-long into a building. The structure still stood.

He got to his knees, intending to help if anyone needed rescuing—but at this time of day the surrounding businesses appeared to be closed. Hearing sirens, he stood anyway, intending to check things out—only to falter.

He was clutching his knee when he saw them: a pair of news trucks, approaching down the side street. Staying to help the police was one thing; appearing—and appearing to be *hurt*—on television was something he wasn't interested in.

The cops were close enough. It was their turn.

Batman tapped his mic. "I need a ride."

When Karlo opened his eyes again, he was still in the bus—but at least it wasn't a hospital room. Only a few seconds had passed, as near as he could tell. The vehicle was smashed, with windows broken and support posts buckled and snapped, and the smoke that had been in the bus now mingled with some from outside.

He looked about, worried. There was nothing but darkness behind him. Wherever Batman had been when the crash happened, he wasn't here now. But he hadn't been a phantom, either. Nothing in his dreamworld had been anything like what he'd seen—or heard, like the sirens that were approaching. Karlo's sick stomach told him what his mind had been slow to accept. He had to admit it now.

This was real. This was his life. What had happened to his face wasn't something he was going to wake up from. And the things he'd done would be attached to him, forever. So would the things he'd be doing from now on.

The sirens were closing in. He had to get moving.

He scrambled over the dashboard and the mountain of debris in the ruined building. Stumbling about, he was thankful no one had been here—especially when he realized what the building was. Wheels jutted out from the debris, spinning madly. They weren't from the bus. Karlo saw a sign and understood. Peden's Bicycle Works was going to need to remodel.

It was a business he'd seen before. It gave him a notion of where he was. Not near his destination, but he knew stacks of slums lay in the blocks beyond; plenty of places to disappear. He just needed to get out before anyone saw him go—and what he found in the back room gave him hope. A hooded sweatshirt, pants, and shoes—*at last!*—and something else that had been spared the destruction up front.

There was no more delusion to hide behind. Marta Babić's little boy had finally stolen a bicycle. And he was terrified that it might just be the start.

THE HOOD ORNAMENT ON the Rolls-Royce glinted in the setting sun as it pulled off the street and into another garage, this one abandoned. Bruce Wayne emerged from the vacant attendant's booth, half dressed and with part of his Batman gear under his arm. Seconds later, he was back in the passenger compartment.

As the police scanner on the dashboard played, Alfred looked back with concern. "Are you injured, sir?"

"No more than usual."

"That does not reassure me."

Bruce groaned as he put his shirt back on. He tried to ignore the pain.

Alfred pulled the car back out onto the street. Police cars screamed past, even more heading for the crash site. "You didn't remain?"

"No." It was true that he had a working relationship with the police now, but he wasn't yet comfortable with the idea of sticking around—especially after an altercation in which he'd been forced to destroy public property. "What are they saying?"

"The scanner reports one injured civilian, apparently from an altercation with the hijacker before you arrived. Nothing else as yet."

Bruce nodded. "It could have ended much worse." He focused again on the police scanner. "What are they saying?"

"Commissioner Gordon is on the scene. But they've not found the perpetrator," Alfred said.

The hijacker had given him every impression it was a suicide run. Apparently, it hadn't worked. "I guess he survived. He was strong—surprisingly so."

"I see. Will looking at mug shots help, sir?"

"I'm going to say that's a definite no."

BRUCE'S LATE BREAKFAST WAS a distant memory when the Rolls crossed the Memorial Bridge heading out into Gotham County. He knew he needed to eat something, and to patch himself up—but he also needed to find out more about the hijacker he'd faced. All three of those things could be done in the Batcave. But the trip was long for a car without an afterburner, and Bruce had looked to try to get a head start while on the drive.

"They still haven't found him." Bruce switched through police channels on the headset he'd plugged into the hidden port facing the back seat. "I'm waiting for them to recover the gun." He looked up at Alfred. "Anything on the news station?"

Alfred gave a slight harrumph, which was about as vocal a measure of distaste as he ever gave. "They are currently debating whether to call the assailant 'The Skincrawler' or 'Meltmouth.' This based on the same eyewitness report, replayed incessantly."

"I'm not fighting Meltmouth." Noticing the sun had set, he had another thought. He removed the headset. "I can't tune to the emergency services channel back here. Can you go back to it?"

"With pleasure." Alfred made an adjustment—and they both heard animated shouting over the car radio.

It took a moment for Bruce to piece it all together. "Sounds like there was an explosion over in Chinatown."

"Not another wayward bus!"

"I sure hope not." Bruce put the headset back on and started checking other sources. By the time the car approached the gates of Wayne Manor, he had a fuller picture.

"An abandoned factory—blew up as soon as it got dark. They're thinking arson." He removed the headset. "Knox's Last Laughs weren't on the bench long."

"That's well away from the hijacker's route," Alfred said. "Do you think the two are connected?"

Bruce frowned. "I don't know." They didn't have to be; knowing Batman and the police were busy across town might have inspired criminals to act elsewhere. He'd started to notice that dynamic. But a connection made sense, too. He needed to check on both cases at once.

He looked at the time. "I'll be going out again."

"Sir, you were out last night—and again this afternoon. Are you—"

"If the police don't get to rest, I don't. Just put a sandwich in the car. The drive-through isn't an option for the Batmobile."

CHAPTER 10

PROFESSOR AUSLANDER HADN'T INTENDED to be anywhere near a television tonight. A local station had filmed his earlier college lecture for broadcast later on a special *Gotham City After Dark,* but he disliked seeing himself on camera. Besides, he already knew what he'd said, and how people had responded. The only reason to watch was vanity.

Instead, it was in his role as *Doctor* Auslander that he found himself in a conference room in Gotham General, intently watching a TV set alongside several members of his staff. He'd kept the workers who'd witnessed Patient Thirty-Five's escape, including nurse Mindy Johnson, after the ends of their shifts in an attempt to gather and manage information about the escape. But as the TV made clear, the problem had metastasized.

Action News was at the scene of the bus crash across town, broadcasting live as Police Commissioner James Gordon stood before the cameras.

"All the passengers are safe," Gordon said. *"No one was harmed in the store. The scene is secure."*

"Secure?" A reporter in a hat piped up. *"Witnesses are saying there was some kind of mutant on the bus!"*

"Fright masks are hardly new around here," the commissioner replied. *"You know it better than anyone, Knox."*

"But the perpetrator hasn't been found!"

"Batman had contact with him until the end. We can only assume he is in pursuit."

"And what about the fire in Chinatown?"

"Please. Give us both time to work, before you—"

Auslander didn't want to hear any more. "Switch it off," he said. An orderly complied.

Masahito Takagi, Gotham General's administrator, stared at the blank screen. Normally ebullient, he looked fraught. "This is dreadful," Takagi said in a grave tone. "That may have been our patient!"

Auslander was firm. "We don't know that."

"Still, we had an escape. We must tell the police."

"Doing that will set off something horrible."

Takagi raised his palms. "People were hurt, Doctor. Property destroyed. Whether or not the courts say we are liable, we *must* say something."

"I'm not worried about money—or our jobs. I'm concerned about the lives of people in this building!" Auslander clapped his hand on the table. "It has already started. Smylex survivors are being refused insurance and getting turned down for jobs. The health department won't allow them to donate blood."

Takagi looked down. "I know. It is shameful."

"Since this ward opened, I've had to deflect all manner of threats to victims," Auslander said. "Mayor Borg and the city government would like to see everything about Smylex go away, so nobody remembers before the next election. The state is choking us for funds. And the federal government is keen to seize control of the whole facility."

That was news to Conover, the young internist who'd handled Karlo's case. "Why?"

Cornered, Takagi answered with reluctance: "Because Smylex was based on *their* weapon."

Auslander pointed out the window. "If these people had their way, every patient's personal record would be an open book to them—and classified forever. We can't even throw our trash away normally. Those black trucks take it away, just in case some foreign power finds we've scrawled a state secret on scratch paper."

Nurse Mindy's mouth went round. *"That's* what that's all about?"

"If a common criminal could make Smylex, so could anyone," Takagi said. "An amateur detective was able to figure it out."

"At least they're only carrying trash away and not patients," Auslander added. "They're afraid of taking too much control because it implies that they were to blame for Smylex—which of course they were. But whether or not that poor fellow Karlo is the one who did all this doesn't matter. If they capture him, he most probably will not get the help that he needs."

Conover nodded. "And they may take our other patients next."

Auslander crossed his arms. "I've dealt with their kind many times, in countries where patients have fewer rights. Innocent people will be hounded, for no other reason than they had the misfortune to come into contact with goods tainted by the madman Napier. We must draw the line here, Administrator, at Gotham General."

Takagi frowned—but nodded. "You make sense."

"And the ward is dependent on Bruce Wayne for funding. I spoke to him, just today. We have no greater friend—but patrons are notoriously unreliable when it comes to bad press."

"I have known Bruce Wayne for many years," Takagi said. "He is resilient to that sort of thing."

"He hasn't set foot in here since we accepted our first patient."

The administrator thought for a moment. "Not everyone likes hospitals."

Auslander waved his hand. "Certainly he'd find fault with the coffee."

The little bit of levity didn't do much for the mood in the room. Many eyes were still fixed on the darkened TV screen. Auslander knew that Takagi was the only one whose opinion mattered—but he got help from an unexpected source when the orderly that Karlo had struck in his escape raised his hand.

"What is it, Victor?" Takagi asked.

"Look, I should be more upset than anyone," Victor said, gingerly tracing the bandage on his jaw. "But Doc Auslander's right. People I know, even my family—they don't like me working here. Like I'll give them some kind of toxin by contact." Victor tried to shake his head, an act which clearly caused him pain. "If our patient stole that bus, we'll find out—and hopefully we'll find out what made him that way. But if we rush to point the finger at him, and it turns out it's one of them crazy Last Laughs instead . . ."

Victor winced and stopped talking—but hearing the name the newspaper was using for Gotham's latest reprobates, Auslander took up where he left off. "The Joker nearly killed everyone in our ward when he was alive. If we allow the fear he created—*or* the panic created by one of his disturbed adherents—to kill the ward itself, he will finish these people from the grave."

All eyes turned to Takagi. He was the same age as Auslander, but often deferred to his celebrity ward chief. He did so again. "What do you need, Doctor?"

"Time," Auslander said. "This patient—this Karlo—needs medical attention. If he seeks it, we'll be there. In the meantime, I need to analyze his past blood toxicology reports. We already knew his case was different. If we can say it is absolutely unique, we may bring down less trouble on our population."

Takagi nodded gently. "Very well. But if the police come to *us*—"

"Of course." Auslander stood and looked to the others. "Do you understand what we need? Complete silence, if you want to save Karlo—and the patients of this ward."

He did not add "and your jobs," but everyone seemed to get the message—even Miss Mindy, a woman who, he had observed, would talk the ears off a living corpse.

He thanked everyone and crossed the room to exit—and deal with the other crisis. One he'd been alerted about before the meeting began.

An elevator and several corridors took him to a building he had never entered during his tenure: a small maintenance garage at-tached to the motor pool. The regular staff was not on duty at this hour, but a driver was present—along with a vehicle.

It was one of the hospital's vans, one that made runs from the Smylex Ward to a special laundry facility across town. The federal government had insisted on that, too. An older man stood nearby, quaking nervously as he smoked a cigarette. The second he saw he wasn't alone, he dropped it and stamped it out.

Auslander ignored that, stepping instead to the front of the van. The grill was smashed, its bumper caved in. A spiderweb of fractures criss-crossed the half of the windshield that remained. The doctor didn't need to be a detective to see the signs of an encounter at speed with an immovable object. "Tree or street pole?"

"The phone kind—I think. I'm Louie." The man looked terrified. "You're the doctor? Dispatch told me to wait for you."

"I am he. I want you to tell me everything about this person you encountered."

"That wasn't no person. He was a monster. A monster who stole my money!"

Auslander raised an eyebrow. This was new. "How much money?"

"Eighty, maybe ninety cents!"

That much? "Perhaps describe him a little more."

Over the next few minutes, Auslander listened as the driver re-counted meeting a "monster" who was certainly Karlo. It didn't sound as though the patient's long period of unconscious immobility had in any way impacted his physical abilities.

Apart from the obvious. "Let me tell you," Louie said, "that guy was B-U-R-P. Butt-ugly, radiation-poisoned!"

"How colorful."

"Freak looked at me with a face like a lasagna that fell on the floor! He was a gruesome son of a—"

"That's enough description. I'm glad you're all right."

"Van ain't. But the radio works." Louie looked at the doctor. "You know, I think that troll is the same guy that 'jacked that bus. I was near there!"

Auslander scratched his beard. They'd reached the important part. "What did the police say to you?"

Louie shuffled on his feet. "I—uh—didn't wait for them."

"You came straight back here." Auslander peered at him. "Why didn't you wait for them?"

"I didn't want trouble." He looked fretful. "I need this job."

"You didn't try to complete your run?"

"Couldn't, with the van in the shape it's in. It just barely got me back here." Outside, sirens blared—as they had been doing since the rampage, bringing the injured in. Louie heard them. "Do you think we ought to tell them this was one of your guys? It was, right?"

Auslander studied the driver. He didn't figure an appeal to humanity on behalf of Smylex victims everywhere was going to work. Fortunately, he had another way to go. He cracked open the passenger-side door and saw clearly what he'd spied from outside.

"These holes. They're from bullets, are they not?"

Louie couldn't argue. "I told you, we fought. He might have taken the van, not just my—"

"Did the troll have the gun?"

The driver didn't answer. He didn't need to, after Auslander climbed inside, reached under the driver's seat, and produced a weapon.

The doctor exited the van and studied the handgun more closely. It was a cheap small-caliber model, like many sold on the streets. He suspected it was unregistered. "Just one more question, Louie."

"Shoot." The driver shuffled on his feet. "I mean, go ahead."

"You aren't supposed to have a gun in a hospital vehicle, are you, Louie?"

"No, sir." He looked down. "The neighborhood the laundry is in is rough." He exhaled. "So's mine."

Auslander tut-tutted. "I understand. In fact, I understand entirely. The reason you came back here is because this weapon is unlicensed. And would I be wrong in saying you aren't supposed to have one anyway?"

The driver shrank. "Yeah. I've had some problems."

"But *we* won't have one." Auslander gestured with the gun, being careful not to point it. "If you keep this matter to yourself, we won't say anything about it either. Do you agree?"

Louie couldn't believe his luck. "Absolutely!" His smile froze, and he looked to the van. "But what about—"

"Think nothing of it. The cost to Gotham General in publicity would be much greater than repair work we can do right in this garage." Auslander nodded toward the exit. "Take the week off."

"But you're not my supervisor."

"I can arrange it."

A stunned Louie thanked the doctor profusely and started toward the door. He turned around just before the door. "Oh, can I have my—?" Seeing the doctor's reaction, he smiled mawkishly and waved his hands. "Never mind."

"I said I'll take care of everything, Louie. Including this." Auslander pocketed the gun in his lab coat.

Louie exited, weaponless but relieved.

Auslander exhaled. The last hours had been trying, but the lid was still on the Karlo incident—for the moment. He exited the shop and used the master key to lock the door behind him. If he wanted to stay ahead of events, every hour counted. And it began with the file waiting for him on the desk of his office.

All right, Patient Thirty-Five. Let's find out more about you.

CHAPTER 11

YOU CAN'T GO HOME AGAIN. That had been the title of the very first production Karlo had worked on at the Capra—an experimental attempt to adapt Thomas Wolfe's posthumous novel. The production had failed, lasting just one night—but it had been enough to make him fall in love with the venue. He'd keep working at the Capra, even if it meant taking tickets.

Though it sometimes felt like it, he hadn't lived there. Karlo had an apartment across town, a unit that his last relative to pass away had willed to him. It wasn't much—a dilapidated walkup in a nasty building—but it meant he could stay in the city. He just couldn't stay there now. The building had several residents that he suspected were criminals; the police were there almost every day, sometimes more than once. There was no going back. As soon as anyone found him, he'd be sent right back to the ward—or worse.

So he'd kept pedaling the stolen bike, always moving on as the shadows in Gotham City turned into night. He kept to back alleys, pausing only to hide behind garbage bins whenever a police car cruised by. He'd only chanced an encounter with other people once.

After riding a few hours, he realized he was starving and had no wallet. Fortunately, he hadn't been forced to steal—thanks to something he'd already stolen. The sweatpants apparently belonged to the owner of the cycle shop; he'd left twenty bucks in the pocket. So he'd gotten a couple of milkshakes at the window of a place that didn't think anything of a guy with a hood pulled tightly in front of his face. He had money, what did it matter?

He drank them eagerly. From what little he knew about people on life support, he didn't think he should be able to tolerate real food—yet he had no problem at all. It was nice to have his body defy expectations in a positive way for a change.

Late evening brought him to a familiar neighborhood. Karlo could see the lights ahead from Theatre Row, but he didn't want to go there. The brightly lit way wasn't for him, not anymore—not the way he looked. But there was one place he could go, one where crowds almost never gathered, despite the best intentions of himself and his friends.

The Capra.

He felt his ire growing as he pedaled closer. More of the fateful evening had been coming back to him. Tolliver Kingston hadn't just sent him out to buy cosmetics on the black market. He'd made him test them. That had transformed him—wasn't that what that doctor had said? If Kingston was there, he'd tear him limb from limb.

Karlo neared the theatre, avoiding streetlamps. As he approached the corner, he wondered what would be on the marquee, and what poor sap they'd gotten to change it. He just hoped it wasn't Tennessee Williams's *A Streetcar Named Desire*. There weren't enough E's or 3's for that.

Instead, he found the lights were out. *The Tempest* was still on the sign, augmented spelling and all. Karlo realized he didn't know what day it was. The Capra was dark on Mondays and Tuesdays. This was probably one, he figured—though usually there was someone inside. He had never doubted that the play would have continued without him; the show must go on. The play must have done really well if it was still running months later. Maybe Kingston had been the star the Goat's Town Players so desperately—

What am I thinking? That can't be it! It wasn't just that he didn't want to give Kingston the credit. The classics never ran that long in

Gotham City. Besides, the ship's wheel he'd gotten for the opening scene was a rental he'd only been able to get for two weeks. Something was amiss. He got off the bike and walked it onto the sidewalk. Seeing nobody around, he went to the once-opulent front door.

A sign there told the tale: closed—for good. ALL PERFORMANCES CANCELED. He pressed his face against the window in the door—and felt his nose flattening against it as he strained to see anything.

A tear ran down his cheek. Clearing it away carved a streak in his jowls. He rubbed his face to get it back into shape.

Hearing a siren on another block, he quickly pulled back. He hustled with the bike to the alley he knew better than any other. The stage door was there—and something else.

Police tape.

He hesitated. The last time he'd passed through the door, his life had gone horribly wrong. Seeing the tape gave him pause. *Was all this because of me?*

The door wasn't sealed; the lock hadn't been replaced since a break-in years ago. He peeled back part of the police tape and ducked underneath the rest. He brought the bicycle in afterward and closed the door.

It was dark and abandoned. An attempt to turn on the lights told him the power was off. That was no impediment, however. It had been shut off before, in the middle of a run of *Mourning Becomes Electra*. "Mourning Our Electric" had been the company joke—until Karlo had saved the day by wheeling an army surplus gas generator into the narrow alley behind the theatre. While Karlo took pride in his work, he was accustomed to nobody giving him credit; this was one of the rare times they had, and thereafter he'd made it his job to keep it ready to go. He fumbled in that direction.

It took long minutes to get it going, but it had plenty of fuel; he'd restocked it just before—*before whatever happened to him*. These things were coming back, getting clearer—and as he stepped back inside the theatre and turned some of the interior lights on, he began feeling restored, himself.

Until he got to the great hall.

The Capra had never been a palace, but it broke his heart seeing what had happened to it. Someone had set some fires on the stage, scorching it. The boards were stained white in several places; given the ashes scattered about, he expected it was some kind of fire retardant. Whatever happened here, nobody had bothered to clean it up. The seats smelled of gasoline, and there were empty wine bottles strewn everywhere.

He sat down on the steps to the stage, breathless. This was worse than any tragedy the Players had ever put on. He'd never gotten to be onstage during a performance, except to fix someone's costume or a dangling prop between scenes. Now he never would. The Capra, in its own way, was just as much a wreck as he was.

Anger washed over him. The island props, scattered about; he'd built some of those. This was an affront. He spied something colorful onstage, amid the debris.

A clown mask. Pinned to the floor, under a fake tree. Not part of the production; he surmised it belonged to one of the vandals that had been here. Hadn't people in this town had enough of clowns?

He let out a deep breath. His rage had nowhere to go. Stomping around, kicking props wasn't going to improve anything. Instead, he spent half an hour tidying up. Just like he had to in the past—but it felt good to do something familiar.

Finally, he got the nerve to walk backstage. He could not remember anything about the day he was exposed, but laying eyes on one of the dressing rooms gave him chills. A chair was tipped over on the floor, and someone had smashed the mirror to bits. He wondered if the vandals had done it, or someone else. Either way, something told him not to enter.

Besides, there was a better room to visit.

Whatever had happened to the Capra, there was a silver lining: Tolliver Kingston was probably out of a job. He had the biggest dressing room, having demanded it when he joined the troupe. Karlo found the door was shut tight, as it often was when the actor was here. But he also knew the trick to get it open.

He still had the knack; the door creaked open. Inside, he found things relatively undisturbed. Kingston's possessions were gone, but most of the rest remained as it was before he'd joined the company. The big mirror, probably too old and big to move; the same went for the large wooden wardrobe. He was surprised when he opened it to find clothing still inside—and wigs, still in the adjacent trunk.

Karlo sat down on what had been Kingston's chair to think. The legend had been that the Goat's Town Players began as a commune; nobody was really sure who owned the building, or what was in it. The building was still here; maybe its contents were tied up in a bankruptcy dispute.

Or maybe nobody wanted them. The same way nobody wanted him—not as he was now.

Karlo sagged in the chair, and looking in the mirror, he saw his face doing the same. He glanced in the mirror at the trunk; there were lots of masks here. *Is this it? "The Phantom of the Capra?" It's been done—and I can't sing!*

There was only one place that might have answers about his condition: the hospital. Surely his wallet and ID must be back there, as well. But he couldn't see returning without winding up locked down in a bed again. In a room there—or worse, after his wild ride.

He looked down—and saw something else, at his feet. Under the dressing table sat a portable television set. Kingston had sent Karlo to find one on the cheap; he'd carted it here from the farthest thrift shop in town. Kingston said he kept the set to see the stock reports, but everyone knew he really used it so he could sneer at the actor who'd replaced him on the soap opera.

Might as well see what they're saying. He put it on the table and snapped it on.

The nightly news was just ending. Thankfully, he'd seen nothing about himself—just the weather report. He had given a sigh of relief when the announcer added a promo at the end. *"Tune in to our morning news for more about today's mad bus rampage—and the deformed hijacker the* Gotham Globe *is already calling* Clayface!"

Clayface? Karlo gawked. *Do they think that's funny?*

He balled his fists and yelled. *"Clayface?"*

He thought to strike the set but decided instead to grab it. Throwing it would do much more damage, and that would be more satisfying. But before he could, he heard the classical music intro to another program.

"Tonight on Gotham City After Dark, *a treat for you night owls who can't get enough of big words. For the whole hour, a lecture, recorded just today, of psychological phenom Hugh Auslander, who's taken Gotham City by storm!"*

The name went with the face he'd seen. Much from the hospital was hazy; he remembered only being able to speak in iambic pentameter. And he remembered the doctor. He recalled that *After Dark* was hoity-toity, the local channel's answer to public television with long chats with authors, actors, and the like. Kingston had worn out his telephone trying to inspire any interest at all in his relocation to Gotham City. Auslander must be somebody to rate a whole hour.

Karlo put the television on the dressing table and sat down on Kingston's chair to watch it. The speaker had an interesting face—and an even more interesting voice. He parroted one of the turns of phrase Auslander had just used. *" 'We think of ourselves as sophisticated primates, but we may owe more to our hymenopteran cousins, the ant and the bees.' "* He smirked. *" 'Hymenopteran.' Who talks like that?"*

Hugh Auslander, evidently—and as Karlo listened more, he continued to repeat the words the man said. His vocal cords had failed him several times that day, impacted by whatever it was that was wrong with him. But he'd spoken much better when he was using someone else's words, and he'd always been a great mimic. *Just like an actor should be.*

By the time the professor-slash-doctor got around to pontificating about Austrian chemists, he had the voice just about nailed.

Then he looked in the mirror—and gasped.

Somehow, in attempting to mimic Hugh Auslander, he'd changed more than just the way his voice sounded. The muscles of his face had shifted.

That's the secret. It took physical effort to modify one's voice, one's mannerisms. Actors did it all the time. Somehow, he was exerting control over his features in the same way.

He focused again at the man on television. Karlo didn't have the beard, and his eyes were a different color. But that could be fixed, and how often did people look into each other's eyes anyway? Karlo looked back at the trunk—and nodded. For the first time all day—and in months—he was going to take control of his life.

"So I'm Clayface," he said out loud. "A role's a role."

WEDNESDAY, 12:32 A.M.

AMAZING BREAKTHROUGH TODAY!
SIMILAR TO REACTION SEEN AT ARMSGARD
MUST RECOVER SUBJECT BEFORE OTHERS DO
BATMAN: NEUTRALIZE OR ELIMINATE?

ACT II

ART, UNTIL SOMEONE DIES

CHAPTER 12

THE CATHEDRAL, AGAIN.

    Batman knew it was a dream, this time—but this one was going exactly as he remembered. Jack Napier had blamed him for creating The Joker—and Batman had punched him in the gut and shoved him through a rotten wall.

It was just as satisfying as it had been in real life.

Batman stalked his nemesis through the darkness. "You killed my parents."

"What?" The Joker turned his head to spit blood. "What are you talking about?"

"I made you? You made me first."

The Joker spoke quickly. "Hey, Bat-Brain—I was a kid when I killed your parents. I mean, when I say I made you, you gotta say you made me. How childish can you get?"

Running out of space to back up, The Joker put on a pair of glasses—his last trick. Batman knew what would come next. And yet—he stopped. "Wait."

"What?" The Joker blinked. "Oh, gotta take a leak, huh?" He took off the glasses and gestured toward Batman's outfit. "Just go in the suit. Nobody will care. I do it all the time."

Batman pointed at him. "You said you were a kid when you killed my parents."

"Proof that even pointy ears work."

"But why did you say it? You don't know who my parents were."

The Joker shrugged. "I just assumed. You said I made you first."

"Right. But I've only been Batman a short time. Why would you think I was talking about people who died decades ago?" He peered at The Joker. "Do you know who I really am?"

Motion, to the side. The Joker looked to the left and saw Vicki Vale cringing behind a column. "Hey, Vick, do you believe this guy? Stopping a fight to play Twenty Questions."

"What are you waiting for?" Vicki said to Batman. "Hit him, again!"

None of this had happened before—but another thought struck Batman, and he had no choice but to go with it. He faced her. "Did *you* tell him who I was?"

"No! Of course not!" She stepped next to The Joker, apparently unafraid of him. "I'd never tell him. He's a lunatic." She looked Batman up and down. "I mean, so are you. But you're better looking. And you've got a limo. And a butler."

A dignified voice came from the darkness. "You called, madam?"

Batman stared in amazement as Alfred stepped into the light.

The Joker gawked. "Who are you? The old man of the tower?"

"I am the gentleman's gentleman, sir." Alfred produced a tray from behind his back. "Martinis?"

The Joker smiled. "Don't mind if I do." He happily took a glass— and Vicki surprised Batman by taking one, too.

Batman moved to confront Alfred. "Did *you* tell him who I am?"

The butler's eyes widened. "Sir! I would never—"

"You would never?" Batman pointed at Vicki. "You let her into the Batcave." Batman poked Alfred in the chest. "The Joker knows. I want to know if you told him."

Alfred scowled. "I won't be spoken to in this manner."

"You're not my father."

"No?" Alfred dropped the tray. He removed his glasses—and transformed. The skin on his face bubbled and boiled.

"Alfred!" Batman grabbed the butler's shoulders in concern.

The old man looked down in pain, white hair falling to the belfry floor in clumps. When he looked back up, dark hair had emerged from his scalp to replace it—and Alfred's visage had been replaced by that of another.

Batman's jaw dropped. "Father!"

The face of Thomas Wayne glared at him. "Release me!"

"Yes, sir." Batman took a step back.

"I'm very disappointed in you, son."

The voice—exactly as he'd remembered it. "Father, I'm sorry. But how—"

Batman looked to Vicki for support—only to see her doubled over on her hands and knees, that beautiful face curdling. She yanked out her hair and screamed as her skin twisted into a new shape. When she looked up at Batman, it was with his mother's eyes.

"Imagine dressing up like that," Martha Wayne's doppelgänger said, standing up. "Mister Napier is right. You *are* childish."

Batman stood transfixed.

"Come with us, young man!" His would-be father grabbed him by the wrist. His mother took his other hand. Batman didn't want to go, but as he tried to pull away, they grew not just in strength—but in stature, their bodies growing rubbery and stretching. Monsters from a wax museum, his perfect parents only in their faces.

They pulled him to where The Joker stood, at the parapet overlooking Gotham City. The villain grinned. "I love family reunions, don't you?"

Shaking as his parents held him near the outer wall, Batman looked to them—and then to The Joker. "The truth, Jack! Did you find out who I was?"

"I'm not telling. Not now." The Joker strolled over and plucked his hat from where it sat on a gargoyle's wing. "Dead men tell no tales."

"And you're dead."

"You sure about that?" The Joker thrust the hat over the side of the wall—and a gloved hand there snatched it away.

Batman gawked. Was there someone else over there, outside, on the ledge? He wrested away from the parent-monsters and turned, intending to look over the side. Before he could see anything, a pair of hands grabbed him and yanked him over.

It had all happened before. But this time, there was no ledge to grab on to, no trick on his belt he could use. He seemed to fall forever . . .

BRUCE WAYNE CRASHED ONTO the floor of the Batcave.

Disoriented, he fumbled about. He'd fallen off his chair. He heard footsteps on the stairs.

"Are you all right, sir?" Alfred asked. He set down the tray he was carrying and offered his hand.

"Thanks." Still dizzy, Bruce got to his feet with his manservant's help. "I dozed off." He opened his eyes widely, trying to reorient. "And I had another dream."

"Oh, dear." Alfred helped him back into the chair. "You really should sleep in a bed if you're going to have these episodes."

"Didn't help me yesterday."

Alfred walked over to his tray. He returned with a steaming cup. "Was it the same dream?"

"Not quite." Between sips of coffee, Bruce explained the nightmare, point by point, right down to the fall. Alfred listened intently—and nodded when he was done. "More mysteries at the cathedral."

"It sounds like a board game." Bruce stared into the empty cup. "I keep turning up more questions about what happened there. At the time, I was so glad for it all to be over—and happy to have gotten Vicki out of there alive—that I didn't really think much about it."

"But do you have any real reason to believe Jack Napier knew your identity?"

Bruce considered. "He knew he shot Bruce Wayne at Vicki's apartment, and when he didn't hear about it on the news, he figured out that I'd lived. One of his surviving henchmen said he assumed I'd had a bulletproof vest or something." Bruce frowned. "But maybe he changed his mind."

"It's paranoia, sir. The mind playing tricks."

"Yeah, it's all mixed up with what I learned about him, and my parents." Bruce shook his head. "My folks being there was new."

Alfred crossed his arms. "You needn't fear your parents' judgment. They were proud of you—of who you were becoming."

"What about what I've become since then? I know what Vicki thought." Bruce stared into the distance at the landing where, months earlier, she had entered the Batcave led by Alfred. He faced the butler. "What do *you* think?"

Alfred smiled gently. "Miss Vale and I both know of the event you witnessed, years ago—and we know that Jack Napier caused it and that you defeated him. To her, it follows that you should be done with your double life."

"And to you?"

"I think, sir, the only opinion that matters is yours. And I believe that you are still deciding." He paused. "My years have taught me that getting justice for a loss does not erase it. The Joker's fate was deserved, but it is no magic salve. When you have done enough, you will know." Alfred took the empty cup back. "As for the grislier parts of the nightmare," he said, "they were surely inspired by the grotesque you encountered yesterday."

Great, Bruce thought. *All I needed was more memories to be haunted by.*

But Alfred was right: the hijacker and The Joker had both been on his mind before he slept. He'd stayed out in the Batmobile half the night, looking for the missing bus thief—and checking into the warehouse fire in Chinatown. The arsonists who'd set a storage facility ablaze had evaded capture, but only physically.

"Got lucky with the fire," Bruce explained, pointing upward. "Monitor three."

Alfred looked up at the grainy figures on the screen. "Clown masks."

"Yeah, Wayne Industries has a warehouse across the street. Security camera caught them leaving."

"The police will want to see that."

"If I know Gordon, he's already watching it. This was from the duplicate recorder."

Alfred tsk-tsked. "More clowns. What was in the storage facility?"

"Nothing. It was new. It seems completely random. But it's across town from the theatre, where Lawrence's people were last." He shook his head. "Strange."

"Speaking of strange, your encounter made the front page." Alfred passed him the newspaper from the tray. "The *Gotham Globe* is calling him 'Clayface.' The press will not be satisfied until everyone in the city has a novel sobriquet."

"I guess it fits better in a headline." Bruce examined the sole photo of the hijacker. Taken by someone on the bus with an instant camera, it depicted only his face—or rather, his lack of one at that moment.

Bruce turned back to his bank of machines, where he'd been taking notes the rest of the night. "He could have boarded the bus anywhere along this route," he said, drawing a line across a monitor with his finger. "I checked out other incidents nearby, to see if anything happened earlier. I came up with this." He handed Alfred a stack of printouts.

"Police call logs." He flipped through the pages. "A report of shots fired. Another report of a runaway van."

"Just another day in the city. But there's more. The emergency line logged that phone service had gone out on Walcott because a phone pole was struck. A hit-and-run."

"That's nearby." Alfred brought the last page closer to his face. "A call from Gotham General?"

"Before everything. A single call, but the police were instructed not to come, were told it was just some sort of test of the phone system."

The butler pointed at the pages. "You did all this research in the middle of the night?"

"Some of it in the car, some of it here."

Alfred's brow furrowed. "When did you actually go to sleep?"

Bruce rubbed the stubble on his chin. "I guess . . . right before I walked into the belfry."

"And you're still there, aren't you? Back in the cathedral."

Bruce shook his head wearily. "It's every night now, Alfred. I don't know what it is. I can't shake it." He looked over at the Batmobile. "I just know I'd rather be awake. Awake, and working."

He went silent.

When Bruce looked back, he saw Alfred was glowering at him sternly. "You're staring at me like your face is about to melt, too."

"I've told you, it's not wise to compound past wounds with new ones. I can't stop you from the physical, but I can suggest something for the psychological. Perhaps it is time to confront another part of The Joker's legacy." He pronounced a single word. *"Smylex."*

That surprised Bruce. "What do you mean? I figured out how it worked. I created the antidote. I've funded the hospital wing. I'd call that confronting it."

"But as you admitted to Professor Auslander, you have yet to visit the wing in person. Why is that?"

Bruce paused. Yes, he was busy—but that wasn't it. He was ashamed to admit what it was. "Some of the victims—their faces are shaped like The Joker's. I know it's not their fault. But I guess subconsciously I don't want to be around that." He exhaled. "The truth is, they're victims of his, just like my parents."

"The difference, sir, is that their stories are not over. You can still do something for them—not as Batman, but as Bruce Wayne. In so doing, you honor your mother and father." Bruce took a deep breath. No, he didn't want to go.

But there might be some value in it. He'd been concerned over the ward's finances.

And then there was the odd call to the police.

"Okay. I'll do it. But I don't want to tell Auslander." He stood up. "Drive me there?"

Alfred studied him. "I'll do more than that. If you like, I'll go in with you."

CHAPTER 13

I T WAS LATE IN the morning when Auslander strode into the reception area of his office at Gotham General and removed his overcoat and hat. He didn't look to see whether his secretary was there before asking, "Any messages?"

Irina appeared before him with a handful of notes. "Lots!"

Wonderful. He hung up the overcoat and snatched the top one, a telex, and read it quickly. He crumpled it and grabbed the next, a telegram. He'd barely glanced at it before he said, "Any messages *not* congratulating me about appearing on that damned television show?"

Irina pursed her lips—and thrust a smaller stack at him. "Here."

"That's better."

"And your newspaper."

"Yes, yes."

She produced several folders. "And here are the other files you asked for—relating to, well, *you know.*"

"The fact that *you* know is a privilege. I'd prefer you to forget about it." He glanced at her, making sure she understood. Then he unlocked his office door. "I'm not to be disturbed."

He didn't wait for her to respond. He shut the door behind him and headed to the desk where he'd pored over Patient Karlo's records until the small hours of the night before. The first note was of little surprise. There'd been no sign of the escapee, either on the grounds or elsewhere. Another memo detailed the personnel status of one Louis Putnam, driver, who had just been given a weeklong vacation as Auslander had promised. Favors were the currency on which human society functioned.

What really interested him was in the files: results from some of the tests he'd ordered on Karlo's last bloodwork. The components that created what The Joker had referred to as Smylex were distributed separately, to avoid detection; what Batman had lucked into was one method of activation, but there were others.

Auslander's team had a good record of the specific mix of products Karlo came into contact with, but nobody had witnessed Karlo during his initial exposure. He had been found collapsed after some kind of seizure, with the muscles of his face frozen into a twisted expression. It was pointedly not a smile, as in all the other cases, and instead of immediately dying, he fell into a coma. Emergency room personnel had intubated him, and he had remained motionless for several weeks.

Karlo was one of several comatose patients brought in after the establishment of the Smylex Ward, and it soon became apparent that his differences went much further. The facial rictus slowly subsided, and he began breathing on his own. Range-of-motion testing had shown no muscle loss; he actually gained weight. A brain scan had showed highly elevated levels of activity, with nearly unceasing periods of rapid eye movement. It was unclear why he was still comatose at all—until he wasn't. There was no doubt now that something extraordinary was going on, both inside and outside his body.

It had also touched his mind in some way—and that, Auslander found the most fascinating. A decade earlier, the idea that both evolution and devolution could be triggered by chemicals and hypnosis had been a scientific fad; it attracted a lot of quackery and was even the subject of a popular horror film. Auslander had looked into it, up until the point when no educational institutions would fund such work. It was career suicide to pursue it as an academic. But Karlo's malady had the potential to blow up everything people thought they knew. Some curses were just misunderstood miracles.

He opened the *Gotham Globe*. It had the photograph he'd seen on the morning news, snapped by a kid with a camera on the bus. Karlo's face had changed just since being in the hospital room. That made it all the more important to get him into isolation, under observation. He couldn't very well send his orderlies out searching or hire detectives. But he had another option to bring to bear.

He reached for the phone—only to have it buzz. He lifted the receiver. "Irina, I told you I wasn't to be disturbed."

"I think you'll want this call, Doctor." She sounded concerned. "It's Harvey Dent."

Auslander's eyes widened. "Harvey Dent? The district attorney?"

"That's what he said."

"Put him through." He waited for the transfer. "Mister District Attorney, to what do I owe the pleasure?"

"The pleasure's all mine," came the response. The caller's voice was rich and personable. *"I'm sorry I didn't make your lecture yesterday, but I caught the broadcast last night. Fascinating stuff. Just fascinating."*

Auslander didn't know what to make of the call. Dent was a slick politician—no intellectual. Most of Gotham City's cognoscenti only dabbled in matters of higher thinking. But there was really only one way to answer. "I appreciate the kind words."

"Listen, Professor—or is it Doctor?"

"Call me Hugh."

"Hugh, there's a matter we really should discuss. In person, if we can."

"I . . ." Auslander froze. "What is this in connection to?"

The voice lost a little of its heartiness. *"As I said—it's a bit sensitive."*

He knows! Auslander's mind raced. If the police knew about Karlo's origins, and the cover-up, it might well warrant a call from a district attorney unwilling to see the hospital mired in scandal.

"Are you there, Hugh?"

He cleared his throat. "Yes, Mister Dent. I will be in the ward here all day." His words receiving no response, he tentatively added, "Unless you want me to come to *your* office."

"No, it's probably better if we avoid that."

A beat, while Auslander exhaled.

"The Flugelheim café has reopened. Let's throw them some government dollars. Shall we meet at one?"

Auslander stacked his papers, pretending to check his calendar. "Yes, yes, I can attend."

"Terrific. Listen, Hugh, I have another meeting that may run late. But don't bail on me, all right? This is important. To me, to Gotham City, and to you."

"I understand. I won't leave."

"Fantastic. Just look at the pretty pictures—and start a tab for the coffee. We'll charge it to Mayor Borg."

The call ended.

Auslander replaced the receiver with both hands—and then stared at it for twenty seconds. He hadn't been exaggerating to his staff about the Borg administration's feelings about the Smylex Ward; his reelection, some time away, already looked in jeopardy. But those prospects wouldn't be helped by learning that a chemically altered madman had escaped from a public facility.

Yes, Dent might be offering a life preserver. It would be smart to at least see what he knew. Certainly, an ally would be useful.

He put the files in his desk and rose quickly. He opened the door. "Irina, I'm going out."

"But you just got here!" She watched, befuddled, as he grabbed his overcoat. "Where should I say you are?"

"Hospital business!"

KARLO SAT AT A PAYPHONE in the hospital lobby and tried to hide his face behind a newspaper. Making the call had been the first acting he'd done in eons, and he'd done it without any of his usual nervousness. It was invigorating.

His first challenge that morning had been finding out which hospital he'd been in. He'd been briefly outside it the day before, but otherwise had only seen the inside of the laundry truck. The clothing bags were labeled GOTHAM GENERAL, but the system had several facilities around the city. Fortunately, he'd found an old newspaper in the Capra mentioning the ward, pointing him toward the midtown location.

Kingston's TV set had inspired the other part of his scheme. Harvey Dent had been on every channel that morning. First doing a press conference about the runaway bus and its missing hijacker—and then at a location in Chinatown, talking about the rise in arson. Karlo had seen Dent before. The man was magnetic, and Karlo had found his voice an easy one to re-create a few minutes earlier during his phone call with Auslander. To be Harvey Dent, one just had to imagine being gifted with more handsomeness, prestige, and charisma than any normal human ever had. Dent always sounded like he was headed for the best seats in the house, with a pocket stuffed full of winning lottery tickets.

Now it was time to switch roles. Karlo's bet that Hugh Auslander would be in his office to take the call had paid off. He watched carefully as the older man emerged from the elevator and strode purposefully across the floor. He was glad to see he'd chosen the right wardrobe; the hat, in fact, was a perfect guess. Auslander had looked like a homburg type—everyone who thought he was Churchill did. The coat was single-breasted with a center vent, and of Covert cloth; similar to the Chesterfield that Karlo was wearing. The color was a little off, but close enough. No intelligence agency could compete with a costume designer with a full wardrobe.

Karlo put on his hat and rose to follow Auslander. Shielding his face again behind a newspaper—horrifically, one with his tortured face on the front of it—he watched from a vestibule as Auslander headed out into the parking lot. Much of the area was cordoned off; construction vehicles were putting in new sidewalks and ramps. Auslander passed the workers without a word on his way to the VIP slots. He got into a cheap foreign car in space number two.

Doesn't care for show, just convenience. Check.

Seeing Auslander drive away, Karlo turned back inside and sought to match his stride. He really was the Big Brain he'd seen on TV, who'd burned his hand with a lighter just to make sure you remembered him, and the point he was making. He was an academic who left almost no time for questions, because what he was saying was probably smarter than anything his audience came up with.

And Karlo wore the man's face.

I can do this.

He advanced toward the elevator he'd seen Auslander exit—and then realized something. He'd gotten the doctor before by calling the switchboard, but all the training in the world wouldn't tell him what floor he was headed for. This would take some cleverness—and a headlong leap into the fire.

He saw a teenaged girl in pink approaching one of the elevators. "Doctor," she said, too shy to look at him.

He figured her for a candy-striper. New enough that she knew Auslander but never talked to him. He spoke. "Good morning, Miss—"

Surprised to be addressed, she blushed a little. "Kellogg."

Okay, Auslander doesn't ask people their names. Let's change the tone. "Miss Kellogg, how long have you been with Gotham General?"

She shrank. "This is just my second week. Pediatric ward."

"But you know your way around, do you not?"

"Um—mostly." She straightened. "I mean, yes, Doctor. I went through the orientation."

"Splendid. Show me to the Smylex patients."

That startled her. "Doctor?" She fumbled, as if fearful she was being tricked. "That's your ward, right?"

"Your career has begun, Miss Kellogg. You might last just the week—or you might be running this facility one day. Demonstrate what you have learned."

"Right away." She stepped to the elevator and pushed the button for him. She stepped back, a bit tentative. "I—uh—have never really seen the patients there."

You're looking at one, he wanted to say. But the fact that she didn't know that was the best thing he'd ever heard.

CHAPTER 14

IN THE YEARS SINCE Bruce's father had helped found it, Gotham
General's midtown location had largely replaced the downtown
original as the medical hub of the city. But while its campus was
more spacious, parking remained an issue for anyone who didn't
want their doors dinged—or whose dedicated founder's parking stall
was blocked by construction.

Consequently, he and Alfred made two circuits of the complex in
the Bentley, their limo of the day, before finding a suitable spot. That
gave Bruce the chance to form some initial impressions, and he mentioned one as they walked to the entrance. "What goes out of a
building can be as interesting as what goes on inside."

"How do you mean, sir?"

"There's a black van parked at the back dock," Bruce said. "It'd
look inconspicuous anywhere but where it was—in between two
municipal garbage trucks."

"I admit I missed that one."

"And over on the west side, did you notice the truck the orderlies
were loading laundry into? It's a rental—one of those pay-by-the-
hour jobs. Seems an expensive way to go."

Alfred grinned. "We did try to raise you with an understanding
of the meaning of a dollar."

The pair traversed the lobby and entered the elevator to the mezzanine. They exited into a round concourse that branched off into several adjoining buildings. All the information desks were busy.

Seeing a young woman in a pink smock crossing the floor, Alfred tipped his hat to her. "Excuse me, miss. We're looking for the Smylex Ward."

"Popular destination," she said. "Follow me."

"We don't mean to take you from your duties elsewhere."

"Oh, no." She smiled. "I was just tested on this!"

As she led them through a maze of halls, several people smiled at Bruce in recognition. Fame had a way of preceding him—and he was, after all, one of the hospital's chief benefactors. His failure to visit the new ward before now didn't seem to have hurt his popularity.

The Smylex Ward was fresh construction, originally intended to serve as a geriatric wing. It might be that again someday, but for now it had been pressed into service to serve an emergency need. The nurse trainee left them before the front desk of yet another lobby, this one painted a muted white.

Bruce had barely introduced himself to the receptionist when he saw a face he recognized—an older lady dressed in civilian clothes. "Lily Booth?"

"Bruce!" Genuinely surprised to see him, she clasped her hands over his. "I haven't seen you since the opera benefit."

"I hope you'll attend the theatre benefit at the Imperial. It's for this place." Reminded of where he was, his eyes narrowed. "Are you all right, Lily?"

"Oh, I'm fine." She gestured behind her. "It's John."

"I'm sorry, I didn't know."

She lowered her voice. "We haven't wanted anyone to know. You won't say anything to anyone, will you?"

"Of course not."

She breathed easier. "Well, as long as you're here, you simply must see him. He doesn't get many visitors." She gave him the room number. "Go right back!"

Bruce nodded. "I will."

After she departed, he whispered to Alfred. "Did you know John Booth was a Smylex victim?"

Alfred clasped his hands together. "Some, I am afraid, consider it socially compromising."

"Why? Contact with the poison was completely random. It's not contagious."

"Things that frighten people are often hard to see logically."

Bruce decided it was as good a place to start as any. He steeled himself as he approached the room. John Booth was a business associate rather than a friend—and the dourest person he'd ever met. A laughing seizure for him would be something people would surely notice. Bruce wondered what he would find.

"Who's that?" a man called out as he opened the door.

"Bruce Wayne."

"*Bruce—?*" In the middle of the room, a man suspended in traction attempted to turn—and paid for it, groaning in pain. "Oh, that's bad."

Bruce and Alfred stepped inside. The man was bandaged from head to toe. "Should we call someone for you?" Bruce asked.

"Call *me*, months ago, and tell me to move to another city!" John Booth gritted his teeth and tried to gesture. "Forget all that. Come in, come in."

His condition wasn't what Bruce was expecting at all. He couldn't really see much of his face, between the bandages and the neck brace. "How are you? I haven't seen you since you were with—what was it? Fourth Chemical Bank?"

"Please don't say *chemical.*"

"Oh, sorry."

Booth winced his way through small talk about his life after leaving the bank. "I had just started my own firm. And then, this."

Bruce apologized again. "I hadn't heard."

"We decided not to send out announcement cards. 'Let John Booth handle your estate planning. Service with a smile.'" Booth started to laugh—and regretted it.

His mummified condition befuddled Bruce. He'd never heard of anything like this before. "Smylex did *this*?"

"You could say that," Booth snarled. "I was exposed to whatever it was, I guess. And when I started laughing, I panicked—right into a heart attack."

"That's bad."

"No, that's good. Somehow, it stopped whatever it was from killing me."

"That's good."

"No, that's bad. I still had a heart attack—and I was driving in traffic at the time."

"You win." Bruce stared. "I hope you're on the mend."

"Life stinks. Can't you tell?"

In the brief conversation that followed, Bruce determined that Booth hadn't changed at all. He asked for some business, and also for Bruce's discretion about finding him in the ward. Bruce had already decided he would offer the latter.

After saying their goodbyes, he and Alfred stepped out into the hall. "That wasn't so bad," Bruce said. "Maybe things here aren't as—"

A Japanese man in a three-piece suit hustled up the hallway. He was out of breath. "Mister Wayne!"

Bruce recognized him. "Masahito-san."

The hospital administrator beamed. He shook Bruce's hand vigorously. "I haven't been called that in a long time."

"And you know I'm just Bruce."

"Of course." Masahito Takagi had been one of his father's hires, many years ago, and he and Bruce had remained friendly. "And hello to you, as well, Alfred. Five different people told me the two of you were here."

Bruce looked to Alfred with mock annoyance. "So much for visiting without creating a fuss. I told you we needed masks."

"There are plenty enough masks in this building already," the administrator said. He glanced about. "Does Doctor Auslander know you're here?"

"Haven't seen him yet. I will—but I'd like to look around, if I may. Find out more about the ward's work."

"Certainly. You've paid for a few hundred million nickel tours—though I caution you that what you may see may disturb you." He glanced to the door. "I see you've met Mister Booth. He is not typical."

"I gathered that," Bruce said. "But I'm prepared. I've toured the burn ward here before."

Takagi shook his head slowly. "You know what to expect, there. These people have suffered harms like no one has ever seen."

KARLO STOOD IN THE HEART of the place he had done everything to avoid being sent back to. And he had no plan.

He'd realized that not-insignificant fact after entering the Smylex Ward and surviving a couple of tests: brief encounters, both of them. A security worker had scared the hell out of him by asking where his badge was. It turned out to be tomfoolery. Nobody would block Hugh Auslander from his own ward.

The second one involved an intern who had stopped him in order to convey some information about a procedure. Karlo had recognized approximately every tenth word. All he had in his arsenal came from his auditions for soap operas, most of which seemed to take place in hospitals when they weren't set at high-fashion design firms.

Karlo had taken the coward's way out by simply responding, "Good work." It seemed to serve, as the intern went on his way with a smile. The real Hugh Auslander apparently did not shower others with praise, but it was worth breaking character a little if it meant he didn't have to pronounce "pericardiectomy."

The encounter caused him to question his whole scheme. Karlo wanted to know what the experts thought was happening with his body—without the experts locking him up. Or, now, the police. He'd heard that there were physicians who worked on the shady side of the law; maybe one would help interpret for him. But he had to get the information first.

He heard her voice long before he saw her. Miss Mindy was at a nurses' station, talking to someone who didn't appear to be listening. Karlo cringed. She'd apparently seen him every day for months, and also during his awakening. There was little chance he could fool her—

—but even less chance of avoiding her. She waved to him. "Doctor!"

His cheek twitched. It was too late for Karlo to hide behind his newspaper or duck away. No, he knew the only way to keep his face looking like Auslander's was to remain in character. He approached the counter. "I'm very busy, nurse."

She leaned in. "I just wanted to let you know I appreciate you bringing me into that meeting yesterday. You really put my mind at ease. And believe me, I won't tell anyone about . . ." She silently mouthed the words *you-know-who*.

Karlo stared at her blankly—before realizing he had an opportunity. "I need the records of Karlo Babić."

"Of who?"

Her answer startled him, and he wondered if his voice was curdling again. "Karlo Babić," he said louder.

Befuddled, she looked at the names on her manifest. "I don't know him. There's *Basil* Karlo, of course."

Karlo flinched. That was his stage name, which barely anyone knew. He spoke carefully. "Do you mean—"

"*You-know-who*," she said. "The one we're not supposed to talk about." She made a motion of locking her mouth and throwing away the key.

Karlo put up his hands in frustration. "Yes, Karlo, of course. The records?"

"Oh, we sent all those to Irina."

He stared. "You sent them to an arena?"

"Your secretary?"

"Oh, yes. That was my next stop."

He stormed away, but could see in the mirror at the corner of the hallway that Miss Mindy was making a different silent gesture to her colleague with her hand: *He's been drinking.*

Karlo didn't care if she thought that. He had an office to find.

HUGH AUSLANDER SIPPED HIS third cup of black tea and stared at the empty seat across from him. The sight of it irritated him—but it was better than looking anywhere else.

Work had been completed on the skylight at the Flugelheim Museum; nobody would have ever known that a masked vigilante had once smashed through it months earlier, attempting to save a photojournalist from a psychopath. Lingering evidence of The Joker's rampage abounded, however. The *objets d'art* Napier and his band had damaged were gone, of course; being auctioned to fools with more money than sense. The paint-stained walls surrounding the café level remained but were hidden behind a series of Eastern-themed folding-panel screens allegedly from the estate of Louis XV. Auslander thought it took a special sort of philistine to make a chinoiserie exhibit do double-duty as a tarp.

He checked his pocket watch again. Still no sign of Harvey Dent. He'd said he might be late—and he definitely had been. If Dent called him amid such a busy day, there must really be a problem.

He knows the hijacker came from our hospital. There's no other explanation.

The waiter stopped by for the fifth time. "Are you sure I can't get you something off the menu? You must be getting hungry."

"The Flugelheim would be of little help there. I've been here long enough to see that the portions are the size of after-dinner mints."

The waiter gave a wry smile. "People come for the ambiance."

And occasional knockout gas attacks. "No matter," Auslander said. "Can you bring me a telephone?"

"No, but I can take you to one."

The doctor hesitated. "I'm reluctant to step away. I'm meeting someone."

The waiter gave a knowing smile. He put his hand beside his mouth and whispered confidentially. "Lunch dates are the worst. Sometimes things don't happen."

There was a growl in Auslander's voice. "It is *not* a lunch date—and I would certainly go somewhere else." He checked his watch again.

"Well, you can continue to wait—but I just wanted to let you know my shift is about to end."

"Some good news, at last." He looked again to the door. *Harvey Dent, where are you?*

CHAPTER 15

"**D**ID YOU HEAR ABOUT *the actress who was gassed with Smylex? She'd had so many facelifts that nobody noticed.*"

Bruce had heard the joke on a national late-night talk show monologue. He was startled then; it seemed the definition of "too soon." But with The Joker dead and the initial crisis over, the world did its usual thing, healing by minimizing, and then forgetting. Even his barber had told him an iteration of the same joke, involving a cheerleader who'd gotten the giggles.

None of those people had set foot in the Smylex Ward. If anything, Bruce had found that Takagi had understated things. Non-fatal interactions with the poison had left some in comas, others dependent on regular transfusions. People who had lost control of their facial muscles were relearning to eat, to breathe, to speak. Others who had only glancing interactions with the substance—such as just a whiff from the gaseous version The Joker deployed in his parade— had developed immunological issues months later.

So many different reactions, and no one understood them all. There was the case of Tonya, the hairdresser, who had come into contact with more different Smylex-laced products than anyone else known to the medical community. Somehow, the various combinations had canceled each other out, preventing death—but not a most pernicious side effect. Several times an hour, she would lapse into the same laughing fit that had first claimed models Amanda Keeler and

Candy Walker—freezing there for five minutes before recovering. It had made it impossible for her to live a normal life.

Everywhere on the ward, Bruce saw people trying to help, to find cures—or ways to cope. Care and research, all in the same place.

"I'm seeing a lot of blood draws," he said to Takagi.

"Ordered by Doctor Auslander. It is important to understand what levels of the compound are in our patients' bloodstreams, and how that changes across time."

"Whether people could relapse, like Tonya?"

"It's more that we want to watch for long-term effects." He gestured to the double doors of the lab. "Tissue and other samples are also analyzed. Doctor Auslander has brought in top-flight researchers—people who studied past chemical exposures, both military and civilian."

Bruce thought of the black van and asked a question he suspected he already knew the answer to. "Is the government involved?"

"We don't tell them about individual patients, but we do report our findings in general. But the cooperation doesn't work both ways." Takagi frowned. "There's a major arsenal just across town: Armsgard. Axis Chemicals was a supplier for it. But they've never returned any of my calls."

Bruce nodded. Jack Napier had brought his own chemistry skills to bear in the creation of Smylex, but he had a head start: DDID Nerve Gas, an abandoned project of the CIA, conducted with assistance from the Defense Department. He guessed that The Joker had likely found information about it in the Axis Chemicals plant after he took it for his headquarters, but Bruce didn't have a lot of details. Blowing the plant up had been an absolute necessity.

He continued the tour. The outpatients he'd been told about existed, and they were putting pressure on the hospital for services. But the needs of most of those in the ward were all too real, and uniformly tragic. And worst of all: many were children.

They returned to an area they'd passed through before—what appeared to be a pediatric ward. Alfred had asked to stay in an activity room, and there he remained: seated in a chair far too small for him, playing checkers with a young dark-skinned girl. The butler looked out of place, and yet not so for Bruce, who remembered the care Alfred had provided him so many years ago.

"You win," he said, as she jumped his last piece.

She did not respond. And indeed, Bruce noticed it was the quietest activity room he'd ever seen, despite the presence of several children. Alfred smiled gently at her and thanked her for the game. Then he joined Bruce and the administrator in the doorway.

"She seems so down," Bruce said in low tones. "All the kids do."

"She explained it to me, sir," Alfred replied. "She is here because she witnessed her mother's death by Smylex."

Bruce's eyes widened. "You mean—?"

Takagi spoke gravely. "She has not laughed since then—and neither have many of these children. Laughter killed their loved ones—siblings, parents, grandparents. They share the same response to the trauma."

Bruce bristled. The room chilled him more than any he had seen. None of the children here bore any physical signs of their interaction with Smylex. Indeed, many had not been exposed to it directly at all. But indirectly, they had all been devastated. He knew what that was like.

"I need to apologize," he said to Takagi in the outer hall.

"Whatever for?"

"I'd heard the people saying the need for the ward was exaggerated, that Smylex was over. I'd also heard there were people here who hadn't been exposed. Auslander had tried to set me straight, but I needed to see it." He looked down. "I know better now."

Takagi listened to his words—but was unwilling to chastise him at all. "Bruce, there are certainly some who have misdiagnosed themselves or who claim impacts that proved ephemeral. That exists for any medical practice. We refer them to outside professionals when we can." He gestured behind him. "But for the rest, the need is real, and every day. We have a masked man to thank that there are not more victims—but we also have you and Doctor Auslander to thank for making this place possible." He put his hand on Bruce's shoulder. "You are heroes as much as Batman."

Bruce glanced at Alfred and saw an approving look. *Okay, I get it.*

There was just one more thing. "Have you seen the reports about the bus hijacker?"

The question surprised Takagi. "Yes, I did see. Terrible, of course."

"People said his face changed." Bruce gestured back into the ward. "Just wondering if you've seen anything like that here."

Takagi stared at him for a few seconds—and then reacted with a start when his beeper went off. "Oh, excuse me."

He stepped to a phone—and returned. "I'm sorry, but I have a prior engagement. If you'd like to see a little more, I could—" He glanced to the right—and brightened. "Wait. *There's* Doctor Auslander!"

Bruce and Alfred looked over to see a man walking across the atrium. He wore a lab coat and had a jacket over his arm. "Right you are," Bruce said, shaking Takagi's hand. "Thank you, Masahito-san."

Takagi nodded to Bruce and Alfred and went on his way.

The white-coated older man had made some distance through the crowded atrium when Bruce and Alfred began to catch up. "Professor Auslander," Bruce called out. "It's Bruce Wayne!"

He stopped to look back. "Mister Wayne."

"Hello again."

"Hello again," the doctor repeated. "Pardon me if I don't tarry. I have a full schedule." He turned again and began walking down a hallway.

Bruce and Alfred quickened their pace behind him. "I'm sorry— I said I would call before I came. Takagi just gave us the tour."

"Takagi?"

"The administrator."

"Oh, yes. That Takagi."

Bruce tilted his head. "You know more than one Takagi?"

"I know many people—and many things. I'm quite busy this afternoon."

"I understand. We've had a look around. Great work you're doing here."

"And I had better get back to it." He approached the door to an office with his name labeled outside.

Before he could enter, the door opened, and a curly-headed woman looked at Auslander, stunned. "Doctor!"

"Yes, what is it?"

She stared at him. "You just called me."

"I just called you?"

She pointed back inside at her desk—and the telephone. "You wanted to know if Dent's office had called back."

Auslander straightened. "Yes, of course. I did that from the lobby."

She bit her lip and looked back. "I could swear that was an outside line."

The doctor pronounced his response a word at a time, impatience evident. "I used the payphone."

"But why would you—" She shook her head. "Never mind. I've got the rest of the records on Patient Karlo."

She offered the files, and he snatched them away.

He briefly turned back to Bruce. "It is good to see you both, but I am busy now. Come back again another day." He turned to the secretary. "I don't wish to be disturbed, Irene."

"Irina."

"Whatever." The inner office door closed with a slam.

Irina looked after him in astonishment—and then turned back to face Bruce and Alfred. She tilted her head apologetically. "Would you like to make an appointment for another day?"

"That's all right."

She closed the outer office door, leaving Bruce and Alfred alone.

Bruce shrugged. "That was odd," he said as they began walking out.

"Indeed, sir."

"I guess even geniuses get temperamental."

Alfred smirked. "I haven't observed that. But I did observe that our professor-physician's accent traveled about a thousand miles while we were talking to him."

"That's impressive," Bruce said. "Almost as impressive as getting three inches taller in a day!"

KARLO STOOD INSIDE Hugh Auslander's office, his back to the door, and hyperventilated. His face fell, literally, losing the cohesion he'd kept during the whole escapade.

He breathed more slowly, wondering if there was a natural time limit to his ability to physically impersonate someone. Certainly he had tired of the act, and nearly broken even before encountering Bruce Wayne. Someone had remarked about his jacket changing colors since that morning, causing him to find a lab coat before heading for his office.

The files he sought were indeed on his desk. There was a lot of material. He thought about walking out with it—but couldn't chance Wayne still being there. And besides, he wanted a look. Just the top page fascinated him, the report from the paramedics who'd been called to the Capra after his exposure. He still remembered nothing at all from that day.

At least one thing made sense now: his wallet wasn't here in the hospital because they'd never found it. They'd gotten "Basil Karlo" from the stage manager there. He tried to remember if he'd ever shared the name with the man—but that, too, was lost in a haze. There was so much more to know.

He looked at the phone, with all its little lights. He searched for and found an instruction page, telling which button he needed to push. He picked up the receiver and did so. "Irina?"

"*Yes, Doctor?*"

"Hold my calls." He paused. "And if you should get another call from an outside line, don't answer it."

"*Whyever not?*"

"Just do as I say!"

CHAPTER 16

WHILE BRUCE AND ALFRED'S visit to the hospital had answered some questions, new ones had taken their place. The peculiar behavior of Hugh Auslander—if it *was* Hugh Auslander—ranked high on that list. The problem was that surveilling a hospital was no easy feat, even if one's family had paid for most of it. The insides of medical facilities were private, and deserved to be so.

That was when Bruce remembered the Batman gear under the seat in the Bentley, still out in the parking lot. Part of the arsenal: a magnetic-mount surveillance camera that transmitted a signal that could reach the screen in the Batmobile—or even the Batcave—via the repeater stations he'd hidden over the last year across Gotham City's rooftops. He'd surreptitiously attached the camera to a piece of construction equipment, where it would have a good view of the hospital's entrance. And then Alfred had driven him home, ostensibly for a night of relaxation and better food, with company in the form of Julie Madison.

Bruce was heading for the Batcave to see if the recorder had picked up anything when Julie called.

"Bruce, sweetie, I'm still at the Imperial. It'll be a while."

She had mentioned this production being more difficult than usual. "Rehearsals running long?"

"No, I'm outside. My cab hasn't shown up. Traffic's snarled by something. It's a mess out there."

Bruce hoped that it wasn't because of another stolen bus. But before he could say anything, he heard her gasp. "Julie, what is it?"

"In the air. It's that thing!"

That didn't sound good. "What thing?"

"The Bat-Signal!"

The spotlight Bruce had provided Commissioner Gordon and the police department was one of the best ideas he'd ever had. It was powerful, both as a light source and as a symbol. Since its installation, its very activation had sometimes dispelled riots and ended hostage situations without need of Batman's direct intervention. And in terms of operational security, it was outstanding. Nothing connected it to the Wayne estate at all.

But while obviously intended for use after dark, it wasn't as effective just after sunset—and it required either him or Alfred to be looking outside. Bruce had a plan on the drawing board for sensors that would detect the signal; he was torn between having them trigger a sound in the house and something more elaborate using mirrors that redirected and amplified the light. In the meantime, he'd been forced to largely depend on word of mouth from others.

Julie's powers of observation had just lost her a dinner. "Listen, just get something in town," he said. "You've got opening night in a couple of days."

"No, no. I said I wouldn't do this to you. You've taken me for granted before. I'm not going to start doing it to you."

"Julie, don't worry about it. Take me for granted. I deserve it. I'll have a pizza and a six-pack and think of you."

She laughed. *"I'll make it up, I swear!"*

Then it was into the iron maiden, one of several routes from the manor into the Batcave. Having seen the signal, Alfred arrived from the kitchen several minutes later. Bruce addressed him. "We've got a situation."

He took off his headphones and switched the police scanner to the speaker. Alfred listened. The Last Laughs had struck for the third night in a row. Not even night; the sun had barely set when they hit their first target. And the adjective was necessary, because there were two suspicious fires, in different parts of town.

"This wasn't random mischief," Bruce said. "This was a declaration. They're telling the world they're here. And that there's more than one group."

Alfred looked at the map alongside him. "If Gordon sent the signal, he must not have the matter in hand." He looked about. "It's fortunate we were upstairs to see it, rather than down here."

"I'll address that—later." Bruce stepped down the metal stairs and headed for the cabinet that held his uniform.

He knew he'd hear about it from Alfred. "You don't mean to go out."

"I got the signal!"

"But you've barely slept. And dinner—"

"Is off." Bruce began putting on the armor. "I've already told Julie."

The butler stood, stone-faced, as Bruce continued to get ready. "I don't recommend this. Even during The Joker business, you rarely were out consecutive nights—much less three."

"It isn't a nine-to-five job, Alfred." Bruce reached for his boots. "Was dinner in the oven? Something I can carry?"

"It's king crab in a crustacean gelée with cauliflower puree and *concombre à la menthe.*" Alfred tromped off.

Bruce shook his head. *Maybe I will hit a drive-through after all.*

THE SUN HAD GONE down outside Gotham General. And Hugh Auslander had been stood up.

He steamed as he walked through the hall toward his office. Three hours, he'd stayed at the Flugelheim, drenched in dreadful tea and waiting for Harvey Dent. He'd finally broken down and called information, which had connected him to City Hall. Not identifying himself, he'd said he was returning the district attorney's call—only to learn that Dent had been called away. Not to the Flugelheim, but rather a meeting at the Hall of Justice.

That, to Auslander, had seemed a reasonable excuse for tardiness; if anyone could pull the strings of a lawyer, it was a judge. Auslander drove then to the court building, hoping to catch Dent on the way out. But it was a fool's errand in a place he found stifling. Universities fed hope. Hospitals worked to restore it. Courts were where hopes went to die.

Auslander's hopes that the annoying Irina had gone home were answered when he reached his office. Yet the outer door was unlocked—expressly against his orders. *Damned fool.* His papers, the hospital's papers, were not for the prying eyes of maintenance workers and custodians.

And one of them was in his office now. He could see the light on, under the door.

He considered calling security—and then thought better of it. The last two days had been about avoiding attention and publicity. The direct method remained. He stepped forward, balled his hand into a fist, and knocked.

Nothing.

He did so again, louder.

He heard muffled sounds from inside. A cough. And then a growl that sounded a little familiar. "One minute!"

Auslander looked around. There, on the secretary's desk, was a snow globe with a miniature cat inside. Irina collected them; Shreck's Department Store issued a new one every holiday season. He grabbed it and took a position beside the door. Irina would just have to do with a hole in her collection. He wasn't going to allow a thief to—

The door opened. "I told you I didn't want to be disturbed!"

Auslander raised the globe—and looked into his own face. *"Mon Dieu!"*

The doppelgänger before him shot out an arm, grabbing his wrist. The snow globe tumbled to the carpet, landed on its base, and bounced. It rolled under the desk.

For long moments, they continued to gaze into each other's eyes.

It was like looking at a wax museum dummy, Auslander thought—one that had gotten his eyes wrong.

But the voice was pretty close. "That's interesting," the lookalike said. "I would have thought you'd say *'Mein Gott.'*"

"I'm from all over. And I know where you're from," Auslander said. "Basil Karlo, from the Capra Theatre."

"Yeah, we've met. You wanted to sedate me."

"And you ran." Feeling the pressure of Karlo's hand increasing, Auslander spoke in even tones. "If you are here to kill me, be aware: I did not make you this way. I was only—"

"Trying to help." Karlo glanced over at the telephone. "I won't let you lock me up."

"But you came back. You must want something. What is it?"

"What's wrong with me?" Karlo released his grip—and his face cracked. Scales appeared in his Auslander visage, and then melted into a clammy morass. The artificial hair around his ears and mouth and on his chin started falling off in clumps. Finally, he was left with just a toupee, which he snatched off and let drop to the floor.

Auslander pulled his arm away and rubbed his wrist. He stared, spellbound. "Amazing."

Karlo sagged, his shoulders drooping. He wore a lab coat, and a jacket underneath. It was hard to read the expression of a man without a face, but he seemed tired beyond measure.

Auslander stepped to the secretary's desk.

"Don't call anyone!" Karlo shouted in a gurgling voice—probably his own.

I wouldn't think of it. Instead, Auslander knelt beside Irina's desk and retrieved her prized possession. He put the globe back in its place on her desk, and a blizzard surrounded a happy cat. "Lock the outer door," he said. "It so happens I have time for one more appointment."

THE BATMOBILE SCREAMED ACROSS the Memorial Bridge into Gotham City. Rush hour had ended, and relatively fewer people were headed into town; everyone wisely moved out of his way.

Well, almost everyone, he thought as a lead-footed semi driver wouldn't get out of his lane. *There's always one.*

It was impossible to protect Gotham City and not have a car, but it also brought complications. The bridges and tunnels into the municipality were chokepoints; they were also an opportunity for people to track him.

What he really needed were multiple Batmobiles stored and hidden within the city, but there were only so many hours in the day and night. Until then, he depended on electronic and radar-baffling countermeasures aboard the vehicle, as well as his main weapon: driving like he was on the way to a fire.

This time, there were three fires—and counting. According to the police scanner, a lighting fixture supplier in the Narrows had gone up; yet another disparate neighborhood. He was unsure where he'd head first.

And then he knew. The Memorial Bridge entered Gotham City over parklands, feeding into an elevated expressway junction. From its colossal height, Batman got a good side-window view of uptown; the fires were in the other parts of the city, far away. But then a tower of flame erupted from behind one of the slums in the shadow of the interstate. Below him, and nearby.

That's my cue. He heard Gordon on the scanner—and decided to chance cutting in. "Commissioner, this is Batman. A tenement has just gone up in Crime Alley—looks like it's on Durant."

"Durant!" The commissioner said a word the federal communications authorities wouldn't approve of. *"The fire department is on its way, Batman. But my units are tied up."*

"I'm on it." He cut across three lanes, zinging just in front of the truck driver who'd been pacing him. Batman waved at the mirror as he tore down the exit ramp. "Sorry I didn't signal!"

CHAPTER 17

LAWRENCE'S NEW BOOMBOX REALLY SPOKE, blasting powerful drumbeats through the alley. He loved it already.

And he also loved a good fire.

Usually in the life of a mob enforcer, success and failure were easily measured. Either the target was dead or he wasn't; either the boss he was protecting survived or he didn't. Some aspects, however, weren't as clear-cut. Lawrence was no good at counting, so figuring takes and percentages was a hassle. And being ordered to just scare a guy always came with silly details to keep track of. It was hard to enjoy breaking bones if you had to worry about which ones to preserve so a victim could do his job and keep paying.

But fires were simple. "Leave nothing standing" was understood, even if he didn't always comprehend why he was burning something—like this time.

Not long after his garage meeting the day before, he'd gotten a call from Shreck's intermediary listing locations to torch. Lawrence figured some were randomly chosen to camouflage the places the businessman really wanted to take out, but he was damned if he could tell which were which. Ultimately, however, that didn't matter. He was a freelancer, offering a service. The customer was in charge.

But Lawrence had *also* done the bidding of the mysterious giver of the boombox. *Stay with it. Recruit. Act.* He didn't have a problem with following both sets of instructions, since they didn't conflict. And as Napier had shown, you never knew who'd wind up in charge.

So he had gone right back to work later that day, leading the uninjured members of the botched Capra fire in a successful arson in Chinatown. So what if the cops were busy with some crazed bus driver? Bouncing back felt good.

And it had been noticed. Lawrence was knocking a few back at what was known to be his favorite watering hole when he'd gotten a call from the same character on the tape. *Nice job. Now do more. Speed up. Be more daring.*

Lawrence was doing just that. Hitting four places on the list at once was bound to impress Shreck, dispelling any doubts. It wasn't that crazy a plan, either. Three of the locations only took one firebug each to torch. They just had to be sober enough to remember to actually start the blaze. The exception had been at this place, the abandoned tenement; these places always had squatters, and he'd brought extra people along to deal with that. If the Last Laughs were ever to be a true successor to The Joker's gang they couldn't just hit places that were closed or deserted. They had to flex their muscles sooner or later.

He was stationed in the alley outside the now burning tenement, his new stereo sitting on the pavement providing musical accompaniment. Music amped people up, giving the punks something to make trouble by. The Joker had taught him the value of that: *"It takes a guy with a drum to make the slaves row the boat."*

Most importantly, Lawrence's music also served as a warning system: if they needed to scram, he'd just turn it off.

The tenement was still shuddering from the gas main in the back being set off when one of the masked clown-faces exited, holding a fuel can. Spotting Lawrence, he ran up to him. "Man, I think there's people in there!"

"Do I look like I care?" Lawrence snatched the can from him. *Full.* He shoved it back in the clown's hand. "This place is huge. Get back in there and finish the job!"

Fearing getting punched, the punk turned and ran—only to somersault through the air when something struck him. The gas can went flying—and so did Lawrence, as he dived behind a trash bin. He recovered quickly and went for his piece.

Pressing his face close against the bin, he moved carefully alongside it. He hadn't heard a gunshot, but he couldn't imagine what else—

Kerrang! Something that looked like a metal hockey puck slammed against the bin, caroming wildly. The vibration slammed Lawrence backward, knocking his sunglasses off and nearly taking out his fillings.

On the pavement, he looked back up the street to see the source of the discs.

Batman. "Not again!"

The Batmobile had fired the projectiles from more than a block away—and the rolling war machine had already closed half that distance. Lawrence forgot about the shades and grabbed his gun before scrambling back to cover. He looked toward the boombox. He needed to shut it off, to warn everyone to get the hell out, but he wasn't going to risk running out into the middle of the alley.

Before he could decide, Batman took care of the problem. Another disc blew the stereo to pieces.

Lawrence swore. "That was brand-new!"

The Batmobile skidded to a stop in the intersection before it got to him. Lawrence didn't understand why, until he saw a few of his rats escaping the burning tenement at the intersection. Either they were tipped off by the musical silence, or they'd seen the car and were just plain dumb. His would-be partners were in the street now, hurling the Molotov cocktails they'd intended for the building at Batman's car.

"Stop! Stop!" Lawrence hurtled out from behind the bin, gun raised. He'd seen this movie before. "Stop!"

It was too late. Having shrugged off a couple of fiery blasts, the car was in the process of wrapping itself into an armored cocoon. The young fools kept hitting it again to no avail, doing more harm to themselves as their makeshift grenades went off. Once the four clown-faces had expended every bottle they had, the shields opened—and Lawrence discovered that the front of the car wasn't the only place that fired the evil hockey pucks.

Seeing his companions fall, Lawrence turned to run. *How many of those damned things has he got?*

The Batmobile roared to life again, rumbling up the alley behind him. Lawrence made a running grab for the bottom of a fire escape ladder. He caught it and hoisted himself up, getting out of the automobile's way in the nick of time.

When he looked down, he realized he hadn't escaped at all. Batman had ignored him. The vehicle continued on, heading around the back of the building where the fire was raging.

Lawrence leapt down to the alley, where he found another victim of the car. His sunglasses, a casualty of the Batmobile's tires. Picking up what was left of them, he realized that success wasn't going to be measured by how many buildings he burned. It was going to be how many of his own people he could keep on the streets, and out of traction.

It's gonna be a long night.

THE BATMOBILE AND A BURNING BUILDING. A familiar combination—only this time, the circumstances couldn't be more different.

Several months earlier, Batman had been the arsonist. He'd driven the Batmobile by remote control into the Axis Chemicals factory and deployed a bomb, taking out the plant that The Joker was using to poison the world with Smylex. The car had survived both a blast in its immediate vicinity and a frenetic drive out of a place that was coming apart at the seams.

This time, he was behind the wheel, driving around an inferno and looking for a place to force his way *in*. This was no empty factory; in this neighborhood, even a shuttered tenement could easily have victims trapped inside. He needed to be in there, too.

He found the least-worst way: an abandoned business on the ground floor. It looked sturdy—and empty, from what he could see through windows that had probably been broken for years. He hadn't stayed aboard the bus hitting the bicycle shop the day before, but this time he clutched the wheel and hung on, smashing through the facade.

It was a good choice. The lower floor had once been a sweatshop for something—probably knockoff designer jeans, from the look of the abandoned desks, shelves, and hampers the Batmobile was powering through. Factories meant strong steel-girder ceilings, for suspending heavy equipment. It was probably why the place was still standing. Apartments atop apartments, and the place might already be coming down.

The blast on the building's east side had impacted every floor, but the fire hadn't reached the center of the structure. Still, Batman could see flames through open doors at the far eastern end of the room. He'd need to work fast. He opened the car's cupola and climbed out, flinching when he felt the heat.

He reached inside for additional gear. He hung a secondary harness over his shoulders; among other things, the assembly included a self-contained breathing apparatus, which connected to a mask that covered the lower, exposed portion of his face. He made for the stairwell, feeling the extra heft. He'd never been a marine, but he was getting used to heavy pack runs.

The apartments started immediately above the factory. Working his way down a second-floor hallway, he saw doors to apartments that had been left open. Nobody had lived in these places in some time, but that clearly wasn't the case for the whole building. Adjusting the sensors in his cowl to amplify sounds, he heard yelling. It was remote, on a higher floor.

He was running for the stairs when he heard a peculiar noise. It sounded like a fire engine—or, rather, someone trying to sound like one.

"Whoop, whoop!" A big man rounded the corner, wearing a clown mask—and above, a red hat with a flashing yellow siren bulb mounted atop it. He stopped before Batman but did not react. "Whoop, whoop!"

Batman stared. It didn't appear to be anyone he recognized from the Capra. "What are you supposed to be?"

"Can't you see?" he said, pointing to his hat. "I'm Fire Truck! *Whoop, whoop!*" He opened his jacket to reveal pockets stuffed with unlit Molotov cocktails. "I bring the fire, special delivery. *Whoop, whoop!*"

"Your ride's here." Batman grabbed him by the shoulders and redirected him toward the window.

"Yiii!" Fire Truck waved his arms ineffectively before hurtling through the aperture. Then he disappeared.

Guess there was no fire escape out there. Batman had no time to care about the fate of someone who'd endanger children—and hearing voices again, he was surer than ever they were present. Before he could search for them, he heard gunshots coming from up a stairwell.

He hurried up the stairs. This part of the building wasn't on fire yet, at least. But he was unsure whether the shots were coming from a Last Laugh or a resident. He figured it was likely the former, having seen Lawrence with a gun in the street.

Batman emerged onto the third floor to more shooting. Bullets were flying in the hallway up ahead. He doubled back around a side corridor, hoping to surprise the shooter.

The shooter surprised *him.* He recognized her tie-dyed T-shirt, and the flames painted on the cheeks of her clown mask. It was the woman from the Capra the other night, the one who'd threatened Knox. She had a bandolier over her chest and was carrying a gun in each hand. One, she fired down the hall. The other, she had pointed in his direction.

"Hey, Batsy. I figured you'd show up," she said, still focused on whatever she was shooting at, out of sight. "Don't bother me."

Batman didn't know what to think—or which of his weapons to go for. He wanted her to stop shooting, but he also wanted to know what she was shooting at, and she didn't seem to mind his approach.

"I'm The Scorch," she said.

It sounded like a disease no one wanted to have. He stepped a bit closer—and saw what she was shooting at. Far down the hall sat several tanks that he figured contained something like oxyacetylene. Batman realized that had been how the Last Laughs had set off their initial explosion outside, targeting the gas meter. She continued firing, but it was clear to him that she had no sense of aim whatsoever.

He took another step. "There are children here," he said. "You can hear the screaming."

She fired again. "You think I should care because I'm a woman?"

"No, because you're human."

"So was The Joker. And you threw him off a roof!"

Wrong on both counts, he wanted to say. Instead, he watched as The Scorch expended her last bullet from the gun in her right hand.

"Damn it!" She tossed the piece to the floor.

"Let me try," he said, advancing with his hands out.

She pointed the other gun at him. "Hey, hold it there!"

"No, let me show you how to do this." He walked the last few steps and snatched the gun from her.

She watched, awestruck, as he stepped beside her, faced the tanks, and drew a bead.

Instead of firing, however, he discharged the clip. It fell to the floor. He faced her. "Yeah, I don't think The Joker would have kept you around very long."

Before she could respond, he faced the nearby window and fired a grapple. She turned her head to watch as it embedded in the wall of the building across the street—and in so doing, did not see that he had clipped the projector to her belt. The motor activated, and The Scorch went rocketing out the window. If he'd figured the cable length and distance across the alley right, she'd have a rough meeting with the wall, ending up suspended just above the pavement.

He turned to go back in search of the voices, worrying anew about the Last Laughs. They were amateurs, for sure. But he'd seen a new wrinkle.

They're giving themselves names, now. That can't be good.

CHAPTER 18

KARLO HAD RARELY GOTTEN to see a real doctor. Having one of the top ones in the country attending to him personally was new. Karlo had allowed Auslander to step out of the office twice, but he had quickly returned each time. The first time, he brought in a cart with instruments. The second, larger cart carried a microscope.

Having doffed the lab coat, he had allowed Auslander to examine him, even using tweezers to take a tiny skin sample. Sitting on an oaken desk rather than an examination table, Karlo wondered if this was what he'd secretly sought all along in coming here. He'd spent hours sequestered in the room, trying to understand a single word from the medical files he'd found. It was futile—and there was no way any two-bit doctor in Crime Alley was going to be able to make sense out of any of it, either.

At least this way he'd have answers. Or not.

"I take it you lived alone," Auslander said, looking through the microscope. "No one sought you out. No family or loved ones?"

Karlo shook his head. "No, I'm alone."

"That's what I thought." He looked up from his slides. "There are limits to what I can do with this equipment, I'm afraid. We should have performed diagnostics as soon as you awoke. But you would not cooperate."

"I was losing my mind!"

"And in your frenzy, you nearly lost even more."

Turning to the notes he'd taken, Auslander explained again that basic Smylex functioned a certain way, whether it was spread through The Joker's tainted products or in gaseous form. Having fallen into his coma earlier during Gotham City's shopping nightmare, Karlo had slept through The Joker's parade and gas attack; he didn't mind having missed out on that. But both his condition and what he was exposed to differed.

Auslander showed Karlo the list of items found near his body when he collapsed. No wallet—but a lot of cosmetics. The attached analysis pages detailed a plethora of unpronounceable chemical names. It was longer than the comparable list for Smylex.

"There is a steroidal component in The Joker's version of the compound," Auslander said. "That's evident in the changes it causes: the sudden reshaping of the face, the stiffening of the muscles. But the blood and tissue samples taken during your convalescence suggest that *your* particular mix of chemicals did something else. It produced an enduring, lingering effect—and it is continuing to do so."

"It hasn't worn off? It's been—"

"A long time. I know. But it does appear that one side effect was a happy one."

"A happy one!"

"Most patients lying in coma suffer physical atrophy. Yet you never lost any weight or muscle tone. Indeed, the steroidal effect appears to have left you healthier than you were. You may even have gained enhanced physical performance. Greater endurance."

"I don't care about any of that. I'm asking about my face!"

Auslander nodded. "There, the clouds arrive." He stepped back to the microscope. "I'm not recognizing some of the features of your cells. I suspect that they're the mechanism for your abilities." He stepped close to Karlo and shined a light on his face while he examined it through an eyepiece. "We all have motor control over our expressions, which we exercise both voluntarily and involuntarily. In your exposure, you have been granted the gift—"

"It's not a gift!"

"—the *ability* to contort your muscles on a minute scale. You can alter both how your flesh and your bone structure appear to others—and apparently for more than just a moment. Any person can attempt to match another's expression. You go far beyond that."

"It—it's difficult. It hurts."

"I can imagine. And when at rest—"

"My face melts!" Karlo hung his head. "It's unnatural."

"Oh, it's quite common, when you think about it. We are creatures whose flesh becomes supple—or solid—at will." He demonstrated making a muscle. "When we flex our biceps, what appears as loose and hanging flesh becomes something that seems tough and impenetrable. Our tongues are muscular hydrostats, like elephants' trunks or octopuses' tentacles. Half the tongue's muscles aren't anchored to bone, and yet it has an enormous range of motion. And consider this: when engorged—"

"I get it, I get it." Karlo put up his hands. He didn't need any more examples. "The Joker's been dead for months, and I've been out for longer than that. Are you sure *nobody* else has shown my—my symptoms?"

"Nobody. Again, your combination of chemicals was unique."

"How did I get so lucky? I have no memory of ever using anything."

"Sometimes our number is called." Auslander put his hands before him in an appeal. "I need you to see the blessing here."

"Blessing! There you go again."

"There are thousands of patients around the world whose daily lives are exactly as yours was. People suffering from terrible injuries and diseases, who are kept alive with extreme measures. If we could isolate what causes your resilience, there might be a silver lining in the nightmare that The Joker wrought."

"This thing could help people heal?"

"Or survive long enough for their other problems to be addressed."

"But you'd have to get it back out of them. You can't have people waking up like me. Nobody would have a face!" Karlo shook his head. "You're missing the point. I need you to help *me*."

"And we will try." Auslander peered at him. "I notice your voice has been improving as we've spoken."

Karlo noticed it as well. "I haven't had anyone to talk to. I'm trying to sound like myself—the way I remember . . ." He choked up. "The way I used to sound."

And the way I used to look. Karlo frowned—and in the mirror Auslander had brought, he saw that his face had reshaped to something familiar. Rubber and unliving—as if someone had fashioned a Sad Karlo mask—but him. With concentration, his features grew even more in relief, color returning.

Auslander watched, spellbound. *"Astounding."*

"But what'll happen when I can't remember what I used to look and sound like? I'll just become a copy of myself, getting worse and worse."

"You have just described aging."

"Don't joke."

"I'm not. All the time, our genes are replenishing our cells, based on the blueprint that makes us *us*. As that picture degrades, so do they. But this is again where you are so incredible. If people could control their bodies on this level, just by concentrating . . ." Auslander trailed off, seeming mesmerized.

"The power of acting," Karlo said.

Acting. At the word, the fog he'd experienced for a day and a half lifted swiftly—and suddenly.

"I remember now!" His eyes widened. Moments that his memory had thus far denied him sprang to the forefront—and his face reshaped itself yet again. "This wasn't supposed to happen to me."

"Yes, it's as I said," Auslander replied. "Fate can be a cruel—"

"That's not what I mean," he said, speaking louder. "This wasn't supposed to happen to *me*. This should be happening to someone else!" A face even more hated than his own appeared in his mind— and his whole body shook as he pounded the desk with his fist. "This should have happened to *him*! To *him*!"

Auslander stepped back, startled by the motion. "To whom?"

Karlo's whole body shook as he struck the desk again and again, shouting the hated name like a curse. *"Tolliver Kingston! Tolliver Kingston! Tolliver Kingston!"*

ACROSS TOWN, THE CEILING SHOOK. Batman took refuge under a doorframe—and then fled through the loft, dodging burning beams as he went.

He'd encountered two more Last Laughs after The Scorch, both of whom had shared their silly names before he'd dispensed with them. Unlike with Fire Truck on the second floor, Batman had made sure there were fire escapes for the perpetrators to forcibly exit onto. Because while he wasn't going to waste any more valuable grapplers on them, he was reluctant to deal with them as severely as he'd handled The Joker's men, months before. He had no reason to believe that "Flameface" and "Ash Tray" were career criminals, and he doubted they stood much chance of becoming so.

But even ignoramus copycats could start a fire that could kill people. Batman had spent precious time trying to make sure they only faced attempted murder charges to go along with their arson. He'd gone from floor to floor and wing to wing, searching and saving. The complex was indeed home to impoverished people, using it as a shelter; those he didn't get to fire escapes, he got out on cables. They'd been worth the expenditure, but it hadn't left much on his Utility Belt—and he'd used just about all his fire-retardant projectiles a couple of nights earlier at the Capra.

At least a ladder truck was operating now. Batman carried a coughing, soot-covered woman toward a window where a fireman perched, ready to receive her.

Before he could finish the transfer, the terrified woman clutched at him. "Listen! My kids . . . they're still in there!"

"How many? Where?"

She bent her head in a coughing fit. Unable to stop, she put up two fingers.

The fireman who took her from Batman heard the exchange. "You can't stay! Come on!"

Batman shook his head. "I'm going back in."

"But we can't—"

Batman didn't hear any more. He knew they were starting to pump water in, but he also knew the help wasn't likely to be fast enough.

He deployed his gear's thermal imaging eyepiece and dashed through the smoke. It had helped to find hotspots during his searches, especially as visibility worsened. It just wasn't as useful for finding victims—flames were much hotter than bodies, living or not.

He crossed back through the blazing wreck that had once been the top floor. The building above the factory space hadn't always been apartments, he'd come to suspect; it must have been converted at some point before it fell into disuse. There were shared bathrooms on every floor, at the end of each hall. It was more like what would be found in an old—

"A hotel!"

Batman considered the floorplan as he'd come to understand it—and worked his way back along the main hall from the now-engulfed stairwell, scanning the walls. He looked this way and that through his imager, adjusting the gain.

There it was: a square-shaped outline on the wall up to his right, cooler than everything else. He approached it. A door, through which more temperate air was escaping.

A dumbwaiter.

Finding the door reluctant to open, he put some muscle into it, ripping it off its hinges. Air rushed up and out, a chimney blast that caused the burning walls behind him to respond with searing heat. He drew his cape up, using it to shield himself until the effect subsided.

He stuck his head into the shaft. There was nothing inside but a cable—and screaming. The haunting yells he'd heard, everywhere else he'd gone lower down in the building. Batman saw the problem: the line was jammed on something above. He took the cable in one hand and grabbed one of the winch grapples on his Utility Belt. It was his last motor, but he could tell from a pull there were a hundred pounds or so inside the dumbwaiter compartment.

"Hang on!" he called down. He held the launcher in position and fired a two-way line—one end into the ceiling of the shaft, the other into the top of the dumbwaiter compartment. He then got out of the way as the winch did its work, bringing the car up.

Too fast! Fearing it would bypass the opening entirely, Batman reached in to stop its progress with the only thing he had handy—his hands. The car rocketed up and struck them, jamming his wrists painfully against the top of the opening. He yelled—frightening the riders inside the dumbwaiter. A boy—maybe five years old—and a girl, slightly older, crouched in the small space. The boy saw the howling Batman and screamed in response.

Batman struggled as he fought against the attempt by his own gadget's motor to take his hands off. *"Climb . . . out!"*

The girl jumped out first. "You're Batman!" she declared.

"For the moment." Batman gritted his teeth.

She saw what he wanted, and helped the boy climb out next. Batman yanked his hands free from the dumbwaiter car, which continued its electrically assisted ride up.

"It got stuck," she said, coughing. She looked around fretfully at the burning hallway. "What are we going to—"

She never finished her question. Seeing the roof starting to give way above him, Batman enveloped the children with his cape and knelt. He triggered the cape's lifesaver protocol, securing the bottom of the garment against the floor. His head tucked down, he felt hot debris raining onto him for what seemed like an eternity.

The cape, secure against the floor, did its job, protecting the children and himself. He dared to look up—and saw a cooler region further up the hall. An arm around each child, he hunched over, walking with them toward relative safety.

Rising, he broke out two junior-sized emergency breathing masks he had in his special gear. He helped affix them to the children's faces. "You're doing great," he said.

"You're full of it," the little girl said, and she was right. She pointed back to where the dumbwaiter had been—an area fully engulfed in flames. Worse, they were still in the center of the building, nowhere near a window.

Think hotel. Think hotel. His eyes traced along the hallways. "There it is!"

He didn't know whether it was a chute for trash or laundry—but it was open, with no door or car blocking the way below. Wooden-walled, it was something he could fit down.

"Hang on," he said, picking up a child under each arm.

The girl yelped this time. "It's five stories!"

"Just hang on." Batman ducked his head and crouched inside the space, looming over the shaft below. There was no fire down there, that he could see, but neither did he have any more cables. Not that he could deploy them anyway, with a squirming kid under each arm.

He spoke to the girl. "What's your name?"

"Manda."

"Manda, do you see that gray button on my gauntlet?"

"What's a gauntlet?"

"Up on my wrist. Push it—and then hold tight." She did so, and he held them tighter. "Hang on!"

Batman stepped fully into the shaft and began falling. His cape expanded as he went, the button-press having triggered the electrical current that transformed the structural ribs within his cape from supple to rigid. It was designed to slow his descent when coming down on a cable, but here it worked just enough for him to spread his legs, slamming the outer edges of his boots against the shaft walls. He skidded all the way down.

By the time he landed in a mountain of trash at the bottom, his ankles were burning much like the building—but at least they hit the ground at less than a bone-breaking speed. Whatever the chute was, the residents had apparently been chucking stuff into it for years. Their sanitation shortcut helped stop his fall.

He released the kids and examined the door in the dark room to see if it was safe to open. It was—and it revealed the factory floor he'd driven onto earlier. It was all now ablaze, save for the area around the shielded Batmobile.

He directed the kids toward it and turned off the shields—a moment that might have driven oohs and aahs from any kids not in a burning building. But the little boy did speak for the first time. "Can that get us out?"

"Trust me," Batman said. "Get in!"

CHAPTER 19

"TOLLIVER KINGSTON! TOLLIVER KINGSTON!"

Auslander clutched the handheld mirror that had been on the desk, protecting it as Karlo raged inside the office. Since naming the name, Patient Thirty-Five had charged around, ranting incoherently and knocking lamps off tables and books off shelves. It was enough ruckus that the doctor was glad it was night, and that his office was situated behind a private reception area.

He had tried to stay out of Karlo's way, protecting his medical equipment and records without getting in the firing line of his rage. Karlo's face was a furious symphony, accompanying his every angry word with a monstrous manifestation. If this was the creature the people on the bus had seen, no wonder their tales had portrayed Clayface as a real-life golem.

Karlo grabbed a chair and threatened to throw it at the window—only to pause. *Perhaps he was remembering his plummet the day before,* Auslander thought. Whatever the reason, he stopped in his tracks, taking deep breaths.

Auslander spoke calmly. "Who is Kingston?"

"The actor I bought the cosmetics for!" Karlo responded, flustered but no longer enraged. "Tolliver Kingston. He's the one that sent me to Crime Alley to get them. That's how I lost my wallet—I remember now. And then he insisted that I test the makeup on myself, first!"

Auslander scratched his beard. "Fascinating."

"It was all hazy. But I see it now, right up to the last minute." He gritted his teeth—and snatched the mirror from the doctor's hands. Karlo looked into it—and then smashed the mirror against the desk. "*Damn him!*"

Auslander watched him carefully. "Please calm yourself."

"Shut up!" Karlo saw the files on the doctor's desk—and swept his hand across the surface, sending papers flying.

"This aggression. It's connected to your evolved state."

"Quit saying I've evolved!"

"I'm a psychiatrist as well as a physician. There may be something I can—"

"I'm not taking any drugs!"

"Their effects are well studied."

"But not on me! For all you know, my face could start sprouting broccoli!"

Karlo looked to the door. Auslander feared he was preparing to leave—but there was no way he could do so without attracting attention. If impersonation took concentration, Karlo was far beyond that now. He seemed to sense it, too, turning toward the window.

"You can't go out that way. There's a drop—"

"I've done it!"

"—and people will know you were here."

But he couldn't dissuade Karlo. He ripped open the blinds—

—and beheld the signal in the sky.

Karlo stared, awestruck. "What the hell is that? The mouth of a shark?"

"No, you wouldn't know." Cautiously, Auslander joined him at the window. "It is a bat."

"A bat?"

"The vigilante Batman—whose acquaintance you made—enjoys a position of public trust because he identified the Smylex components—and he killed The Joker."

"Killed him!"

"The official story is that The Joker did it to himself, but official stories are rarely true. At any rate, that symbol means the police are requesting his aid with something they cannot defeat."

Karlo stared at the light. "You mean me. Something like me!" His voice now a feral growl, he turned and grabbed Auslander by the neck. "You told them I was here!"

"I did not. I don't have that power."

Karlo tightened his grip on the doctor's throat. "You're lying!" He pulled Auslander toward him—and then shoved the older man backward, throwing him against the desk.

His back on the desk, the doctor saw the phone. An idea formed. "Please. I can clear this up."

"Don't touch that!" Karlo growled.

Auslander put up his hand. "This isn't what you think."

Karlo seethed—but held off when Auslander toggled the intercom and pressed a button.

"Lab," a female voice said.

The doctor quickly composed himself. "This is Auslander."

"Up late again, I see."

"I have samples to send up. I'd like them prioritized."

"Yours always are."

"One more thing. Your office faces downtown, like mine. How long has that signal been shining?"

"It appeared just after sunset. More of those fires, all across the city—radio says Batman's been rescuing victims. Uptown's burn unit is handling intake, ours is on standby."

"Good to know." Auslander ended the call. "You see, that light in the sky had nothing to do with you."

Karlo stared at the phone—and then threw himself into Auslander's chair. He put his face in his hands. "I'm sorry," he said in something closer to his own voice. "I don't know what's been coming over me."

Auslander stepped away, straightening his collar. "I told you I can help—and there is another option besides medicating you." He drew out a golden pocket watch on a chain. "Hypnosis."

Karlo gawked. "Oh, here we *go*. You do the full mad scientist. Does a book on this stuff come with the beard?"

"The mind is surprisingly pliable."

"Wrong term!"

"I am saying it adapts. In just a day, you've taught yourself to impersonate someone you've barely met."

"It's called acting!" Karlo bolted up. "No, no. I'm not doing this. The second I zone out, you'll be back with your needle. And then I'll be locked away!"

"I will not. I promise—"

"Forget it! You don't just want to study me to find a cure. You want this—this thing that's in me!"

Karlo wasn't having it. He put on his suit jacket. He strained, and Auslander's face returned—only without the beard, eyebrows, and hair.

"Don't do this. People will notice—"

"Shut up." Spying a surgical mask, Karlo put it on. "It's late. Nobody will stop me."

"*I'm* trying to stop you." Auslander continued to plead with him as he reached the doorway.

At last, he got the actor's attention. "Mister Karlo—Basil—I will try. Perhaps there is something in the samples I've taken today. But I implore you to stay out of sight. Events like what happened on the bus—or stunts like the one you pulled today—must stop. I cannot protect you from the police—or Batman."

Karlo looked back from under his hat, eyes full of rage. "If he comes for me, it'll be Batman who needs protecting!"

Auslander remained in his office after Karlo departed. It wouldn't do for anyone to see the two together, for certain. He tidied a bit before venturing to the window, to wait.

There he is. He continued to watch as Basil Karlo receded into the shadows outside, leaving Gotham General's grounds for the second time in two days. This escape was much more peaceful.

Auslander exhaled. Karlo's case had surprised him in every

way—and yet, it also had not. He knew there were connections between the mind and the body that had largely gone unexplored by man. He had not lied to the actor about the potential break-throughs his condition might portend—and not just medical ones. Patient Thirty-Five could open doors people had never considered trying to unlock.

The Bat-Signal was no longer on, he saw; that, he figured, would assuage Karlo as he fled into the night. In many ways, the actor was an imperfect vessel for so many hopes. Erratic, emotional—it was clear to a trained observer that he was, in his previous life, a character of little consequence.

Yet, that was also a great advantage. Nobody had missed Karlo, and nobody would be searching specifically for him now. And better still, his acting abilities had given him a handle on his physical ones in a remarkable short period of time. A thespian had figured out in thirty-six hours what might take another test subject years.

Yes, it could all be useful—especially as Karlo was on the outside, on the run. *He will not be found unless he wants to be,* Auslander thought. *But I will know where he is.*

He had already made sure of it.

SIXTEEN. SIXTEEN PEOPLE HAD been inside the tenement that the Last Laughs had burned to the ground.

Boots soaked from the spray of fire trucks still fighting a lost cause, Batman reflected on the number. *Sixteen.* He had saved every one, according to the count of the people who'd escaped. That was a success. But it remained that the Last Laughs had no compunction about burning those people alive. Their comical failure at the Capra had given him two kinds of hope: that they were incompetent, and that they preferred an abandoned target. Tonight's attacks had dashed those prospects. They were indeed capable of pulling off a major crime—and they didn't care who they hurt doing it.

They hadn't all escaped, but Lawrence had, and he expected that the perps now being handcuffed were the ones of the lowest quality. This had happened during The Joker's reign of terror: between Batman's efforts and Napier's own internecine violence, his gang had been culled down to just the smartest and most dangerous felons by the end. Here, Batman was doing all the winnowing himself. Yet the Last Laughs hadn't run out of people—and if things kept up, they'd be getting better and better.

If I'm their training program, what are they training for?

More sirens sounded in the night. Commissioner Gordon tromped through the puddles toward him. "We owe you again, Batman."

"We owe somebody else."

"Indeed. We're questioning the perpetrators we caught. They aren't being cooperative."

"I'm shocked."

"It takes a certain sort of person to idolize a dead clown. It also seems to be the same sort that likes to set fires at random." He looked at Batman. "If they *are* random."

"We'll see." He could tell Gordon was hoping to hear his ideas—but he was too tired to think about it. He was about to pull his disappearing act when an ambulance's arrival caused Gordon to step away instead.

Batman saw the children he'd saved. They ran from where the paramedics were caring for their mother. "Thank you, Batman!" they said in unison.

"Anytime." Batman knelt next to the young boy. "Thanks for driving, partner."

The girl embraced him—and stepped back. She'd stepped on something. She bent over to pick it up. "I think this might be yours," she said, handing it to him.

Another clown mask.

"Thank you," he said, and they ran off to rejoin their mother.

He walked back to the Batmobile, wondering if he'd actually won tonight. Yes, he'd saved people—including part of the next generation. Poor kids, who were on the margins of society. Maybe they'd remember that someone had acted to help them.

But many of the Last Laughs were probably on the margins as well. And what lessons had they taken?

Suddenly feeling despair, he tossed the clown mask away. *This is never going to end,* he thought. *The Joker just won't die!*

THURSDAY, 12:53 A.M.

FRUSTRATION TURNED TO ELATION TODAY
NOT SIMILAR TO ARMSGARD,
SOMETHING BEYOND!
CONTAINMENT NOT ACHIEVED,
BUT BATMAN AT BAY
KEEP HIM CHASING THE WRONG QUARRY

CHAPTER 20

THE GOTHAM CATHEDRAL, YET AGAIN.

This was getting ridiculous. Batman saw it every time he slept, now. And yet something in his half-dozing state told him that it would be the last time. That, at least, would be worth sticking around through one more dream.

It definitely *looked* like the end. The Joker had paid the ultimate price for his crimes. Batman had attempted to prevent him from escaping by lashing him to a gargoyle—and it had been Jack Napier's executioner, toppling off the church and pulling him down to his death. Batman and Vicki had escaped the same fate only barely, through the use of his longest cable and grapple. They had swung, suspended, across the face of the great edifice, a pendulum of relief in the searchlights. The danger was over.

They'd conveniently come to a stop near a parapet; reaching it was a simple matter, relative to everything else he'd had to do that night. Once he was sure Vicki had a safe route down, he'd leave. He wasn't ready to interact directly with the police yet; he felt confident that Vicki wouldn't reveal his secret to them.

But she stopped first, and turned to look over the side. "He's down there."

"And?"

She looked at him, eyes pained. "I'd like to make sure. Wouldn't you?"

This is new, the dreamer thought. But she had a point. *Let's see where it goes.* He went inside with her.

The rest of the way down was a blur of shadows, an improvised descent all the way. But they exited the cathedral just as the people of Gotham City, scared away by the open warfare on their streets, gathered to see for themselves what he and Vicki were interested in.

A mix of police, reporters, and passersby had gathered on the pavement. The gargoyle, having struck nearby, had shattered into pieces, leaving a crater and stone fragments everywhere. But the largest grouping was to one side; a creepy, robotic laughter came from the center of the throng.

Vicki didn't turn away; she'd seen death in Corto Maltese. But she still didn't want to approach too closely. "Can you make sure?"

"Yeah."

Alone, he strode into the circle, drawing mesmerized looks from the bystanders. But he was nothing compared to the sight on the ground. The Joker lay in his own cracked indentation in the street, half in deep shadow. In the light, Batman could see Commissioner Gordon kneeling beside The Joker's bloodied, smiling corpse. Gordon rose holding a smashed pouch: a broken laugh box, the source of the eerie sounds. He'd heard about the moment, but never seen it.

Then something impossible happened. The flattened Joker stood up—and snapped the laugh box from Gordon's hand. "I'll take that, if you don't mind." He sneered at Gordon. "Thief."

Batman clenched his fists, on guard—and around him, the gawkers stepped back in horror. The Joker reached down and removed the cable that had gone around his ankle.

"I'll never explain this to my tailor," he said, strutting about with one leg longer than the other. He cracked his neck so loudly it produced a groan of horror from the watchers. Then he shook like a dog, trying to re-inflate his crushed form.

I've seen enough. Batman tried to wake up—but found he couldn't. Instead, he stepped forward and seized The Joker's shoulders. "How are you alive?"

The laugh box in Gordon's hand singsonged, "How did I survive the fall? Maybe I never fell at all!"

Batman looked at it—and then looked up. Something was descending through the air from near the top of the cathedral: The Joker's helicopter. As it approached, Batman could see The Joker in its window, holding a megaphone—and shouting words from an old song, just as he had when he escaped Axis Chemicals.

"Into the air, Junior Birdmen!" He laughed. "Missed me—again!"

It's all running together, Batman thought. *Why?*

Baffled, he turned back to see The Joker on the street was in motion. Moving like lightning, he grabbed Batman and lifted him from the ground. It wasn't possible—he wasn't strong enough, nor tall enough, even after his experience—but the hero's boots dangled over the street nonetheless. He writhed helplessly, getting no assistance from anyone.

Batman looked into The Joker's eyes. "What *are* you?"

The Joker pulled Batman's face toward him. "Funny thing about Jokers. There's two in every deck!" His face melted, and his mouth opened—a laughing maw that consumed the universe . . .

BATMAN WOKE UP THRASHING. He kicked and punched, disoriented. It took him several seconds to realize where he was.

He'd fallen asleep in the Batmobile.

Wincing, he triggered the cupola to open. The rush of cool, dank air told him he was in the Batcave. Squinting, he touched the control next to the dashboard monitor. "Alfred?"

Static—and then Alfred appeared on the screen, sweeping the kitchen. He looked up at the camera. *"Ah."*

"Do you know where I am?"

"Of course, sir."

"You didn't come get me?"

"The biomonitor in the car told me you were there, and uninjured. The camera told me you were simply asleep. I chose not to interrupt you." He put away the broom. *"I'll join you presently."*

"Bring coffee. And aspirin."

And maybe a neck brace, he thought, trying to clamber out of the car. His uniform was singed and soot-covered from the fire, and when his boots hit the parking island, he had to steady himself so he didn't pitch forward.

Bruce had shed a trail of gauntlets, cape, and armor behind him by the time Alfred came downstairs with a tray. He rubbed his neck. "Cramps."

"I can't imagine sleeping in the suit was any more comfortable than sleeping in a car," Alfred said. "But people do what they must."

Bruce looked back toward the opening to the cave. Sometimes a little light would peek in, but this time he saw nothing. "I must have only been out an hour or so."

"No, sir. You arrived two hours before dawn. It is now two hours after sunset. You slept the whole day."

Bruce looked at a screen depicting the time—and took the mug. He moved, shakily, toward the stairs to his observation station.

Alfred brought the tray up to him. "You must shower and eat, sir."

"No, I have to see what the Last Laughs have been up to." Bruce rubbed his bristly chin as he stared at the screen. He exhaled. "No fires."

Alfred stepped to his right. "In fact, sir, tonight's fires already occurred."

Bruce looked up at him. "What?"

"There were two, right after sunset again." Alfred pointed to one of the screens. "But they were both on the waterfront."

"Why didn't you wake me up?"

"The police scanner said they were unoccupied structures."

Bruce was glad of that, but something about it rubbed him the wrong way.

As Alfred descended the stairs from the platform, Bruce called after him. "Did the signal go up?"

Alfred continued walking.

Bruce put down the mug and stood. He called over the railing. "Alfred, did the Bat-Signal go up?"

The butler stopped. He turned his head. "It did."

"And you didn't let me know?"

"I told you, the structures were unoccupied. There were no injuries—"

"But also no arrests."

"None that I know of." Alfred faced forward again and continued walking toward the entrance to the mansion.

Bruce stormed down the metal stairs, after him. "I can't believe you didn't wake me up!" He reached the old man's side. "Alfred, that signal is a pact with the city. I've earned their trust. I *have* to respond!"

"They shut it off almost immediately, sir. I told you, the threat was—"

"*I* needed to decide! Alfred, this isn't like not answering the doorbell!"

Alfred stared at him, cold as stone. When he spoke again, it was with a tone Bruce hadn't heard since he was a teenager. "I am going to attribute that comment to a lack of sleep. And respect."

Bruce hung his head low. "I know, I know. I'm sorry." He lifted his eyes. "What I was trying to say—very poorly—is that I've never missed their call before."

"And you have said yourself that it was going to happen eventually." Alfred gestured to the rest of the Batcave. "You intended to serve as an insurance policy for the city, a last resort. But you cannot be expected to respond to everything." He frowned. "Nor do I think it wise for you to let the commissioner believe that every emergency requires your intervention."

Bruce sighed. Alfred was right, as always. "I saw Gordon last night, in fact. He's very stressed."

"You see? I suspect he regrets sending tonight's signal."

I doubt the people who owned those warehouses would feel the same way, Bruce thought. But he kept that to himself as Alfred headed up the stairs.

When the butler returned, he was bearing a plate. He carried it back to the platform, where Bruce was catching up on the day. Bruce had a forkful in his mouth before he even saw what he was eating. "Salmon?"

"One struggles to find meals that could serve as either breakfast, lunch, or dinner." Alfred stood back by the railing and clasped his hands together. "Did you dream again?"

"Did I ever. It was a doozy. This one was the worst of all." Bruce explained it between bites.

Alfred repeated some of the same refrain from earlier days. "Professor Auslander said The Joker inflicted a collective trauma to the city. This one affected you personally and directly. It was going to arise eventually."

"I just want to make sure *he* doesn't arise."

"You know there's no chance of that. I continue to contend this was triggered by the so-called Last Laughs—and your faceless pugilist."

Bruce snapped his fingers, reminded. "Let's see what we caught."

Bruce called up the video captured by his camera in Gotham General's parking lot in the hours after his visit the day before. He cued through it, keeping his eye on the entrance and a particular parking space. Hugh Auslander arrived after the sun had set, entering the hospital.

"Our professor works late," he said. "I wonder who cooks for *him*."

"Perhaps we can share recipes." Alfred studied the images whizzing past as well. "Pause there."

"I missed it," Bruce said, slowing down the tape. Then he looked more closely. "Or did I?"

Making a note of the time codes, he put the imagery from two different moments on adjacent screens and played both in slow motion. Well after dark, someone resembling Auslander exited, only to walk past his car, continuing out of frame. Fifteen minutes later, a second Auslander left the building.

"He looks around, gets in the car, and drives away," Bruce said. "Weird." He remembered the person they'd met whose behavior had been strange. "What's out of frame where Auslander Number One went?"

Alfred sat before another terminal and pulled up recent satellite images. "The bicycle racks, sir. A path leads off campus from there."

"A bicycle," Bruce said. "As in a bicycle shop." A timeline took shape in his mind. "We've got a canceled call from the hospital to the police just before the bus incident. A phone pole that gets hit on Walcott. Do we have anything else?"

Alfred looked reluctant to speak. With a sigh, he reached for a folder. "I received word from the Wayne Industries insurance lab on your Walcott sample."

Bruce nodded. When he had gone back out as Batman the night of the bus incident, he'd visited the site of the phone pole that had been struck. The police hadn't done any forensic collection, but he had, obtaining samples of paint from the pole and broken glass from the scene. He took the file from Alfred and read.

"No pigment in the bumper paint, but there's a particular acrylic in the clear coat. Two layers of paint from the hood . . ." He trailed off. He pointed. "I was right about the kind of laminate in the glass."

"Your experts agreed, though they have no idea what they're agreeing about. But what you have there is a stock service van—"

"—repainted to match Gotham General's fleet." Bruce snapped his fingers. "What if this guy—this Clayface—fled the hospital and came back the next day?"

"To what end, sir?"

"I'll find out." Bruce sprang from his chair.

His action startled Alfred. "You're going back out?"

"If nothing else, I've got to retrieve our camera." Bruce trotted down the stairs to the floor of the Batcave.

Alfred followed him as he collected the parts of his costume. "You're weary beyond measure. You can't mean to go back out yet again."

"You sound like someone else."

"And when you wouldn't listen, Miss Vale took an assignment that carried her out of town."

"So are you going to run out on me too?"

When he didn't hear an answer, Bruce stopped and looked back to see Alfred smoldering. "Again, I'm sorry. I'm just—"

"I know." Alfred spoke slowly. "After your parents died, Master Bruce, I was advised that surviving children often test their remaining loved ones, to see whether they, too, will abandon them." He turned toward the stairs. "They just never told me the phase could last this long." He turned and walked back up the stairs.

CHAPTER 21

"PERLUIGI'S! WHADDYA WANT?"

The phone was ringing off the hook at the pizza place, as usual. The shows were letting out, leading to the inevitable nightly moment when theatregoers divided into two camps. Those with reservations, connections, or good fortune got tables in restaurants. Everybody else called Perluigi's for a pie.

At H-Hour—Old Man Perluigi was a veteran—a small army of drivers and cyclists entered through the back of the restaurant to re-supply. New ones signed on every week; he rarely bothered to learn their names. So when one reentered just five minutes after departing, he thought nothing of it. After all, the guy had the hat and jacket. "You're fast, kid."

"Gracias," Karlo said, pivoting and walking out with three boxed pies, at least one of which he hoped had the sausage he liked.

He didn't figure the driver he'd impersonated would get in trouble; Karlo had moonlighted at Perluigi's while at the Capra, which is why he still had the jacket and hat. Things were so hectic that orders went astray several times a night. Nobody could ever get through on the phone to complain, anyway—and the old man was such a horrible boss that Karlo didn't feel the least bit guilty. Interacting with others was a risk—particularly someone who had once known him—but discovery and morality both paled before the gnawing in his stomach.

If Auslander wanted me to hide, he should have given me some money.

He dined al fresco, on the fire escape that had been his home away from the Capra that day. He'd sat there reading the abandoned magazines and newspapers he'd collected from behind the newsstand down below, learning more about what had gone on while he was unconscious.

It was all astonishing. Everything about The Joker's campaign of chaos had made national news, and with good reason. Karlo had skipped over the stories about Smylex—that wound would always be raw—but marveled at what had happened during the night of The Joker's parade. Learning the villain's fate had given him mixed feelings; Karlo was happy he was dead, but sorry he'd missed the chance to tear him limb from limb.

Karlo was also astonished at how much Batman was in the news. He worked directly with the police now; worrisome, given the fact that the paper from that morning continued to mention his bus battle with the hideously deranged Clayface. What a peculiar character Batman was—and a horrible one to have gotten on the bad side of, even though it was completely unintentional.

I guess I'm lucky he didn't come after me in a plane.

Karlo took solace in one thing, at least: he'd moved below the fold in that morning's newspaper. Joker copycats—how wretched could you get?—had tried to burn a building with families inside. Batman had come to their rescue. Maybe he'd have his hands full chasing them.

I'll just lay low. Auslander will find a cure—and I'll forget about Batman.

He finished off his second pie, well aware of how impossible his ability to eat was this soon after his coma. But he was still famished. He reached for the third box, hoping to find his favorite kind.

Under the light from the nearby streetlamp, he saw Perluigi had just changed his menu for the first time since opening his doors. Black olives sat atop the cheese, forming the shape of a bat.

Karlo shoved the box off the fire escape. He'd lost his appetite.

———

"I TOLD YOU BEFORE, have Doctor Conover see the patients," Auslander shouted into the phone in the hospital hallway. "My research is at a critical juncture!"

He slammed the receiver on the cradle. Nobody at Gotham General knew that he'd encountered Karlo the night before; he'd barely been able to keep a lid on the fact the man had escaped from the Smylex Ward in the first place. Auslander had hardly slept over the last twenty-four hours, retreating to the top-floor private lab that had been a prerequisite of his joining the staff. The samples he'd taken from Karlo had kept him busy; he'd emerged only to run out to other parts of the facility, to commandeer additional equipment.

He'd discovered something amazing having to do with Karlo's skin and its resilience. The tissue samples exhibited such astounding properties that he felt he understood the mechanism behind Karlo's autonomous responses. It took his breath away—and it caused him to drop everything else. *No more interviews. No more visitors. He had to be left alone.*

So he was surprised to discover, after unlocking the door to his lab, that the light switch didn't work—and that someone was inside, moving about in the darkened room. He thought about leaving for help—but instead he put down the equipment he was carrying and closed the door behind him. He picked up a scalpel from the counter.

"If you are looking for narcotics, you will be disappointed," he said, edging forward in the dark. He thought about Karlo's arrival the night before and added: "Unless it's *you.*"

"That depends on who you were expecting," said a low voice.

Auslander's eyes widened as a silhouette took form against the low light from the windows facing outside—a figure topped by two wedge-shaped horns.

The doctor stepped forward, unbelieving. "Batman!"

Gotham City's hero was in his lab, standing behind rows of beakers and imaging equipment, looking at something with a flashlight.

The doctor proceeded carefully, a step forward at a time. "I admit surprise. I thought your arrival would be heralded by a light in the sky—and a war machine in the parking lot." He looked to the ceiling. "Or perhaps you landed your flier on the roof."

"I can teleport now."

"Will wonders never cease?" Auslander put down the scalpel and advanced a little farther. He watched as Batman lifted test tubes before his light, reading as if he understood what he was doing. "Finding anything interesting?"

"You already have."

Auslander smiled in spite of himself. "Yes, I suppose so. Actually, I should greet you as a colleague. That was marvelous work you did, isolating Smylex and determining how it was distributed."

"Lucky guess."

"I don't believe that for a moment. Either you—or someone in your employ—is a chemist of the top order."

"I only had to be as good as Napier," Batman said.

"I'm not sure how good Napier was. An amateur, drawing upon the work of others." Auslander watched as Batman moved from one counter to another. "What brought you here? What are you looking for?"

"Basil Karlo."

Auslander deadpanned, "Who's that?"

"You know who he is," Batman said. He lifted a file. "He was your Patient Thirty-Five. He awoke from a coma two days ago, having undergone some kind of transformation. He lashed out—and then he leapt out."

"So you know."

"And I know what he did after that. He hijacked the D27 bus."

Auslander chortled. "What an outlandish claim. *That's* definitely not in the file. And it's quite outrageous."

"It was him."

Auslander listened as Batman recounted clues he'd found connecting Karlo to the bus incident. The vigilante had connected

Karlo to the laundry van accident—and that had somehow led him back here. "He returned to this facility last night—and left again."

Auslander wanted to know how he knew that—but instead said, "Go on."

"These blood and tissue samples are from him, time-stamped from last night. You're working on his case personally."

"It's quite the case that *you've* built." Auslander looked Batman in his dark eyes. "Have you informed the police about it?"

"Not yet."

"I suppose you think I'm hiding him here."

"No, I'm certain you're not. He left yesterday and hasn't returned."

Auslander expected Batman to elaborate on how he knew that, but he never did. There was no point in prevaricating further. "Very well. I did see him. He came here, asking for help."

"In disguise."

"In a wig and hat. It is the only way he feels he can travel."

"He was impersonating you."

"I'm a public figure, for good or ill. There is some comedian in a local nightclub who has worked up an act around me." Auslander decided to cooperate, seeing as Batman already had the file in hand. "Karlo was exposed on the date you see there, while working at a theatre called the Capra."

The masked man's head turned slightly. "The Capra. Really?"

Auslander nodded. "Yes, the site of the arson attempt from the other day. I read about your intervention. He was exposed to multiple different tainted products there. Paramedics brought all the substances here, as you see."

Batman rounded the corner of the lab table. He loomed in the dark. "Where is Karlo now?"

"I don't know. And if I did, I wouldn't tell you."

"He's dangerous. He nearly killed people!"

"Extenuating circumstances. Diminished capacity." Auslander

crossed his arms. "You're no law enforcement officer—and Karlo is no hardened convict, escaped during a prison transfer. He's a well-meaning innocent—I would almost say, a nebbish—who has been trying to cope with the most extraordinary changes."

"One of those changes stole a bus."

"And I guarantee you he won't do it again." Auslander gestured to the glassware. "That man's body contains secrets, Batman. Secrets which could change the world. I only want to understand them—and use them."

"Use them?"

"To cure others, of course." He spoke freely. "The government continues to deny it has any information on DDID Nerve Gas—Smylex—and so we have been forced to reverse-engineer everything we know about it to help our patients. It's plain that Karlo has had a very different reaction. But there are aspects of it that could help people—and not just those in this facility."

Batman glanced again at the file. "You mean his resiliency, during the coma, and after."

"From bedridden to bus-napper in less than an hour. Wouldn't it be amazing if The Joker had somehow stumbled over something that could cure, as well as kill?"

"Survivors said The Joker worked with a chemist at Axis Chemicals to prepare the Smylex shipments. We never found him—or any notes." Batman shook his head. "That's a dead end."

"Karlo is a walking record. You have seen the things he can do."

Batman crossed the room and stared out the window, clutching the file in his hand. He seemed to be brooding over something, but Auslander had no idea what.

His surprise was complete when Batman spoke, without turning. "This resilience Karlo has. Could anyone with the same exposure have his abilities?"

Auslander blinked. "That's what I'm trying to find out. Today's patients could be—"

"I don't mean today." Batman turned his head. "Could Napier

have been exposed—accidentally or intentionally—to whatever it was that made Karlo so resilient?"

The doctor gawked. "Are you asking if The Joker could survive a fall of hundreds of feet?" It was an incredible suggestion. "They pulled his corpse out of a crater!"

"But Karlo was as good as dead, too. And he woke up."

Auslander stared—and then laughed. "I had thought you brilliant. Now I believe you're quite mad." He shook his head. "Do you know what happens to bones that strike the ground at terminal velocity? Can anyone walk away from such a fall?"

"I have." Batman turned away. "But not from that high."

How peculiar, Auslander thought. Whoever was behind Batman's mask was clearly an obsessive character—possibly fitting several criteria found in the *Diagnostic and Statistical Manual of Mental Disorders,* if not a whole new chapter. It was astonishing he would even consider that The Joker might have survived.

As fascinating as Batman was, Auslander also saw an opportunity. He turned, heading in search of his tape recorder. "If you don't mind, I have a few questions I'd like to ask of *you.*"

He turned back and saw that Batman was gone. Auslander crossed the room quickly. Karlo's file was sitting there on the table, and nothing was missing. Nothing save his visitor. The doctor stepped through a side doorway into a small room and looked around—and then up. The ceiling panels were gone, permitting access to the crawl space above.

File in hand, Auslander scratched his beard and thought about his two very different nocturnal invaders. His career plans had changed—and changed again—over the last year. But it was a poor scientist who did not adapt to reflect new information.

And he had just gotten a *lot* of it.

"Jo Jo's." THE CURLY-HAIRED BARTENDER listened for a moment before she called out. "It's for you, big guy."

Lawrence paused his pummeling. It was true, what they said: once you'd worked as a bouncer, you could never set foot in a bar again without smacking someone around. The fools he worked with happened to deserve it, particularly once the clown masks came off and they started to celebrate. He shoved the drunk to the floor. "I'll be back."

Lawrence walked out onto the party deck behind the bar. Jo Jo was an ex-con who knew the town and knew the score; she paid the right people, making her tavern a sanctuary for those on the wrong side of the law. She also had a big garage, useful for hiding things— and people. "Keep it short," she said, handing him the cordless phone.

He turned his back on the chaos inside. "Yeah."

"Six hits in two days. We're impressed."

Lawrence knew the voice. Max Shreck would never make such a call; his partner, Fred Atkins, did a lot of the dirty work. Still, Lawrence was careful not to use his name. "We aim to please. And the guys they pinched stayed quiet."

"Too bad they got caught. But that rat-trap needed to go. Good job."

Dealing with anyone else, Lawrence would have expected some carping about the families in the building. But the Shrecks were cold customers.

"You've really stepped up to the plate—but lay off a bit. Batman raises the temp too much."

Before hanging up, Atkins told him where he'd find their pay for the week's work—and how much. It was good. Enough to keep recruiting. Success had bred success; for every fool that had gotten caught, two more had shown up to get in on things.

Lawrence hadn't left from behind the bar when the phone rang again. Jo Jo grabbed it and listened.

"Seriously?" She held out the receiver to him. "I'm not your damn answering service."

Lawrence ignored her. They were laying down enough scratch to cover the booze and the damage to the place; phone calls should come with the package. He snatched the receiver. "You forget something?"

"No, my memory is perfect. You've done well for yourself."

Lawrence recognized the electronically distorted voice from the tape. He held the receiver closer to his ear. "We're getting it together. Why do *you* care?"

"I have many interests."

"Listen, pal, unless you're hiring—"

"I do have a job I need performed, in fact. But it's quite unusual. Listen closely . . ."

CHAPTER 22

CLAYFACE WAS BASIL KARLO. But Basil Karlo wasn't anybody.
Batman had left Auslander's lab with a lot of information, including a name—but the latter hadn't been of any help. He'd called it in to Alfred, who had reported that Basil Karlo was not in any database they had access to, under any possible spelling.

He'd gotten that information while on the way to the Capra for the second time in several days. He'd tried to shield his surprise in front of Auslander but hearing the name of the theatre had alarmed him. It tied Karlo together with a place the Last Laughs had tried to burn. What if it wasn't a random connection?

He had exercised care in entering the Capra, though he hadn't really expected to find Karlo there; in the same position, Batman doubted he'd have wanted to return to a place where his life went wrong. Visiting the corner where his parents had been killed once a year took a lot out of him. Indeed, Karlo wasn't there. Somebody had tidied up some, and the power was back on; that wasn't much of a surprise, given all the developers who wanted the site.

What interested him was the room Karlo had met his fate in. It appeared undisturbed; months of dust covered everything, and he hadn't been able to find any good fingerprints. He already knew from the police investigation that Karlo hadn't left any on the bus. The Capra expedition came up empty.

Fortunately, Alfred had not. *"A pull of the Capra's phone records shows dozens of local calls over the years to and from a Karlo Babić."* He provided an address in a poorer part of the city. *"Both numbers are out of service."*

"Thanks, Alfred. I feel bad about keeping you up so late. Go to bed."

"Just try not to do too much property damage when you fall asleep in the car tonight."

Batman knew he wasn't joking. He suppressed a yawn and made his way across town.

IT WAS A NICE NIGHT *for a walk,* Karlo thought. His hunger addressed for the moment, he dared to venture back to the Capra along his favorite street: Theatre Row.

The crowds had dispersed, and some of the lights were out, apart from the houses that stayed lit all night long. That meant he was able to safely walk, knowing that nobody could easily see his face in the shadows. He could will a new appearance if he wanted to, but it was chancy to do without a mirror nearby and hair to add for effect.

More than anything, he wanted Auslander to find a cure. But if he was condemned to live beneath and behind stages, interacting with others only through false faces, that might not be the worst thing. As fates went, at least it was artistic. He thought again of *The Phantom of the Opera,* a French novel he'd read in high school; he wouldn't be joining the musical for that either, if it ever came to Gotham City.

It was with a little spring in his step that he chanced to approach The Post. Once part of an impossibly large tree, it stood in a circular island of grass amid Theatre Row, bathed in spotlights from the ground. Tacked to it were layer after layer after layer of posters and playbills. Regular odysseys to The Post had been part of his chores for the Capra; his flyers were usually covered immediately by bigger and more colorful ones.

This time, someone had gone to town. Shiny posters encircled the wooden column, climbing up well above eye level. Impossibly, nobody had torn any down, or tacked anything over them. Taking a closer look, he understood why. They were for charity. The Wayne Foundation was sponsoring a benefit night for the Smylex Ward at Gotham General. And not just any night: the opening for *Pygmalion*, at the Imperial.

Karlo was impressed. That was probably why Bruce Wayne was looking for Auslander the day before, he figured. The actor didn't think much of billionaires—much less ones who went around town with their manservants—but this made Wayne sound like a good egg.

And *Pygmalion* wasn't just any play. It was one of his favorites. Karlo preferred it to its musical version; he could mimic singers well enough, but his own singing voice wasn't the best. And he knew Professor Higgins by heart.

"The science of speech. That's my profession; also my hobby. Happy is the man who can make a living by his hobby!"

Karlo cited more lines aloud as he walked from the circle to a shuttered souvenir stand. Still outside was a mirror, used for people buying sunglasses. He looked up into it—and saw the angular features of Leslie Howard, one of his favorite idols from the Golden Age.

"Of course!" Howard had played Higgins in 1938, and Karlo knew him well. The actor had given Bogart his big break, and had played a major role in drumming up British support for the Second World War. There were even rumors Howard was a spy for the Allies; the Nazis shot down his passenger plane over the Atlantic.

Karlo smiled. He'd rather be Leslie Howard than Basil Karlo anyway. Why not wear his face? It gave him more confidence as he walked toward Theatre Row, chattering lines from Shaw as he went.

He came, at last, to the center of the universe. The Imperial had just finished a run earlier that night, and the workers were wasting no time changing the marquee. He envied the workers their scissor lift; the Capra had only a rickety ladder. *I bet they never run out of letters!*

He watched as they spelled out Julie Madison's name. Of course she'd get top billing; she was the scion of Gotham City royalty. The

Goat's Town Players thought little of her. Roles were hard enough to get without having to fight nepotism.

Then he jumped at a sound: the *whoop* of a police siren.

Karlo hustled toward the shadows. *They've found me!*

BATMAN KNEW EVEN BEFORE he picked the lock that he'd come to the right place. The mailbox outside the door was stuffed with months of mail; some of it had fallen on the floor. Overdue bills, cutoff notices—and magazines. Lots and lots of film magazines.

The door creaked open, unleashing musty air. Where someone had at least been trying to clean the Capra, the small apartment hadn't been maintained at all since Karlo's hospitalization.

Even so, it wasn't a strikeout. Batman shone his light on the walls. Poster and lobby cards depicted movies from the silent era through the previous year. Most of the other memorabilia came from stage productions; some from Gotham City, some not. Cast recordings sat gathering dust alongside an ancient turntable. It was evident Karlo had little money—and this was how he spent it.

And scripts. So many scripts, from big-name movies to small shows way off Theatre Row. Many of them had dog-eared and flagged pages. He'd either run lines out of them, or gone to auditions. But there was little evidence that his ambitions had made a dent. That became apparent when Batman found a stack of playbills from the Capra.

One playbill after another from the Capra mentioned Karlo Babić, usually about twenty names in and always getting his last name wrong. He seemed to have revolving jobs—roles everywhere but onstage. Batman frowned. He couldn't have been making much money—*any?*—working there. Yet he hadn't gotten anywhere.

Batman stepped back and surveyed the room. Perhaps Auslander was right in saying that Karlo meant no harm. An actor who could change his face at will could be a formidable foe—especially one with an uncanny capacity to absorb punishment. But despite the blows they'd exchanged aboard the bus, nothing in Karlo's apartment suggested much propensity for villainy. Thwarted ambition, perhaps, but almost every actor everywhere dealt with that. It was rare that anyone had everything handed to them—

His eyes narrowed. Batman snatched one of the more recent programs from the table and flipped through it again. He recognized something—and touched a control on his gauntlet.

"*Yes?*" Alfred said dryly over the transmitter in his ear.

"I thought I told you to go to bed."

"*Very humorous, sir.*"

"Seriously, what night is that play of Julie's?"

"*Tomorrow night, sir. A helpful fact for you to know, since you are sponsoring the show.*"

"Then I guess I have tickets." He looked at the playbill again. "I'm coming home."

THE POLICE HAD NOT, in fact, found Karlo. After hiding behind a phone booth, he'd seen the reason that the squad car had made an alert noise. Some juveniles were hanging around, after the shows had ended; the cops were sending them on their way. And then the cruiser itself was gone.

Karlo slammed his hand against the phone booth, infuriated. The glass cracked. Here he was, starting to feel good for the first time, and the mere sound of a police car was able to scare him out of his shoes. Shoes that had come from a defunct theatre's costume department, because that was all he had.

Joker wannabes were trying to burn the city down. Didn't the cops have anything better to do than bother people on Theatre Row?

He looked at what he'd done to the phone booth—and his hand, unharmed—and quickly stepped over to an alleyway. He stopped before a wall and leaned his head over, breathing deeply. He needed to keep calm. Things were bad enough without him doing something to lose control.

I'm okay. I was happy. He put on a smile. *I am happy.*

He ventured forth from the alley, heading back toward the front of the Imperial, quoting Higgins again. *"You have caused me to lose my temper: a thing that has hardly ever happened to me before. I prefer to say nothing more tonight. I am going . . . to . . . bed . . ."*

He trailed off as he gazed, astonished, at the workers finishing the marquee above the Imperial. And then the lights went on, blazing the name of Julie Madison's leading man: TOLLIVER KINGSTON AS HENRY HIGGINS.

Karlo's arms drooped to his side, and his face melted. But then his fingers balled into fists, and he spoke lines from the original play too harsh for inclusion in any musical.

"There's only one way of escaping trouble. And that's killing things!"

FRIDAY, 8:04 A.M.

BATMAN . . . WHAT A PECULIAR PERSON!
PARANOIA, ESP. RE: THE JOKER,
WILL BE OF SERVICE
PESKY SOCIAL ENGAGEMENT LOOMS TONIGHT
WHILE THE REAL BUSINESS IS ELSEWHERE

CHAPTER 23

OPENING NIGHT AT THE IMPERIAL, and the Gotham City paparazzi were out in force. "It's Bruce Wayne—and his grandfather!"

"I am wounded," Alfred said quietly. "I am an elder uncle at most."

Bruce smiled, and not just for the cameras. To listen to the chatter on the red carpet on the way in, the leading candidate for Alfred's identity was "that actor from that movie." *Which could be either a good or a bad thing.* But it was nice to see Alfred get out the bow tie for something other than a function at Wayne Manor.

More limousines disgorged passengers. The benefit was looking successful already. Several members of the *Gotham Globe* staff were present, as were their rivals from the *Gazette*. The political reporters, the society reporters, the theatre critics; this event had an angle for everyone.

"Mister Wayne, is the fact Mayor Borg isn't here tonight a sign Gotham City is tired of hearing about Smylex?"

"He's a busy man—and we've got a packed house. Everyone wants to support the cause."

"Mister Wayne, is there any truth to the rumor you and Julie Madison have been secretly married for years?"

"I don't know how these things get started."

"Mister Wayne, did you get Julie Madison the role as leading lady?"

"That's nonsense!"

His answers got shorter every time. In fact, the mayor *was* balking, *Julie* had started the rumor, and her mother, the chair of the arts council's board, had gotten her the role. But Bruce Wayne was pretty good at keeping secrets.

And then he ran into Alexander Knox.

"Didn't think this was your scene," Bruce said. "Isn't there bigger news out there?"

"City Desk figures any big event these days could be ripe for my kind of breaking news." Knox shrugged. "It's all right—the copyclowns seem to be taking the night off."

"Copyclowns?"

"Copycat clowns!" He threw his hands out, only to get no response from Bruce. "No good?"

"Maybe not."

"You're right. 'Last Laughs' is better."

Bruce was glad to hear his enemies for the past few nights were taking a breather—licking their wounds, probably. He'd have to break them once and for all, but not tonight.

"I can't believe I'm setting foot in a theatre at all," Knox said, "after what happened at the Capra."

"I read about that. Glad you're safe."

"You know, the leading man tonight used to work over there, with the Goat People."

"With what?"

"You know, the Goat's Town Players," Knox said. "I still don't get that name."

Bruce glanced at Alfred. *This one's yours.*

Alfred obliged. "*Gotham* is Old English for 'goat home,' sir. It was intended as a pejorative."

A light went on for Knox. "I missed that class in J-school." Then, remembering his job, he brought out his recorder. "While you're here, Wayne, I could use an interview—"

"Good thing there's plenty of subjects available." Spying an opening through the crowd, Bruce began walking.

Alfred joined him, nodding to the reporter. "Enjoy the play, sir."

Left behind, Knox called out, *"Hey, I never got my grant!"*

Bruce and Alfred stopped for champagne. Bruce barely sipped, as always; he'd sworn to Alfred he wouldn't go out yet again as Batman, after so many nights in a row, but there was no sense changing his habits. Besides, he was working, even here. He'd heard Kingston's name from Julie; she'd complained about him constantly, calling him an insufferable *prima donna*. Seeing the actor's name atop the recent playbills from the Capra in Karlo's apartment had led him to hope he might speak to the man.

"I'll talk to Kingston after the show," Bruce said. "If he and Karlo were friends, maybe he can give us a lead on him."

"Reasonable," Alfred replied.

"You're not going to say something about how I can't let a social engagement go by without detective work?"

"I had a different observation, if you'll permit. This is the third time you've included me in a trip recently."

"I couldn't bring a date, not on Julie's big night." He and Julie Madison had no kind of understanding, but they'd been seen together enough in the last couple of weeks that the gossips would surely talk. "Besides, I figured you'd like getting out of the house—or the cave, as it were."

"Certainly, sir, and I'm glad to accompany you. But it does recall another time. An *earlier* time."

Bruce remembered. After his parents died, he and Alfred were inseparable. Learning about Napier had brought it all back up again, but he'd had Vicki at his side then.

Vicki. I wonder where she is, tonight?

Applause interrupted his pondering. He turned to see Hugh Auslander entering. He wore no tuxedo; just the same ensemble he'd had at the university lecture. Nobody was interested in his sense of fashion anyway.

Gotham City's latest celebrity tolerated the flashbulbs and questions for just a few minutes before spotting Bruce. The two were united in purpose, this evening; they shook hands for the cameras. Flashes went off as the two smiled.

"At last," Auslander said when the gaggle moved away. "Escape!"

"I'm glad *you* were able to escape . . . work," Bruce said, checking himself. He'd almost said *lab*. Batman had seen Auslander in his lab the night before, but Bruce Wayne hadn't seen him since the university lecture, clay-faced imposters not included.

"I understand priorities. This is good for the ward."

After Auslander greeted Alfred, the three stepped into an alcove. The doctor kept his smile for several seconds, perhaps to allow Bruce to see it was forced. When the doctor spoke, he was direct. "You visited the ward while I was away."

Bruce had to think for a moment. "Yeah, we did."

"I asked you to let me know when you were coming." Auslander raised an eyebrow. "What did you think you were doing? Some sort of surprise inspection?"

"Not at all. Takagi showed us around—I really saw the importance of the work." Bruce looked to Alfred for support. "Didn't we?"

Alfred nodded. "Oh, yes, sir."

"Fine." Auslander seemed placated. "So there'll be no more talk of restricting funding."

"Of course not," Bruce said, pausing to wave to someone who had passed by. "In fact, I might like to bring some more people on board."

Auslander froze. "More people?"

"Yeah, as I understand it, you work nights—and I imagine you do a lot of lab work on your own."

"That should come as no surprise. I am no figurehead, but a working scientist."

Bruce nodded. "True, true. Still, it's important not to burn the candle at both ends. With your schedule, lectures and all—"

"My schedule is none of your concern, Mister Wayne. My celebrity activities, for want of a better term, are part of what attracted you to bring me on board. And I dare say I am calling more attention to this charity tonight than the misbegotten pantomime that's about to start!"

Bruce put up his hands. "I didn't mean to offend you. I was just trying to help."

"Sign the checks, Mister Wayne. Leave the rest to me." He stormed off.

Bruce watched him go. He didn't expect Auslander to say anything about Karlo, but neither had he expected to be warded off with impunity. The doctor had just dealt a brushback pitch worthy of a major leaguer. Bruce looked to his companion. "Alfred, what was that all about?"

The butler tilted his head. "We did say that geniuses are temperamental." He looked up as the overhead lights flashed. "It's time for us to take our seats."

"TWENTY MINUTES UNTIL CURTAIN! Twenty minutes!"

The Imperial's stage manager stopped her announcements when she saw a newcomer carting a horseshoe wreath. "For Tolliver Kingston," Karlo said.

She pointed behind her. "He'll be glad to see those. Or not. He's in a crappy mood."

There were two kinds of people with immediate backstage access, Karlo knew: financial backers, and florists. The arrangements he'd been able to swipe had gotten him into the Imperial with no problem. He tried not to marvel at the building, so much more elegant and refined than the Capra. He had a delivery to make.

As he reached the star's door, he nearly collided with someone on the way out. Older, bald, and bespectacled—and carrying a tool chest.

"I wouldn't go in there," the weary handyman said. "Unless you can fix the lights the way he wants you to."

"How's that?"

"To make him look ten years younger."

Tolliver's room, all right. "I can give it a shot." He offered the old man the floral arrangement. "Let's trade."

The handyman laughed and handed Karlo the toolbox. He admired the horseshoe. "They'll love this at the bar. But if you're going in there, you're the one that needs the luck!"

Toolbox in hand, Karlo entered the room and closed the door.

"Klaus, I told you to get out of here!" yelled the man at the dressing table.

"It's not Klaus." Karlo set down the toolbox and approached Kingston from behind.

The elder actor looked in the mirror at him. "Carlyle?"

"Karlo."

Kingston turned in his chair. "This is quite a surprise."

"For me, too."

"I was devastated—simply *devastated,* dear boy—with what happened to you. They told me you were off convalescing."

"You could say that."

"You look different. Fatter in the face."

"That's kind of you to say."

"Vacations can do that. Mine was too long!" Kingston explained that after the breakup of the Goat's Town Players, he had drifted—but only briefly. "It turns out that Julie Madison's beloved mater is a lifelong fan of my soap opera!"

"Really."

"Oh, yes. Just the sort of nut that business thrives upon—she would write letters addressed to the characters themselves. It appears she had a particular affinity for me and was devastated when I left."

She was devastated over you, you were devastated over me. Uh-huh.

"She hadn't heard I was at the Capra—who had?—but when she learned that I was in town, she decided it was high time that I trod the boards of the Imperial." He smiled broadly. "I'll take a patron, no matter how foolish."

Kingston went back to fiddling with his makeup. "So why are you here? After a job, I presume?"

"You could say that."

"The Imperial is a damn sight better than that Capra pigsty, but my makeup artist keeps disappearing on me." He gestured. "He's lacquered on the rouge—I look like a mannequin that's been through a fire." He gestured to his cheek. "Could you take care of this, like you used to?"

"Sure."

"Splendid! Just like old times."

Karlo stepped forward and began working. It was indeed just like they used to do. An 8"x10" glossy on the mirror depicted Kingston from an earlier era—perhaps the Pleistocene—and it served as a model for what the actor wanted. It was a challenge, but Karlo remembered exactly what he'd done before.

He rubbed some of the excess off with a rag. "How's that?"

Kingston sighed. "You're out of practice. But that will have to do. Bring over Higgins's hairpieces."

Karlo did so.

"Fine." Kingston reached toward the wig, only to pause in thought. He covered his mouth. "Oh, I'm afraid that even now, I still haven't gotten over the jitters." He gestured with his thumb. "Be a good boy and clean up in there while I'm onstage, won't you?"

Karlo looked back where he was pointing. It was the bathroom.

That's enough talk.

He grabbed the top of Kingston's head with one hand and jammed the makeup rag into the man's mouth with the other. Kingston struggled as Karlo twisted his arm behind his back and got him up out of the chair. Elated to finally be fighting back, Karlo turned him to the side and shoved him toward an empty trunk.

Seeing that he wouldn't fit standing up, Karlo spun him about so the two were face-to-face. Kingston, eyes wide and watering, stopped his muffled shouting and stared at him in astonishment.

"The role of Tolliver Kingston tonight is being played by his understudy!" Karlo punched Kingston in the gut, causing him to double over. Then he jammed him into the trunk, shut it, and locked it.

Hearing Kingston thrashing, he heaved against the trunk, pushing it toward the other side of the room. "I'm the one with the fat face, huh? You weigh a ton!"

Satisfied that it was far enough away from the door that no one would overhear the noise, Karlo turned toward the dressing table. He'd sat at Kingston's old one at the Capra; this one was so much nicer. And better stocked—with cosmetics that weren't likely to put him in a coma.

Not that he'd need many. He stared at the photo of Kingston and began reshaping his face, putty in his hands, creating.

From outside the room someone called out, "Five minutes, Mister Kingston!"

Karlo smiled with the older actor's face—and called back to the door in his voice. "I wouldn't miss it for the world!"

CHAPTER 24

"**W**HAT! *THAT IMPOSTER! THAT HUMBUG! That toadying ignoramus!*"

Onstage, Henry Higgins flew into a rage, prompted by the mention of his most hated rival. Karlo was not Higgins, of course; neither was he Tolliver Kingston. He was attempting the highest-wire act of all: playing both convincingly at the same time, while also keeping his condition under control.

As he yelled at Julie Madison's Eliza Doolittle, Karlo could tell the audience was taken aback, uncertain where his character's anger would take him. As hard as it was for Karlo to believe that the play was new to anyone, there were certainly rich philistines present who had no knowledge of the source material, musical or otherwise. *So be it,* he thought. The play was about using acting and language to transcend class. He'd happily school them all.

His Higgins was a pompous professor, teaching Julie's Eliza to speak and behave like a duchess. He had lorded over her mercilessly for the whole play, and Julie had tried to give back some of what she had gotten. Karlo didn't think she had succeeded. She hadn't been his equal. He was a tour de force, a whirlwind. Years of pent-up desire was bursting forth in the form of one of the greatest performances Gotham City had ever seen. He had hit every mark, stolen every scene.

And while he'd forgotten a few lines over the years, each time he'd saved himself by saying something that his character *might* say. It was easy. Higgins was a preening popinjay—and so was Tolliver Kingston. Playing Higgins as Kingston would play him was simply playing Higgins. It was barely acting at all.

At last, Karlo and Julie reached their final verbal duel in Henry's mother's drawing room. As written, Julie's character was to get the better of it, and Karlo took care not to let it seem otherwise. A good actor was a generous one. But he had carried the play on his back, and when she said her final line and stormed out, it was clear the star was still onstage.

Only the actress playing Henry's mother remained with Karlo. She set him up for the play's final line, as he mocked Eliza's suitor. "She's going to marry Freddy!" Karlo burst into incredulous laughter. He repeated the name, tears in his eyes, practically driven to his knees with hilarity. "Freddy! *Freddy!*"

Karlo and the actress playing his mother froze—and then it happened: the moment he'd waited for all his life. Someone in the pricey seats rose—and then everyone did. *A standing ovation.* Applause bubbled up and became a wave of adoration, concentrated and amplified by the Imperial's wonderful space. It was seismic, as well. He could feel it through the floor.

Karlo rose from his doubled-over position, smiling, the tears in his eyes now real. He took his bow.

And yet, as the roar continued, he heard a name shouted—and a sudden realization came over him. Everyone had seen Karlo's portrayal. But they were cheering *Tolliver Kingston.*

He blanched. Sure, Karlo was soaking up the raves right now, but it would be Kingston the newspapers would love. Once Karlo released him from the trunk, Kingston would have no compunctions at all about taking credit for tonight. He would be the one to do the interviews, whose agent would get calls. Kingston would leave Gotham City behind for bigger and better things—and not just daytime television, either. People would say it all began tonight—

—when really, it was all on account of a performance by an actor whose existence was completely unknown to them. Karlo's name wasn't in the playbill; he probably wouldn't go to the after-party. He'd never held someone else's face this long. And when had he even gotten to go to a reception at the Capra?

Karlo smiled, as befitting the man of the hour. But his mind was hours, days, and months ahead, contemplating the terrible crime he had just committed against American culture.

Dear God, I've made Tolliver Kingston a star.

He stood fast—only to realize that the leading lady was coming out for her accolade. She'd be last to bow; that was the tradition. He took a step back and to the side, as he'd seen thousands of other actors do. She beamed, her flower-girl-turned-duchess now a queen, holding roses that he had delivered. She carried them like a scepter.

And as people cheered, he thought: *She wasn't that good. I made her look good.*

That, he could live with. But the rest was something else.

He stepped forward again, reaching for her hand like a robot. These things always ended the same way. The two leads would bow, and then the whole company would clasp hands and do the same. When she grasped his hand, he'd already decided.

He raised his other hand for calm, startling Julie—and clearly unnerving the others onstage waiting for their final turn. "Excuse me!" he shouted. "I'd like to say a word about our charity."

That quieted the crowd, who took their seats—and it calmed the others onstage. He'd interrupted their moment without telling them; poor form, but certainly excusable given the occasion.

What's coming next won't be.

"We appreciate all of you coming out to support a good cause," Karlo said. "The research Doctor Auslander is doing is very important. You should give everything you can to make sure *every* Smylex survivor is made whole!"

That drew applause, and a spotlight turned to shine on the doctor in one of the boxes. The old man, startled, stood stiffly and bowed.

"I'm glad you all came out to see us," Karlo continued. "But it would have been damned nice if *any* of you had come to see poor Tolliver Kingston while he was in Purgatory over at the Capra!"

That drew scattered, surprised laughs, probably from people who knew Kingston's recent past.

Karlo could see how his words had played with them. To them, it was just a bit, an extension of Henry Higgins's unsociability. He added more menace. "I'd also like to thank our friends in the press for coming out tonight—though once again, you couldn't be bothered to mention the Capra unless you were reporting a medical emergency. Or a fire!"

More laughs, but from substantially fewer people. Yet still forgivable; looking past a squirming Julie, he caught a knowing smile from several members of the troupe. After what he'd just said, Tolliver might even become a folk hero with the local acting community.

Karlo couldn't have that.

"And I want to thank Miss Madison for her performance."

She smiled awkwardly, and relieved audience members responded by beginning to applaud. But his next words ended that.

"Tolliver Kingston would *never* say that another actor got ahead because of who their parents are, or whom they're dating." People gasped. "But if I did say it, I'd make sure my accent didn't change from word to word!"

Julie recoiled, ripping her hand away. Bursting into tears, she turned toward the actress playing Henry's mother—who hustled her off to the side.

Catcalls began. Someone in the audience called him a son of a bitch. Karlo saw horror in the seats—sheer horror. He was tempted to show them what his face really looked like. *That'd* be horror.

But he wasn't done. "You know the difference between the audiences in the little theatres and here? They go to see a show. You go to *be* the show!"

Shouts of anger from the crowd. "Who do you think you are?"

He slapped his hand on his chest. "I'm Tolliver Kingston. I was too big for the soaps, too big for the Capra, and too big for Gotham City. Send the award to the next place I wind up!"

He turned around and stormed backstage.

Now, that's *an exit!*

THE CURTAIN CAME DOWN on a shocked acting company—and the lights went up on pandemonium. Bruce had never seen anything like it. Julie had told him that Kingston was an insufferable prig in rehearsals. But attacking the leading lady, the press, the audience? All the energy that had gone into cheering the lead actor was nothing compared to the booing now.

In their luxury box, Alfred said it best. "That was perhaps taking Method acting a bit far."

Bruce stared in awe. "I guess the interview idea is down the drain. I don't think that guy's anyone's friend."

"He may not be well. And certainly Miss Madison will not be."

"You're right." Bruce looked across the theatre and saw Auslander in the box on the other side. While some were in shock, he looked mesmerized, his hand on his chin as he stared at the stage. "Come on."

He and Alfred worked their way around the outer hallway to Auslander's box. Auslander was still sitting frozen when they entered.

"Professor, I think Julie may need medical attention," Bruce said. "And that actor, too. If not now—when the leading lady gets done with him."

Auslander considered. "Yes, of course, you're right." He rose and turned toward the exit. "I'll get my bag from the car."

KARLO RIFLED THROUGH THE WARDROBE in Kingston's dressing room. He'd sprinted here and closed and locked the door; he figured he had mere minutes before the deluge. Finally, he found clothes similar to what Klaus, the handyman, had been wearing. Changing into them, he could still hear the boos.

He could also still hear Kingston, scratching at the inside of the trunk.

"Do you hear that?" he called out to the box. "That's for you, on behalf of everyone you stepped on. Everybody you've ever made miserable. You, and people like you!"

He turned back to the mirror. "And it's what you get for turning me into *this*!" Karlo rubbed his hand across the face—and Kingston-as-Higgins disappeared, his eyebrows falling off. "You've ruined my life. Now I've ruined yours."

He was removing his hairpiece when the pounding on the door began.

Karlo paused—and began to think. He'd been living on adrenaline the entire time he was onstage, and his fury had boiled over again. But as he glanced in the mirror at the trunk, hearing Kingston's name being cursed outside, he felt a small pang of regret. Kingston had forced him to poison himself, yes—but he hadn't *known* that would be the result. And he certainly hadn't created the chemical.

That was The Joker.

Karlo blinked. *There's no time for this.* He had to snap out of it. Too many people were outside. "I'll get you out in a few minutes," he told the trunk. He reshaped his face to match that of the old maintenance man. That was easy; he had the benefit of being bald. Armed with the new look—and glasses to hide his lack of eyebrows—he grabbed the toolbox, steeled himself, and opened the door.

He looked not into the face of a member of the company, but rather Auslander. Karlo nearly broke character then and there.

Holding a medical bag, Auslander peered at him—and then past him. "Where is Tolliver Kingston?"

"Dunno," Karlo said, pretending to be hard of hearing. "I fixed his plumbing. And this lock."

"Where the hell did he go?" the show's producer demanded.

"He ain't been here." Karlo stepped aside as she and her assistants bulldozed past him. "Have you checked the stage?"

With all the commotion outside—and now inside—he hoped they wouldn't hear Kingston scuffling. But they were getting close to the trunk. Too close—

"Where is that bastard?"

Everyone went to the door. Julie Madison had arrived backstage, surrounded by others. The chaos drew the gaggle out of the dressing room and into a large open area, milling with people. Karlo thought it best to follow the crowd until he could find a spot where he'd be safe from further questioning.

He located one by a water fountain. He knelt, tinkering with it as he glanced at what his righteous anger had wrought. Julie was a wreck, being consoled by others—and now security escorted the billionaire Wayne backstage as he cut through the crowd to her. The throng closed around Julie again, but Karlo could hear her high-pitched wails. And she was not alone.

Karlo had to look away. He'd never had a plan, not since his arrival. Impersonating Kingston had been an impulsive act; assassinating him onstage had been, too. He'd never thought in the moment about what a single sentence would do to Julie—or what his malicious act would do to the production and the company. More than the performers were in pain, here. Yes, he'd been turned down for everything on Theatre Row long before landing with the Goat's Town Players—but weren't they all in the same family?

His eyes shifted again to Kingston's dressing room. He had to get in there when this cooled down. Earlier, Karlo had envisioned letting Kingston out hours later and confronting him with his great reviews; later, during his tirade, he'd relished the thought of showing him the horrid headlines. Karlo honestly didn't know what he'd say to the man now. But he needed to be the one to let him out.

At one point, he thought he saw Auslander staring at him through the crowd—but decided it was just his imagination, or perhaps his need for a rescuer. Karlo needed to be healed before he harmed anyone else.

This has all been a mistake.

He spotted another water fountain down a more secluded hall and decided to relocate there until the crowd thinned out. Until then, he couldn't bear to watch any longer.

AUSLANDER HAD OFFERED Julie Madison a sedative, but she had refused it. He had backed off then, more concerned about the missing actor.

He had no doubt that he had just watched Karlo impersonating Kingston, his purported enemy. It had taken Auslander minimal research days earlier to learn that Kingston was starring at the Imperial; had the doctor's attendance not been obligatory, he would have gone anyway for the chance to spot Patient Thirty-Five.

Auslander just hadn't expected to see him onstage, giving a reputable performance. *Quite extraordinary, indeed.*

He glanced around the crowd. He thought he had guessed which person was Karlo, and where he'd come from, but the place was buzzing with too much activity for him to approach. And much of it centered on Madison and Wayne—their personal controversy compounding a public calamity.

"Don't touch me!" she yelled, shrinking away from his attempt to comfort her.

"Julie, it's all right. I'm here—"

"You haven't been here, through this whole production." She rubbed her mascara-smeared face. "You're not here when you *are* here! You're constantly looking around! Like now!"

Wayne nodded. "We're all trying to find Kingston, honey."

"Don't 'honey' me! I don't care about him!" She turned to her friends. "I'm ruined! *We're* ruined!"

Auslander thought it all a bit much, but he'd seen her act and it was all of a piece. Turning again, he found his suspect had moved. He started walking, eyes darting everywhere. He had just spied Karlo again down a side hall when Wayne's butler arrived down the stairs.

He watched Pennyworth cross the room, navigating the mob.

Having gotten Wayne's attention away from his paramour, he whispered something in his ear.

Wayne's face went white.

Too far away to hear, Auslander saw the billionaire turn back to the devastated actress. She screamed at him anew—and he beat a hasty retreat from the area, heading up the stairs with his butler.

Funny, I didn't think the markets were open anywhere.

Auslander resisted the impulse to follow—and to check his watch. He knew what time it was, and what else was happening tonight. And he knew where Karlo was, and he had a good idea why he was still hanging around the theatre.

The play was over. It was the doctor's turn to act.

CHAPTER 25

WHEN A PRODUCTION DIED, people never wanted to sit around long looking at the body. Karlo had been the last one left in the Capra after several opening night disasters; the actors broke speed records heading to the bar. The benefit situation was different. But things began clearing out after Julie's friends mercifully spirited her off somewhere. Most figured that Kingston had either absconded to a bar or the airport; either way, the Imperial was the last place he'd be.

So only a few people remained when Karlo, toolbox in hand, got the nerve to return to Kingston's dressing room. He quietly shut and locked the door before removing his fake glasses and approaching the trunk.

He stood before it and clasped his hands together. "Tolliver—Mister Kingston—it's Karlo again. I'm going to let you out, but I need to say this. I told you what you did to me—and what I did to you. But I think I did too much."

He looked back toward the mirror—and saw the handyman's face melting. Watching it reshape into his own, he knelt until he could no longer see his reflection.

"I hurt everyone here, and I'm sorry. This thing that's happened to me—it's turned my life upside down. I'm upside down. I get mad, and carried away, and nothing makes sense." He clasped his hands together, pleading with someone who couldn't see him. "I just ask—give me some time to get away. I'm going to get help. I promise."

Spent, he rose and worked the lock on the trunk. He opened it. "Tolliver?"

Kingston was inside, motionless. Karlo assumed he'd gone to sleep, and jostled him. But he did not rouse.

"*Tolliver?*" He pulled the rag from Kingston's mouth. A moment later, he reached for the actor's wrist. He felt nothing. "Tolliver!"

Karlo hauled him out of the trunk. Kingston slumped on the floor, a dead weight. He leaned in close to see if he was breathing. He'd learned first aid as a teen. But mouth-to-mouth resuscitation did nothing.

He rose and looked about in panic. There was no phone in the room. Without a second thought, he rushed the door and unlocked it. He drew it open—

—and just as before, looked into the face of Auslander. Only this time, Karlo was wearing his own face—and glad to see him. He snatched the doctor's arm. "Come in, quickly!"

Auslander did, and Karlo shut the door behind them. "Over there," he said, pointing.

"My word!" Auslander hurried to Kingston's side.

Karlo knelt alongside as the doctor tended to him. "He was locked in the trunk. I thought he could breathe—"

Just as Karlo had done, Auslander attempted mouth-to-mouth resuscitation.

"Should I get someone?" Karlo asked.

"I am someone." Auslander began to apply CPR. Karlo watched and prayed.

Karlo was rocking in a fetal position by the time the doctor stood up. "He is dead."

"Dead!"

"I'm afraid so." Auslander cleaned his hands with a cloth.

"How can that be possible? He couldn't have suffocated." Karlo scrambled over to the trunk and turned it so the handholds worked into the trunk's frame were visible. "Look here, there's air holes!"

"He's an older man. Much older than his photo, there." He pointed to the dressing table. "I would suspect cardiac arrest." Auslander looked toward the door. "Did you lock that?"

"No. I can still get someone—"

"That won't be necessary. But we need time to talk." He crossed the room and locked the door before returning to examine Kingston further.

Karlo was beside himself. "I didn't mean to kill him! It's just the way I act now—"

"I believe you," Auslander said. Then his tone grew more ominous. "I believe you, but I also think I know what you did tonight. And if others find out—they will not believe this was unintentional."

Karlo looked about, frantically. "We can put him in the chair. Say he had a spell, right after being onstage."

"He scratched the inside of the trunk lid. Material from it is under his fingernails." Auslander held up the dead man's wrist.

Karlo went to his knees, looking to see for himself. Then he began weeping. "I didn't mean to kill him."

"His instructions did lead to your transformation."

"They did. I know. I hated him. I envied him before that—I resented him. But he didn't deserve this." He looked down. "I guess you have to turn me in."

Auslander stewed. "I am thinking."

Karlo didn't know anything he could do to help. He sat back, resigned. It was the end of a very long and bizarre week, and it was always going to end with him in a cage. He deserved no better.

Auslander rose. "The timing is tragic. I had hoped you would return to me." He stared right at Karlo. "Since I saw you last, I made a discovery. *There is a way to reverse your condition.*"

Karlo sprang to his feet. "When do we start?"

"We cannot."

"Why not?"

"The resources we need—experimental pharmaceuticals and testing data—are not readily available. Further, I now believe your condition results from a specific formula, one the government already has. But the secrets behind Smylex are classified. They are not likely to help."

"Even to cure what they caused?"

"Even then."

Karlo frowned. Then he had a notion. "What about Bruce Wayne? He funds the ward. He made tonight happen. Surely he could get us what we need."

"He is also not a partner we can trust." Auslander paced around the room. "Just this evening, he threatened to put his own researchers in the ward. Oh, he described it innocently enough. But a man who runs a corporation involved in so many industries may have *other things* in mind."

"You mean he wants to make money from the cure."

"Or from *not* finding a cure. The military of this nation—and many others—might well consider Basil Karlo as more than a human being. You are a prototype."

Karlo was speechless.

"Indeed, I think it possible that Batman himself may be another government project. It certainly explains the willingness of the authorities to brook his involvement in police affairs."

Everything Auslander said made sense to him. The whole world was against him. Karlo sagged. "So that's it. I'm like this forever."

"I said the timing of my discovery was tragic. I did not say I was giving up." The doctor clasped his hands together. "Certain things have already been set in motion."

"What do you mean? You just said nobody would help me."

"Nobody you named—but there are other allies, willing to help. Unorthodox ones, whom I have come to know since arriving in this city." He gestured to the body on the floor. "They can help you get out of this situation."

Karlo stared. "Allies—*who would hide a body?*"

"We both know Kingston died naturally. They can deliver him to another place of repose, unconnected to what happened here tonight. They will do it because of what you bring to the table. And then you will both help me to get what I need for the cure."

What I bring to the table? "This sounds illegal."

"And so is what you have done here." Auslander put his hand on Karlo's. "Yes, these people operate outside the law. You will need to put aside your scruples, but I guarantee that your enemies are their enemies. And they will get us what we both want."

Karlo hung his head. It was a slim reed, but it was something. Eventually, someone would want into this room—where he was sitting with a corpse.

Any way out of a nightmare. "Get me out of this mess—and then tell me what you want me to do. Then I'll think about it."

"You won't need long to decide. It's a thing you're going to like."

IT FELT LIKE ANOTHER bad dream. Batman ran through the graveyard at midnight, paying no mind to his usual cares about being seen. Amid the chaos at the Imperial, the Bat-Signal had gone up. Alfred had gone to the car to check the police scanner, where he had heard just enough to know where Batman was wanted: *Castle Hill Cemetery. Now.*

It was where Jack Napier was buried.

Bruce Wayne had been needed at Julie Madison's side—but that paled in comparison to what he feared. And cresting the hill, he now saw it: a crime scene, lit by the flashing lights of parked police cars and ambulances.

He recognized Gordon by his silhouette. The veteran protector of Gotham City for so many years—the most recent one more bizarre than all that had come before—looked weighed down. Flashlight on, he directed Batman to a location on a rise. "I assume you know what this is."

Batman did. Jack Napier's grave had never been marked, to protect it against vandalism both from those who admired and hated The Joker. But the location had changed. Mounds of soil had been dug up on all sides, leaving a yawning hole in the ground.

His heart skipped a beat as he approached. He clicked on his light and looked down—on something he never expected to see. "Two bodies."

"Uniforms mark them as Castle Hill employees," Gordon said. "Attendants, probably."

Batman's stronger light revealed their wounds. "Both shot in the head. But they were killed somewhere else." He examined a stretch of ground nearest the hole. "They were dragged here on something."

"We've found it." Gordon led him several feet away to a canvas, discarded on the ground.

Batman examined it. "Mud on one side, blood on the other. They were killed, dragged on the tarp, and dumped in."

Gordon agreed. "The poor souls probably caught the people who were defiling The Joker's grave."

"The Joker defiles any ground he's in. But he's no longer in it."

"He didn't go far." Gordon led Batman around a line of tombstones. There sat a muddy casket, its lid open. And farther, down an incline in a small wooded area, was a motionless body.

Batman descended into the hollow, careful not to disturb any of the footprints on the ground. The vile stench told him it was an older cadaver even before he brought his light to bear. A face he never wanted to see again stared up at him from the ground, just as in his nightmare. Muddied from rolling downhill, The Joker's pallor had taken on an even ghastlier tone, with months to start decomposing.

Batman brought a camera out from his Utility Belt. "Be my guest," Gordon said. "Just don't touch anything. Not that anyone would want to."

They had the beginnings of a working relationship, but Batman knew Gordon had to be concerned about evidence and crime scenes. He took care not to disturb the corpse as he took several flash images.

After examining the imprints on the ground, he looked up and saw that a one-lane drive lay beyond a clearing through the hollow. "They arrived over there," he said, before leading Gordon carefully back up the rise to the open coffin. "They rolled The Joker out of the casket and onto the tarp," Batman said. "To carry him back to their vehicle—but they didn't get far before being discovered." His eyes traced the muddy slope back down into the hollow. "They rolled him off the tarp—"

"—so they could use it to drag the victims up here to dump in the grave." Gordon let out a heavy sigh. "What does that tell you?"

"They expected they'd have more time to get away with The Joker's body. But they didn't finish what they started." He glanced at Gordon. "They were interrupted again?"

Gordon nodded. "The shots were reported. When a squad car approached, they skedaddled."

"Without The Joker."

"We should have put him in the prison cemetery at Blackgate. But he wasn't a convict."

A forensic worker stepped away from the casket. "All done, Commissioner."

"There are prints everywhere," Gordon said. "But I'll bet you dollars to donuts we don't even need to run them. It's the Last Laughs."

It was too late to complain about the name having caught on. Batman agreed with him. "There were no fires tonight."

"None. First night in days." Gordon eyed him. "What would they gain from stealing The Joker's body?"

"Chaos. It's a recruiting tool."

"Or some sick initiation ritual." Gordon shook his head. "Could be random—or connected to their arson wave." He peered at Batman. "Do you have any more about *that*?"

"No—but I've got a lead on your bus hijacker." *A lot more than a lead,* Batman did not say, but he didn't want to reveal his conversations about Karlo with Auslander at the hospital. He wanted to give him more time to find a cure. "What are the arsonists you've arrested telling you?"

"Marching orders through Lawrence—but I can't believe he's the mastermind behind all this. That man would burst unless someone told him to pee."

Batman frowned. "Maybe it's someone on the outside."

"Someone who had The Joker's ear?"

"Maybe."

Gordon heard the *whoop* of another car arriving. "I can give you a few more minutes here, but that's all." He studied Batman. "This is a bad time. And this is a horrible place to see again—for all of us. Get some rest." He turned back to supervise his officers.

Batman took the opportunity to return to The Joker's body. He expected Gordon would be eager to get the corpse in the casket and back in the ground—here, or someplace safer.

We should have cremated him, Batman thought as he stared at The Joker. But the ashes of his madness were already on the wind, infecting others. Others who were being run by someone else, someone with as little disregard for life as—

Batman stopped.

He looked over his shoulder to see if anyone was looking—and then knelt by the corpse. His gloved hand reached down, finding rotting flesh. A fold gave way without much effort. He placed it in an evidence pouch on his Utility Belt.

He didn't know who else Napier had collaborated with in Gotham City's underworld. But Batman definitely had The Joker's ear.

One of them, anyway.

I've got to make sure.

LAWRENCE HAD DONE A LOT of dirty work in his day, but tonight had been the pits. Literally.

He'd arrived back at Jo Jo's after closing. He was paying five hundred a day to crash in the apartment over the bar, but that didn't include the use of the shower. She'd wanted four times the daily rate on seeing—and smelling—him after his trip to the cemetery, and he'd gladly paid it. It was necessary—and the money he'd been promised had made it worth it.

He wasn't surprised to get a call, long after the bar had been closed. "Lawrence."

It was the distorted voice again. *"Did you do it?"*

"Yeah, yeah." He shook his head. "When I get the other half, I'm done. I've got plenty of work, and none of it's as loony as what I did tonight."

"You disappoint me, Lawrence. You never used to question orders."

"What do you mean? Who are you?" Lawrence glared at the receiver before putting it back to his face. "Tell me or I'm out!"

"Touchy, touchy. But fine. I guess we can dispense with this now."

The next voice Lawrence heard was not distorted—and it nearly caused him to drop the phone.

"Hello, Lawrence. It's your old pal, Jack. Miss me?"

"Joker?" The big man sputtered. "B-but how?"

"The healing power of laughter strikes again, my friend. And with your help, so will I!"

SATURDAY, 4:05 A.M.

GREAT PLANS ADAPT TO NEW OPPORTUNITIES
THEY TOOK IT ALL AWAY FROM ME
NOW I WILL GET IT BACK
THEY WILL LEARN

ACT III

THOSE WONDERFUL TOYS

CHAPTER 26

"WHEN YOU HAVE ELIMINATED *all which is impossible, then whatever remains, however improbable, must be the truth.*"

Bruce had committed many of Sir Arthur Conan Doyle's lines to memory during his life—and commended more to his heart. The author's works had convinced him early on that it was necessary for Batman to be more than simply a midnight protector who made use of his fists and his gadgets. He also had to be a detective, able to interpret the clues he encountered. Doing so would keep him alive—and it would also guarantee that he only struck against deserving parties.

But Bruce now felt Sherlock Holmes's quotation had failed to address something. What if *all* the options were impossible—including the one that most of the evidence pointed to?

There were no more bad dreams. He was living one.

He rubbed his eyes and tried to focus again on the microscope in the Batcave. *Let's take another look.*

He'd switched slides for the tenth time when he heard someone walking down the stairs.

After their evening at the theatre had led to an unscheduled trip to the cemetery, Alfred had conveyed Bruce straight home—only for Batman to leave in the Batmobile again to find more evidence. Bruce had retreated straight to the Batcave after that. He hadn't surfaced since.

"I suspected you were here," Alfred said. "Did you have nightmares this time?"

"I never slept."

"So the answer is no."

"I wouldn't say that." Bruce rubbed his forehead with the side of his palm. "Has Julie called?"

"She has not. The newspapers are full of reports from the theatre—including many stories about Tolliver Kingston's past dreadful behavior toward the cast and others who knew him. But no one expected anything like last night's antics. He has still not surfaced."

Bruce looked down. "I hated to leave, but . . ." He would try to reach her later, but he doubted she'd take his call. There was no explaining what had drawn him away.

"You had quite the busy night. The tracking device said your last visit was to Marbury Heights. There's nothing there but the old juvenile reform school. One last brainstorm before dawn?"

"A fishing expedition."

"You would barely have room for the catch." Alfred looked astonished by the array of materials Bruce had set out for study. He stopped at the first station. "Your gauntlets."

"The ones I was wearing that night in Gotham Cathedral, when I punched The Joker. His blood is on them."

"You never cleaned them?"

"Nope, stored them."

Alfred stared at him. "All this time I thought the multiple outfits were utilitarian. It turns out you were starting a trophy collection."

"That's just one sample. I had already collected several traces of The Joker's DNA from before that night. Everywhere he'd been— Alicia Hunt's apartment, Vicki's apartment, Grissom's office."

"A treasure trove of detritus," Alfred said. He looked to the table Bruce was working at. "And I suppose that is the corpse's ear. There is nothing like going to the source."

"He didn't argue."

Alfred hadn't believed Bruce the night before when he'd said he had taken the ear, and he hadn't approved. That had not changed. "Napier's grave was hardly a holy sepulcher, but it seems wrong to have taken it."

"I wasn't the one who dug him up."

"Ah, the legal theory of 'finders, keepers.'"

Bruce turned his bleary eyes upon him. "Are you done?"

Alfred clasped his hands together. "No matter. What have you discovered?"

Bruce explained that gravity had drained much of the corpse's blood from the ear to lower parts of the body; the rest had congealed and dried out. There'd been enough material for him to test, however, and he'd found it matched Napier's known blood type. It was also the most common, however. That left DNA analysis: a relatively new technique, parts of which were beyond the technical capacities of the Batcave and his own knowledge.

"I've already sent out to our partner labs," Bruce said.

"*Labs?*"

"In triplicate—I need to be sure."

Alfred turned to look at the monitors for the first time since his arrival—and nearly gasped as he saw the bloated faces staring at him. "The photos from the death scene, at the foot of the cathedral."

"And from last night," Bruce said. "It's pretty clear the body in the casket's been dead for months."

"*The body in the casket,*" Alfred repeated.

"Yeah, it sounds like an Agatha Christie novel."

Alfred looked back at Bruce. "I don't understand this road you've gone down. Suddenly seeing Napier's body again has you questioning—but there *is* no question." He stepped over to files Bruce had placed on a counter. "We have Coroner MacReedy's report. The Joker died of severe trauma caused from a fall from a great height." He looked back at the cracked face on the screens. "This clearly is the case with the body you saw last night."

Bruce sat back from the microscope and crossed his arms. "Yeah."

"And whether before or after, they both have the same smile. It's unique."

"It is, and it isn't." Bruce rose and pointed to the screens. "The Joker's smile came from reconstructive surgery after I deflected a bullet into his face. But what we see in Smylex victims is similar—and of course, a surgical result can be duplicated."

"I certainly wouldn't patronize *that* surgeon again," Alfred said, staring at the dead Jokers. He turned to face Bruce—and let out a breath. "I understand that the nightmares have instilled doubt in your mind. But there must be *more* than that."

"Take a look at this." Bruce invited the butler over to the microscope.

Alfred settled in behind it and looked. "There's pigment in the creases—and flakes atop the tissue. Something white."

"The ear was coated with the material." Bruce looked at a printout. "The pigment is titanium dioxide. It's bound in paraffin wax and calcium carbonate."

"Face paint." Alfred looked up. "But Napier's look was natural—if you can call it that."

"It's hard with the decomposition to tell where the coating starts and the tissue begins. The Joker's skin was tainted by many chemicals. But paraffin wouldn't have been one of them." He frowned. "This coloration was applied later."

Alfred thought for a moment. "The Joker did use makeup."

"To hide his true skin color, not to look like The Joker."

Alfred nodded. He stepped back from the counter. "I can see why you have been here all night."

"I thought it was still day." Bruce started to move back to the microscope, but instead he watched as Alfred rounded the table with purpose. "Do you need something?"

"An apron."

"I brought down food. I don't need—"

Alfred opened a cabinet, took out a lab apron matching Bruce's, and put it on. "Tell me what tests you were going to run next."

Bruce shrugged. "This is a one-person job."

"Then we have one person too many." He took Bruce's seat behind the microscope. "If you will not rest until this work is done, I will work—and you will rest." He raised an eyebrow. "I'm told that's how it used to be with masters and servants."

"You're a marvel, Alfred."

"NOW, I CAN BE THEATRICAL—*and maybe even a little rough. But one thing I am not—is a killer!*"

Karlo paused the tape. He'd been comatose during The Joker's televised announcement of his impromptu bicentennial parade— and the carnage that had followed. But now he'd seen it, as well as the crazed criminal's other on-camera moments from his short but murderous career, a dozen times.

Auslander had been as good as his word. He'd made calls from Kingston's dressing room, after which they'd waited until after the Imperial was closed and locked. Then they'd let in a peculiar assortment of shady characters, who had dealt with removing Kingston. They hadn't shared where they were taking the body, and Karlo hadn't really wanted to find out. He was glad when Auslander finally whisked him away from the theatre.

He'd spent the time since in the one place he'd wanted to get out of: Gotham General. In Auslander's private top-floor lab, Karlo had rested fitfully, grappling with what his life had become. He'd felt terrible stealing a bicycle. Now he was an accidental murderer, indebted to the kinds of people who didn't care.

And yet, for the first time in his life, someone wanted him to act.

He studied the tapes the doctor had provided. Karlo ran back the one he was watching one more time. He splayed his fingers apart as he'd seen The Joker doing. Then he aped the voice. "But one thing I am not—is a killer!"

"Well done," Auslander said, entering. "I can definitely see you've been practicing."

Karlo looked back at him—and asked a question he'd already asked a half-dozen times. "You're sure you want me to play *this* guy?"

"I'm sure. And you've made progress. You sound quite like him."

"I'm close. But acting's not about doing impressions," Karlo said. "I need to think as a character thinks. Especially if I'm going to be ad-libbing everything." He pointed to the screen. "The Joker's mannerisms are pretty easy to get, and that voice is iconic. But I need to match his cadence and insert jokes from time to time the way he does. And there's other little tics I need to capture."

"Such as?"

"Sometimes he butchers the expressions he uses on purpose—especially from other languages. *'Commence au festival.'* *'Mano y mano.'* He wants to look like he has class, but he doesn't want to seem educated. It's disarming—man-of-the-people stuff." Karlo studied the face onscreen. "He reminds me of the actor from that movie that was set in the asylum. An everyman, on the edge."

"Napier is playing two roles," Auslander said, "just as you did with Kingston and Henry Higgins. The Joker is a persona—and so is this reasonable version he presented here on television."

"But it's a lie, too. He says he's taken off his makeup—but in fact he's put on makeup to change his appearance." Karlo frowned. He definitely knew what that was like.

He played a different line back. "*. . . the man who has brought real terror to Gotham City: Batman.*" Karlo repeated the words again and again. "*Bat Man. Bat Man.*" He looked to the doctor. "You hear that? He's got a little stop there between the words."

"It is purposeful," Auslander said. "He is trying to make his enemy seem more like an animal. *He* is the lead in his story."

"The hero."

"Not the hero. Napier saw himself as a destroyer of heroes—and of life. A true solipsist. The human he was died when he fell into that vat of chemicals."

"I know the feeling," Karlo fretted.

"What remained in The Joker's case was a walking corpse, dispensing revenge. You can escape that fate, my friend. But to do so, you must learn *him*." He gestured to the screen. "It is the only way."

Everything about Auslander bewildered Karlo. He'd first seen the man as a medical doctor; then as a brilliant lecturer. He'd seen his willingness to bend the laws in not turning Karlo in. But since Kingston's death, Auslander had revealed another layer. He professed to be familiar with secret things in the government, and clearly knew players in the underworld. The people who had come to fetch Kingston's body certainly weren't official agents. *All in the quest of—what?*

Auslander had been evasive about that. But he had done something nobody else ever had. He'd treated Karlo with respect. An actor lived to find a director who listened, who gave good feedback. Auslander did both.

The problem was all the other stuff.

Karlo pressed him. "You do everything. I saw that lecture you did. Psychology, sociology, medicine, all of it. But you helped me hide a body—and now this," he said, nodding to the TV. "I don't understand."

The doctor appeared to choose his words carefully. "I see—and have always seen—more to human potential than others were willing to accept. I reach further, for things others consider forbidden."

"The things that will cure me."

"And they will be forbidden no more, and you and I will usher in a new age for medicine. Basil Karlo in a hospital bed is a prisoner; in a jail cell, he is a freak, and forgotten. But in the guise of The Joker, he may just cure himself—and countless other people around the world. No Nobel Prize winner will have done more than you and I have. It simply requires a willingness to cross lines."

"It still sounds dangerous."

"Your new gifts will protect you."

"You keep saying that. I saw the people that came in to get the—" Karlo couldn't finish the sentence. "The people who came in to get *Kingston*. Those were tough guys!"

"And so are you. I suppose I must prove it." As Auslander approached him, he produced a lighter from his pocket.

"I didn't think doctors smoked anymore," Karlo said, until Auslander grabbed Karlo's wrist and brought the lighter underneath the actor's hand. "Wait!"

"It is a demonstration."

"I saw you do it in your lecture. I know how it ends!"

"Really?" Auslander ignited the flame, which burned tall beneath Karlo's writhing palm.

Karlo tried to wrench away—only to realize it wasn't hurting him. Instead, the skin on his palm seemed to bubble and coalesce, moving to the area touched by fire. He gawked, unbelieving.

"You see? You are better than you were. Understand that, and you will fear no one."

Karlo yanked his hand away—and marveled as the flesh returned to where it had been. His larger concerns, however, lingered. "Those guys were one thing. But Batman was something else. I never want to see him again."

"And I told you, steps have been taken. Batman is quite occupied." Auslander pocketed the deactivated lighter and picked up a stack of files. "I have more supplies to obtain before your performance. Resume your studies."

As he left, Karlo turned back and looked into a mirror. His face was featureless again, a zero in every way. That was where his aspirations and morals had gotten him.

But now he had a role, as challenging as any actor had ever taken on. No one could hope to succeed with it, even if they had to. Karlo *did* have to—and as he glanced between the mirror and the television set, his longing to be something went to work. His visage transformed, matching the contours of Jack Napier's face onscreen. He lacked the hair and proper coloration, but he was getting there: Karlo, pretending to be Napier, pretending not to be The Joker.

He pushed Play. "I have taken off my makeup," he said in unison with the set. "Let's see if you can take off yours."

He smiled. Uncomfortably at first—but growing more confident by the second. *Somehow, I doubt there's an awards category for this!*

CHAPTER 27

DURING HIS CAREER WITH the Gotham City Police Department, James Gordon had taken a lot of strange walks. He'd once conducted into the station an entire festival crowd of muddy and sweaty revelers, not one of whom was wearing a stitch of clothing. He'd guided an entire troupe of drunken mimes into their cells; they weren't handcuffed together, but they pretended to be. And he'd delivered a clown-faced corpse to the coroner's office not once, but twice.

Now, not long after, he was entering the morgue in the middle of the night alongside a masked man wearing a cape. Gordon had no hotline to Batman; that wouldn't have made much sense for someone concerned about protecting his identity. But Gotham City's new champion had reached out to him as he had after the end of The Joker's rampage: with a letter, left on the dashboard of Gordon's personal sedan. His *locked* sedan. The commissioner had wasted no time in arranging a meeting. The matter under investigation was too important.

Gordon had ordered his officers to stay away, to ensure Batman would be comfortable entering the official building. But the hero didn't show any unease at all—saying very little as usual, always using the same low voice. "You didn't rebury him."

"The Castle Hill people don't want him anymore," Gordon said. "I don't blame them. And I won't stick guards on a grave like he's a war hero. Besides," he said, his tone growing darker, "you and I share the same concerns."

Stepping through the doors into the autopsy room, Gordon removed his hat by reflex, remembering only afterward whose disrespectful corpse he was coming to see. At least, he *hoped* that was whose corpse it was, being examined by the gray-haired woman in a lab coat. She barely looked up when Gordon addressed her. "Miss MacReedy, this is Batman."

She barely gave the hero a glance and responded in a scratchy voice. "Thanks, Jim. I couldn't have guessed."

"Madge is our best cutter," Gordon said. "She can tell you what he had for breakfast when jazz was still king."

"Masks and gloves or stay back," she said. She pushed up her glasses and looked at Batman. "You've got the gloves, but the mask's on the wrong half of your face."

Gamely, Batman put on a mouth covering from his belt and approached the table. The commissioner noticed that he didn't blanch when he saw the body. That usually took trainees years, and some never got used to it.

"I thought we had all the remains," MacReedy said. "But he's pulled a Van Gogh on us."

Gordon watched as Batman produced a plastic pouch like a stage magician. "Here."

The medical examiner raised an eyebrow. *"You took his ear?"*

"I brought it back."

She snatched it from him—and Gordon chortled. "Better Batman have it than the Last Laughs. They'd open a shrine and sell tickets."

"Well, whatever your training is, Mister Batman, the information you gave Jim was on the money," MacReedy said. "This person certainly did die in a fall—or he fell, at any rate. But it is not Jack Napier."

"Saints preserve us," Gordon said.

MacReedy went over what she had learned. "Napier's only dental records were at Blackgate, during his last incarceration. They were destroyed in that fire, years ago. A riot *he* started."

Gordon brought up the document Batman had left with his note: a copy of Napier's police record. He wasn't going to ask how Batman had gotten it. "We know Napier had been stabbed twice before—and had part of a slug in his shoulder nobody could ever get out. What'd you find, Madge?"

"No trace of either."

Batman studied the corpse. "The tissue degradation could hide scars and perforations. And Napier could have had the slug removed later."

MacReedy looked at Gordon. "Your hero's a skeptic."

"They're the best kind."

"Well, the other thing he asked about should convince even him." She stepped to the side of the corpse. "It's gut-check time, Mister Batman."

Batman looked down into the hole she'd opened in the abdomen. He scowled. "There it is."

"There what is?" Gordon asked, unable to see.

Batman responded without pause. "An appendix."

MacReedy produced a manila folder that had gone completely yellow with age. "Napier had his out when he was fifteen, during a stint at Boys' Home. They weren't even aware they still had these records until Batman told us where to look." She glanced at him. "Bats know attics, I guess."

Gordon's stomach sank into his shoes. "So that's it. This can't be Napier. So who is he?"

"No idea." She directed Batman to her report on the nearby counter. "Be my guest."

Batman took it. His eyes scanned it quickly as he flipped through the pages. "You've started genetic testing."

"There's no database, of course—so all we can really do is compare the John Doe with Napier's samples that you sent. That's all gone to the lab." MacReedy shook her head. "Nobody I know can do that stuff overnight."

Batman didn't respond to that. He turned the page. "Toxicology?"

"That takes even longer. But whoever he is, this guy is full of chemicals. That, we'd expect—the real Joker swallowed plenty of crap. But as you told Jim, the pallor's painted on. And I also checked the face, like you asked. No evidence of surgery."

"So someone painted up a Smylex victim," Gordon said. *How ghastly could you get?*

Batman faced the head of the corpse. "This isn't Napier. But was it his body that was brought in off the street?"

"We assumed so," MacReedy said.

"Assumed? You did an autopsy."

MacReedy crossed her arms. "Shortest one on record. City Hall was in a hurry to get this monster in the ground, procedures be damned. And it wasn't like there was any doubt who he was."

"We all saw him fall," Gordon said. "There was no question, not in anyone's mind."

Batman moved to the other end of the body and began examining the John Doe's leg.

"What are you looking for?" MacReedy asked.

"The gargoyle," Batman said.

"How's that?"

"I lashed Napier to a statue before he fell. The weight would have torn all his tendons and dislocated his knee." He looked up at Gordon. "If the bodies were switched, Commissioner, we'll know it. But if this is the man who fell, then The Joker never fell at all."

"ALL RIGHT, IDIOTS. You know where to go!"

Lawrence had suspected his days of running the Last Laughs from Jo Jo's were numbered. The new recruits had done more damage to the place in a couple of weeks than she could get fixed in a year, even if it was paid for. And no amount of graft could hide the fact that such an undisciplined, disorganized bunch was being run out of the place. He had to shift part of the zoo somewhere else.

Fortunately, a destination awaited. Lawrence rode shotgun as his pickup truck loaded with mask-less hoodlums made its way down Theatre Row. The performances were over for the night; the Saturday show at the Imperial had never gone on at all, for good reason. But the lights were still on, and a lot of couples were still milling about. The animals in the back hooted at them, making a nuisance of themselves—but Gotham City teenagers did that all the time. It was amazing that the same group of people who'd burned down buildings could drive right past the cops without incident, simply by not having their masks on.

Maybe Batman had something there.

The truck rounded the corner onto a side street, just as Lawrence had done earlier in the week. But this time, multiple vehicles converged on the Capra. Passengers hopped out, and the cars and trucks cleared the scene.

Seeing the lane deserted in front of the darkened theatre, Lawrence led his party across it. When several of his followers started making for the alley and the stage door, he shouted for them to return. "This way."

He led them through the front doors. Past the ticket counter and the concession booths that they'd ransacked the week before, and back into the auditorium. The people behind him started putting on their clown masks. Lawrence didn't figure it mattered, but he let them do their thing.

The auditorium was fully lit when he entered. Someone had cleaned up some from the other night, he noticed, and had drawn the stage curtains closed. A new boombox was sitting in front of them; it had a bow on top.

Behind Lawrence, hoodlums started fanning out. "Burn, baby, burn!" one of them yelled.

Another clown flicked a lighter. "I'm ready to go! Where's the gas cans?"

"No!" Lawrence shouted. His voice boomed through the hall. He pointed to the seats. "Siddown!"

The punks looked at one another—but complied.

They were still fighting with one another over who got front-row center when Lawrence climbed onto the stage. The boombox was identical to the one he'd been given a few days earlier. He knelt and saw the note taped to it, written in crayon: PLAY ME.

He brought it to center stage, put it on his shoulder, and did exactly that. The tinkling strains of "Beautiful Dreamer" came from the stereo. The animals in the audience reacted to the lame elevator music with hoots and curses, but Lawrence found that hearing it transported him to another time.

Except that time was now. A voice everyone in the hall had heard before interrupted the music, shouting as a pitchman: *"Preeee-senting, in his revival tour, the most stupendous act Gotham City has ever seen! An oldie, but a goody. A bit moldy, a bit sooty. From a broken back, he's back to breaking: laws, hearts, records, you name it, he'll break them!"*

The words paused, and Lawrence droned his appointed lines. "All hail the new king in town, same as the old one!"

The boombox shouted the rest: *"The Joker!"*

Lawrence stepped aside as the curtains opened and music returned in the form of a twangy old Western beat. The most famous and hated figure in all of Gotham City arrived dressed as a dime-store cowboy, riding awkwardly onto center stage atop the world's most terrified mule.

"Come on, jackass!" The Joker kicked at the creature with his spurs. "We're not getting good gas mileage!"

The clowns in the audience sprang to their feet, waving their arms and shouting. Some happy, some angry, all astonished. The mule decided then and there that he wasn't going farther. The Joker held the bridle and swung one leg and then the other comically off the mule—who registered his thoughts about the situation by leaving a deposit behind him.

"I just polished that floor!" The Joker slapped the ass's ass with his ten-gallon hat. The critter responded by turning around and bolting backstage. His rider looked down at what he'd left behind. "I've gotten some bad reviews before, but this is ridiculous."

Lawrence stared over, mesmerized. Between the voice and the act, it was in every way the boss he remembered.

Noticing the crowd for the first time, The Joker bowed. "I love seeing so many smiling faces."

"But you're dead!" one of the listeners shouted.

"I went off into the sunset, sure enough. To the Happy Hunting Ground." The Joker smirked. "Turns out I like the hunting here better."

"You fell off the cathedral!"

"Can't a man bounce back?"

Several of the listeners apparently didn't think so. The clowns began scrambling onto the stage from the orchestra pit, furious at the supposed sacrilege before them. *"You ain't him!"*

Lawrence started to take a step toward them—but The Joker waved him off. "I always like to meet the fans."

The first of the goons to reach The Joker grabbed for his arm. He got a painful mousetrap-around-the-fingers for his efforts. The second lunged for The Joker and got two fingers in his eyes, right through the holes in his clown mask. When the injured goon tried to pull back, The Joker kept his fingers in the mask—releasing them only when the elastic around the mask had reached its limit. The mask snapped back on the punk's face loudly.

By the time several other would-be attackers climbed onto the stage, new music began on the boombox: a square dance. As one clown after another lunged for the man dressed as their hero, The Joker sometimes avoided their attacks with a do-si-do; other times engaged them by swinging his partner. Every one landed on the floor.

"Roll away to a half sashay!" he called out—only to wind up staring right at Brickhouse, the self-named tower of a clown who rivaled Lawrence for bulk.

"You ain't Joker," Brickhouse growled.

"O ye of little faith. You haven't seen the light." The Joker pulled a cigar from his vest pocket. "If you have seen a light, I can use one!"

Brickhouse slapped at The Joker's hand, knocking the cigar away. Then he punched the smaller man in his midsection. The Joker took the hit without wavering at all.

"I always heard the bad guys wore masks," The Joker said. "But I've got the sheriff's badge."

Ignoring him, Brickhouse started to deliver another punch. Before it landed, The Joker grabbed his wrist with his left hand—and stabbed it with the item in his right. Brickhouse howled and pulled back, the pin from The Joker's sheriff's badge embedded in his skin. "I told you I had the badge. Nobody listens!"

Clutching his bleeding arm, Brickhouse screamed in anger and charged. The Joker stepped nimbly away, using his assailant's momentum to steer him into what the mule had left behind. A noisy and messy pratfall followed.

The music stopped. The Joker looked at the people on the floor—and then those still in the audience. They weren't yelling now. All were staring at him, dumbfounded.

"Yes, I'm back—and a little better than before," The Joker said, stepping over one of the fallen assailants to reach the side of the stage. "Now, we can keep screwing around like this, or we can really get down to business." He gestured to Lawrence. "My friend there has been playing the music, but I'm calling the tunes. I'm going to finish what I started. There's a Golden Age coming for Gotham City. Come along with me—and you'll all live like kings!"

Lawrence stared at the man onstage—and then at his listeners. He smiled. *I don't know how he did it, but he did it.* "Give it up for the boss!"

The cheers began—and The Joker took a bow, his smile a mile wide. "Who doesn't love an encore?"

CHAPTER 28

*I*NCREDIBLE.

Hugh Auslander had just watched Basil Karlo perform on-stage for the second time—and his act before the Last Laughs at the Capra was even more incredible than his performance at the Imperial. He had observed from backstage as Karlo convinced several dozen fanatics of The Joker that their idol had come back to life. And now they were ready to do anything for him.

It had transpired completely according to theory. The initial veneer of skepticism was just millimeters thick. They truly wanted to believe.

The only non-fanatical viewer, Lawrence, seemed convinced as well, although in his case it was because he was tragically dim. The tough had stepped backstage after Karlo's improvised hamming extended into a second hour. Auslander had introduced himself to Lawrence as a business associate of The Joker's and the goon had accepted it—answering questions about the recent activities of the Last Laughs. That was the newspaper's term for them, and it was as good as any. A plague needed a name.

He and Lawrence had spoken for several minutes before the behemoth raised his sunglasses and squinted down at him. "I *have* seen you before."

"I have been on television," Auslander responded.

"Don't own one. Someplace else."

Auslander was implacable. "When you remember where you saw me, you will know you can trust me." Auslander gestured in the direction of the stage. "This is how it will work in the future, Lawrence. I'm to remain behind the scenes, literally and figuratively."

"Is there a difference?"

"Never mind. I'm back here. You're out there. Do you understand?"

Lawrence put his index finger to his forehead in a salute.

"Now prepare your people. And don't forget your stereo."

"Oh, yeah." Lawrence marched off.

Auslander heard cheers and applause, but it wasn't for the enforcer. Karlo strode backstage, beaming. He spied Auslander and tipped his cowboy hat. "What's up, Doc?"

"Come along. Lawrence will handle the masses."

Auslander led Karlo into the dressing room the actor had taken for himself. He'd been surprised to learn that Karlo had been using the Capra as his home since being on the run, but it made perfect sense—as had the fact that Karlo had chosen the late Kingston's dressing room for his living quarters. The actor had expressed unease a few times on remembering Kingston's fate, but the exhilaration of performance had put a stop to that.

Karlo took off his hat and gushed, still speaking in The Joker's voice. "Did you hear them? They completely bought that I was The Joker."

"They did."

"I pulled it off. I can't believe it!"

The actor's exhilaration was palpable, Auslander saw. It had overcome all fears about what he was doing, any concerns about whom he was portraying. "Your talent did this, Karlo. That, and preparation."

"For sure. It was the right move starting with a costume they'd never seen him in."

Karlo had contributed a lot to that decision. The purple suits Napier had worn publicly as The Joker were now available in any costume shop, but he was concerned about how well they would hide his extra bulk. Karlo also had some height on Napier, so a cowpoke's hunched posture while wearing boots that were really flats distracted from that.

"I told you not to be concerned. No one was looking at your feet," Auslander observed. "Your performance made sure of that." He studied Karlo. "I am curious. Which applause mattered more? That at the Imperial or tonight's?"

The eyes of the Not-Joker beamed. "It's all great. But that just now? Those were all my words. Nobody wrote that for me!"

"They believe you. *And they will follow you.*"

Auslander had expected no less.

He watched as Karlo sat in the chair before the dressing table and looked at the mirror. The actor had done a masterful job as well on his hair and makeup, Auslander thought—from the green wig to the face paint and lipstick. It had taken some effort to convince Karlo that the makeup was safe, but it was clear now that the actor trusted his word.

"You're the director," Karlo said. "What next?"

"I've been speaking with Lawrence about whether the Last Laughs can obtain the items we need. He currently does not have the tools—or the numbers—for that."

"What about all the people out there?"

"They are a start. And there will be more. Right now, he's having them put the word out into the underworld that this is more than a cult, that the old organization is re-forming. And while they are being urged not to say The Joker is alive just yet—I expect the rumor will spread." Auslander examined a clipboard. "The tools we will get from another place. And before anything, we require capital."

He saw Karlo frowning at him in the mirror. The rush had passed—allowing other considerations to creep in. "I'm not telling them to rob a bank!"

"That's not what I have in mind," Auslander said. "Lawrence had a business arrangement going with Max Shreck."

"Shreck?" He gawked. "The department store guy? With the creepy cat?"

"The same. Like many of the rich and powerful in Gotham City, he has made his millions through activities that are not always legal."

Karlo shook his head. "He always charged too much for underwear."

"Meeting him will be your next test." He stepped behind the chair and clapped his hands on Karlo's shoulders, looked at his reflection in the mirror, and spoke. "You have convinced the puppets. The puppet master is next."

Karlo stared at him. "What are you, some kind of Crime Doctor?"

"Not exactly."

"Then who *are* you?"

"There will be a time when everyone will know," Auslander said. "Until then, who I am isn't important. Who *you* are is."

BATMAN'S HOPES FOR DETERMINING whether the corpse belonged to the person who fell from Gotham Cathedral had come to nothing. The John Doe's injuries from the fall were simply too catastrophic to demonstrate any injuries caused by the gargoyle. Batman had more questions, but he'd thought it unsafe to remain longer at the coroner's office. He trusted Gordon and those that the policeman considered reliable friends—but he remained cautious nonetheless. The mere existence of the Batwing broke a host of federal laws, to say nothing of the forbidden weaponry he used. Those were lines he was willing to cross for the greater good, but there was no sense causing trouble for people like Gordon and Dent.

Still, the present circumstances demanded they continue their conversation—on the rooftop of Police Plaza, the complex where Gordon had mentioned needing to pick something up. Batman kept vigil beside the unlit Bat-Signal until Gordon emerged from a doorway onto the breezy rooftop.

"Watch your step," Batman said.

"I was a navy man during the Big One. You should have seen me skitter up the radar mast." Gordon braced himself against the searchlight. "I didn't want to talk about this in front of Madge. You've got a theory, don't you?"

"Two, and neither one makes sense. One is The Joker never fell. The other—it's worse for us. *Much* worse."

"Start with the better one."

Batman paced the rooftop, his cape billowing in the wind. "When I destroyed Axis Chemicals, The Joker already had his parade plan under way."

Gordon nodded. "The floats, the balloons, everything. The mayor had postponed the bicentennial. So he made his own."

"He told his crew he wanted to kill a thousand people an hour. Why did they go along? *He* was the maniac. What was in it for them?"

"I sat in on the interviews with the survivors myself," Gordon said, clamping down his hat against the wind. "Our guess was he intended for them to knock over local businesses. They'd be able to walk right into every jewelry store."

"And Lawrence and Phil—the gymnast—never told you why they were in the cathedral."

"Right."

Batman reached the edge of the roof and looked toward the colossal stone edifice across town. "We assumed mass murder was The Joker's plan. But that might not have been the *only* plan. He killed there. He might rob there. But he never intended to die there."

He turned and saw Gordon watching him. "I'm following you."

"A foreign government launches a chemical weapons attack on an American city. What happens next?"

"The Feds come in. They take over—and strike back."

"Correct. Napier might dream of setting himself up as king over a charnel house. But the ring would close tight."

"And fast," Gordon said. "Too late for the people of Gotham City—but they'd come."

"He never wanted ransom. He just wanted to *keep going, keep killing*. Axis Chemicals is gone. The police have seized Grissom's properties. The Joker has to leave the city—and he has a helicopter. But that won't get him far."

"Not with the National Guard on the way. They'll track him wherever he goes. Shoot him right out of the sky."

"So he stations men in the cathedral, because that's how he intends to leave. Because he has one last trick to pull."

Gordon stared through the darkness. Then Batman watched as his eyes went wide. "Oh, no. He pulled a switch!"

"The Feds want him dead. He has to give them a body. Napier already knows you don't have his dental records."

"So he paints some poor sap to look like him and throws him off the roof?" Gordon shook his head. "But you were fighting with him!"

"All we had was the full moon. There were times I couldn't see him. Including the last moments—after I knocked him over the side." Batman squinted. "After that he was dancing, telling jokes—or so I thought. I was hanging from a ledge and trying to help Vicki Vale."

"That'd occupy anyone." Gordon frowned. "So what happens to The Joker?"

"He stays in the cathedral, until he can slip away."

"Diabolical. But I wouldn't put it past who we're talking about." Gordon blanched. "You said your other theory boded worse for us. I'm not so sure I want to hear it—but I'd better. Tell me."

Batman hesitated. He didn't want to get Auslander in trouble or cause Karlo to be targeted—but the biggest reason was that it was so outlandish. So he chose his words carefully. "There's some evidence that a certain Smylex variant might provide incredible physical resilience." He paused. "Even to the point of allowing someone to recover from a coma and walk out the door."

Gordon stood silent for several moments. "You don't mean—"

"The Joker could have recovered from his fall. Back there in the morgue."

"And he walked out *that* door. Good Lord." Gordon took off his hat and scratched his head. "Madge MacReedy wouldn't approve. She likes her guests to stay put."

"She definitely wouldn't like the science."

"But then who's on the table now? We buried a body killed by a fall."

"I said it makes no sense."

They both stared into the darkness for several moments. Batman worried that he'd said too much—broken his aura of mystery, of invincibility. He thought to recant the theories and speed away.

Instead, it was Gordon who broke the silence with somber words. "I spent a lot of years as a detective—and then I taught them. I don't pretend to do what you can do, Batman, but I've been at it long enough I can tell you this: A tough case will break you, if you let it. The mind's not designed to consider so many conflicting things at once."

Batman was surprised to be given advice—but he readily accepted it. "So what's the answer?"

"Focus on the clues you can see, can hold." Memory jarred, Gordon reached into his jacket pocket. "I totally forgot the reason I asked you over here. I got this out of storage for you." He drew a green cloth bag from his jacket.

Batman took it. The mechanical parts moved around inside as he held it. He squeezed—and it began to emit a cycle of stilted, robotic laughs.

"His laugh box."

"I've had it since that night. Took it off The Joker's body myself." Gordon then added, "Or whoever it was."

Using a flashlight from his belt, Batman examined the bag and found a clasp. He saw some of the expected electronics inside—and something else he didn't expect.

"There's an antenna coil." He looked up. "It is a laugh box. But it's also a ventriloquist's trick. A receiver. I need to study it."

"It's yours." Gordon looked sick. "Batman, if he survived, what would we do?"

Batman wasn't sure. But he was sure he knew who he would warn.

CHAPTER 29

"OH, MISTER SHRECK! You surprised me!"

"That's odd," Max replied. "You never surprise me."

Every day, Max Shreck's secretary arrived in the office atop his skyscraper an hour early in a futile bid to impress him. And every day, Selina Kyle seemed to leap a foot in the air when he walked up the stairs from his private elevator. Max didn't suspect it was because she was rooting around in anything she shouldn't; that would require a creature capable of independent thought. But by now he figured she would at least listen for the *ding* announcing his arrival.

Max strode past her, removing his overcoat. Without looking behind him, he reached to the left and dropped it, assuming she would be right behind to grab it. He didn't notice whether she caught it or not—or care. He was already on to the day's work, adjusting his bow tie as he walked and talked.

"I want a letter sent to Mayor Borg about the bicentennial. Either he decides on scheduling a do-over this summer, or I'm dumping all those T-shirts we've got in storage on his front lawn." He tossed his hat behind him.

"Mayor, T-shirts, front lawn," Selina repeated.

He glanced back to see she had caught his hat—just barely, given her awkward pose. "I told him merchandising the bicentennial was a dumb idea. Nobody's going to want to walk around wearing the number 200. For half our customers, it's a target weight!"

"Um—I have an idea."

"You don't get to have ideas."

"Just that there are five states with bicentennials coming up."

Max stopped walking to consider. "Yeah, have Atkins send the gear to a sweatshop and get the city name stitched over. Then unload them on wherever it is." He headed for the coffee urn. "I love it when I start the day with a good idea. Shreck scores again."

He poured. Atkins handled a lot of the dirty work for Max's businesses, of which there was plenty. Eventually, he'd know too much, Max figured; there were ways of dealing with that. He never needed to worry about that with Selina, who was as oblivious as she was scatterbrained. Not the worst thing for someone who worked closely in his orbit—and wanted to continue to.

Seeing her stumble along behind him, though, he sensed this morning was different. "You seem more nervous than usual. Which is impossible, unless the building is currently on fire."

"It's because of the fumigators in the conference room."

"Fumigators? I didn't call for fumigators." He looked over to the conference room and saw plastic drapes had been pulled across the wide entrance.

Selina fidgeted as she faced the protective curtain. "They were waiting when I got here," she said. She winced with discomfort. "I hate bugs."

Max did, too, but for a different reason. He had his offices swept regularly for listening devices; with an ambitious D.A. like Harvey Dent in charge, he'd doubled the frequency. He wasn't a crime lord like Carl Grissom had been, but his gloved fingers were in so many pies that sting operations were always a threat.

But fumigators? That was too clever by half. *Amateurs.*

He strode toward the curtain, ready to expel the invaders. Selina balked. "I don't think I'd go in there!"

"And why not?"

"One of them was already in a *gas mask*."

"And?" He looked back at her. "What firm, pray tell, did they say they were with?"

"I wrote it down." Selina turned toward her desk and went rustling through a mountain of papers. At length, she found what she was looking for. "Here it is!" She pushed her glasses back on her nose and read. *"Lawrence Pest Control."*

Max stared. *Lawrence?*

He looked to the drapes. "Selina, go downstairs."

"What?"

"Take your coffee break."

"Um—I make coffee here."

"Take an hour." He grabbed her shoulders and turned her around. "If I'm not here when you get back, call my son."

"But—"

"Scoot!" He marched her to the elevator and saw her off.

Once the doors closed, he turned back to the conference room. He approached the temporary curtain, steeled himself for anything, and gave it a tug.

Indeed, Lawrence was sitting inside the round room, accompanied by several of his companions. All were wearing service-worker uniforms; that would have gotten them past security. At least they had left the clown masks at home. Most of them, anyway; there was someone he couldn't see in his usual chair across the room on the other side of the circular table. The chair was facing the window, and the storm clouds gathering outside. Nearby, someone had defiled his spherical cat's-head bust by hanging a gas mask over it.

Max felt his rage overflowing. "What the hell are you doing here?" He stepped into the middle of the room, approaching where Lawrence had his feet on the expensive table. This didn't feel like a sting; just stupidity. So he spoke openly: "You meet me where I tell you to, and when!"

Someone else responded. "Lawrence is no longer handling the family business."

Max looked over to his chair. The voice sounded familiar—and the second the chair pivoted, he saw why. Holding a cup of coffee over a saucer, someone who looked just like The Joker smiled at him. "Hello, Maxie."

"You!"

"People keep yelling that, but I never see any sheep." The clown looked left and right. "What is it with people?"

Shreck took a step back. "You're dead and buried!"

"I held my breath." The Joker lookalike put his forehead in his gloved hand and sighed. "I'm sick of hearing about it. Can we get something else on the menu, please?"

Max stared at him. While over the years he had occasionally found common cause with crime lords like Vinnie Ricorso and Antoine Rotelli, he'd tended to steer clear of Carl Grissom's gang. He'd known what a menace Jack Napier was long before his transformation. But his deranged reign of terror had upset apple carts and then some, threatening all commerce in Gotham City—some of it, Max's. The Joker's presence would have been unwelcome then; this person's arrival was just some kind of sick game.

He looked to Lawrence. "I get it. You've dressed someone up like him. Is that the joke?"

Lawrence shrugged.

"Jokes are *my* business," declared the clown, who put down his drink. "Lawrence doesn't speak for me anymore—and that means he doesn't speak at all." The would-be Joker stood up. He was in the same kind of service uniform, but everything else about him resembled the man Max had seen on television. "I'm telling you, Maxi-poo, I'm legit! A lot more than those fancy watches you sell downstairs."

"Ridiculous! Nobody could fall out of a building that high and live!"

"I bounced off an awning, okay?" The clown began walking—and as he did, his companions rose, too. They blocked the exit behind Max.

Max glared at them. Imposter or not—and he surely was—this

invasion of his sanctum was unforgivable. But he wasn't going to be cowed. "I want all of you to leave. You don't know who you're dealing with."

"Oh, I know," the clown said, entering the central area. "But it's important that *you* know who you're dealing with. And if you don't believe I'm The Joker, then we can't do business."

"Is that so?"

"That's so. So let's just shake hands and say goodbye." He approached Max and proffered his hand.

Max looked at it—and tilted his head. "Nah." He'd heard about what had happened to Rotelli; The Joker had burned him like a brisket. He couldn't imagine a more terrible way to die. If there was even a chance this guy was The Joker, he needed to act as if he was. "I'll pass on the handshake."

The Joker saw it in his eyes. "Now we're getting somewhere." He withdrew his hand and paced around Max. "Let's talk about Lawrence and the Last Laughs. You know, I loved their last album!"

"Get on with it," Max said.

"I hear you've been doing business with them. A bold choice, helping out the plucky young entrepreneurs—even if you're embarrassed to be seen with them." The Joker looked around. "I saw all your pictures on the wall with famous people. You like the limelight."

Max's eyes followed him. "Is that what this is? *Blackmail?*"

"Oh, heaven forfend!" The Joker looked up innocently. "I like the spotlight, too—at a time and place of my own choosing, of course. No, this is a renegotiation, reflecting the needs of the new—or should I say, *old*—management."

Max rolled his eyes. "What do you want?"

The Joker turned toward him. "The Capra."

"The theatre?" Max shrugged. "I don't own that."

"It's no longer for burning."

Max didn't understand. "Why do you care about an old rat-trap like that?"

"I used to fiddle around in the balcony with the Fitzgibbon Sisters. I'm kinda fond of the place." The Joker glowered. "It's off-limits."

"But my parking garage—"

"This isn't a negotiation." The Joker began another circuit of the room. "And there are other matters."

"I can't wait to hear this."

"Lawrence has plenty of experience collecting debts—but deal-making was never his department. He's been woefully underpaid."

Max shrugged. "He's running a crew of amateurs."

"*My* crew. My prices. Or it's 'cleanup on aisle three.'" The Joker stepped away, and Lawrence and the others took that as a signal to advance closer to Max, surrounding him.

Max raised his hands more in frustration than fear. "All right, I get it! I'll deal."

The Joker called his hoodlums off. "A blue-light special on good sense!"

Now that he knew they weren't going to kill him, Max figured it was safe to play for something else. "If you really are back—or not, it doesn't matter—I want to be on the ground floor." Glancing at the windows surrounding the room, he quickly rephrased. "Not that way!"

The Joker looked back, startled. "A piece of *my* action?"

"Peace of mind. You avoid hitting my businesses."

"But where will we get our overpriced factory seconds?"

"Easy. Granders is opening a discount supercenter in the suburbs. I'd like it to be closing."

"Hit Granders?" The Joker looked hurt. "But they give out free popcorn!"

"You'll be able to afford to pop your own." Max took a pen and pad out of his jacket pocket and wrote a figure. "Half now, half after."

The Joker snatched the paper from him. His eyes widened on reading it. "All those zeroes in one place. It's like watching a junior prom."

"I don't care how you do it. Just make sure it doesn't open—and that it isn't traced to me. Pick a reason. Labor strife. Angry locals protecting their backyard."

"Crazed clowns hopped-up on discount Halloween candy."

"That'll work." Max nodded toward the exit. "Take the stairs. They go to my elevator leading out, down to the private garage. Nobody will see you."

"Ta-ta, Maxie. I'll make an appointment next time." The Joker crushed the paper in his hand and marched toward the exit. The others filed out.

Max followed them to the curtain to make sure they had left—and then looked back to see the gas mask was still on the cat's-head bust. Refusing to call them back for that, he stepped over and yanked the apparatus off. Then he saw it.

The Joker had painted his own face onto the cat.

Max stared at it for a moment, before shrugging. "Eh, maybe I can auction it as art."

CHAPTER 30

ALEXANDER KNOX DIDN'T WRITE his headlines; they came from the *Globe*'s copyeditors, who knew how much space was available in the layout. Nonetheless, he had suggested a slew of them, occasionally with bribes from the candy machine or the donut shop. When everyone involved in the transaction worked at a newspaper, they tended to keep their prices realistic.

Knox had long since run out of eye-catching puns about burning buildings the previous week, and had been afraid that readers were growing numb to the subject. The Last Laughs had gradually gone from an above-the-fold headline to a daily nuisance, and there had been a chance their crimes would fade from the front page altogether. Until last night, however, when the Last Laughs committed their most surprising and coordinated attack yet on a place most Gothamites were familiar with.

Having only barely filed his report in time for the morning edition, Knox hadn't seen the headline they chose—and instantly regretted it after tromping through the rain back into the *Globe* after a few hours' fitful rest. The first word stared out at him, a 144-point hammer to his gut:

BAT-ACLYSM!
BATMAN TOO LATE TO SAVE NEW MEGASTORE

He didn't like the word choice, but he couldn't argue with the accuracy. The Last Laughs had invaded suburbia, looting a store before it could even open for the first time. A low cloud ceiling had prevented the Bat-Signal from being seen past midtown; rain and a parking lot the size of an airport prevented the fire from spreading far. The Batmobile had pulled up only after the perpetrators had fled out the back, vanishing in a dozen cars and directions.

Knox carried the copy toward the city room. He was almost there when a man with a briefcase stepped from an alcove in a raincoat and hat. "Knox."

The reporter spun—and dropped his newspaper when he saw who it was. "Wayne!"

Bruce Wayne leaned over to pick the fallen paper off the floor. The mogul was so out of context, Knox barely recognized him. Normally, the rain stopped for billionaires; Wayne looked drenched. And where he usually owned whatever room he was in—sometimes literally—the man kept his head down, even when he straightened up. Knox noticed that he hadn't shaved. "Jeez, you scared the hell out of me!"

"Sorry." Wayne saw Knox looking around in the hallway. "What are you looking for?"

"The hidden cameras. It's not my birthday, so this must be a practical joke." Seeing none, he smiled. "So are you here to buy a newspaper? Or maybe *the* newspaper?"

"I'm here to see you."

Knox's eyes bulged. He had no idea what Wayne wanted—but it didn't matter. Billionaires did *not* make house calls. "All right, all right."

He searched in vain for someplace to take his guest. The conference room was full—and the city room didn't seem like a good idea at all.

"Don't you have an office?" Wayne asked.

"It's more like a shoebox open on one side, and without a lid," Knox said. He hurried Wayne right past the bullpen. "You don't want to go in there. There aren't enough chairs. Besides, they're a bunch of idiots. And they smell."

Bruce said nothing as Knox directed him down a hallway to a break room. Seeing people through the open door, he stopped. "Pardon me, Your Grace." He reached around Wayne's neck and put his collar up so his face was even more obscured. "It's for your protection. Trust me."

Knox entered and approached the two reporters who were loafing around in front of the snack machine. "Sorry, guys. Machine's going to explode. You need to evacuate."

He grabbed their arms and proceeded to initiate the bum's rush. They were halfway through the door when they looked at Knox's guest. "Is that Bruce Wayne?" one asked.

"No, it's Liza Minnelli." With Wayne safely inside, Knox shoved them out the door. "Get out of here. Go cover a fire. Or a store opening."

"You already swiped that story from us last night!"

"Tough toenails! Get out!"

Knox slammed the door shut and propped a chair under the knob. *Why couldn't they get their own billionaire?*

Turning, he looked past Wayne to see that one person remained: Norman Pinkus, a mawkish, bespectacled young man with tousled, unkempt hair. As usual, the copy boy—a strange title for someone who was easily past thirty—was huddled in the corner, headphones on, working all the competition's word puzzles before starting to work on his own.

Wayne looked back at him. "What about him?"

Knox shouted at the guy, "Pinkus! Pinkus!"

He expected no response, and got none.

"Pinkus can't hear us," Knox said. "He listens to his college courses on tape until noon. He doesn't even know we're here." He gestured for Wayne to take a seat at a table.

The billionaire removed his hat and coat and did so—and placed in front of him the newspaper Knox had dropped. Wayne looked tired as he spread the front page out before him. "'Bat-aclysm,'" he muttered.

"Yeah. I don't think I've ever seen Batman arrive someplace too late to help before."

Wayne folded the paper so he couldn't see the headline. "Big city, big job."

"I guess he's not invincible. Or everywhere at once." Knox stepped over to the coffee service and found the least disgusting mug. "The coffee here sucks, but it could come in handy if your limo needs an oil change. So to what do I owe the pleasure? Have you finally got my grant?"

He turned and looked to see Wayne's response—and was startled by the deterioration in the billionaire's appearance just since the benefit. "Jeez, Bruce, you look like hell."

He passed him the cup. Bruce took it and drank without complaint.

"You ever let a minute go by without a joke?" Bruce asked.

"Jokes didn't used to have a bad name in this town. Back—"

"I'll cut to it." Wayne glanced over at the silent puzzle-worker, rocking back and forth in ignorance, before addressing Knox directly. "I need to get in touch with Vicki."

"Ah." Knox took a step back. It all made sense, now. Wayne's appearance, wandering in from a monsoon. Losing a fox like Vicki could break anyone. "You know I can't help you."

"Knox—"

"No, no. I know how you feel—believe me." He paced the break room. "Trust me. I'd be a puddle of goo by now. But she asked to take the assignment, knowing it would take her away for months. She didn't want us giving out her forwarding address."

"Vicki needs to hear—"

"Seriously, guy, you need to let it go. Someone like you should be able to—"

"Alex, this isn't about us!" Bruce slammed the mug on the table, spilling some of the coffee.

Knox searched for a rag to wipe it up with. He took care of it quickly. "Sorry, I need to get this. Or it'll eat its way down to the basement."

But as he did, he saw Bruce fumbling for his briefcase.

"Oh, no," Knox said. "You've brought a million dollars." He dropped the dripping rag on the floor, walked to the chair across from Wayne, and threw himself in it. *He's brought a million dollars!*

And it didn't matter. *More fool, me.* Knox put his hands before him. "Bruce, I appreciate the thought, but I don't dish on sources. And I'm certainly not gonna break my word to Vick. That's *golden.*"

"It's not money," Bruce said. He opened the case and produced a file. "Here."

Knox exhaled. "I'm not trading the phone number for a lead, either. Even a big interview."

"Just read it!" Bruce pitched the file in front of Knox, right near his fingertips. One of the items inside slipped partially out. A photo, of the world's most dangerous person, *The Joker.*

That was enough for Knox to see. He snatched the file and opened it. For the next ten minutes he read the confidential police report. "How did you get this?"

"Gordon wanted me to see it."

"He sure as hell wouldn't want *me* to see it!"

"He shared it with Batman, too—who *also* shared it with me. Do you understand now? They did that because they think I can reach Vicki. They think she may be in danger."

"Well, duh! If there's a chance that S.O.B. is still alive—" Knox snapped his fingers. "I bet that's why Batman was too late to save Granders! He's probably busy checking this out!"

"I wouldn't know," Bruce said. Then he added, in lower tones, "It sounds like a good guess."

Knox flipped through the pages. "But wait. This stuff in here. It's crazy. It's impossible. How could The Joker survive?"

"There are theories. But that's all they are."

"And then the Last Laughs dug up The Joker—and found someone else. Who was it?"

"Nobody knows. A John Doe. But when they didn't succeed in stealing the body, it caused Gordon and Batman to take another look."

"Maybe Lawrence was trying to hide the fact it wasn't The Joker buried there," Knox said.

Bruce agreed. "Gordon told me he's never thought Lawrence is smart enough to be running a criminal organization on his own."

"Yeah, he's strictly muscle. The kind of guy that eats corn flakes with just a knife."

Bruce closed the briefcase. "Do you get it, Alex? You need to call Vicki, right now. If you care about her as much as I did, you'll warn her."

Knox looked at the dead man's photo—and nodded. "I can do that. I *will* do that." Then he paused. "But there's another problem." He jabbed his finger at the file. "The people have to know."

Bruce shook his head. "I didn't bring that to you as a journalist. I brought it to you as Vicki's friend."

"I never stop being a journalist. But set that aside. I'm a citizen of Gotham City. The Joker's loons put me in the hospital. If there's even a chance Napier is back and that he's been running the Last Laughs all along, people need to know."

"You'll start a panic."

"They *should* panic!" Knox stood from the table abruptly. He pointed again to the file. "They need to know."

Wayne stood, as well. "What if we're wrong? With everything this city has been through . . ." Wayne trailed off. After a few moments composing himself, he spoke softly. "Think about this. If The Joker is alive, he hasn't told the world yet. Maybe there's a reason. You might force him to pull the trigger on something."

Knox saw the reason in that. "I get it," he said more calmly. "But I've got a job." He looked at his watch. "Here's the deal. I'll reach out to Vicki. Tell her what's up, tell her to hide. Then I'll give Gordon and Batman forty-eight hours before I go public."

Wayne blanched. "I'm sure a week would be better—"

"Seventy-two, and I'm only doing that so I can say I won a negotiation with Bruce Wayne."

Bruce assented with a nod. He offered his hand, and they shook on it.

The rich man picked up the file and put on his raincoat and hat. Knox got the door for him. The reporter paused to offer some unsolicited advice. "Two things. Better go out that door over there—fewer idiots to dodge."

"Thanks. And number two?"

"You develop a story based on what you have. You tell Batman if he wants to find The Joker, I'd start by finding out who Chuckles here is." He tapped his finger at the photo of the corpse.

Bruce's eyes narrowed. "You know, maybe you're right."

"What can I say? I'm a pro. And tell Batman I still want an interview!"

CHAPTER 31

SEE THE SAD CLOWN, KIDS!

Karlo wasn't really sad. He was as exhilarated as he'd been since he'd taken the stage at the Imperial. But back in his private dressing room in the Capra, he could relax his muscles—and with The Joker's toupee off and his makeup still on, his resting face looked like a painting one would find in a motel with more rats than guests.

If the Last Laughs ever saw the man behind the curtain, they might sooner take orders from a random pedestrian. But they had followed him with fervor on his first field mission the night before, and they'd made the new Granders department store significantly less grand. Karlo hadn't gone inside until the place was secured; Auslander had said it wasn't the time or place for his public debut. The troops saw him, however, and they had done their damnedest to impress their guru.

Many of them were back in the auditorium now, their new haunt, enjoying the merchandise they'd looted from the retailer before—some, *while*—they set the store on fire. Karlo didn't understand them. He'd gotten to know some of the Last Laughs by name, if sobriquets like Overdoze and Next-of-Pumpkin counted as names. Meeting them hadn't helped. He'd been poorer than poor in life, too, and treated awfully. But he never turned to crime.

I guess they didn't have the theatre. Then again, it took theatre to turn me to crime!

Hearing a key turning in a lock, Karlo looked over to see the only other person who had access. Auslander entered, wet from the rain, with several items under his arm. He put them down, removed his hat, and locked the door behind him.

"The money from Shreck's man has already arrived," he said. "Lawrence's more able recruits are distributing those dollars where they need to go for the next stage."

Karlo hoped that didn't mean destroying any more stores he liked, but he was happy that it had been overnight when nobody could get hurt. "Did The Joker ever do mayhem for hire?"

"No, but Napier certainly did. And the spray-painting is consistent with his brand." Auslander opened the late edition of the *Gotham Gazette* to a picture of one of the surviving walls of the store, and the new graffito.

Karlo recognized it. "I told them to paint 'NIMBY' like you asked—'Not in My Back Yard.' This is one of the few places where they spelled it right."

"I'm told Shreck loved the touch. He is quite satisfied. A rival retailer is diminished, and The Joker's adherents are now seen to be in league with the local anti-business groups. As they have been agitating against his intended power plant, he considers that a bonus."

Karlo shook his head, bewildered. Businessmen using criminals to battle competitors and citizens' groups—with a renowned doctor directing the bagmen while he coordinated their next moves.

Auslander noticed his agitation. "Are you unwell?"

"Sorry."

"You needn't be nervous. I've told you, raising the specter of The Joker's return functions as self-preservation on your part."

"I know—nobody's looking for me, because they're all looking for someone else. Who is also me!" He shook his head. "Everything just feels topsy-turvy. Like I woke up in a Marx Brothers movie."

"The world changed while you were lying in bed. Batman

changed it. The Joker changed it." Auslander paced as he pontificated. "The old authorities—the police, the legal system—were usurped by Batman, to the point where they now readily work with him. Likewise, The Joker took the structured power system of organized crime and shook it like a tree."

It had all happened practically overnight, Auslander said, and Karlo realized the man either had a whole university lecture on it or was preparing one as he spoke. The actor had never met anyone who was a deep thinker on such a vast range of issues. It started to make sense to him that Auslander had never mentioned a wife or family. Karlo doubted anyone could keep up with him conversationally.

But the message of what was to happen next was simple. "Get me the tools and I can cure you," Auslander said. "And then, I will change the lives of millions."

"What tools? Where? How?"

Auslander put up his hand. "We'll talk tomorrow, once all the pieces are in place. Just don't let the Last Laughs see you like this."

"Don't worry. I'm fine here—and fully stocked." Karlo looked behind him to the stolen refrigerator, liberated that morning from Granders. His eyes followed Auslander to the door. "I guess you're headed home."

"No, to work. I still have a job, you know."

Karlo watched as the door closed behind him. *I've heard of moonlighting before, but this is ridiculous!*

Indira Panesar Wilburn, age 59.
Terrance John Wilcher, age 12.
Chester Aaron Wilcox, age 34.
Marigold Mae Wilczynski, age 77.

One twisted smile after another sped past Batman's eyes as the data reader in the archives of Gotham General's Smylex Ward ran. Every image belonged to a victim of Smylex-laced products before Batman's warning went out.

Some of the records were stamped DECEASED; the living were in the Smylex Ward or somewhere else. One of the initial goals for the facility was to develop a database of all victims of The Joker's attack; Bruce Wayne's money had made sure it was on a modern system, but it had no connection to the outside world. The only way to see everyone was as he was doing now, in the middle of the night in a darkened room.

And while the micro-camera he'd directed at the screen was recording every one for later evaluation, he'd realized two things. First, the true scope of Napier's crime. From the disfigured to the dead, the first chemical weapons attack on a major American city had a far greater impact than those in power wanted to admit.

And second: none of these people matched his John Doe.

Having given Alfred a night off that the butler was surely using in the Batcave doing more research, Batman had arrived at Gotham General after dark by clinging to the top of a service truck. After hours of watching an electronic carousel of smiling sadness, he was barely clinging to hope at all.

Or wakefulness, for that matter. He was so mesmerized that he barely noticed when the sensor he'd placed outside the door went off. Someone was approaching. He was in the process of grabbing his camera when the door opened behind him—and a familiar voice rang out.

"It's one thing to invade my laboratory, but *this* is a new low."

Batman looked back through the darkness to see Auslander entering, wearing a lab coat. A coffee mug in one hand and a clipboard in the other, the older man didn't seem surprised by the invasion at all.

"I still haven't seen Karlo. Nothing you'll find there will help you, I can assure you."

"This isn't about Karlo." There was no sense beating around the bush. "A body was found," Batman said.

"Tell the police."

"It was the police that found the body."

"Then I await their warrant to see these materials."

"There's no time," Batman said. "The whole city could be in danger."

Hearing that, Auslander closed the door behind him and locked it so no one else could enter.

Batman pulled a folded photo from his Utility Belt. "This is delicate. I need your discretion."

"A curious time to ask, while violating others' rights." Auslander stared at him—before sighing. "I suppose my refusal to help won't cause you to stop."

"It's important."

"Let me see." Auslander snapped on a desk light and reached for the photo. He immediately reacted to the face of the corpse it depicted. "Is this a prank?"

Thanks for not saying "joke," Batman thought. "It's not Jack Napier. It's a John Doe, painted to appear like him."

Auslander peered more closely. "Are you sure? This cadaver looks as if he died from a fall."

Batman pointed to the chin. "We now know the rictus isn't surgical like Napier's. And the first toxicology just came back. The dead man was exposed to Smylex." He sank a little. "But I agree he also fell."

"A parade of misfortunes," Auslander said. He looked over to the electronic reader. "Have you found a match?"

"Not so far. But I'll have to look more closely. The corpse is a man Napier's age, race, and build—and we know some other things about him that narrow it down. But the police don't have any reports of Smylex victims whose graves have been robbed."

Auslander looked at him—and then back at the photo. He brought it closer to the light. "Hold on. With glasses . . ." He trailed off.

"What is it?" Batman asked.

"I was visiting Gotham City for a medical conference years ago. There was a man with these features." He pored over the image. "Yes. The forehead. The zygomatic arch."

Years ago? "How can you tell?"

"Eidetic memory, my dear Batman. I forget nothing—and no one. And I work daily with faces. You might say they are my calling." He traced his finger across the face on the photo. "Yes, we sat together for four days of lectures. He was no one important, but he sang the praises of Gotham General, which is part of what brought me here."

"You mean he works for the hospital?"

"Not anymore, not that I have seen. His name is David. Or Davis—something like that."

"At this branch, or another?"

"I have no idea." Auslander handed him the photo. "I suppose this means you will be invading yet another sanctum here—human resources. I should alert you that the administrative wing functions twenty-four hours a day and that the office is always occupied. I will help you no further, but I admit I would be amused to learn how you will solve that particular problem."

Batman looked at the picture for several moments. If it was a break in the case, it was his first—and even it wasn't going to come easy. He put the photo back in his belt.

Auslander turned the desk light so the bulb glowed before Batman's face. "You seem overwrought—much more than the other night. I renew my offer. You don't seem to want medication, but hypnosis could be calming. I have an audio treatment that is particularly relaxing."

"Another time, Doctor." Batman closed up the camera device and made for the window.

He was in earshot long enough to hear Auslander's response. "When the mind fails, the body follows. Take care or the next fall may be yours."

WHILE BRUCE WAYNE HAD changed to Batman in the limousine often in his short career, changing to Bruce Wayne while in the Batmobile was another story. There wasn't nearly as much room, and of course it wouldn't have done for Bruce to be seen climbing out of the vehicle, at any time of day. But he had hidden the shielded car in an abandoned midtown junkyard the night before, so as the sun rose, he marched right into the same hospital he'd broken into the night before.

He hated to drop in on Takagi unannounced again—but not half as much as he hated to prevail on their friendship. He didn't think he could present the photo of the John Doe without alarming the administrator about The Joker's possible survival—but then he remembered his deal with Knox. The clock was ticking down. Soon all of Gotham City would know. So Takagi had taken him to the records department, where Bruce had privately repeated what he'd said to the reporter about Batman sharing the photo with him.

The story astonished Takagi, but his eyes widened more when Bruce mentioned the names Auslander had suggested. He sprang up from the desk and immediately turned to the file cabinets.

"There," he said, plopping open the file to a sheaf of documents. A yellowing photograph sat atop it. "Arthur Steven Davis. I'd never forget that face."

Bruce goggled. The staff ID photo depicted a balding man with glasses and a pronounced nose; someone he could have encountered on any street. But he could see how both Auslander and Takagi could have recognized him. Apart from the clown makeup and the twisted smile—and months of decomposition—the photos were a good match.

Bruce felt his blood surge. "When did he die? How?"

"I didn't know he was dead at all," Takagi said, shaking his head. "I haven't seen Art in several years. Not since we released him."

"Released? You mean fired?"

Takagi gave the smallest of nods.

"Why was he fired?"

The administrator pulled back. "I can't say." He gestured about. "We are literally in the human resources department, Bruce. As an executive, I'm sure you understand. I shouldn't even have implied we dismissed him."

"I respect that," Bruce said. "But what's at stake—"

He paused—and stopped himself. Batman was about acting when others would not—but Bruce wasn't going to make a good person do something he shouldn't. "I'm sorry," he said. "But can you at least say when? Or an address?"

"We last employed him six years ago. His address—" Takagi stopped to think for a moment. Then he looked about and leaned over, looking across clasped hands. "It wouldn't do any good. Davis dropped out, and moved—more than once, I'm told. I doubted he was even in Gotham City." He looked down at the photo and shook his head. "This is sad. But it's all I should say. Speaking to investigators would be a different matter."

Bruce thanked him. The name, at least, was something he could pass along to Knox and Gordon—and he urged Takagi to call the commissioner, to fill him in on anything else he was allowed to. "We're all praying The Joker isn't back. You could help us know for sure."

"Together we've created a whole building devoted to saving his victims." Takagi began to nod—and then did so more vigorously. "Yes, I'll do exactly that."

Bruce started to leave—when for the second time in the space of hours, someone in the hospital expressed concern for him. Takagi grasped his sleeve. "You need sleep, Bruce. This must be stressful for you, given what this could mean for Vicki."

"And the people of Gotham City."

"But also to Vicki." He released Bruce's arm. "Please try to take care of yourself."

"I don't need a B-12 shot, Masahito-san. Just peace of mind."

"Find it for all of us. I'll be rooting for you."

WEDNESDAY, 2:05 P.M.
....

PARANOIA SOWN, REWARDS REAPED
BATMAN MUCH DIMINISHED
TONIGHT, THE WEAPONS
THEN THE PRIZE

CHAPTER 32

RAINDROPS PELTED THE BATMOBILE like bullets. The headlights illuminated the car's destination up ahead—and the limousine waiting there beneath an underpass. It was as good a spot as any for a meetup, Batman thought. The hydrophobic properties of the Batmobile's windshield limited the need for wipers to the most extreme circumstances, but he still had to get out of the car.

He found Gotham City's district attorney standing outside the limo, smoking a cigar as he clenched his overcoat tight against the wind. "Hell of a night," Harvey Dent said. "But it keeps the firebugs away."

"It didn't help Granders," Batman replied. A ten-million-dollar store, ruined before it could move a single tennis shoe. "I'm still trying to track where the Last Laughs are based. If they have a base at all."

"Big city. When you only have to take off a mask, you can melt away." Dent gestured to the Batmobile. "Present company excepted. Traveling in style comes at a cost."

Batman hadn't interacted with Dent during Napier's reign of terror, but Bruce Wayne knew him. People considered Dent a competent, ambitious prosecutor. They also used to consider him lucky. Not anymore, not with The Joker appearing just after the start of his term. Few could survive that, but Dent had tried. He'd been glad to endorse Batman's successes publicly, even as he remained cautious around him. Gordon working with a vigilante was problematic enough. For a D.A., things were even more complicated.

They were unified on one subject, however. "I spoke with Gordon," Dent said. "Tell me it's all a bad dream. Is The Joker back?"

"There might be more than one answer to that question."

"Wonderful."

Batman now knew Takagi had been as good as his word, contacting Gordon and revealing the name and photo of the man who matched the corpse found outside The Joker's grave. Now Dent knew—and it clearly sickened him.

Batman got straight to the point. "We think the grinning corpse is Davis. But there's no evidence anyone matching his name or description died of Smylex exposure. The database at the Smylex Ward came up empty."

"Wait a minute. Gordon told me it'd take days to find if there were any matches!"

"There aren't any."

"How could you possibly—" Dent looked at him and paused. "No, I'd rather not know."

That's for the best. Batman didn't consider his most recent hospital invasion his finest hour, but at least he knew what *wasn't* there. "By now, that victim file is supposed to be comprehensive. Every patient known to Gotham City Health Services—and the federal government supplements it weekly with anyone from out of town. So either Davis died without anyone knowing about it or someone didn't put him in the database."

"Don't look at Health Services." Dent snorted. "It's the one thing in this city that's working."

"I want to know if the Feds kept Davis out of the victim file."

"Why would they do that?"

"I don't know. But I don't have time to find out." Batman peered at Dent. "And there's something else. I need everything the government knows about Smylex."

The cigar drooped in Dent's mouth. "Say what?"

"DDID Nerve Gas. All the data on what The Joker used, plus known variants. Everyone—from me to people like Doctor Hugh Auslander—has been forced to work from the other end, trying to reverse-engineer what it was and what it does by looking at the victims. But if there's a variant that lets people come back from traumatic injuries, one might have allowed Napier to survive. We need to know about it."

There was a growl in Dent's voice. "Smylex zombies. That's all I need!"

Batman still thought that was the less likely of his two theories for The Joker's survival. But Karlo might be the missing link—and he couldn't leave the stone unturned.

Dent was still dazed. He took the cigar out of his mouth and pointed at him with it. "Batman wants *me,* a local prosecutor, to go after the federal government. The CIA and probably the Pentagon, too. Is that all?"

"Yes."

"You're as crazy as The Joker was." He threw the cigar on the pavement and stamped it out. "They're going to wipe their asses with my subpoenas—after they're done laughing. We signed the chemical weapons ban. We're busy destroying the shit we pretended we never had!"

Batman nodded. Some of it was being done at the military depot in town; everyone denied it, but Bruce Wayne's contacts knew.

"Can't you get this information yourself?" Dent asked. "By doing—you know, what you do?"

"Breaking into Armsgard wouldn't endear me to the people you have to work with."

"Yeah, we'd be back to shooting at you." Dent steeled himself against the moist breeze and thought for a moment. "I'll drop paper on them—but it'll help if I can say The Joker is back. And that's the one thing I *don't* want anyone to know. Mayor Borg would need a volume rate on heart bypasses!"

"If the knowledge would get cooperation, use it. While it's still worth something."

Dent stared at him. "Wait. What do you know?"

Batman didn't want to reveal his deal with Knox. But rumors in the underworld were already circulating. "Move before the clock runs out."

The district attorney stared at him—and chuckled. He took a silver dollar out of his pocket. "Heads, you're crazy. Tails, I'm crazy for listening to—"

Before he could finish—or toss—the passenger door to Dent's limo opened. A beautiful young woman peeked out. "Harvey, phone! It's urgent."

"Even here, they find me." Dent pocketed the coin and stepped to the car, where she handed the large phone receiver to him.

He tried to listen for several moments. "Wait, I can't hear you." He looked up at the underpass and grumbled. "This damned thing!"

Batman drew an object from his belt. "Try this," he said, clipping it onto the back of the phone. It did its work—so well that he could hear the person on the line just as clearly as Dent could. "Can you hear me?" the district attorney asked.

"*Yes! I said, it's Schreiber from the security warehouse on Twentieth. The truck is on the way.*"

"Truck? What truck?"

"*Like you asked. You called me and said The Joker case might be reopened, so you wanted his stash taken to lockup in Police Plaza.*"

Dent looked startled. "I never called you!"

"Turn them around!" Batman yelled. "Now!"

If Dent did as asked, Batman never saw it. There was no time to wait. The Batmobile blazed from beneath the bridge into the rainy night.

"LICENSE AND REGISTRATION, PLEASE."

Karlo had always wanted to say that. Playing a cop was an easy day, for easy pay. But he'd never imagined saying the lines *to* a cop—and particularly not while he was posing as The Joker, standing underneath an umbrella held by Lawrence. The Last Laughs had thrown up a roadblock, stopping the police transport.

The driver of the armored van didn't seem to find the reverse traffic stop amusing. "Get those cars out of the way!"

Karlo felt insulted. "Can't you see who I am?"

"I see a nut. The Joker's dead!"

"Dead people have just as much right to hijack as anyone else. Just the other day, a shape-shifting ghoul stole a bus." Karlo pulled a pistol from his jacket and waved it about. "That guy was a great inspiration!"

His cohorts had already surrounded the van; with guns pointed into the cab from the passenger side as well, the driver and his partner wisely surrendered. The doors to the cab opened.

"Go easy on them, boys," Karlo shouted to his companions as the cops clambered down onto the puddling pavement. "No rough stuff. Treat 'em right and drivers across Gotham City will be asking for Joker-brand hijackings by name!"

His minions—it was so strange to think of them that way— escorted the disarmed officers to the side of the street. Karlo let out a deep breath. The real Joker was prone to random acts of violence, even against his own people. Karlo didn't want to hurt anyone, but it was hard to play the character without that element. No one had yet noticed that he was using jokes to cover his acts of mercy, but improvising was getting to be a challenge.

Worse, he'd spent so many hours lately wearing The Joker's face and speaking his words that he worried about getting lost in the role. It was tempting. Madness had a gravitational pull. But he wasn't there yet, and he hoped he wouldn't be.

With a jaunty "Hot-cha!" Karlo took the umbrella and rounded the cab as Lawrence settled into the driver's seat. Karlo made a show of pitching the umbrella into the breeze before climbing into the other side.

He took a glance back into the darkened cargo area. It was the laundry van writ larger, with no windows and a lot more armor; in place of laundry bags were racks with sealed cases. The tools Auslander had wanted, brought special delivery by the police themselves thanks to Karlo's second telephone impression of Harvey Dent in as many weeks.

Karlo rapped on the dashboard before Lawrence. "Home, Jeeves!"

"Huh?"

"Drive, you imbecile!"

The cars forming the roadblock pulled back, and the van lurched into motion. Within seconds, six cars had surrounded the armored truck: two flanking it on each side, with one before and one behind.

The Last Laughs' mobile brigade was an aggregation of personal cars and pickups, stolen and otherwise; they'd accompanied Karlo on the attack on the department store. The difference tonight was they were no longer anonymous. On Auslander's orders—passed through Karlo—his adherents had decorated their cars. A few had been repainted purple and green in the manner of The Joker's old allies, but there'd been so little time that others had settled for smiley faces painted slapdash on hoods and doors.

Karlo hadn't seen the sense in calling attention to themselves like that, but Auslander had made his usual point. Keeping the police and Batman's focus on The Joker meant nobody was looking for the so-called Clayface. By promoting The Joker, Karlo was thus protecting himself.

"They are your sentinels," he'd said, leaving out only a mustache-twirl. "Each car a recruiting symbol for anyone who has heard rumors of The Joker's return." Similarly painted cars were spreading out all over town. But the important ones were surrounding the van, a rain-swept convoy of chaos.

"Take the bypass," Karlo said into his multicolored walkie-talkie. "Make for Belford!"

He leaned back in his seat as the van accelerated up the on-ramp, flanked by cars that were scraping the barriers. Belford was nowhere near the Capra, but the Laughs had branched out, securing an abandoned warehouse there. Once a target for burning, it'd give them a place to go through the contents of the truck, whatever they were, in safety and—

Karlo's thinking the word *peace* coincided with the loudest noise he'd ever heard. Something blacker than the night blasted through the barrier on the overpass above and rocketed off the bridge, plunging toward the convoy head-on. The hurtling menace from above caromed off the roof and trunk of the car in the lead, causing Lawrence to swerve maniacally to the left. Thrown from his seat, Karlo could hear crashing all around—and a horrific grinding noise.

He didn't know what was going on or why—but he knew they had to get away. *"Floor it!"*

As Lawrence mashed on the accelerator, Karlo scrambled back to his seat and looked in the mirror. Past the remaining flankers, he could see the bludgeoned lead sedan burning in the road behind them. That car's occupants weren't the only ones trying to scramble out; Lawrence's reflexive move had driven their forward-left flanker into the retaining wall. The car behind it had rear-ended it; it was also out of commission.

And far behind, a black blot, a shadow in the rain, had come to a complete stop. Karlo knew nothing on wheels should be able to stop so fast—

—until he realized it wasn't on wheels anymore. Squinting, Karlo could swear he saw the shape rise on some kind of stalk, some hydraulic lifter. It rotated 180 degrees before setting down again.

Then Karlo heard a sound that he hadn't since his days working at the airport: a jet revving to take off, far too close for auditory comfort.

It took a second to realize the roar wasn't coming from a plane—but rather the car, which started to move, giving chase.

The Batmobile!

Karlo had learned of the car from the newspapers; their reporters were evidently the ones who'd named it, just as they'd named his plane and everything else about the masked man: "unknown vigilante's vehicle" didn't make for snappy headlines. It was thundering after the van now. Between Batman's arrival and Lawrence's reaction, the number of defending vehicles had been cut in half.

Karlo finally found his radio. "Get back there, boys!" The other drivers really didn't have any choice. Lawrence, seemingly gripped with terror, had floored the van, racing well past its escorts. Karlo knew the tough had faced Batman before, just as he had. Neither was looking for a rematch. If they could just get to Belford and hide—

Gunfire! First from the passengers of the escort vehicles, leaning out the windows and shooting at the metal marauder with pistols and submachine guns. Then, from the Batmobile itself, which had deployed automatic weapons of its own from locations ahead of the invisible driver. The bullets from Karlo's allies appeared as meaningless flashes on the battle machine's hull; the rounds from the Batmobile found their targets, blasting out the tires of the middle defender screening the runaway police van. The disabled car swerved and flipped, rolling longways up the highway. Upside down, the vehicle had barely stopped moving when the Batmobile struck it, sending it spinning on its roof like a top.

This is no good! Auslander had planned everything, but he'd also said he had kept Batman busy. The chess master had lost—

—or had he? Karlo looked up and out of the passenger-side window and spied a helicopter. For a moment, he thought it brought rescue, until he recognized the WXRX-TV logo on the side. His car chase was on TV, probably live.

He knew it for sure when the receiver in his jacket buzzed. *"I see you,"* Auslander said.

"See me?" Karlo shouted. "Save me!"

"Everything you need is right behind you."

"Batman is right behind me!"

"Right behind you—in the van."

Karlo nearly jumped out of his seat until he realized Auslander wasn't talking about Batman, but rather something else. He stood. Steadying himself as he went, he made his way back between dark racks, laden with deliverance. What the doctor had suggested was the most dangerous option, but Karlo also knew it would come from the character, from diving deeper and asking the key question: *What would The Joker do?*

"I've got this," Karlo said, shutting off the transmitter. "Straighten the curves, Lawrence. Your Uncle Bingo's going to have some fun!"

CHAPTER 33

BATMAN FLOORED THE ACCELERATOR, charging up the Belford Bypass after the runaway police van. The rainy night had kept most people off the road, but not all of them, and it was those civilians causing him the most trouble, rather than the two jeeps that were all that was left of the hijackers' defense. The riders in the jeeps were just firing automatic weapons at him. Saving the terrified drivers scrambling to get out of the way was another matter.

As the rump convoy barreled past, a church minivan swerved and began hydroplaning. It spun out and swung toward the Batmobile. Batman veered, changing his angle so he'd only sideswipe the van— and then he toggled a trick he hadn't used before. At the punch of a button, powerful electromagnets in the Batmobile's right side activated, clamping onto the steel body of the veering minivan with a jolt.

Saddled with a taller, bulkier sidecar, the Batmobile swerved as the minivan's rotation transferred to it. Batman steered into the curve, gently applying his more powerful brakes to prevent whiplash for anyone in either machine. Gradually, he brought the minivan over to the side of the highway and released the magnets. Parishioners saved, the Batmobile was back under way after the police van.

A call over the police band told him what he already knew. The van held the gadgets The Joker had deployed during his campaign of terror, from electrocuting joy buzzers to music-box machine guns—and also others he hadn't had a chance to use publicly. Napier was whip-smart and good at inventions, but the origins of some of them remained befuddling. The technology to hijack a local television signal had already been used a few times by vandals, but not all channels at once. Then again, Gotham City was an intellectual powerhouse. A madman with money to burn and a willingness to steal could do a lot.

Batman wasn't going to let the Last Laughs get the same equipment, even as souvenirs. It was time to end this. The traffic cleared as they approached the low bridge over an inlet separating Gotham City's islands. The two jeeps raced along ahead of the Batmobile in adjacent lanes, allowing the gunmen aboard to concentrate their shots against the windshield. Nearly blinded by the flashes, he heard the alarm stating that the window, as strong as it was, was beginning to be compromised.

Same song, different verse. Batman gunned the car forward onto the bridge to get directly between the jeeps—and this time deployed the electromagnets on both sides. He saw astonished looks from the jostled attackers riding shotgun as they were suddenly joined to the Batmobile. Batman smiled in their direction—and deciding they were not on their way to scripture lessons, swerved violently.

The trio of vehicles spun forward on the drenched pavement. Batman hit the emergency brakes and deactivated the magnets at the same time, causing the jeeps to fly away, literally—catching enough air to go over the barrier on the side of the bridge. A wet landing on a wet night awaited.

The Batmobile having come to a stop in the wrong direction, Batman triggered his lifter again to rotate the car. He was only partway turned when something colorful came hurtling from the darkened sky. A ball—*or was it a balloon?*—the size of a basketball struck the pavement in front of the Batmobile and burst, sending liquid flying.

But it was no mere water balloon. The Batmobile's hood took a glancing shot from some of the liquid, which began to sizzle. And ahead, a boiling pothole opened up in the middle of the bridge where the object had landed.

An acid water balloon! Batman had no time to contemplate how such a thing might work when he saw where it came from. Up ahead on the other side of the bridge, the police van had stopped, its motor running—and he could just make out something moving between its open back doors. Someone was operating a mortar out of the back of the van—and it fired another bright red object high into the air.

Batman didn't take chances this time. He deployed the car's shields and waited as the cocoon enveloped him. He couldn't hear an impact, but the Batmobile's sensors reported one: one balloon and then another had struck the car. And whoever was running the artillery had gotten the range. The last one had landed right over the passenger compartment.

With an alarm telling him that even the Batmobile's mighty shields were at risk, he knew he couldn't hunker down forever. Counting the seconds between balloon impacts, he waited for the right moment to retract the shields. The Batmobile's turbo roared to life, sending the car ahead, bumping through the smoking crater the first launch had created. He was just in time; another projectile landed behind him, right where he'd been parked.

There was nothing to do but close the distance with the minivan as quickly as possible. Whoever was using The Joker's arsenal was likely to be a novice at it; that was something he could use. When another mortar round launched from the police van, he noted the trajectory had changed. This one was heavier, a wounded duck that promised to miss him altogether.

Instead, the hurtling container burst open in midair, showering the soaked street with bouncing pieces of metal. Caltrops, like the ones the cops prepared for the runaway bus—only these resembled a child's toy. Jacks, but for the razor-sharpened edges.

Batman drove toward the clanking cloud without concern, knowing his sturdy tires were proof against anything so small. But they never settled on the ground. Rather, they continued bouncing, embedding themselves in the Batmobile's armor as he neared—including its underbody.

Jumping jacks. I get it. Even in death, The Joker was having a good time. But Batman wasn't. The INTEGRITY COMPROMISE POSSIBLE light came on, indicating that something had punctured one of the more sensitive nodes beneath the car.

He was out of patience. Whoever was in the rear of the van had abandoned the mortar and turned back inside, no doubt in search of another toy. Batman closed to forty feet, stopped the car, and toggled the police channel.

"This is Batman. Are any officers still alive in the van?"

He heard incredulous sputtering—and then an answer. *"No, they were released."*

Odd. But it was what he needed to hear. He prepared one of the car's missiles. He wasn't happy about having to damage police property, but he'd be a lot safer if the van was resting on its roof—and if it meant some of The Joker's tricks were damaged, the world would be safer, too. There were press helicopters watching the end of the bridge. They could easily be the Last Laughs' next victims.

Batman was targeting a spot beneath the van when a figure stepped out from the passenger door. He saw him immediately, lit by the spotlights from the helicopters.

The Joker. Or an amazing facsimile in purple, shielded from the rain by his hat—and drawing something from his pants pocket. A gun with an extended barrel, longer than his arm. Batman's eyes went wide—and he did not wait. *"Shields!"*

The metallic shield began to fan out—only to fail in mid-deployment, compromised by damage from the caltrops to sensitive points. The clown fired. Batman already knew what it was—and what it could do.

In taking over the other gangs in Gotham City, The Joker had gotten hold of something really nasty: an experimental military rifle shell that fried electronics. It had allowed The Joker to down the Batwing with a single shot. Now it did the same, a flaming charge launching into the hood of the half-shielded Batmobile. One system after another rebelled against him.

This was no bicentennial parade, however. He was already on the ground—and ready and able to engage his enemy on foot. Or so Batman thought. As electricity crackled around the driver's compartment, he fought to toggle the emergency latch allowing him to exit. But the half-deployed shield was not retracting, and he couldn't get the hatch open.

He was pounding at it when he saw the evil leer ahead of him. The Joker—or whoever it was—returned his gun to its original size and strode confidently toward the Batmobile, lit from above. Batman punched angrily at the missile control panel, trying to get it to fire. Nothing worked.

The clown stopped right before the hood. Batman couldn't hear what his assailant was saying, but he could recognize the finger he was holding up. Then he looked straight into the lights from above, doffed his hat, and blew a kiss. Batman didn't need to be able to read lips to understand what he said next.

"I'm back!"

KARLO HURRIED TO GET back into the van. The flourish had been the capper to the performance of any actor's lifetime, live on the world stage—but it had also been incredibly dangerous. He'd been lucky to find the right weapons at the right time, and to use them in the order necessary to stymie Batman. But he had no idea how long he'd have before the Batmobile started working again—or the police blocked their way.

Lawrence sped forward as soon as he was inside. Karlo used his portable radio again. "They saw me, Doc."

"As planned," Auslander said. *"Cut back through the tunnel and then to Belford. You will lose them all."*

Karlo turned off the transmitter and collapsed back in the passenger seat, spent. Everything about it had been terrifying—and also exhilarating. He could easily understand why The Joker had gotten off on his macabre showmanship, even if he didn't share his blood-lust. But enough was enough. He hoped that Auslander now had everything he needed.

As the van entered the tunnel, he reached into his vest pocket and pulled out a handkerchief. Finding that it was a trick one, with multiple squares of cloth tied together, was a nuisance, but it served the job as he tried to wipe sweat and rain from his brow.

It was when Lawrence stopped the van suddenly that he knew he'd made a terrible mistake. His sunglasses already off, he turned on the map light. "Your face! What's happened to your face?"

Karlo looked in the rearview mirror—and saw that the moisture and motion had combined to put a lot of his pallor as The Joker onto the multicolored handkerchief. Rattled, his face fell—and his features melted into his resting faceless state.

Lawrence pulled a gun from his jacket and pointed it at him. "What are you, man?"

Karlo put up his hands. "Lawrence, no! Stop!"

"*What are you?*"

"*I'm an actor!*"

"You ain't no actor! You're a monster."

"I'm a monster who's an actor." He pleaded with the tough. "I was hired to play The Joker. By Auslander!"

"Who?"

"The doctor. The professor. You know, the old guy backstage!" Karlo looked in the side-view mirror. Nobody had followed them into the tunnel yet, but it was just a matter of time. "You can't say anything about this, Lawrence. He's promised things. To me, and a lot of other people, if we'll get him what he wants."

Lawrence stared at him, wary. "But then who sprang me from the joint?"

"Auslander's done everything from the start. He said he needed you to bring the gang together, for something he's got planned."

"But it's all a scam! This is gonna ruin the whole thing when they find out."

"Then don't let them find out, Lawrence. You want to be part of a successful gang, get me back to the Capra without anyone seeing me."

Karlo heard sirens going behind him in the distance—a sound that seemed to have an impact on Lawrence as well. The driver put away the gun. "Me and that doctor are gonna have words."

"Don't hurt him. I need him, or my face will be stuck like this forever."

"I wouldn't count on it," Lawrence said as he put the van in gear. "My ma said 'ugly is forever.'"

Karlo was tempted to ask whether she was referring to Lawrence at the time. But he decided that was his role as The Joker talking, and that it would be better to shut up.

CATASTROPHIC. THERE WASN'T ANY other word for it. Batman had gotten out of the car at last—and was quickly retracting the damaged parts of the car's protective shell by hand. The two helicopters had lingered to get shots of him and his fancy car in its damaged state before lightning and even harder rainfall forced them to depart. But they already had what they wanted—more news than they ever could have imagined to ask for.

At least the car had recovered. He'd hardened the electronics some after the Batwing incident; this had been the first field test. Clearly it was only a partial success. Batman was settling back into the seat of the Batmobile and preparing to leave when a pair of cars pulled up. One a squad car, a clunky old sedan. Commissioner Gordon and Alexander Knox approached from either side. They both looked as bleak as he felt.

"So it's true," Gordon said.

Batman didn't answer, because he didn't know the answer for sure. Instead, he tuned the television inside the car to WXRX-TV—

and saw what the rest of Gotham City was seeing. Amazing footage of the culmination of a nighttime chase with the ringleader in full view. There was little mistaking The Joker, and the caption on the screen screamed it for anyone who had.

Looking in from the other side of the car, Knox's face fell. "There goes my exclusive."

Gordon looked at the reporter. "What exclusive? What are you talking about?"

Batman didn't know what to say in response. "I've got to get after him. Whoever he is."

"Wait!" Knox clapped his hand inside the Batmobile's cockpit, causing Batman to abort closing it up.

Gordon glared. "Let the man go, Knox!"

Knox didn't give up. "I came for a different reason. I can't believe I'm going to say this—but the real story isn't here."

Batman and Gordon looked at each other. "What are you talking about?" Batman asked.

"You both need to see this." Knox backed up and gestured to the Batmobile. "If this thing still works, I need you to follow me. If not, I guess you can ride with me." He called back as he ran toward his tiny car, "Just don't get your cape stuck in the door!"

CHAPTER 34

"*I* CREATED A MONSTER. *This is my confession.*"

Batman shined his light down at the letter, written by a quivering hand. From the date, it appeared to have been written months earlier, but it had never been sent. It sat beside a large open mailer addressed to the Gotham City Police Department. No return address.

Knox had led Gordon and Batman to a walk-down at the end of an alley, past blinking red neon advertising a live show of the kind people didn't tell their neighbors about. A simple sign read SURGERY, but Batman found the place was anything but sterile. The power was off, and his and his companions' flashlights had revealed dust and debris all over the place. There was no hospital bed; just an old surplus barber chair, apparently used for stitching up people who had to get back on the move.

Batman had visited this part of Gotham City but never the alley, not even on patrol. And yet he knew what he was looking at. The Joker had been born at Axis Chemicals. But someone had assisted with the labor—and had done it here.

And now he knew who it was.

"This isn't exactly surgery for the stars here," Knox said, his shoes crunching against the glass on the floor. "But once I got Davis's photo and name, I ran them past an ex-con I know." He chuckled. "It was weird—my notebook at work just happened to be open to the guy's number. That led here."

Gordon had been perturbed by Knox's presence all along. "How did *you* get the photo?"

"Bruce Wayne sent me a copy."

"Never trust a celebrity," Gordon grumbled. "I thought he was one of the good ones."

Batman had no interest in debate. He examined the floor for the source of the glass and found something: a broken hand mirror. He deployed an eyepiece from his belt and switched his light to ultraviolet. "No prints. Whoever held this wore gloves."

Knox watched from the side. "There's been someone piecing criminals together for years. Some rogue doctor. For years the cops thought it was a guy named Thorne. Not Rupert—*Matthew*. But Thorne cleared out—and gave his practice, such as it was, to someone else. *This* practice."

"We knew the place was here," Gordon said. "Just not who was running it now. Why nobody ever tried to run him in, I have no idea."

Batman had the answer. "We're near Axis Chemicals. Whose beat was this?"

Gordon and Knox looked at each other and said the name at the same time. "*Eckhardt.*"

It was known that the late Lieutenant Eckhardt was on the take from the Grissom Gang. Apparently that wasn't his only source of income. "Industrious little bugger," Knox said.

Gordon filled in what he had learned from Takagi. According to the hospital's personnel records, Davis committed no less than half a dozen actionable errors as a surgeon for Gotham General. "Malpractice insurance wouldn't cover him anymore—and he lost his accreditation. They released him."

"And he landed here," Batman said. It made sense.

He was accustomed to being the solver, coming up with the information no one had. But this was an occasion where Takagi had something he could only tell Gordon—and Knox had the final piece.

Alfred had once told him that bringing the right people into one room was what detective work was like for people who didn't wear masks. He was clearly right.

He looked again at the letter. "Dated just before the first Smylex attack."

"But where's the confession?" Gordon asked.

"Right here," Batman said. He walked carefully to a location in front of the chair and found a collapsed tripod. A video camera sat atop it. It had a small screen for playback, but its battery was dead.

One Utility Belt gadget later, he had the camera up and running on the restored tripod. He rewound the tape—and then the three gathered around it to watch.

The image depicted Davis. A fusty-looking nebbish with wire-rimmed glasses, he wore a bloodstained lab coat. He backed up and sat in the chair to speak to the camera.

"*I am Davis,*" he said in a thick accent. "*It's not the name I was born with—as you might guess. I've changed it several times. It's been hard to get work—to keep work.*" He clasped his hands together nervously. "*There have been so many mistakes. I meant well, always. But my skills never matched my ambition.*"

Onscreen, Davis opened his coat and took a bottle from the pocket inside. He uncapped it and began to drink.

"I see what scotched his career," Knox said.

Gordon growled at him to shut up.

Davis gestured around him. "*This is the only work I can find, here. Carl Grissom sent me many customers. Him and his rivals. But those people are all dead now—because of my great mistake.*" He hung his head. "*Jack Napier killed them all, in broad daylight, not long after I pieced him together.*"

Batman understood. They weren't far from Axis Chemicals.

"*The damage to his skin, to his face—he was too far gone. It drove him mad. He spared me—but no one else, it seems. I should have let him bleed, let him die. I set this loose.*"

Onscreen, Davis took a last drink and put the empty bottle on the surgical table beside him. Batman glanced to see that it was still there, uncapped, months later.

"I am sending this so you will know it was Napier who killed the other bosses. He is alive, because of me. I am leaving Gotham City, before he comes back for me. A new town, a new name. But nothing will erase the shame of—"

"Well, well, well." Another voice came from the player—silken and serpentine. Familiar. Davis responded by sitting up straight and looking around. New people entered the frame. Batman recognized Bob, The Joker's henchman, immediately.

"Stop!" Davis said. *"You can't come in here!"*

"Oh, I certainly can." The speaker entered the shot. It was The Joker. *"Making a little commercial, Doctor?"*

Batman heard Gordon gasp. But his eyes remained fixed on The Joker, who advanced toward Davis. Bob and another tough held the surgeon by the shoulders, keeping him in the chair. *"You must leave,"* Davis said.

"Don't you like repeat customers?" The Joker put his gloved fingers around Davis's chin and looked around. He tsk-tsked. *"Have you ever considered investing in a broom?"*

Fearful, Davis began to sob. *"Don't hurt me."*

"Perish the thought, Doctor. I have other plans for you. It'll make things right between us." His next words were darker. *"Once—and for all."* The Joker released hold of Davis, and someone threw a bag over his head. Then the clown advanced toward the camera. *"Ciao!"* he declared, before giving the camera a swat.

The image turned sideways—and then darker, focusing only on scuffling feet. Davis's helpless cries were clearly audible. The tape ended.

Batman broke the silence. "It tracks. Davis was The Joker's surgeon—and he's our body."

"I can get a forensic team here," Gordon said. "Find out how long the place has been closed."

"He gave us the date." Batman scowled. Theory One had just got-

ten a lot stronger. "The Joker that fell from the cathedral was someone he had every reason to hate. He used Davis as a prop in his show."

Knox looked around, startled. *"That's* what you're thinking? A
switch?"

"You should hear the theory about him getting up and walking
away," Gordon muttered. He shook his head. "The fact remains, Batman, that we have *a* Joker on the loose. And now the public knows.
Whether it's *The* Joker is immaterial."

"No," Batman said. "It matters."

He heard footsteps on the staircase. One of Gordon's patrolmen
entered.

The commissioner addressed him. "What is it, Jennings? I told
you to stand watch outside."

"I stepped away to follow a noise," the officer said. "When I came
back, this was on the door." He handed the commissioner a sheet of
paper. A bit of tape was attached.

Gordon opened it in front of Batman's light. It was a simple piece
of graph paper bearing a message composed of single letters cut out
of a newspaper and pasted on. He shook his head. "I've been telling
people for years the police only got these kinds of messages on TV.
Guess I have to change my story now."

Batman read it. *"When is a stranger not a stranger?"*

Knox squinted at it. "Some of those letters are the *Globe's* headline typeface."

Batman took a closer look at it. In fact, one of the letters was
wrong. The article in the first occurrence of "a stranger" was actually an "e." He pointed to it.

"Son of a bitch," Knox said. "Nice to know even crackpots make
typos."

"Who knew we were coming here?" Batman asked.

Gordon shrugged. "I told dispatch what neighborhood. But we
didn't know the address until Knox showed us."

"I didn't tell anyone," Knox said.

Batman photographed the message before handing it to Gordon.

Then he hurried up the stairs. He had so much to do. He had to fix the Batmobile, if it could be repaired—and he had to find The Joker. He'd spent so much time on the question of whether The Joker was the genuine article that he'd overlooked almost everything else—and Gotham City might pay a price for that.

If someone's trying to keep me busy, they're doing a great job of it!

CHAPTER 35

Every hour in the Batcave was the darkest hour. But this one seemed darker than all the others.

The place had been Bruce's haven for so many years while he was preparing for his double life. He'd never let the setting dampen his mood, except for the one time he'd learned Napier killed his parents. It was all happening again. It seemed a dark, wet, hateful place. He was buried, and The Joker wasn't. Only Bruce was underground of his own free will.

That's not right. I have to be here.

He leaned over the Batmobile, soldering connections as he'd done since limping home with the car. He was going to have to come up with a countermeasure for the electromagnetic pulse charge, or his next tussle with the Last Laughs would end the same way.

He saw Alfred descend the stairs without speaking. Bruce had recounted his engagement with the hijackers and the discovery of Davis's workplace on arriving the night before and had immediately set to work on the car. There was no point trying to guess where The Joker—he was tired of mentally adding "if that's who he is"—would strike next. He had all his weapons. He could strike anywhere, at any time of his choosing. It fell to Bruce to make sure Batman was ready.

Alfred had helped work for as long as he could keep his eyes open, before finally retiring. He'd returned several times since sleeping, trying to offer Bruce any kind of sustenance. Bruce had refused it all.

Now Alfred held no tray at all. Just a long, lingering gaze at his master, which Bruce saw whenever he glanced up from his work.

"You're near collapse," the butler said. "You cannot keep going like this."

"You know what I know. Those helicopter shots of The Joker are everywhere. The Last Laughs are probably recruiting like crazy now. This is going to be a war on the city, bigger than anything Napier tried earlier."

"And you will fight this war. Alone."

"Not alone. Gordon and Dent—"

"—were outmatched months ago and promise to be no more help now. These kinds of opponents are simply beyond their capacity to defeat."

Bruce looked up. "So what do you want? For me to start an army? Assemble a league of like-minded billionaires?"

"You're one of a kind, and you know it. And that has always driven you." Alfred took a deep breath and sagged. "Do you know why I let Vicki Vale into the Batcave?"

This? "I assume she rang the doorbell."

"You had already decided to tell her your secret when you went to her apartment, but you were unable to. When it didn't happen, I took the final step upon myself—because I feared for you." Alfred gestured about. "When this . . . *project* of yours began, I saw it as therapeutic. Your exercise routines, your combat training, tinkering with machinery. When you went into action, I was initially trepidatious—but grew less so when I saw how you fared. Purse snatchers and hoodlums on rooftops were no match for you."

"Successful operations."

"They also had the benefit of being finite. You stopped crimes, one at a time." Alfred paced around the Batmobile. "But The Joker represented a step beyond. Even before we knew he was Jack Napier, and what he had done to your parents—he had already become a second obsession."

"Number two of a series, collect them all."

Alfred was undeterred by the attempt at levity. "At the time I brought Miss Vale here, it looked like a story with no end. You had decided already that you could trust her—and she looked like the one chance I had to save you from destroying yourself." He looked toward the Batcave's exit, where the day's last light was still creeping in. "Now, the second obsession is back. And you are in worse condition than you were then. And I have no ally comparable to Miss Vale to bring into this chamber."

"Yeah, I don't expect Julie Madison will be finding her way here." She had already left a half dozen messages telling him where to go after his failure to stick around after the *Pygmalion* incident. That relationship was beyond repair. But the car wasn't.

He put his head down under the hood and continued working. "I don't have a death wish, Alfred. It's a *life* wish, for the people of Gotham City."

"I wonder if you include me in that number. What kind of life do I deserve, if any?"

Bruce took a breath. He'd never contemplated life without Alfred, and yet it had always been out there. The possibility that his only companion would judge his works—and find that he could no longer continue.

He put down the wrench he was holding and rubbed between his eyes. He could hear it in Alfred's voice: Bruce taking a meal or a nap would not assuage him, not this time. There might not be a way around it. Batman couldn't take a vacation, but Alfred could.

But would he come back?

Bruce saw no alternative. "Look, maybe it's best if you—"

A chime interrupted him.

Alfred turned and walked to the platform with the monitors. "A car drove up."

Bruce stepped over. The screen dedicated to the door camera was black, as it had been all week. Maintenance had taken a back seat to everything else.

"We'll do this the old-fashioned way." Alfred pressed the intercom button that connected to the door. "Welcome to the Wayne Residence," he announced. "Who is this?"

"Vicki Vale!"

VICKI WOULD NOT ENTER THE CAVE.

As Batman, Bruce hadn't given her any choice about visiting it, the first time. He'd needed the photos she'd taken of him, before his anonymity could be spoiled; he'd also needed her help to get his Smylex research to the authorities. She'd entered the second time, down the stairs, at Alfred's request.

But she had never once entered the Batcave in the days after, when they had been seeing each other.

She would wait for him. She would help patch him up. She would console him when things went wrong. But she would do it all in the mansion above. They had been partners, but not in fighting crime.

And then she had left. Bruce couldn't really remember why.

Now she stood before the incredibly long dining room table, the initial site of their first date. They'd never used the room again. But he had, spreading out newspaper reports, printouts, and science journals across the length of the table.

Vicki sifted through it all, mesmerized. "Autopsy reports. Chemical manuals. 'A clinical study of resuscitation in Order Rodentia.'" She held up a book and stared at him with incredulity. *"Frankenstein?"*

Bruce attempted a smile. "Fan of the classics."

"You never used to bring your Batman things upstairs."

He nodded. "Security risk."

"But now?"

"State of emergency."

She dropped the book on the table. "You're talking like him."

Alfred brought in her camera bag and suitcase. "Is this all, Miss Vale?"

She brightened immeasurably to see him. "Alfred, I told you I would get that!"

"I detected that you would prefer to talk alone."

"Don't *you* start detecting on me." She gave a wan smile, which he returned.

"I'll put these in the bedroom," he said as he headed up the stairs.

"The guest bedroom," she interjected.

"I will select one of the hundreds."

"Surprise me."

Bruce was surprised, sure enough. She hadn't called, written, or telexed. She was tanned—and tired, he could tell. "Corto Maltese again?"

"There are other trouble spots in the world."

"Don't I know it." Bruce sipped from a glass of water, his first in hours. "I told Knox to tell you to stay away."

"He did."

"Then what are you doing here? I begged him to tell you to hide."

"Alex did. But he also told me why." She clasped her hands before her on the table. "I thought about it, Bruce. I even started to leave for somewhere else, a different country. A trail of different countries." She looked up. "But then I realized that if The Joker is still alive, there's only one place in the world where I can be safe. And that's wherever you are."

Bruce stood dumbfounded for several moments, searching for something to say. Finally he said, "I appreciate the vote of confidence. I'm not sure it's correctly placed."

She studied him. "You look like a wreck."

"What do you expect?" He picked up a photo of The Joker from the table. "I plan for years, hoping to help this city. And I'm barely out there when this *demon* appears, a twisted mirror image matching me, answering my good with his evil. And—oh, yeah—not only that, he killed my parents." He threw the picture down. "Then as soon as I think I've dispelled him, it all starts up again."

"We had months without him. But you still—" Vicki put her hands in the air on either side of her face in frustration and stopped talking. When she began again, she threw her hands down. "Here we go. I told myself we wouldn't do this."

He took a step in her direction, arms extended. She took a step back. "We're not doing *that,* either," she said. "This is just about The Joker." She looked down at the material on the table. "Run me through it."

Bruce did, slowly making sense of the evidence he'd found and the theories he'd developed. The disappearing plastic surgeon, winding up in Napier's grave. The faceless man who walked away from a coma. And a sense that he'd never had the whole story of the night in the cathedral.

Vicki looked increasingly unconvinced as he spoke, and when he finished, she rummaged through the printouts with his timelines. "You really think Napier switched places with Davis on the ledge of the cathedral? And that The Joker somehow threw his voice?"

"Through this," Bruce said, picking up the laugh box and offering it.

It began laughing. She recoiled from it. "No thanks!" She walked along the table. "Bruce, we were both there. He was joking, dancing on the ledge. It was him."

"There are drugs that—"

Vicki put up her hand. "I'm sure there are. I'm sure your mounds of research has found every possibility—including, now, a Smylex variant that raises people from the dead."

"Comas. Death hasn't been tested."

She buried her face in her hands in frustration. "I'm barely here and I'm back in the madness."

Bruce wanted to tell her that things would be all right, that he had a handle on things. But he couldn't. "To tell you the truth, I'm kind of lost."

She looked up at him. "You'd better find yourself, before you find yourself dead."

Silence hung between them for several seconds until Alfred entered, begging their pardon. "I regret to say something on the television interrupted my nightly stories."

Alfred led them into one of the dens. The set was already on, depicting The Joker, white-skinned and cackling as he sat in an easy chair before a fireplace. In one hand he was holding open a book that looked like a Bible; his other held reading glasses. He had a champagne glass on the reading table beside him. It was footage Bruce hadn't seen before—and he soon realized why. This fireside chat was on every channel, live.

"—apparently my little set-to on the bypass got people talking," The Joker said, pursing his lips. "Lousy paparazzi. Here I was planning a proper announcement, and they horned in on my fun."

He rolled his eyes, closed the book, and placed it on the table. It wasn't the Bible, but rather an old book titled 1001 Jokes for Gentlemen's Parties. He uncrossed his legs and leaned forward. "It's been a while, so I have a few things to get off my chest. Buckle up, buttercups!"

Vicki looked fretfully at the screen—and backed up toward the couch. She shuddered. "I guess we'd better sit down for this."

"I guess," Bruce replied. He sat down beside her. But she did not take his hand.

CHAPTER 36

I**N THE GOTHAM CITY** neighborhood of Burnside, Drake Winston worked late trying to get the dents out of the door of a sedan. Royal Autobody had gotten plenty of cars in recently, given all the body work that the chase on the bypass had generated. The teenager knew that wherever Batman went, service jobs were sure to follow. He'd once told the owner that it might be worth inventing a Bat-Signal just for the garage, to make sure his next pursuit helped the local trade.

Jerome Otis had, of course, shot the idea down, with the usual additional splash of cold water. "Crime in Burnside's enough to make Batman take a second home here." He was right, of course. Drake liked Mister Otis and felt lucky to have the work. He was learning a trade, and the old man was even talking about letting him get a computer to help with the billing. Royal had become his second home.

Usually Drake had the TV on in the evenings to catch the games while he worked, but tonight the channels had been hijacked— again—by a grinning clown. Drake knew all about The Joker, of course; everyone in Gotham City did. Smylex had hurt friends and family members. The Last Laughs and their fires had been indiscriminate, too. The fact that Burnside had nothing to steal was no protection, not with a character like that.

"Now, I know you've probably seen me on the news, and you're all in a tizzy," The Joker said. He clasped his hands together antically and mimicked an old woman's voice. *" 'Oh, my! Look, Harold, the scary clown has returned! Put the children in the basement! Cancel all the magazine subscriptions! Find the ball-peen hammer!' "*

Drake's eyes narrowed. The guy had the patter down, but it was obviously some copycat. He had to be. The Joker had fallen flatter than flat; one of Drake's cousins had seen the cops prying the body out of the crater.

But somebody like that being on TV was still dangerous. People without hope were always looking for something, and people he knew were already responding to the Last Laughs' attempts to recruit. It was better to keep this stuff out of the ears of the impressionable.

Like his coworker Tyler, who walked in. He looked up at the set. "What's that fool on about?"

"No idea." Drake found the remote and turned the set off. "It's a rerun, I guess."

IT WAS THE THIRD TIME The Joker had scared the daylights out of Selina Kyle.

Months earlier, Max Shreck's secretary had been frightened along with everyone else during the villain's reign of terror over Gotham City. Convinced everything in her bathroom contained Smylex, she'd emptied her cabinet shelves of everything but cotton balls and emery boards.

Days later, she had been on the street coming home late from work when The Joker spooked her. He was emerging from the Flugelheim Museum—after vandalizing it, she later learned. Heading for his car, he'd tipped his hat to her and said, "Love the librarian look. Maybe I'll read a book!" She'd called out of work and spent the next week huddled on the couch with furniture blocking the door, convinced he had followed her home.

That experience explained how he'd been able to scare her again, just now. She had been falling asleep before a television show about the lifestyles of the rich and famous when she'd heard The Joker's famous voice declare "Hello there!" Convinced in her half-awake state that he was in the room and reading her novelty neon sign, she'd fled to the bathroom and slammed the door. It had taken her a while to realize she'd just heard a voice on TV, interrupting her program.

Having emerged to find that The Joker was on every channel, she curled into a fetal position on the couch, buried between stuffed animals and holding one of her stray cats. He looked like he'd never been away, never fallen off a building—and he sounded as if he'd never forgotten a slight.

"—turns out that during my little sabbatical, a lot of people have been taking my name in vain. Speaking ill of the dead. Such behavior! Sister Margaret would have slapped your hand with her ruler, if she wasn't out back sneaking a cigarette. I may have to teach this town some manners—"

She clutched the cat tighter. "I don't think I'm going outside anymore, Miss Kitty. Maybe ever again."

NORMAN PINKUS SAT IN the *Gotham Globe* break room, working the competition's puzzles—in permanent ink, as always. Other employees were milling around and ignoring him, as usual; this time they were looking at the TV mounted high on the wall beside the fridge.

The others were prattling on about how The Joker was back—when they weren't shushing one another so they could listen to the broadcast. Most were insufferable. Alexander Knox, usually their ringleader, seemed more serious than usual, more fixed on the television. He quieted them as the unhinged rant onscreen continued.

"—because I've heard you people talking. Talking, talking, talking—your vowels in an uproar, always getting things wrong. Those guys at the Globe *should skip the middleman and go straight to wrapping fish!*"

Shouts of "Whoa!" came from the others at the speaker's slight against them.

Norman glanced up at the clown onscreen—and cast his eyes right back down. He'd already solved *that* puzzle and acted at great personal risk to tip the forces of good in the right direction. Everything a hero should do. But he couldn't do *everything* for them. At some point they had to figure things out for themselves, didn't they? They were supposed to be good at this game, to understand the rules that any child knew.

Funny thing about Jokers; there are two in every deck.

They *had* to figure it out. Just what he'd done already to intercede had made him nauseous. Thinking about it rattled him such that—

He looked down at the nearly finished crossword from the *Gazette*. He'd entered an "E" rather than an "A." No fixing that—and fixing it would be cheating. Every time he'd been tempted to turn an "I" into an "E," his stomach had rebelled. He'd be looking at that day's puzzle years later, and he'd know that he failed—and tried to cover it up.

Nope. He stood abruptly, in the middle of the False Joker's speech.

Knox looked at him, startled. "Where you going, Normie?"

Norman responded in a tiny mumble. "I have to buy a new paper."

"HEY," THE GIANT CALLED OUT. "I got frozen pizzas melting back here!"

The clerk at the all-night market on McSparren Street barely glanced at him—and neither did anyone else in line. They were transfixed on something else.

Normally, seeing the huge bodybuilder got people's attention; hearing him bark always did. It had made his Strongman character a popular attraction for the Red Triangle Circus. Things had gone wrong, there, sending him and the whole gang underground, literally. But even in civilian clothes, as now, he nonetheless was used to getting fast service when he surfaced to get the groceries the gang couldn't find in the trash.

Not tonight, though. Not with the television going behind the counter and everyone transfixed. The Strongman rarely saw much

TV; his boss was stealing cable but kept it on the naughty channel all the time. But The Joker had dominated the airwaves both before and after his reported death—and now he appeared to be back.

The Red Triangle Circus—now the Red Triangle *Gang*—didn't think much of The Joker horning in on their circus theme, but their boss had liked his style. The Joker had just shown up one week and turned the city upside down the next. Something to aspire to.

Wherever The Joker had been keeping himself, he'd apparently been stewing for a while, as he'd been on a nonstop rant, defending himself about one thing after another.

"—*know that I am innocent of all charges! What you called a chemical weapon was just me doing a musical number at a street fair, introducing a new fragrance. Poh-tay-toe, toh-mah-toe.*"

The Strongman remembered the Smylex panic well. The boss had thought it pretty ballsy—even if it did threaten everybody who spent any time in Gotham City's sewers. Half the people in the city had dumped their shampoos, perfumes, and colognes down the drain. It resulted in a toxic brew underground that even he was afraid to go near, though he had to admit it made the place smell marginally better.

Realizing The Joker was just getting warmed up, the Strongman shoved the shoppers in front of him out of the way and slammed a few bucks on the counter. It wasn't the gang's way to pay for anything, but this place sold the only pizzas even close to the ones the boss really liked. There was no way of getting those, of course; nobody was going to deliver to a sewer downtown.

He took the bag and made for the exit. No matter what, he knew the boss would want to hear about The Joker. He made mischief, and whenever the cops and Batman were preoccupied, that made for good times. More scraps, more leavings available for those who lived on the fringes.

Or under them.

———

BARBARA GORDON HAD WORKED everywhere in Police Plaza, from the range to booking to vice—anything to shake the impression that her name had gotten her work. It wasn't her fault that Gotham City only had one police force to work for. A caped crusader could decide to freelance in that line, but that option was hardly available to everyone.

Finally a detective trainee, Barbara had been stationed on a floor where she had no choice but to encounter James Gordon at work. They did a good job of ignoring each other outside situations where she had to directly report to him, though those who knew them clearly found the pantomime almost comical. The biggest hazard was running into him in the elevator—

—or now, as she entered the control room where incoming calls were taken. The emergency lines had been on fire ever since The Joker had been seen battling Batman on the bypass—and whatever had just happened a few minutes ago had knocked her out of the call she was on. The commissioner was here, with several of his captains, standing amid the madhouse—but none of them were looking at the busy operators. They were looking up.

Barbara had to walk nearly to her father's side to see the large television, its volume turned up high enough to be heard.

"—know you've all been wondering about the fires lately," The Joker said. "Yes, my little friends have been engaging in some impromptu urban renewal. Call it the enthusiasm of youth. In some cases, we've been looking out for you. I have it on good authority that the snack bar at the Granders department store was going to use fake butter on its popcorn. Who needs that?" The Joker clasped his hands. "But let's talk about the future, and my plan for Gotham City. It's one I want to bring you all in on!"

She saw her father sag. Years before, she'd have offered a hug—but not here, not now. Barbara had worked to become a tough cop. That couldn't be her, not anymore.

Still, she had to ask, in the quietest whisper: "Tell me you've got this figured out." Her eyes went to the ceiling—and the beacon she knew was mounted on the roof. "Tell me he's got it figured out."

"I would if I could," he said sadly. "I would if I could."

―――

LEO BORG CLUTCHED HIS SIDE. His ulcers had ulcers, and if he took any more antacids he was in danger of exploding the next time he had a soda. Not that he'd had many, lately. Since the Last Laughs started their rampage, the mayor of Gotham City had been strictly on the blackest coffee, round the clock. City Hall was a war room again, despite everything he'd done.

He'd worked for months to get people to forget the Smylex panic and The Joker incidents. No American mayor had ever faced such a nightmare, and most could never hope to survive such a thing at the polls. Borg knew he certainly couldn't. He didn't have the Teflon of Harvey Dent's charm, and while he knew his district attorney acted one way to the cameras and another for everyone else, nobody else ever saw that. Leo Borg they saw as always reacting, never acting— and completely ineffectual.

There had been hope. Batman was a wild card, a rogue element— but for the moment the mayor considered him an asset. The people of Gotham City loved the idea of the guy, and it was Borg's nature to find the popular thing and pretend to be in favor of it until it was no longer useful. Things had gotten better. He'd even started to take Shreck's idea of restaging the bicentennial celebration seriously.

But it was all happening again. The nightmare was back, on the trio of TV screens in Borg's palatial office, outlining his "plan" for the city.

"—truth is, my friends, I do have a problem. I'm a little cash-poor after dumping all my money on a parade—literally. I've got an itch to raise a little scratch!" The Joker cracked his knuckles. "So let me tell you what I'm going to do—and how you can get a piece of the action!"

Borg rubbed the side of his head. Next time, I run for dogcatcher!

CHAPTER 37

"TELL ME YOU'RE RECORDING THIS," Vicki said as the clown on-screen rattled on.

"In the Batcave," Bruce said. "If there's enough space to get it all. He sure loves the sound of his own voice."

"That hasn't changed."

I guess the afterlife makes you long-winded, Bruce thought. But at last The Joker came to the point. He made a show of putting on glasses and reading from a card.

"Sometime in the next week, as soon as my schedule opens, I'm declaring that every bank in Gotham City will be open extra hours for one night. And those that aren't, we'll open—if you know what I mean." He raised an eyebrow and made a meowing noise. *"I invite all of you to come on down, whether you have accounts or not. Anything we can't carry out, we'll share. Bring your wheelbarrows!"*

"Merciful heavens," said Alfred, who remained standing by.

"I know, some of you think this is a trick. But your old Uncle Joker is on the level. There's no big bad balloons. I blew the deposit on those and they won't rent to me again." He ripped the card in two and threw the remnants over his shoulder. *"I'll pop on the old set here to give the signal when it's time. So get ready to drop on by your local branch that day. Give us a smile, and we'll give you a hundred. Hot dogs will be served. Extra mustard for the best costume at each location!"* He took off his glasses and smiled. *"Lassie la bone temps roolay!"*

As a spinning animation of The Joker's head replaced his face, Bruce let out a deep breath. "Let the good times roll," Bruce said. "But not the way he says it."

Vicki stared at the screen, almost hypnotized by the motion. Bruce used the remote control to turn it off. He looked to her hands, flat on the couch at her sides. She wasn't shaking.

"That wasn't him," she said.

He looked at her. "I can't tell. But you talked to him more than anyone."

She nodded—and then shook her head. "I don't know. Maybe it is. Maybe I just don't want him to be alive so much—"

Bruce looked to Alfred, standing a respectful distance away. They locked eyes for a moment. "Tell us why," Alfred said. "Why don't you think it's him?"

She pointed at the blank screen. "He goes on too long. The Joker was snappier. This guy was ad-libbing, stalling for time." Her head tilted. "But why would he do that?"

Bruce stared. "To make sure everyone saw it. The longer it's on, the more people tune in, see the message. The more likely I see the message."

Alfred spotted something—and went to the window. He peeked past the curtain. *"My word."*

Bruce rose from the couch. "Is it—?"

"The signal is in the sky."

Vicki joined them. "Already?"

"Gordon probably wants to go over war plans," Bruce said.

Alfred turned toward them. "Your metaphor is apt. This is a *provocation.* Someone wants you out there, dealing with many things. In many places."

Bruce nodded. "Like the fires."

Vicki got the idea. "Perhaps to cover something else?"

Bruce let out a deep sigh. "It doesn't matter. It's the kind of problem I have to deal with. I have to go." He scowled. "Checkmate."

Vicki gave him a sad look that said they'd been in this place too many times before. "I'll wait," she said finally.

But before Bruce could leave, he noticed Alfred looking to the side. His memory jarred, he called out. "One moment, Master Bruce."

Bruce turned. "Yeah?"

"It totally slipped my mind. There's something I wanted to show you." Alfred stepped toward the door. "I promise I won't be long."

As Alfred disappeared, Bruce looked again at Vicki. She looked lovely as always, but tired. He knew the look—and the feeling. "Have you eaten anything?"

"On the plane," she said. "What about you?"

"You know, I can't remember."

BACKSTAGE AT THE CAPRA, Hugh Auslander peeked through the fireplace scenery that Karlo had found. Karlo had finished his broadcast, to the delight and applause of the burgeoning number of Last Laughs, many of whom had been recruited in just the last few hours. They were where they most wanted to be: ringside at the resurrection of the greatest agent of chaos Gotham City had ever seen. And before a static camera—and a sophisticated piece of equipment with a bunch of cables leading outside—he had just declared war.

A war needed weapons and now they had them, thanks to Karlo's quick actions on the bypass. The Capra had storage areas at the front and sides of the house, and the captains Karlo and Lawrence had appointed were sorting through everything.

Auslander was scribbling notes on his pad when Karlo repaired backstage and spotted him. "Did that really go *everywhere* in town?"

"Everywhere," Auslander said.

"What did you think?"

"You went a tad long. You don't need to check boxes, using a variant of every expression Napier used. Don't go overboard."

"The whole thing's overboard." Karlo shook his head. "*Every* bank?"

"You and I need to be in the one place Batman and the police are not, tomorrow. If you want your cure."

Karlo let out a deep breath and touched his face. His skin puddled under his touch, as if to remind him that his malady still existed. "Excuse me," the actor said, heading back to the dressing room. He'd be needed as The Joker again to coordinate efforts.

One person passed through backstage—the one person who was allowed to: Lawrence. "Did you shut down the signal capture device?" Auslander asked.

"I did what you said." Lawrence stood before him, silent and motionless behind his sunglasses.

Aware, Auslander looked up from his notepad. "Yes? What is it?"

Lawrence stared at him. "I thought that guy was The Joker."

"And now you know he is not. Did he tell you?"

"I found out." He loomed over Auslander. "You put him up to this? To fool me?"

"No, Lawrence, to fool *them*." He pointed toward the stage. "This is what you told me you wanted. The Last Laughs are organized, growing, formidable. You needed a leader."

Lawrence took a few moments to catch on. "*You* were the voice on the tapes? The calls?"

"I even arranged for your escape, so you could reconstitute the beginnings of what we have now. We needed personnel."

The brute clutched his hands into fists—and then snapped his fingers. "I know who you are. I know where I saw you." He pointed. "*At Axis Chemicals.*"

"I had a different name there. But that's what I meant. We are on the same side. And with your help, we can take what had been the madness of a common criminal—and turn it into something that will change the world."

Lawrence scowled. "I just want money."

"You'll have that, too."

————

BRUCE DIDN'T HAVE TO wait long. Alfred returned to the den bearing a photocopy of the anonymous message that Batman had found affixed to the door of Davis's surgery. "I've been thinking about this since you brought it here, last night."

Vicki read it. *"When is a stranger not a stranger?"*

"When he's someone you know," Bruce answered. He'd come up with that not long after seeing it. "I was going to say 'friend'—but not everyone who isn't a stranger is a friend."

She frowned. "Someone's playing guessing games at a time like this?"

Alfred stepped toward her. "If I may, Miss Vale, there's something else." He passed her his magnifying glass. "Examine the letters in the first occurrence of 'a stranger.'"

She did. "It's actually '*e* stranger.'"

"Correct."

She handed it to Alfred. "You thought there was a wrong letter," the butler said. "But what if it's intentional?"

"Instead of *a stranger* it's *e stranger*?" Bruce asked. "What could that mean?"

"On its own, nothing. But together, you get *estranger,* the Middle French word meaning 'foreigner.'"

"Sure. And?"

"It connects to the history of a particular surname in English," Alfred said. "'*Strange.*' I'm sure you recall that the parallel surname in German is much different."

Bruce did. *"Someone we know."* He nodded as he said the name. *"Auslander."*

THURSDAY, 11:59 P.M.

ALL IS IN READINESS
I WONDER IF THEY KNEW
AFTER WHAT THEY DID TO ME
WHAT I WOULD GO ON TO DO TO THEM

ACT IV

WHO DO YOU TRUST?

CHAPTER 38

"EVERYTHING IS REFLEX," the great professor said. "Everything is reaction."

He stood before the lectern in the Gotham State University auditorium, just as he had a couple of weeks earlier. But while he began his speech the same way, what he had to say differed—beginning with the photo that appeared when he started the slide-show.

"Regard Hugo Strange," he declared, gesturing to the kid with thick glasses in the black-and-white school photo being projected on the screen behind him. "He was born Hegesias, after a talentless Greek writer who was the target of much scorn from his colleagues in the ancient world. The fact he had been given that name when Victor Hugo was *right there* had irritated him no end."

Laughter echoed in the auditorium.

"His idiot mother had found the name in a book, probably one she came across while cleaning someone else's house. Had Magda Strange read even a little, she might have seen the original Hegesias was a chronicler of the exploits of Alexander the Great. What was wrong with *that* name?"

More laughter.

"Birth was not destiny, however, and neither was a name. He had already determined that when his father, a violent simpleton and petty thief, uprooted them from their squalid home for the fifth time in as many years in search of another town to rob."

The slide projector clicked through scenes from different European towns before holding on the image of a pastoral estate. "It would end only when young Strange—now *Hugo*—emancipated himself and came to the attention of a prestigious academy. His parents little noticed. They were breeders, who put no more thought into bringing him into the world than they put into what liquor to buy. His genius was his. His story, his own."

He clicked through images from the academy—and the next one, and the next one. Each one, more prestigious.

"Everything is reflex," he said. "Hugo Strange's teachers recognized his talents and encouraged him. But his fellow students envied him—and despised him. Hierarchies everywhere change with the addition of each new member—often to defend the old order. And everywhere Hugo went, the same story happened."

He gestured to a sequence of candid photographs showing a series of awkward moments. Teenaged Hugo alone at a dance, alone at a table in a crowded lunchroom, alone on Parents' Day.

"In the animal kingdom, dominance comes from might and coercion, rather than knowledge and persuasive ability. Sexual desirability, too, comes from traits beyond higher logic. And so it was that wherever Hugo went, the body social reacted against him, like an invading bacterium. Rejecting his superior knowledge. Mocking him for his low birth. Abusing him for his lack of physical strength."

The next photos were instant-camera shots of Hugo as the butt of practical jokes. Hugo, holding his smashed science project. Hugo, wearing a dripping paint bucket on his head. Hugo, walking off a highway with only a traffic cone to cover his nudity. His enemies had snapped the photos to humiliate him, and he had saved them all. Sympathetic sounds were heard throughout the hall.

"I would be glad to say it improved as Hugo grew older. But as he earned doctorates in medicine, psychology, and biochemistry, the same dynamic always remained. The behavior of crowds convinced

Hugo that individualism was a myth. That *Homo sapiens* was actually seeking the caste system of cooperative species, like bees."

The screen changed quickly from one creature to another.

"When Hugo suggested the human condition could be altered with chemistry, his sole refuge, the body academic, rejected him. *Eugenics,* they called it. But Hugo wasn't seeking to create a master race, or supermen. Rather, something else entirely—suggested by a chap I've already mentioned."

Alexander the Great appeared onscreen. Laughs of recognition followed.

"Alexander of Macedon reinforced his ranks in every land he entered by bringing many of the conquered into his army. That tactic survives, in some form, to the present day—but it has always been an inefficient solution. Pressed soldiers and sailors who cling to their former national identities are apt to be less efficient—and the first to flee in the face of setbacks. In the worst case, they could rebel."

The professor gestured to an image of the young student, now older. "Hugo Strange understood that subjugation was not enough— but eliminating whole populations was wasteful, and likely to rouse one's enemies to unite in opposition. No, the answer was conversion—or as one of his papers had put it, *transformative mercy.* Enemies could be turned into pliable, willing warriors for one's own cause. All it took was a combination of chemicals and a knowledge of biology and evolution."

The screen framed through a sequence of chemical formulas, some labeled with the title PROJECT HEGEMON, as the professor's voice reached a crescendo. "A master race is nonsense. What Hugo Strange proposed was altogether different. The defeated would step back down the evolutionary chain, becoming the neo-Neanderthals. Better physically, but completely at the beck and call of their leader through a combination of hypnosis and other controls."

Illustrations of armies of brutes flashed across the screen.

"More than one dean had told Hugo that he would never improve himself by putting others down. *How wrong that was!* It could be done

with whole countries, whole races. By making men monstrous—
Monster Men!"

Loud applause came from before him. The professor put up his
hands to still it.

"Of course, the universities would never support such revolution-
ary ideas. But fortunately, Hugo Strange found others who had
broader minds—if not nearly the same level of smarts."

Behind him, an overhead image of the Pentagon appeared. Raucous laughter followed.

"Hugo worked with the CIA and the Defense Department on a
variety of gases designed to trigger major reactions. DDID—the
basis for Smylex—was one. What if it could be altered to make minds
pliable, while making bodies resilient? It became the basis for *Hegemon*, his greatest concoction. He was in the process of testing it
when the worst happened. The Chemical Weapons Convention
banned Hugo's research. He was fired."

He waited for the *aww* sounds to end.

"Truth be told, his jealous colleagues had already been agitating
against him. But this time, he had nowhere to go. All his research was
locked away, seemingly forever."

He let the moment linger before starting again. "Hugo was
bereft—but he was not lost. He had developed several alternate identities over the years, publishing his works under a number of pseudo-
nyms. He had never been interested in celebrity anyway. He was able
to move, to function, as he needed to. But he never lost sight of reclaiming his prize. And that brought him here!"

Gotham City filled the screen. Applause, again.

"More specifically, the Armsgard Defense Depot. Where Smylex
and other chemical stocks were being destroyed by the government—
and where all Hugo's research was kept. Even satellite and aerial photographs aren't permitted, but it's a place many of you drive past
every day. Hugo wanted a way back in. But this time, he played the
game, looking to get close to power. The *real* power in Gotham City."

The late Carl Grissom appeared onscreen, prompting gasps of
surprise.

"Hugo knew that Boss Grissom had connections, but he had to get access first. He got it by setting up as a psychiatrist—a therapist who made house calls, with a prescription pad and no-questions-asked." Images of Gotham City mobsters flashed past. "Hugo had become like the exiled Doctor Davis, serving criminals—and yet he was *nothing* like Davis. Davis was a reptile, scratching out a meager survival by stitching up stab wounds and removing bullets. Hugo dispensed medications to the crème de la crème of the Gotham City underworld—including Grissom's own girlfriend!"

The slide changed to depict Alicia Hunt, on Carl Grissom's arm.

"Many was the day Hugo visited Alicia, listening endlessly to her petty problems and vapid dreams, learning information that would give him leverage over her lover." The professor turned. "There was just one problem—her other lover."

Jack Napier's mug shot appeared, provoking more sounds of shock.

The professor shook his head. "Alicia had gone from success in the modeling world to being the escort of a mobster—and she was in the process of blowing it all up through her assignations with Grissom's loosest cannon. It was a dangerous day when Napier and Hugo met unexpectedly. Once the maniac realized Hugo was a head-shrinker and not a rival, he relaxed. 'Just don't try to psychoanalyze *me*,' he said."

Loud, long laughter.

"Napier's physical transformation to The Joker was a freak accident; who he became was no surprise at all. He was sick, twisted, deranged—these are technical terms, of course—"

More laughs.

"—but he was also brilliant, going without sleep, devising tools of violence. And he had a way of commanding attention, even self-destructive loyalty, from those who simply could not stop staring at him." He looked down. "One was Alicia Hunt. Hugo watched her descent into the madness of this Caligula of Crime. And when Napier again noticed Hugo, it was to threaten to kill him. But like The Joker, Hugo had a card to play."

A folder appeared onscreen depicting the words DDID NERVE GAS.

"Axis Chemicals had been a contractor during production—and maintained files in a safe that Grissom had emptied. When The Joker found them, he realized what he had. Overnight, his brilliant, warped mind concocted a method Hugo had never considered—lacing products with the components of what he called Smylex. And that was where Hugo came in. He pledged loyalty—and a willingness to act as the man in the coat with the clipboard, working for The Joker inside Axis to make sure everything got out." The professor smiled. "'Through a whole new door,' to use Napier's phrase. Hugo never found out what that meant."

The slides cycled through the famous headlines of the Smylex panic. The professor began to pace.

"The Smylex that products were laced with was *not* the tool Hugo had intended, and certainly not the tactile method of transmission. But hoping to perfect Hegemon, Hugo took the opportunity to tweak a number of chemicals, creating variants whose formulae he recorded—and then sent out into the wild in controlled tests via black-market sellers. Over a hundred such variant samples went out before the entire project ended suddenly."

Batman's shield filled the screen.

The professor tut-tutted. "Rodents are rarely welcome visitors—but Hugo expected that *something* would stop The Joker. He was ready. Hugo fled moments before the destruction of Axis Chemicals by Batman, carrying his record of the variants he'd made. It remained to then reconnect with the victims. And that meant activating one of his oldest aliases, an identity who had all the university credentials, complete with the requisite paperwork . . ."

A publicity photo of Auslander appeared, looming large behind the speaker. He heard cheers and took a bow. "Yes, I am that Hugo Strange. The rest you know. I found a patron in Bruce Wayne and a place to evaluate Smylex victims. And I found the most fascinating one—Patient Thirty-Five, Basil Karlo, who coincidentally appears to have been altered by my Variant Thirty-Five."

Pictures of Karlo—comatose, and from Auslander's office post-transformation—appeared onscreen.

"He unlocked everything. His unique theatrical talents have helped me gather the money, weapons, and personnel needed to get back *all* that I have lost!"

Deafening applause.

"And as for the random element—Batman? He has been neutralized. He proves to have been quite human after all—paranoid, and easily misled." The professor returned to his position behind the lectern. "Batman and The Joker thought to be titans, towering over humanity as they worked their will. In fact, it will be a human who will do the towering. *The new Alexander!*"

Hugo Strange—more recently known as Hugh Auslander—smiled amid the clapping—and looked into the darkened auditorium. "All of you are probably wondering why you are hearing this. Here, now, and from me. It is a very simple matter."

He paused—and switched off his microphone. "That's enough, Lawrence. I'll record the rest once we have everything in order."

In the middle of the aisle, Lawrence stared as if in a daze.

Ah, yes. I forgot. Strange spoke sharply. *"Lawrence!"*

Lawrence jarred as if from a sleep and gave a thumbs-up. He turned off the video camera—and then his boombox, the source of all the crowd noise. The hall went silent.

Strange stepped over to turn up the lights. The auditorium was empty, but for the two of them. Turning, he saw a face peeking through the small window in the door. He unlocked the chamber and recognized the university maintenance man he knew. "Yes, Felix?"

"All done, Professor?"

"We're quite finished," Strange said. "Thank you for allowing me the auditorium. I wanted to practice my next address."

"Anytime."

Hugo closed the door behind Felix and saw Lawrence approaching with the tripod, camera, and boombox. He eyed the lummox. "You recorded everything?"

"Yep. But I still don't know why you needed me to."

"Did you understand everything Jack Napier did?"

"No."

"Of course not. How about what I said? Did you understand any of that?"

"Sounds like you were looking for a way to make people dumber—and stronger."

"Rest assured I would never consider it in your case. I doubt anything would make *you* stronger." *Or dumber,* he did not add. "Will we have a problem?"

"You're the boss."

"Good man," Strange said. *And you will remain a man, as long as you obey!*

CHAPTER 39

ENTERING GOTHAM CITY on Monday morning was like driving into an armed camp. Bruce had never seen anything like it.

Within an hour of The Joker's late-night televised address days before, Bruce had wearily responded as Batman to the commissioner's signal. But other forces were already in motion. On arriving that night, he'd learned Mayor Borg had declared a state of emergency in the city. He had even set aside his numerous differences with the governor and called in the state's National Guard. That hadn't even been done in the initial Joker crisis.

That had put Gordon in a predicament. He likely wouldn't be in charge of his own plan to protect the city's banks—and he told Batman the higher powers weren't likely to be amenable to cooperating with a costumed vigilante. Nonetheless, Batman had parted company with the commissioner promising he'd still contribute in his own way—and that it would be a way people would notice. Gordon had laughed. "I'm sure of that!"

Now, after a weekend of frenetic preparations—and too-frequent after-hours patrols with a barely repaired Batmobile—Bruce wondered if even that amazing car could get back into the city. Vicki had wanted to venture out to see Alexander Knox, and Bruce had insisted on accompanying her. It seemed safe to go during the day, given the "after-hours" part of the televised threat to Gotham City's banks. But it had required them waiting with Alfred and the limo for an hour on the bridge to get through the roadblock. There was no VIP lane where the National Guard was concerned.

The rains finally having stopped, they'd met for lunch in what was, currently, the safest public place in all of Gotham City: the financial district. Almost every major bank in the world had an office here, and Gordon and the governor had placed tremendous resources in the area. Officers, armored vehicles, barricades all across the plaza; they could see it all from the windows of the third-floor restaurant Bruce had chosen.

Knox pushed back his empty plate. "The grub was okay, Wayne. But I'm surprised nobody else is here." He looked about. "Or did you book the whole room?"

Bruce shrugged. "It's my building."

"I hate you." Knox looked across the table to Vicki. "But I get the privacy thing. It's good to see you—but I don't want anyone else to."

She rolled her eyes. "If I knew I was going to have to hide my face all the time, I could have stayed where I was."

Knox snapped his fingers. "Now I know why they call you Vicki Veil."

Vicki winced at him. *"Allie!"*

"Sorry," Knox said, uncomfortably. He put his fingers on his temples. "Always working. I can't shut it off."

"Try."

Vicki had explained that she'd gone to stay at Wayne Manor because it was remote—and that Bruce had the resources to get her anywhere in the world. Knox had seemed to buy that.

Bruce was glad she'd seen her friend, but it wasn't just a social meeting. Not for him.

While Batman had a working relationship with Gordon, Bruce remained reluctant to have his alter ego reach out to Knox. Batman and the police shared similar goals. The reporter served different masters—and many of his coworkers would sell their grandmothers for a scoop. It was better for Batman to keep some distance. So having already opened a channel over their mutual concern for Vicki, Bruce had asked for further off-the-record help.

He glanced at the folders beside Knox. "Got 'em?"

"Oh, yeah." Knox put the thinner of the two folders on the table between Bruce and Vicki and opened it. "Direct from the *Globe*'s morgue, I give you *Hugo Strange*," he said, trilling the "r" in "Strange" comically. "And boy, does he look it."

Bruce sifted through pages printed off microfilm. There were things in a newspaper's archive he couldn't get anywhere else, and Knox's librarian had found them. Articles in competing papers and international editions about a young prodigy from decades earlier winning competitions and scholarships. All showed the same dour, mousy young man. Sometimes as an adolescent, sometimes as an adult.

"There's nothing newer than thirty years ago," Vicki said.

"That tracks," Bruce replied. His eyes fell on the other, fatter folder. "And that?"

"Easy-peasy," Knox said, passing it over. "The head of the ward you funded has a clip file to rival Zsa Zsa." The folder was filled with clips about Hugh Auslander. His lectures. His book deal. His TV appearances. And most of all, his work with the Smylex Ward at Gotham General.

There was just one thing, which Bruce quickly noted. "Nothing before a few months ago with a photo of him."

"He took the town by storm. You should know. You hired him."

Vicki's eyes narrowed. "All the ones with photos are from local papers. Didn't the librarian pull up anything else?"

"Just clips of what he was doing here," Knox said. "What, does he owe money or something? Didn't you and the hospital vet him?"

Bruce had already checked into that. "Auslander did have degrees in his name, did have papers published—including the first on Smylex. Did have residencies on his record in the last dozen years, though my people can't track down anyone who actually knew him before that."

He put the two folders side by side. Young Hugo, old Hugh.

Knox's eyes bugged. "Wait. You don't mean he's the geek?"

Vicki examined the images with a photographer's eye. "He's had work done."

"He would have." Bruce took a deep breath. He'd spent part of the weekend running the name *Strange* through databases available to Batman and checking through the records of Wayne Industries' defense companies. "A man named Hugo Strange has been working with various intelligence agencies over the years. Looks like he was canned by the CIA when it discontinued the program that gave the world Smylex."

Knox stared. "So *Auslander*'s an alias?"

"He'd never have been able to publish under his own name—and certainly not about the effects of something he worked on. The agency thought Strange had defected. But maybe he didn't."

"Cover identities," Vicki said. "Very cloak and dagger."

Bruce looked again at young Hugo's citations. The subject areas all fit.

Knox compared the pictures again. "You have a source on any of the CIA stuff?"

Bruce shook his head. "Not that you can use."

"Figures. There's no story without it—just a couple of guys who may be the same person. But I can see why you asked me about it. And I bet his boss might be interested."

"Among others."

Knox chuckled. "Let's see if Commissioner Gordon is as charming to him as he is to me." He rose from the table. "This has been nice, but I have to get back to the fall of Western Civilization over here."

He gestured to the windows overlooking the financial plaza, and they followed him to it. There hadn't been much of a run on Gotham City's banks yet, but the only reason was nobody could get to them.

Knox shook his head. "I've talked about Gotham's greed before, but this is next-level shit."

"An armed camp, sitting on everyone's money," Vicki said.

"Not everyone's money. The little local banks get a senior citizen with a nightstick," Knox said. "Of course, my money is in a shoebox." He glanced at Bruce. "I'm sure yours is all buried under that estate of yours. Or some other state. Maybe Montana."

They walked Knox past the empty tables to the elevator. Outside it, Bruce offered his hand. "Thanks, Knox. Seriously."

The reporter shook it. "Anytime." He turned to accept a hug from Vicki. "Stay safe, Vic. Don't go near any tall buildings."

"You can see we're eating on the third floor. That's my limit."

Knox stepped into the elevator. Inside, he called out to them. "Good thing we were away from the paparazzi. You two together— what would Julie Madison think?"

Bruce winced. Vicki looked at him. "Julie Madison?" she asked.

Knox looked at them both—and his lower lip sagged. "Don't get the social pages where you work, I guess." He shrank against the back wall of the elevator car as the doors began to close. "Oops."

Bruce reached out to call a new elevator car. "We should go. Alfred's waiting."

"He's got a book," Vicki said, shoving her hand in front of his, preventing him from touching the button. She faced him. *"Julie Madison?"*

Bruce shrugged. "We're not even talking. She's mad—"

"But Julie Madison? The actress? She thinks, that is."

Vicki had met Julie before. It had seldom gone well—but that was then. Bruce put up his hands. "Vicki, we're in a restaurant—"

"Where you paid everyone to be somewhere else." Vicki crossed her arms. "How long?"

"How long what?" Bruce shuffled. "How long have I been seeing Julie, or how long did I wait?"

"Pick one."

He began walking away from her. "You left. We'd broken up."

"I know. But—"

He stopped and looked back to see her fighting for words. "You're angry," he said. "Hurt." He lifted an eyebrow. "Jealous?"

"More like insulted. *Offended*. Julie Madison is a dandelion."

"I've known her for years—"

"That's what I mean. She's pretty, she's always around, and you can't get rid of her. And as for substance?" Vicki made like she was holding a dandelion bloom and blew. "Gone with the wind!"

"Dandelion," Bruce muttered. "I get it."

"Who else?"

"What, you want a list? Phone numbers?"

Aggravated, she charged away toward the window overlooking the plaza. He followed, against his better judgment.

When he reached her, she spun, speaking in just over a whisper. "I'll tell you what you're doing."

"What am I doing? I'd like to know."

"You're doing what I thought you'd do. You're dating arm candy. Pretending to have relationships, so you can cover your—*your nocturnal activities.*"

He looked around, making sure the restaurant floor was still empty.

"Oh, nobody's here." She grabbed his wrist. "You'd never let someone like Julie in on your secret. So she becomes a prop—or *whatever else,*" she said, icily. "All so you can get to date without ever having to deal with the other half of your life!"

Bruce put hands behind his neck. They were back to this again. Right where they were before, in the entry hall of Wayne Manor weeks back when her bags were packed.

He took a breath and spoke calmly—and softly. "Vicki, there's no point. No one would accept that I can't quit being Batman." He looked at her. "*You* didn't."

She shook her head. "I just don't understand why you didn't quit when you learned The Joker killed your parents." She reached for his hand. "You got justice. It's done."

"You didn't argue when I kept on after the cathedral."

Vicki looked away. "Well, you were triumphant. They had a big ceremony. I didn't think you'd quit your other life just like that, but I thought you were getting there." Her eyes met his. "I thought I was your next stage."

So did I. Bruce stared at her, wanting to say the words he'd just thought. He wanted to tell her the city didn't improve as fast as he'd hoped. That it was hard to disengage from something he'd put so much time into. He also wanted to kiss her.

But he knew better. About everything.

Instead, he put his other hand over hers and whispered, an inch from her face. "It didn't end with Napier—because it was never about Napier. It was about my parents' murder."

"But aren't they—"

He shook his head. "Not the same thing. I see my parents' killer in the face of every criminal I punch. I even fought a man without a face a couple of weeks ago. All I could see was a man with a gun, threatening my parents—*someone's* parents. And I had to stop him."

She closed her eyes, and a tear fell. "Then you'll never be done. Until one of them kills you."

"And I do everything I can to make sure that never happens. It's like I've told Alfred. I don't have—"

"—a death wish, but a life wish," she finished for him. She opened her glistening eyes. "You need some new psychobabble."

"Maybe I'll ask Doctor Auslander—or Hugo Strange, that is. When I see him." He released her hands. "I'll be talking to him now, anyway."

"Back to business again," she said. Vicki let out a sigh. "I swear, these villains will be your only long-term relationships."

He chuckled. "Maybe I need to find someone like me."

"Someone who's also split down the middle?" Vicki asked. "It'll be a great romance until you both retreat to your separate holes in the ground."

Bruce started to laugh—before snapping his fingers. "You just gave me an idea—if the Last Laughs will give me time to check it out!"

He turned and hurried toward the elevator. He could see her chasing after him in its mirrored doors. "You will *never* change!"

CHAPTER 40

THE MILITARY TRANSPORT RUMBLED through Gotham City at sunset, bypassing National Guard checkpoints. Karlo fidgeted in the passenger seat as he saw the hard faces of the people he passed.

He checked his makeup in the mirror. He'd been willing to play dead bodies in war stories before, cannon fodder; never did he dream of being cast as a soldier with a name, much less a full-fledged general. He looked the part, for sure; Karlo had the face of a hard-bitten man in his fifties, ready to spit nails.

His driver, Lawrence, looked less convincing in his ill-fitting MP uniform. The sunglasses didn't help. Lawrence had known about his face-changing abilities since their battle with Batman; it hadn't seemed to matter to him. When Karlo had told the doctor that Lawrence knew, Auslander had included him in their plan. The doctor was riding in the back, wearing civilian clothes.

Karlo looked over the seat to him. "Shouldn't I be back *there*, Doc? I'm the VIP."

"No. Consider my role."

Karlo smiled. It was amusing to think they were *all* acting for a change. "What do I call you again?"

"Hugo Strange."

Karlo chuckled at the funny-sounding name. "Really?"

The doctor's expression hardened. "Yes, really. You will understand. Just play your part."

Karlo didn't press. Auslander had been the only constant in his life since his awakening, but he didn't think they were exactly friends. He'd had so few in his life, he didn't know how to tell. "Hugo Strange" had sometimes acted the wizened sage, and sometimes a mad Rasputin, making little sense. He'd protected Karlo like a prize, not necessarily anything else.

Karlo shook his head—his thoughts, again, on an old movie he had loved. A late-show horror flick in which a man robbing a grave had looked upon a cadaver's smile only to find that his own face had frozen in that same grotesque position. In the film, Baron Sardonicus had turned villainous, blackmailing a doctor he hoped could reverse the condition. Karlo didn't consider himself a villain—and it was the doctor asking him to do questionable things in exchange for a cure.

Please. Just let this be over.

The drive, at least, came to an end. Karlo saw a large sign ahead:

U.S. Army
Armsgard Depot, Gotham City
Keep Out

The last line hardly needed to appear; the high stone walls and barbed wire said enough. And behind it was something out of the gates of Hell. Towering smokestacks burning who-knows-what loomed behind, belching foulness into a bloody sky. Karlo could only imagine what Fritz Lang could have done with it in black-and-white.

He gestured for Lawrence to lose the shades, and he did. The wheels screeched to a halt before a checkpoint. *It's showtime.*

A soldier came up to the driver's side window. His initial shock at seeing Lawrence gave way to respect when he saw Karlo sitting next to him. He saluted. "What can I do for you, General?"

Karlo clenched his jaw. "You can get your C.O. out here to let us in there."

The kid nervously flipped through the pages on his clipboard. "We didn't have you on the—"

"Just make the call, son. We'll do the rest."

As the sentry disappeared into the guardhouse, Karlo pulled the transmitter from his pocket and made a call of his own. In The Joker's voice, he said, "Run tape, boys. It's time."

BRUCE HAD COME AWAY from his lunch with Vicki and Knox with several leads—but he had only had time to make a few calls. Hugo Strange or not, Auslander was not in his office at Gotham General. His boss, Takagi, had never made it into work, either; their receptionists suggested they'd probably both gotten stuck in traffic someplace. Bruce found that easy to believe, as he quickly realized he needed Alfred to get Vicki back to the mansion as quickly as possible. It wouldn't do for them to be stuck in the city should the expected call to action come.

It came shortly after sunset, about as early in the evening as the Bat-Signal would be visible. It was no surprise, because Gotham City's television stations had seen their transmissions hijacked again. "It's showtime," The Joker announced. "Banks are open late tonight. Free samples. Come on out!"

An unusually terse announcement, it repeated every ten seconds. Bruce wasn't surprised. If the idea was to get people out onto the streets, there was no need to filibuster, keeping viewers inside waiting to hear what The Joker would say next.

Bruce had remained in the city on purpose. Having realized how well protected the financial district was, he knew the softer targets would be spread all across town—and his usual methods of movement as Batman wouldn't do. The Batmobile would never get everywhere in time. Fortunately, since the Batwing's destruction, he had been able to supplement by bringing a couple of additional systems online.

He found one of them where he'd deployed it. The tractor-trailer driver, hired anonymously, had no idea what he'd brought to the warehouse, also rented under a false name. The trailer had sat there since, untouched, waiting for Bruce to need it. In the lengthening shadows, he entered the facility and reached for his control unit.

A press of the button opened the back doors of the trailer—and a lot more. A seam along the middle of the shipping unit's roof split open, and the walls of the trailer folded outward. As components whirred into place, Bruce climbed a short ladder to the platform where a Batman uniform was stored in a chest. Systems started coming online as he donned it.

He went for the radio scanner first. Gordon was speaking on his channel, appealing for Batman's help.

"I'm on it," Batman replied into the transmitter. "But I also want you to get a message to Coroner MacReedy."

The commissioner sounded flustered. *"This isn't a good time right now, Batman. For you or me!"*

"I know. But I think it'll be worth it. I'm on my way!"

KARLO COULDN'T TELL WHO was more scared: himself, or the privates who'd just gotten a surprise inspection from a general. They stood at attention inside the gates of Armsgard beside the parked transport. Lights were beginning to come on across the compound, illuminating garages and warehouses.

As Lawrence opened the door for the doctor to exit the transport, Karlo noticed a small bunker, off near the smokestacks. A door opened, and a female officer emerged from it.

Salutes were exchanged. "I'm Major Peltz," she announced. "What's going on here?"

"Hastings. Buck Hastings," Karlo said in his best Burt Lancaster. He gestured to Lawrence, who handed the major a packet of documents. "I'm here with someone you're gonna want to see." Karlo indicated Auslander, who was in handcuffs. More props from the Capra.

Peltz looked over the trio—and then the papers. Seemingly satis-fied, she handed them back. "The company guys are coming upstairs. We'll see what they say."

Karlo had been told that most of the facility was underground. He clasped his arms behind his back and did his best commanding strut around the driveway before the truck. "Not much to see up here."

"Things are almost done downstairs, General." Peltz pointed to the smokestacks. "We'll finish destroying all the hazardous materials and close up shop. This'll probably be an EPA Superfund site in a couple of years, and then who knows—maybe a shopping mall."

Karlo gave a belly laugh. "Think I'd get my milkshakes some-where else!"

Peltz chuckled along with him.

The major explained that much of the staff was away. "A lot of our civilians decided not to come in—that Joker business. Some are Guardsmen, got activated."

"The Joker," Karlo grumbled. "Damned maniac."

"Well, this place sure didn't need the attention before. Now that he's back—"

Two men in black business suits exited the bunker and ap-proached. Even just past sunset, they wore shades that would be the envy of Lawrence.

The taller of the two introduced himself. "I'm Agent Walsh. This is Dowell." He spoke sharply. "What's going on here? What's this about?"

Karlo identified himself and launched into his lines. "This is Hugo Strange," he said, gesturing to the captive Auslander. "Worked on the covert side developing some of this crap you guys are destroying here."

The shorter agent, Dowell, gawked. "*Hugo—?*"

"You're putting me on," Walsh said. Looking the doctor over, he pointed. "I saw you on TV the other night. You're that professor!"

"I assure you I am Hugo Strange," the doctor said. He recited a serial number which he said would identify him. He looked around.

"It has been many years since I last visited this place—or was in your service. I do not look as I did then—but you will find my biometric data unchanged."

Karlo snorted. "Would you believe? This sumbitch has been back in town for years. Skulking around, trying to get close to this place. He's even been running the Smylex Ward at the hospital. Can you imagine? Fixing what he broke."

Auslander stood firm. "There is information here on Smylex and its variants. It would be helpful to my patients now."

Karlo had to give the doctor credit. He didn't know how Auslander had dug up this Hugo Strange character, but it had gotten them in the door. Now it remained to see what he could get out of them.

"Strange was sneaking around the veterans' hospital when they grabbed him," Karlo said. "When he told the cops who he really was, they called our field office. We figured he belonged to you, so here we are."

Agent Walsh scratched his chin as he glared at the doctor. "Hugo Strange. I've heard about you. They said you vanished. Joined up with somebody else."

The doctor looked down at his handcuffs. "I joined the human race, gentlemen—and I invite you to assist. I already know that much of my research is here, including my samples. What you haven't destroyed yet could help all of humanity."

He glanced at Karlo, who was glad to hear his words. It was Karlo's cue. "Is any of Strange's stuff even here? Or is he crazy?"

Agent Dowell shook his head. "That's classified, General."

"Take a breath, Dowell." Walsh chuckled. "Yeah, of course. We're burning the stockpiles—but we'll never let go of the prototype samples or the recipes. No sane government would do that."

"Then let us see them," the doctor said. "For humanity's sake!"

"Nothing doing, Strange. This is national security we're talking about. You should know that. If you've got a complaint, write a letter to your congressman. I think they've got paper at Leavenworth!"

The agent gestured for Major Peltz to call over the sentries. Karlo hesitated, not knowing what the next play was. "Now, wait a minute. Maybe we can—"

"Save it." Agent Walsh eyed him. "Why have I never heard of you, General?"

Karlo glowered. He'd suffered through so much, only to now have everything taken away. Here, right at the final moment where he had been promised deliverance. He saw Walsh reach for a walkie-talkie.

Then Karlo's mustache fell off. And then his eyebrows.

Major Peltz's eyes widened. "What the hell?"

Not now. Not now!

Karlo felt his face melting again—and his rage rising. When he looked up again at the officer, his anger exploded. "Give the doctor what he wants!" He lunged forward and grabbed Walsh's wrist with both hands. He pressed hard, causing Walsh to yell and drop the radio.

The sentries left the doctor's side and moved toward Karlo. He yanked Walsh toward himself and then shoved, hurtling the agent toward the sentries. Peltz unholstered her sidearm and gave a yell. "Halt!"

Karlo turned on her with blinding speed, grabbing the weapon and knocking her away before she could point it. The gun discharged and fell to the pavement.

The sound ringing in his ears, Karlo turned on Dowell as the others scrambled to get to their feet. A scrum developed as they tried to keep him from the agent—but his strength was too much. Amid the pile, Karlo drew Dowell close to him and screamed in his face. *"I told you, give the doctor what he wants!"*

"I can get it myself." Auslander triggered the trick handcuffs, and they fell off his wrists. He glanced over to the parked transport. *"Lawrence!"*

Leaning against the truck, Lawrence pounded the side with the back of his hand. At the sound, the back doors burst open. Eight people bounded out. All members of the Last Laughs, all in clown masks. Each was decked out comically in commando gear that had been painted not in camouflage, but in bright clashing colors. And every one carried a submachine gun.

They were the most trusted of the Fake Joker's adherents, and they fired into the air on exiting just as instructed. Everyone who had piled onto Karlo scrambled to get away—and he hurried to get to his feet, as well. He rushed toward cover on the other side of the transport.

Chaos ensued, as other personnel on base, alerted by the noise, appeared—either running toward safety or heading to join the fight. But the agents and soldiers nearest the transport had either fled or fallen. The Last Laughs had surprise on their side—and the doctor soon stood next to Karlo.

"Secure the tower!" Auslander called out to Lawrence. "No one enters, no one leaves!"

Shocked by the sight of so much violence, Karlo felt his rage abating. *My cure isn't worth this!* He turned to the doctor. "They're shooting!"

"This is serious business, Karlo. These people stand in the way of the future!" With the bulk of the fighting moving away from their location, the doctor stepped to the ground where an injured Major Peltz had fallen. One of the Last Laughs handed Auslander her sidearm, and he pointed it at her. "I need access to everything, Major."

"You won't get away with this, Strange!" she said. "This city is crawling with troops!"

"All of whom are elsewhere, responding to emergencies that we engineered. You said much of your garrison had joined them. I assure you, no one will be coming to save you."

For the first time, Karlo spotted something to the side—in the sky. The Bat-Signal. "What about *that?*"

The doctor barely gave it a glance. "He is the busiest of all." He opened the door to the transport and pulled out an empty satchel. "Put on a clown mask, before Lawrence's lackeys see you without a face. Then come along. We're going shopping!"

CHAPTER 41

"*LAST LAUGHS ON TOP of Byars Mutual Bank and Trust!*"

So was Batman. The Gotham City Police Department had barely gotten the alert on the scanner before he was on the scene and on the roof. Four clown-faces were there with giant orange-and-green battery-operated water guns—only rather than water they held more of The Joker's highly concentrated acid. They'd been firing at the rooftop itself, wearing away person-sized holes leading inside. Meanwhile on the ground, greedy onlookers, having overwhelmed police, were bringing ladders from wherever they could find them.

While he didn't think climbing through a hole still dripping with acid was the smartest move anyone could make, Batman had obliged the Last Laughs by taking the threat seriously. He bounded across the rooftop, belting one clown-face after another. One tumbled off the roof; another plummeted down the hole he'd made. By the time two others brought their acid cannons to bear on Batman, his Batarang was in the air. This time he made sure to pick it up after it had done its job. From there, he leapt back onto the hovering conveyance that he'd arrived on.

The Roost.

Six blasting turbines held the bat-shaped platform aloft, adjacent to and at the height of the roof. Twenty feet across, it provided a stable surface as he headed for the relative safety of its control station. Standing in the platform's center and protected on three sides by metal shields, he operated the yoke to move the flying raft—for that was what it was—away from the building.

Seconds later, he turned it toward the crowd and descended, buzzing eight feet off the ground. It posed no threat to the civilians down below, but its angry jets had the intended effect, causing people to hit the ground and abandon their plans to storm the bank. Then it was back into the air and off to the next location.

The Roost's creation had been a response to what had happened at The Joker's bicentennial parade. The Batwing had been able to stop the balloon threat and had driven most of the hoodlums from the streets. But while it had precision-guided munitions, it was somewhat of a blunt instrument when it came to surface threats. It could cause rioters to disperse but could not select individual rioters from the innocent.

The thinking in policing had tended toward riot tanks, but he didn't need protection from the crowds. He needed mobility and the ability to see and act against specific threats. The Roost wasn't a fully functional aircraft; it didn't have the range to take it into the city from Wayne Manor, hence the need to station it inside the city limits beforehand. But it was capable of hovering anywhere from three feet above the ground to three stories, serving as an elevator where none existed.

Gotham State Credit Union, up ahead, didn't have anyone on the roof using any of The Joker's insidious acid. But that wasn't the only weapon that had been stolen from the police truck. As a pair of beleaguered shotgun-wielding police officers stood in the doorway of the bank warning people off, four Last Laughs were attacking the other side of the building with, of all things, a comical rainbow-striped drill.

It took all four of them to operate the unwieldy thing, and it was sparking madly against the brick of the old bank building. Batman brought the Roost down the alley on a speed run and fired discs at the device, causing it to explode in their grasp. Not every one of The Joker's ideas was a gem.

He spun the Roost about, sweeping over the crowd again. Someone fired shots. Batman couldn't tell where they had come from, but he didn't want things to escalate. Spotting the gunman in the crowd, he put the Roost back on autopilot and made a running slide to the edge of the ebon surface. Grasping a handhold, he leaned over the edge and fired a cable at the shooter. No sooner had it lashed around the man than Batman had connected the other side to the Roost's hull.

The result was the gunman being yanked from the crowd—and his falling weapon—as Batman got the platform back under way. He deposited the shooter roughly in a public swimming pool across the way.

The scanner went off again. *"Last Laughs have breached Burnside National Bank!"*

Batman turned the aerial barge hard around and headed north. There weren't many Last Laughs at each site, and this clearly wasn't the cream of the crop he was fighting. He wondered where the A-team was, if they had one. And The Joker, real or not, had not appeared.

Needle in a haystack, Batman thought. *Lots more banks to go.*

Or maybe it was all a feint, and Alfred was right. He often was.

DURING HIS YEARS DEVELOPING CHEMICAL, biological, and psychological weapons for the Cold War, Hugo Strange had visited Armsgard several times. It was a place to hide Secrets Man Was Not Meant To Know: the wild successes as well as the terrible mistakes. Much of what Strange had developed was entombed here, including everything associated with Hegemon; some of it he had walked into the storage chambers himself. He'd just never expected then to be fired, to never see his work again.

After years on the outside, he was rectifying the situation. He knew from his tenure with the criminal that The Joker—brilliant and mad—believed in excess, particularly when it came to strength. To that end, he had created far more weapons using the vile stores at Axis Chemicals than he had used. There had just been no chance of getting and deploying them. Karlo had changed all of that, supplying not just the manpower and the weapons, but the distraction and the way into Armsgard.

With the facility itself likely to be decommissioned when the last of its disposal work was done, Strange had always doubted that the government would have paid to update the doors and locks. He was right. The way in was barred by an enormous metal door.

"Acid," he ordered.

Two of the three masked Last Laughs with him stepped forward with oversized squirt guns. Part of the genius of The Joker was in his ability to make cheap and commonplace things into weapons; the otherwise simple plastic of children's toys was highly resistant to acid, making it suitable for storage and delivery devices. Strange stood back as the minions blasted away at the locking mechanism.

The third masked clown-face sidled up to him. "You've been here before," Karlo said, clearly sounding rattled. "I thought you were pretending to be this Hugo Strange guy—like me with the general. But you're really him, aren't you?"

"I've been known by many names. And I was here often enough to know that your cure is here, too. The formulae are here. So are the products."

Gunshots rang out from beyond the bunker. "This is crazy. Those soldiers out there are shooting!"

"They are bottled up in another building while we do our work. They created the poison that harmed you and many more—and they are even now trying to prevent you from finding an antidote." Strange glared at him. "You were willing to fight them earlier to get me what I want."

"Yeah, but—"

Strange saw Karlo sag. The actor's resolve came and went with his ire. *Weak.*

Something else strong had now been made weak. A sizzling hole burned through the locking mechanism; the enormous door gave way, creaking open.

Strange pushed through, leading his companions inside. An anteroom lay beyond, with forklifts, trailers, and carts parked along the sides. Equipment used, daily, to deliver his precious potions to the incinerator tower. He could make use of them.

But first, there was El Dorado. That's what his colleagues had called it: a long concrete-lined hallway with cells on either side. Each was behind a vacuum-sealed door with an electronic lock.

"It'll take all day to open all those," said one of the acid-sprayers.

"Yeah, and I'm nearly out," said his companion.

"Don't worry." Strange stepped toward a control panel at the front of the hallway and found an electronic interface. It had been, in its day, an advanced security reader; it required a palm print and then a specific code to open a single door. He gestured to Karlo. "You're up."

Karlo snapped out of his silent ponderings and reached for something in his pocket. It was part of The Joker's personal weaponry, but it would be of use here: the megavolt joy buzzer. With it attached to his hand and a hidden line going to the battery pack under his uniform, he pressed against the palm reader.

Enormous current surged into the device, melting the glass panel and then frying the electronics within. At once, every door in the hallway snapped open. Karlo drew back his hand and ripped the buzzer off his hand, happy to be out of contact with it.

Strange walked down the hall and surveyed what was within the doors. Vats of green, yellow, and orange ichor, each one the product of years of his and others' research. But mostly his—including Hegemon. He had been in time. They had not destroyed it yet.

He opened his empty satchel, ready to receive the documents of years past. "Bring in the others. Prepare the convoy!"

———

SOME IDEAS WORKED BETTER than others. The Roost was previously untried, and while it functioned properly, Batman had discovered some unanticipated problems over the hours Gotham City's financial institutions were under siege.

It had efficiently delivered him to eleven different attempted bank invasions, including eight where he had leapt from the hovercraft to engage in hand-to-hand combat. He'd gotten his aerial "sea legs" quickly, nimbly walking the upper hull to wherever he needed to go. And the fearsome sight and angry sound of the thing had dispersed not just the civilians, but sometimes the armed Last Laughs he confronted. He hadn't been forced to even deploy the machine guns encased in its hull, much less use them.

But at the same time, the Roost in action had encountered issues he hadn't considered. Batman had designed several recessed handholds near the edges of the hull—above and below—so he could operate while standing on the platform or hanging beneath it while it was on autopilot. Those had proven to be a two-way street. In Elmwood Heights, he'd hovered over a street clogged with cars and people to deal with Last Laughs on a fire escape outside John Booth's old bank, Fourth Chemical. But on returning, he'd found that several rioters had scaled the tops of cars and grabbed the handholds beneath the platform. Batman realized when he lifted higher into the air that his Roost had hanging bats of its own.

He expected many of the rioters were really just people looking for the free money promised to them on television—unlike the gunman earlier, little danger to anything but property. Batman eased the Roost out away from the bank he'd just saved and the crowd below, and headed for a small park. Putting the craft into a gradual spin, he watched as one stowaway after another tumbled down onto the grass.

As his dislodged but uninjured passengers swore at him from below, he guided the Roost away and looked again at his digital display. The Last Laughs had used relatively small numbers at each location he'd visited, relying upon The Joker's invitation to the people to serve as a force multiplier. No masked criminals at all had struck the financial district, leaving it entirely to the masses. He'd seen no pattern at all to where they'd actually struck—other than that the disparate locations seemed optimized to keep him busy and on the move.

"Fifty-Fifth and Melrose!"

Batman paused as he recalled the neighborhood. "There's no bank there," he mumbled.

He checked his vehicle's gauges. The flying platform had enough fuel for one more stop before he needed to get it back to its storage truck. But if one location wasn't like the others, that was worth checking out. Batman turned the Roost about and headed southeast. There was still work to do.

CHAPTER 42

THE CONVOY WAS ON the move. The Last Laughs had arrived together in the back of the surplus military transport that Strange had obtained a month ago; now they were all departing individually into the night, driving jeeps with trailers carrying the barrels and equipment he required.

A full satchel over his shoulder, Strange stood beneath a light post and watched the vehicles departing the military base through the unattended front gates. No one would stop a military convoy moving after dark during what the radio had called "The Joker's Bank Panic." And nobody on the grounds of the Armsgard depot attempted to stop them.

And Karlo had apparently figured out why. He emerged from the Quonset hut that the soldiers and agents had retreated to and stumbled about in a daze. Then he saw where Strange was and stormed over.

As Auslander, Strange had lectured that a smile was the simplest and most universal emotional visual cue. When Karlo yanked off his clown mask, Strange saw in the lamplight a face that could well have made the same case for anger. Distorted and misshapen, Karlo's face spoke fury in every sharp line.

Karlo's words were equally sharp. *"You killed them!"*

Strange looked blankly at him. "Killed whom?"

"The soldiers. The agents. They're dead!" Karlo shoved at Strange, knocking the older man backward. "Somebody threw a grenade in there!"

"Ah," the doctor said, recovering glasses knocked sideways. He took out a handkerchief and polished them. "It was actually Lawrence—and it was one of The Joker's fragmentary satchel charges from the truck you liberated. I believe he had labeled it a 'whoopee cushion.'"

"I didn't know you were going to do *that*! You're a doctor, for God's sake. Or you're supposed to be!"

"We've only done what was necessary."

"Killing people? Stealing from the government?"

"They stole from me. And you've killed too, or have you forgotten? Tolliver Kingston!"

Karlo took a step back as if struck. "I didn't mean to do that!"

Strange glanced over. The last vehicle had left the compound. It was time to put a stop to this. He opened his satchel. "Would you like to see one of the things I recovered?"

Karlo stared blankly at him as he pulled a spray can out of the bag. "What?"

Strange shook it up as if to spray it in the air above him—only to turn the nozzle toward Karlo. He blasted him with an icy gas that glowed blue under the light. Karlo screamed, clutching his face. Bathed in approaching headlights, Strange continued spraying until the can emptied. Karlo hit his knees and fell to the ground.

Lawrence pulled up with the transport and got out. He'd seen what had happened. "Is he dead?"

"Knockout gas. He required a triple dose."

"Sure that wouldn't kill him?"

"I should know. I invented it. But I expect he appreciates your concern. Place him in the truck." He looked down on the actor's limp body. "I'm not finished with him yet."

———

By the time Batman and the Roost reached Fifty-Fifth and Melrose, he thought he'd misunderstood the radio call. There was no crowd at the corner, and of course, no bank. And certainly no sign of the Last Laughs.

He put the Roost down on a warehouse rooftop and leapt out. Lightning was on the horizon and the winds were up; the brief respite from the cycle of rough weather looked about to end. A police car drove up, sirens blazing, and parked beside the building he was on. He walked to the edge and looked down.

One of two figures in shadow below yelled out. "There's one!" A second later, a shotgun blast rang out. The shot was just in the air, missing him—but Batman took no chances, leaping from the rooftop and landing with a flourish of his cape beside the gunman.

"Wait!" yelled a woman—the person who had not fired. "It's Batman!"

Batman already had his hand on the shotgun, ready to take it away—and paused when he realized he was looking at an older male in uniform: a security guard. The person who had spoken was a policewoman. "Sorry," Batman said, releasing the weapon.

Once over the shock, the security guard apologized. "I thought you were one of them!"

"Who?"

"Those clown people." The security guard explained that he worked at the car dealership across the street but had seen people breaking into the warehouse. "They made off with all kinds of stuff. Truckloads!"

Batman saw that the garage door of the warehouse had been smashed in. A sign identified the business: BUG ME NOT.

"What is that?" Batman asked.

"Pest control supplies," the old man responded.

Batman looked across at the car lot. There were luxury sports cars behind the rail fence and in the showroom, all untouched. It made no sense. "They hit this place—but not the dealership?"

The police officer laughed. "I guess they got the wrong address. Or maybe they've got a bat problem!"

If they don't, they will. Batman clenched his jaw and headed back to the Roost.

KARLO HADN'T SLEPT MUCH since emerging from his coma. He had already been asleep for too long, and he'd been forced to sleep sitting up. One night waking up with a face visibly flattened by his pillow was enough.

Strange—or Doctor Auslander, or whoever he was—had dosed him with something that had laid him out completely. No dreams, this time, no Shakespeare. Not even a sonnet. And when he came to, it was in a place he recognized even in the dark.

I'm in the Capra.

He was sitting third aisle, orchestra section, in a middle seat—one of the best seats in the house. He was also bound tightly with chains. He strained against them, to no avail. He was too groggy, the chains too strong.

A spotlight appeared. The curtains opened slightly, and Strange looked out. "Ah, you're awake."

Karlo looked about. None of the Last Laughs, who'd used the theatre as their home base and play place, were around. "Where is everybody?"

"Gone to secondary lodgings," Strange said, emerging onto the stage. "We couldn't bring all that material we took back to the Capra, of course." He chuckled. "This area has a parking problem. Maybe Max Shreck was right to want a garage!"

Reminded of that past meeting, Karlo resumed struggling. "I'm not dressing up as The Joker again. We're done!"

"I only need you to do it once more—and there is another small role first. You'll be in a television studio. You'll like it."

"Forget it!"

Strange looked down on him—and adjusted his glasses. "I wouldn't speak so abruptly. You need me. I will still cure you—and the world. But you must accept that there are enemies to progress—"

"And my enemies are your enemies," Karlo parroted in Strange's voice. His facial muscles changed with his words. He couldn't see himself, but he imagined it was a pretty good Hugo Strange. "I told you, I've had enough."

Strange stared down at his image on Karlo's face and shook his head. "Still remarkable." Then he turned back and looked inside the curtain. "Are you ready, at last?"

As if in response, the curtains opened. As they mechanically drew back, they revealed two colossal speakers stage left and right.

Karlo gawked—and his face changed shape again. The speakers were very Lawrence, for sure, but in the Capra they were an abomination. "It's an opera hall. What does it need with a sound system?"

"You'll see—or rather, hear." Strange looked on them with admiration. "These weren't stolen, by the way. A gift from Max Shreck, for your earlier job well done."

Karlo sat and steamed. Lawrence emerged from behind one of the speakers and gave Strange a thumbs-up. The strongman exited offstage—and seconds later, a crackle said that the speakers had been turned on.

"I often practice my speaking to a recording that has sound and laughter," Strange said. "Do you thespians do the same?"

"No," Karlo responded. Before his transformation, the only applause he ever received was in his own mind. But now applause spilled from the great speakers. First lightly—and then in waves.

Next came laughter. Titters, chuckles, and genuine belly laughs, booming across the hall.

"What do you think?" Strange asked.

"I think you missed a class somewhere. We don't use laugh tracks in live theatre." He strained to look behind him. "And why would these sounds be coming from the stage?"

"For your benefit. I invite you to listen. I have work to do." And with that, Hugo Strange walked backstage to rapturous applause.

Karlo could do nothing but sit and listen to it, while wondering what kind of person he'd gotten mixed up with. *And people thought The Joker was a maniac!*

THE SIEGE WAS OVER, but Batman's night was not.

He had gotten the Roost back to the warehouse just in time. The approaching storm was creating dangerous and sudden downdrafts, and it was nearly out of fuel. It had taken more than an hour to button it up, during which the skies finally let loose. Batman's mood was just as dark. The vehicle was an interesting idea, and it had been useful—but it seemed impractical on balance. Sometime after travel in and out of the city was restored, a truck would be by to haul the container someplace where he could securely get it to the Batcave.

Beaten and exhausted, he had planned to shed his costume and pick up a car from one of his office buildings to take home. But before powering the Roost down entirely, he decided to check the police scanner one more time.

Gordon was on, sounding more beleaguered. And not a little frantic—which was odd, considering that the Last Laughs he'd fought had either been captured or fled, ending the bank attacks.

Batman broke in and identified himself. "What's happened, Commissioner?"

"Something's happened at Armsgard," Gordon said. *"Something bad. Very bad."* He paused. *"The Army won't tell us what."*

Batman sagged. So that was what the night was all about. Alfred was right.

"And Madge MacReedy wants you to drop by," Gordon added as an afterthought. *"But I know what I'd check into first."*

Batman knew, too. He just wondered how he would find the energy to do it.

TUESDAY, 4:57 P.M.

EUREKA!

CHAPTER 43

R AIN HAD POURED ALL DAY after the depot attack, but for Strange, all was beautiful. He had gone immediately to his private lab when he reentered Gotham General that morning, and it had been the most fruitful workday in his entire career. Equipped with his old notes and the samples from Armsgard, he had seen the roadblocks of a dozen years fall before him. He understood now what had happened in Karlo's unique case—and how to alter Hegemon in order to make his achievement complete.

Administrator Takagi had left a half dozen messages for "Doctor Auslander," and Strange's receptionist had nearly pulled out her hair by its different-colored roots dealing with his schedule. But the understanding had always been that he needed time for his public engagements, fundraising, and research. Now centrifuges were whirring in his private lab. The great irony of Gotham General's Smylex Ward would be that it would be the source of bringing his work to completion.

And all done with Bruce Wayne's money.

After the better part of the day, he drove back through the sloshing streets to the Capra. Newly added to the stage inside was a large screen. A new movie projector sat out in the middle of the house. The applause tape was still running on its endless loop, and Karlo was still sitting there. Placid, but awake—and listening. Strange walked to the center of the stage, between the booming speakers. "Good evening, Karlo."

His mouth sounding dry, Karlo responded. "Good evening."

Strange waited for a break in the sound effects. "Applause, laughter—these are the most infectious of sounds. They are aural social cues that go to the preternatural animal brain. Even if people do not find what is before them humorous or worthy of praise, they will join in the noisemaking." His words grew disdainful. "So as to be alike. Hidden from harm, as part of a crowd."

Karlo nodded. "That's nice."

Strange made for the stairs at the side of the stage. "In my psychiatric work I have developed a series of sonic waveforms that trigger the brain's frequency-following response. They do not create a trance, strictly speaking, but they do calm the listeners—and make them receptive to suggestions that follow."

Karlo nodded. "That's nice."

"I encoded the recorded laughter and applause you heard with these effects. I theorized that it would work particularly well upon people prior to the exposure of Hegemon. A mental anesthetic, so to speak—preparing the psyche for the loss of identity in the transformation to come." Entering the seating area, he glanced back at the speakers. "I am immune to the sounds, of course. I developed them."

Karlo nodded. "That's nice."

"You were exposed to Variant Thirty-Five and not Hegemon, and your exposure was much earlier—but the audio does seem to have pacified you." Taking a key from his pocket, Strange thought back on Karlo's awakening in the hospital. "You did later report to me the belief that during your coma, the words of Shakespeare ran incessantly through your mind. By applying the aural hypnotic, I ensure that the dominant voice a listener hears is mine."

Karlo nodded. "That's—"

"Yes, yes." He found the padlock holding all of Karlo's chains together. He used the key and pulled the chains from the actor. "To your dressing room, please, until I call for you."

"Yes," Karlo said, standing. "Yes."

"And you have soiled yourself. You may take care of that, too."

Karlo looked down, noticing for the first time. "Thank you."

"I have two last jobs for you. The first is a new character, but one you should be able to capture easily."

"Yes," Karlo said. He looked back. "And the second?"

"A different kind of capture," Strange said. "We will catch Batman—and kill him."

Karlo climbed the steps and disappeared backstage. Lawrence entered—and looked to Strange, who signaled him to turn the great speakers off.

"The projector is working?"

"Yep."

Strange did some mental math against the count of Last Laughs who remained free after the previous night. "I'm heading to the secondary site. You're to tell them the team from last night is to assist me directly—on The Joker's orders. Understood?"

"Check."

"And then call your safe houses. I want sixty of your people to assemble here at four in the morning. They're night owls, they won't mind." Strange added, "And do not let Karlo leave his dressing room."

"Check."

Strange was reasonably sure Karlo would follow the directions he'd been given. The actor was weak-willed, just a bit more sophisticated than Lawrence—and they were both just above snails. But he wasn't sure exactly how someone with Karlo's condition would respond to what Strange had planned.

It would be interesting to find out, but that would need to be an experiment for another time. *So many new horizons to explore!*

VICKI WAITED.

Bruce had never come back to Wayne Manor the morning after The Joker's bank run. Neither had Batman, and while they were of course the same person, they arrived back at the house in such different ways that she had grown used to having to check both the front door and the ways up from the Batcave to see if he had returned. It was exhausting.

And it had been exhausting, back whenever she had stayed here before.

Vicki had a fine apartment in Gotham City, obtained quickly through one of the modeling agencies she frequently shot for; spacious and tasteful, it probably cost more a month than many of her new colleagues at the *Gotham Globe* made in a year. She had not abandoned it after Jack Napier fell from the cathedral, but it often felt like she had. She had never moved into Wayne Manor, but it was so far out of town that almost any trip there was already an overnighter—and her date kept leaving while she was there. Every visit became a vigil.

It didn't matter how many times he had told her she didn't have to wait or how confident she was in his ability to take care of himself. Vicki had found herself constitutionally unable to make her way back to Gotham City before knowing what had happened to him. Alfred had seemed to deal with it, somehow, displaying that steady demeanor he always had. But as she spent increasing numbers of breakfasts—and then lunches—with him, she began to see through even his cloak of calm. He had more information than she did about where he was, but even that was limited.

And when he came back alive, he was dead. And not just tired. Vicki had dated doctors, had known people married to firefighters and others who worked impossible hours. This was different. If being Batman was when Bruce Wayne was most alive, it also drained him of life. Even when he did not return bruised or bleeding, he was completely spent—and was rarely interested in talking about what he'd been out doing. On the rare occasions when he returned with energy, it was because he wasn't done being Batman. Some lead kept him from ever coming upstairs from the Batcave.

Around the tenth time she had gone downstairs to find him, it was to tell him she was leaving the country. She'd had a dangerous career, too. It was better to return to that than be a helpless spectator for someone else's.

And now I'm back—and he's not. She looked again at the grandfather clock, the only noise she'd heard all day besides the rain pounding against the windows. Alfred had been gone most of the day as well. If Batman was supposed to protect her from The Joker, this was a damned funny way of—

A chime sounded. In spite of her reservations, Vicki hastened to the entry hallway. Outside, headlights in the rain heralded the arrival of the Rolls. Alfred discharged Bruce out front, before pulling around.

Vicki opened the door. Bruce staggered in, sopping wet—and very nearly fell into her arms. "Are you hurt?" she asked.

He looked at her in a daze. "Mom?"

"You're drenched. Why didn't Alfred bring you in through the garage?"

"I told him. Stairs hurt."

She supported him through the foyer into a parlor, where he collapsed in a chair. She swore she was not going to help him take off his shoes, but he seemed unaware of what he had on, anyway.

"Got to get the costume off," he muttered.

"It's already off."

"Oh, yeah. I changed in the limo." He squinted at her. "That's not easy to do."

Vicki thought if he had tried to operate as Batman any further, his five-o-clock shadow would have given him away. "You've been gone since Monday morning—since lunch with Alex."

"That sounds about right." He tried to move—and groaned.

Alfred entered from the garage. "I'll get the pain medicine."

Bruce shook his head. "Just a sandwich. And a pillow."

As he slumped in the chair, Vicki followed Alfred into the kitchen. "What happened?"

"His plan was to store the Roost and call for a cab to leave the city.

But Commissioner Gordon needed him somewhere else. So he traveled across town through the rain atop a military vehicle as Batman to cross town. He called for me to pick him up once he was finished."

"Finished with what?"

Alfred's grave look told her she'd better ask Bruce herself.

Vicki walked back out into the sitting room. "What did Gordon want?"

Bruce looked up at her, his face fraught. "There was a massacre. At Armsgard, a military depot."

"Military?"

"It's a chemical weapons storehouse and destruction facility. Stuff like Smylex."

Her eyes widened at the word. "Who did it?"

"We don't know. All the cameras were destroyed, and there were no survivors." Bruce rubbed his eyes. "But nobody saw The Joker anywhere last night, not at a single bank attack."

Vicki nodded—and, feeling as if struck, sat down in the chair across from him. "The Joker and Smylex. Not a good combination." She had a thought. "But wait. What about Hugo Strange?"

"I told Gordon that Strange had worked for the government—and that I thought he might be Auslander. He didn't know what to do with that. There's nothing connecting them besides the photos—"

"Which I brought here with me," Vicki said. "I guess you should have kept them."

Bruce shook his head. There wasn't anything to do about that now. "I even called Takagi, who confirmed that Auslander was in his lab all day—and his schedule said he had been the night before. But he wasn't taking visitors."

He explained that he had scoured Armsgard for clues with Gordon until the Army officials arrived. Gordon had fought to remain—these were homicides in his city—but Batman could not. He spent the rest of the afternoon and evening trying to follow the trail the thieves had taken, to no avail.

Alfred brought him a sandwich and a whole pot of tea. Then he produced from his jacket pocket a container of painkillers. "Just in case."

Bleary-eyed, Bruce reached for the plate before nearly knocking it off the table. "Wait. I nearly forgot," he said. "The coroner. I was going to follow up—"

"You're not going anywhere," Vicki said, grabbing the plate. She handed him his food. "You're no good to Gotham City dead. Or us, either."

I can't believe this is happening again, she thought. *And I can't believe I'm doing this again.*

CHAPTER 44

THEY HAD ALL LAUGHED at him.

The Last Laughs were the dregs of society, Strange knew. Uneducated, unambitious losers willing to follow anyone with a yen for destruction. People always tore down things they didn't understand, and the dolts Lawrence had rounded up didn't understand anything.

The sixty seated in the Capra hadn't understood why Lawrence had instructed them to go to the theatre before dawn, and they hadn't comprehended why they were being forced to watch "some egghead professor," as the one aptly named Brickhouse had called Strange, speechifying to them on the big screen. They had laughed at his image, poked fun, thrown things at the screen. Strange had seen it all through the peephole behind the stage—and had seethed. It wasn't until Lawrence had brought Karlo out dressed as The Joker that they'd taken their seats.

"Just watch the little ferret-face and shut up," he'd said. "You might learn something."

Karlo had retired backstage after that, as instructed. The video Strange had recorded at the university resumed, its volume turned up to shut out the thunder outside. As the tape continued, the Last Laughs began to calm down. It was the pacifying effect of the sonic waveform in the applause, laughter, and other sound effects. By the time the recording got to the part Strange had added that evening, they were captivated—and captive.

"—*you are probably wondering why you are hearing this. Here, now, and from me. It is a very simple matter.*" The Strange onscreen launched into the new material. "*Those of you watching this are just like the people who belittled me all my life. You accept me now, because of my title, my financial connections—but history will know what I now know.*"

Backstage, Strange mouthed the next words even as he put on his gas mask. "*I have perfected Hegemon, my greatest invention. I told the truth: celebrity does not interest me. But those who stole from me, ridiculed me, belittled me? They will learn my name. And nothing after that.*"

Gas mask firmly in place, Strange snapped the switch on a power strip.

"*My quest is at an end. As are your lives as human beings.*"

Next to the speakers onstage, fog machines spun up. But instead of combining water with glycerin or some other component to generate a low-lying cloud, the devices churned out something else: Hegemon, laced with Smylex Variant Thirty-Five and aimed toward the audience.

The screams were expected, as were the convulsions. He had seen some of it in his prior practical testing for Hegemon—both for the current government and previously for foreign ones. Years ago, back before everything had been banned and he had been fired. The Last Laughs stood. Wrenching off their clown masks, they howled, racked with immeasurable pain. The subjects literally ripped their hair out in agony.

It proceeded as he expected. The Joker's Smylex had caused immediate tightening of the facial muscles; Hegemon did it to *all* muscles, causing skin to swell and crack. It was not a bloody ordeal. Rather, the human integumentary system responded by going almost reptilian, stepping down the evolutionary ladder to something scalier.

The howling stopped, leaving in the theatre hall only the bomb-shelter echoes of thunder beyond.

Strange watched carefully. This was the moment when, in past trials, subjects died from the strain. Every one, without exception. But things were different this time. He'd made them different. Karlo's exposure had been through skin absorption of highly concentrated levels of Variant Thirty-Five. It had put him in his coma—a pupal state, Strange now believed—and transformed his tissues and provided him with strength and hardiness, even as his skin grew pliable.

Consumption in gaseous form produced changes that were more immediate, and dramatic. Karlo's system had taken months to adapt to its new condition. The Last Laughs—now the First Freaks—had collapsed into their chairs, exhausted from writhing. But their eyes, beneath bulging troglodytic brows, were wide open.

Strange looked down and scribbled notes as he watched. "Fascinating."

He stepped out onto the stage where, confident that the gas had dissipated, he removed his gas mask. "Stand," he commanded.

They did. Some slower than others—but eventually, all sixty were on their feet. Apart from their clothing, he could no longer tell who had been whom. Men and women, bulky and skinny—all were now of the same hairless, muscular body type. No one could gain mass from thin air, but they now existed in a state of constant tension, their bodies hardened. He'd imported the resilience from Variant Thirty-Five without the protean characteristics.

He already had one changeling. He didn't need more.

A simple battery of tests would follow, to make certain that the subjects would follow him and no others. They had heard his voice through the auditory waveform; in their suggestible state, they would imprint on him now. His hold on Karlo was considerably less absolute, but it had served so far and would probably get him through the last couple of things Strange needed from him. One of those would follow, later in the day.

If Karlo wanted a place in the world after that, he would have to apply again. *This day belongs to the Monster Men,* Strange thought. *And all the days after!*

———

BRUCE STAGGERED DOWNSTAIRS. He had slept alone, as he had all during Vicki's stay—but that was for the best in more ways than one. He had actually slept, although he figured the experience probably more resembled what astronauts might do on the way to Saturn someday. He would have been surprised to learn he had registered a pulse.

When he entered the den, the rain was still coming down outside, and Alfred had a fire going. Bruce saw Vicki before the TV set. "Noon news?"

"Evening. But it looks like you were busy this afternoon."

"I couldn't remember how to get the shower to work."

"That's not what I mean." She gestured to the set, where the newscaster was speaking in studio with Julie Madison, Hugo Strange—identified in the chyron as HUGH AUSLANDER—and a surprising additional guest.

Bruce Wayne.

"*—wanted to make the announcement myself,*" the Bruce on set said. "*The Smylex Ward Benefit Performance is back on.*"

Bruce sat down on the couch and put his hand at the side of his head. "Was I sleepwalking?"

"*The previous benefit was overshadowed by the breakdown of one of the actors, and that's a shame,*" TV Bruce said. "*It tainted a fine performance and hurt the charity.*"

"*The breakdown of Tolliver Kingston,*" the newscaster interjected. "*Who has not been seen since that night.*"

Julie Madison spoke. "*I forgive him, and I hope he gets the help he needs.*" She put her hand on TV Bruce's lovingly. "*But Bruce here had the wonderful idea of our putting on another benefit this Friday. And I'll be starring in it!*"

"I guess you're back together," Vicki quipped.

"It's news to me," Bruce said. He saw Alfred enter. "Have you seen this?"

"I've been watching in the kitchen," the butler said. "I was half afraid I had hallucinated bringing you back home last night."

"You and me both."

Julie went on to say that the company at the Imperial would be staging *Heartbreak House*, Shaw's next work after writing *Pygmalion*. It was the play the Imperial had canceled due to the Smylex crisis, so everyone knew the cast and the props were ready to go. *"I play the lead, Ellie Dunn. Geraldine Fitzgerald made her debut as her in the Mercury Theatre Production!"*

"Her *American* debut," Alfred said. Alfred knew everything.

Bruce figured it would be meaningful to all the viewers born in 1910—but Julie seemed delighted, and quite reconciled to him—or, at least, the him that was onscreen. The camera turned to Strange, who appeared even more elated by the news they were reporting.

"I feel the important nature of the benefit has been lost after the previous unfortunate incident," he said. *"I intend to make a presentation beforehand this time. Demonstrate the vital work of the Smylex Ward—and introduce some of our patients."*

The newscaster agreed that it was a nice idea, but he had concerns. *"After the events earlier this week, are you at all concerned that The Joker will strike?"*

"Mayor Borg and District Attorney Dent have both today endorsed the performance," TV Bruce said.

"But after the events coming to light out of Armsgard—"

"A terrible tragedy," Strange interjected. *"But this town will not cower in fear."*

As the telecast moved on to talk about tickets and scheduling, Vicki stared at the screen. *"Heartbreak House.* I hope that play title isn't on the nose."

Alfred explained. "The lead's father is a mad inventor trying to create a weapon of mass destruction. No one in the play is really who they pretend to be."

"On the nose is right," Bruce said. "Maybe Strange can play the dad."

She looked to Bruce. "Well, one thing's for sure. That definitely wasn't you."

"You think?" Bruce asked.

"You'd never wear a tie like that. That jacket wasn't even pressed."

Bruce stewed. He'd been impersonated—but he wasn't the only person that had happened to lately. He'd seen someone pretending to be Strange—or Auslander—at the hospital. And he still wasn't sure about The Joker one way or another.

Alfred handed him a cup of coffee and the afternoon edition. As the broadcast had indicated, news of the deaths of service members at Armsgard had gotten out. The FBI and other government agencies had locked down the site. But nobody had any leads, and the copy made clear that Batman had been consulted—and had come up empty-handed.

He looked up at the television, wondering what more could happen. The broadcast had moved on to the weather, and the rainiest cycle Gotham City had seen all year. The forecast for Julie's play later in the week was good, but the downpours of the past week were taxing the city's drainage system, and municipal teams were moving out to see what they could do.

Always something going on under the ground, Bruce thought.

He looked up, memory jarred. "The coroner. I was going to check in on something."

Seeing him get up from the couch, Vicki stared at him. "You're leaving?"

"I'll eat first. But I've got—"

"Right, right—got to go to work. Aren't you the least bit concerned about someone on TV pretending to be you, alongside what may be a dangerous scientist?"

"Of course I am." Bruce gestured. "I don't want people to think I dress like that."

CHAPTER 45

HOURS AFTER THE FALSE Bruce Wayne spoke on television, The Joker spoke on Gotham City's airwaves again. Batman had just finished getting the information he sought from the coroner when the airwaves were hijacked, just long enough for a brief message. He had watched it in the dark on the Batmobile's dashboard monitor.

"Twice now I've tried to introduce you folks to the wonders of Smylex," The Joker declared. *"And twice you've rejected me. You can lead a horse to water, but you can't make him drink. So how about I shoot the horse and throw him in the water—and make you drink!"* He grinned. *"If you don't get it, you will soon—and you'll be smiling along with me!"*

The message had sent the city into spasms once again, as people asked the obvious questions. Was the water supply safe? Did Smylex work in water? Did it have something to do with the stuff that was stolen from Armsgard?

Batman had checked on the water supply before returning to Wayne Manor the next morning, but it had done nothing to alleviate his concerns. When he went out in the rain on the night after that, it was to try a new theory. He was looking at the threat from the wrong end. Smylex worked as a solid, but also as a gas. What if the idea was to send it *up* into neighborhoods, through storm drains and people's sinks?

Gotham City's infrastructure was a mad jangle of the old and the new. More modern areas had a separate sewer system that routed untreated stormwater to natural bodies by gravity. But many neighborhoods used an older, combined system, where everything was connected. As he'd seen on the news the night before, pump and tanker trucks were out, drawing some stormwater back into surface retention pools so it didn't overwhelm the wastewater treatment plants downstream.

And one of those trucks had just been reported missing.

He took the Batmobile on a tour of impromptu pumping sites—wherever there was a lagoon near the system. He'd seen nothing out of the ordinary until he saw a truck being backed up to an intake basin—and a man with an umbrella standing alongside it, guiding workers to bring a great hose into position.

The Joker!

Batman gunned the Batmobile down the street. The workers—clown-masked, he now saw—dropped the hose and went for their weapons. He thought about toggling his machine guns, but a lot of people lived in this neighborhood, and he didn't know yet what was inside the tanker. He instead fired discs that rolled crazily up the road ahead of the car. Flash-bangs, they detonated behind the tanker, sending Last Laughs stumbling away in all directions.

The car screeched to a halt and the cupola opened. He fired a bolo, which caught The Joker mid-run as he tried to flee. Batman was on the wet pavement in an instant, being set upon by the few hoodlums who'd regained their footing. He belted one and kicked another. The Joker was bound, but still running ahead.

The tanker's motor hadn't stopped. Someone put it into reverse, attempting to back over both Batman and the people he was struggling with. Batman rolled just in time, ensuring the tires barely missed him—but there was a new problem. It had backed over his cape—and stopped. With an uninjured Last Laugh trying to wrestle with him, he slapped the control disengaging the cape. Freed, he got enough range of motion to jab his enemy repeatedly in his cockeyed clown-masked face.

He scrambled out from beneath. The cape was pinned, but there was no time to free it. Another Last Laugh was heading for the open Batmobile. Batman couldn't wait. He grabbed the handheld communicator from his Utility Belt and activated the car's shields—after which he ordered "decommission cape." The electrical system inside the cape went into overload, frying itself beneath the tire so no one could plumb its secrets.

The sacrifice was necessary. The Joker had escaped the bolo; Batman spied the cable on the ground, sizzling with acid. Under the glow of a streetlight, he saw the umbrella discarded next to an open grating. His enemy had gone downstairs. Before the Last Laughs could charge him, he threw a smoke pellet into their midst. Then he looked into the hole and leapt inside.

He landed with a splash. Batman knew the drains in this area could accommodate standing movement; children had been known to play in them, and not a few spelunking college students. He triggered his light and saw the ankle-deep current running up what he knew to be a line parallel with the street. He worked his way forward, the only way to go. As he did, he heard The Joker's crazed laughter.

If it was a trap, Batman would be ready. Deciding the quarters were too close for a Batarang, he selected a launcher that fired a stun charge. As long as he didn't fire it below the water level anywhere, it wouldn't come back to bite him. He headed down one tunnel, made a turn, and went down another.

He rounded a corner and entered a wide area, ringed by waterfalls. Days of rain, spilling down from gratings above. There was a viaduct up there, he calculated; drainage was miserable. The water was knee-deep in the tunnel and flowing west, heading for the Gotham River.

The maniacal laughter filled the chamber—and stopped as Batman flashed his light from alcove to alcove. There, off to the side, he looked into the face of his old enemy—and a new one. Hugo Strange was dressed uncommonly well for a man in a sewer. He wore a bowler hat and carried a lantern. His other hand held a pistol. Beside him, The Joker was halfway up the rungs of a ladder leading up and out.

He stopped moving when Batman spoke. "Strange place for a house call," he said. "Doctor Hugh Auslander. Or should I say Professor Hugo Strange?"

Strange seemed indifferent. "Your choice."

"Let's go with professor." Batman didn't think too much of him as a man of medicine. "What's your plan down here? You're not poisoning anything but the fish."

"There are many ways to introduce terror into a city from below."

I'm sure. Maybe it was an attempt against the treatment plant—or the plan was to pipe something up through the storm drains all over town. It didn't matter now. They were trapped. Batman gestured to the figure on the ladder. "Who's your friend?"

Strange lifted his lantern—and tugged at his companion's vest. "Turn and have a look at him."

Batman held his weapon in place and watched carefully as the man he'd chased into the sewer stepped down from the ladder and faced him. Water dripped down from high above, pelting his purple hat.

Strange sneered. "The great Batman. Battered. Exhausted. Are you so tired you don't know your mortal enemy anymore?"

"He's not my mortal enemy. He's not The Joker."

"What makes you say that?"

"Because The Joker is dead."

Strange smirked. "Wishful thinking."

"You had me nearly convinced," Batman said. "I started to think The Joker had switched places with Davis atop the cathedral—or later, in the morgue. You even suggested to me who Davis was, knowing I'd spend time looking for him—and finding him."

"So?"

"Davis *was* painted to look like The Joker—and dressed in The Joker's clothes. But the fall came *after* he was dead from Smylex exposure." Batman held his weapon tightly as he announced what he'd learned. "I had the coroner take another look at his body. His clothes had traces of mud, but it wasn't from Castle Hill Cemetery. The combination of soil and chemicals exist in one place in Gotham City: down the slope behind Axis Chemicals."

Strange simply stared at him.

"The toxicology report came back. The Smylex concentration in Davis's blood was immense. There's no way he could have been alive up on that roof. He was already dead before he fell."

"That's lunacy."

"No. Davis hit concrete, not asphalt. I think The Joker took him from his office, poisoned him, and threw him off the top of Axis Chemicals." He pointed. "Lawrence would have known that. And he would have known where the body was, when you needed one to paint up and fool me."

Strange stared at Batman—and nodded. "You are sharp. But you don't have it all. You see, I was present when The Joker exposed Davis to Smylex. He was *Patient Zero!*"

At that, the lookalike stared at Strange. He hadn't said anything, not since Batman had appeared. His eyes looked blank, as if drugged.

"Napier blamed Davis for his condition," Strange said. "His henchmen dressed and painted the surgeon to resemble The Joker, but that humiliation was always just the prelude to his real role—as an unwilling test subject. Little did Napier know I would find a use for Davis's body months later. Lawrence and his lackeys were to switch the bodies—and leave the job unfinished, so you would find Davis—and a sea of doubts that would drown you." He grinned, impressed with himself. "It worked perfectly."

"Where's Jack Napier's body?" Batman asked.

"I have no idea," Strange replied. "All Lawrence said was it was someplace appropriate. The Last Laughs are deranged when it comes to The Joker. Perhaps it is in a place of honor—if their kind knows any."

Batman thought it was perverse to hear Strange talk of honor. "I imagined a world in which The Joker might have survived—and I made the mistake of telling you. So you gave me one. But I'm willing to bet that's one of your patients. Basil Karlo."

Now the lookalike stared at him.

"And you know this how?" Strange asked.

"I knew from his home he had been an actor who likely worked with Kingston. You distracted me from following up on him, but I finally did. From what I've learned from the other Goat's Town Players, there was no love lost between them." Batman pointed. "He escaped from the Smylex Ward—and then he impersonated you, with whatever facial skill he has. And because of that, you shielded him. Brought him into your plans."

Karlo took off his hat and shook it. Makeup started to stream down his face.

"He also impersonated Bruce Wayne on television yesterday," Batman said. He tilted his head. "You must have known Wayne would have told someone."

"Of course," Strange replied. "But he would never speak out to cancel the restaging of the benefit. Not a bleeding heart like him— and especially not if it would disappoint his woman." The professor smiled. "It was very easy to convince her to put on another show. Vanity is all."

"You won't have any part of it," Batman said.

Strange looked to his side. "Perhaps you should ask how Karlo here feels about it."

"Why?"

"Because that hospital ward—and my work—are the only things that will restore his features." He reached out and grabbed Karlo's chin, which reshaped itself vulgarly in his clutches. "I told you, vanity is all. Among the rich—and even the desperately poor, like Karlo. What is an actor, but someone who pretends to be rich and beautiful?"

Karlo said nothing. Water and paint dripped from his face, running in rivulets down the wrinkled canyons of his skin. He looked like an abused animal. "I don't—"

Strange released Karlo's chin and pushed him forward. "If you want your cure, defend me."

The actor hesitated. "I'm not—"

"You're a *killer*. Go!"

Batman held his ground. "Karlo, you don't have to do this."

"I do," Karlo said, stepping forward. "It can't all have been for nothing. Everything he's done—everything he's made me do. *Everything I've done.*"

"What have you done?" Batman asked.

"Didn't you hear?" Karlo gave a shout as he lunged forward. "*I'm a killer!*"

CHAPTER 46

KARLO GRABBED BATMAN'S LAUNCHER, causing him to pull the trigger. The stun dart embedded in Karlo's chest and activated.

He shook as electricity soared through him—and into the water at his feet. The charge wasn't strong enough to electrocute them both, but Batman saw the impact in Karlo's face. The flesh twisted and reshaped, going from an expressionless muddle to a screeching cartoon. Karlo's teeth glinted in the light as he wrested the weapon away from Batman. He ripped it to pieces—and then yanked the dart from his chest.

Batman took a step back, trying to get into a defensive stance. The slickness under his boots made that difficult. When Karlo launched himself at Batman, both went backward into the water. It was several feet deeper there, fed from runoff above.

Showered by cascades of rainwater, they struggled with each other in the slough. They tumbled. Sometimes Batman going underneath the water, then Karlo. As they tangled and spun, Batman occasionally emerged long enough to see Strange. He was still standing in the drier alcove, holding his pistol. But he didn't fire. He seemed to be enjoying watching the fray.

Batman versus Clayface. Audience: one.

Karlo had rage and a propensity to take a punch, but he wasn't a fighter. They sparred for half a minute before Batman began gaining the upper hand. He drove Karlo back, a foot at a time. At last, nearing a side wall of the chamber, he clasped his hands together and swung mightily. The blow sent Karlo reeling. He struck his head against the wall and collapsed into a spot where a current had formed. He sank beneath the water.

Batman waded in that direction, intending to check on him. As he did so, he looked back at Strange. The so-called doctor made no effort to try to help locate his ally. "He works for you," Batman said. "Don't you care?"

"Not anymore," Strange said. "I just wanted to see what he would do." He looked up to the ceiling of the chamber and shouted. "Lawrence!"

All around, Batman heard loud clangs from the overhead apertures. To his right, something dark fell from one of the chutes to the surface world. It landed with a colossal splash. And then something else did the same, off to his left.

It was a person that rose from the water. But not one like he—or anyone else—had ever seen. Batman looked into the face of something that seemed from a prehistoric age. Human, but not. Musclebound, and soaked—and furious.

Batman was horrified. "Strange, what have you done?"

"Your government dollars at work," Strange said. "Many governments, in fact. Hegemon and Smylex Thirty-Five—the perfect combination."

A third creature landed with a splash—and then a fourth, fifth, and sixth. There was never a plan for the storm drains. The trap, Batman realized, was not for Gotham City—but for *him*.

He turned. He was already running when Strange commanded the brutes, "Monster Men, kill Batman!"

Batman dashed forward—and looked up, startled. Another shaft, another Monster Man, being introduced into the concrete tunnel like white blood cells in a vein. And like leukocytes, they had a mindless devotion to one thing: attack. Elongated fingers grasped at him from behind and from the sides. He dodged them, knowing it was just luck that he didn't have on his cape. They'd have had him by that for sure.

He charged through ever-deeper waters, hoping for a breath, a heartbeat, a single moment when he could deploy something from his Utility Belt. The best he could do was another smoke pellet, which he hurled against the ceiling to break. But the tunnel was already dark, and it didn't seem to be stopping the Monster Men. There was only one direction to go, anyway. Forward—and down, ever downward, descending with the incline of the land.

He made it into another chamber, nearly pitch black. Wider, it had a raised concrete platform jutting out of it along one wall. *Probably something connected to the waste system,* Batman thought. Unable in the darkness to tell which waterlogged tunnel led out, he used the few footsteps' lead he'd gotten over the horde behind him to hoist himself up onto the shelf. Hearing water pouring in everywhere, he hoped there might be a shaft he could rappel himself up. He just needed to be able to see it. He hurled a phosphor grenade against the platform and shielded his eyes as it lit the chamber.

All around, he saw even more Monster Men rising from beneath the surface of chest-high water. They'd been here, lying underwater in wait. Dripping specters, they snarled and gnashed their teeth as they converged on the platform.

How many of these things does Strange have?

STRANGE HAD NOT SKIMPED on Monster Men for his trap. It had been the mistake The Joker had made in the cathedral, months earlier; not bringing enough forces to the fight. Strange hadn't spared anyone for this ambush.

And he wasn't done. Emerging from the storm drain by the maintenance ladder, he saw Lawrence waiting outside with a pickup truck full of Last Laughs in the pouring rain. Seeing what they were armed with, he climbed into the cab and ordered Lawrence to drive him up the street.

A few hundred yards uphill, they stopped near what he'd spied from afar: a railyard. There was an old-fashioned water stop there, a big cylindrical tank where Gotham City's steam trains used to take on water. And up and down the lightning-illuminated yard were tanker cars parked on the rails.

Strange and Lawrence exited the truck. The doctor directed Lawrence. "Get your acid sprayers to take down that big tank. And blow open those tanker cars."

He looked down the street. He had a good idea where it would all wind up.

"Some of these ain't water," Lawrence said.

"Doesn't matter."

BATMAN HAD ONLY INTENDED to pause on the raised surface within the chamber long enough to get his bearings. It had become a last stand.

There was no way forward and no way back—and no shaft above that Batman could launch himself up. Indeed, the apertures he could see were just admitting more Monster Men, like demons reentering Hell. Batman was nearly exhausted, as was his Utility Belt, but he couldn't think about that. He and the creatures were playing a child's King of the Hill game, only underground amid a flood. He had to win to live. He hadn't held back. He'd deployed the metal prongs on his boots and bars on his gauntlets; they were harsh medicine for normal opponents. Against the Monster Men, they were proving to be the only thing that got their attention—and kept them off his concrete island.

Every few seconds he had to spare brought another weapon into play. His precious Batarangs were having a field day of a field test, smacking four, five, six Monster Men in the head before returning. But no sooner would the targets disappear under the black water than others would surface. And eventually, his weapons didn't come back. He could hear the small explosions as the brutes snapped the Batarangs in half, triggering their internal charges.

Stun charges like he'd used against Karlo were completely useless against the Monster Men, and there wasn't enough current in anything he had to possibly electrify the water. A chemical bomb that created and ignited an oil slick caused many of his opponents screaming pain, but they simply went back underwater and returned again elsewhere.

There was no going back—and the only way out appeared to be an aperture far into the darkness, past a host of enemies. He could already see there was a metal grating there, filtering the water for whatever purpose. It looked solid, and something to shoot for, but his cables were for swinging. He had no idea how he would traverse—

Thunder sounded, and not from the shafts above. The entire chamber seemed to quake. Monster Men trying to scale his platform fell backward and away. Batman looked past them, back the way he'd come, and knew what was on the way. More water—far more than had been entering the system.

Strange believes in overkill!

Batman saw his only chance. He put his small portable rebreather unit in his mouth and bit down, holding it. Then he took the cable launcher he'd been saving for a shot at a ceiling shaft and pointed it at the grating far ahead. He fired.

A miss. The dart slapped against the grating and rebounded, flopping against the water. Batman quickly toggled the electric retractor. Given the rumbling, he'd only have one more chance, if that. And now the Monster Men were half on the platform, grabbing at him while he was distracted.

He fired again. The second shot was true, zinging through the bars of the grating and pulling taut. Batman grabbed hold of the launcher for dear life and held on as water exploded from the tunnel he'd entered from. He flew across the black surface, smacking against Monster Men like a fish being reeled in through a waterfall.

The wave caught him before the retractor could finish its job. It struck with the force of a dozen Monster Men, and carried that many or more toward him. His eye protectors deployed; he saw swirling shapes as he slammed into the far wall. Battered by the deluge, he felt bodies striking his, some grasping at him—at anything.

Yet he held the retractor. As thousands of gallons pummeled him, he spun with the line, trying to keep from getting tangled. For long seconds, he feared the grapple hadn't held, and that he was lost. There was no surface to reach, not anymore.

At the last hopeless instant, the retractor stopped, and he felt the grating against his face. He released the launcher and confronted the new problem: the crushing current, surging past him through the grating. Whether it opened in or out didn't matter. The only way was through, before he got pulverized against it.

That meant his final trick, the one he'd been saving for any gratings above: his portable handheld blowtorch. The waterproof tool ignited, blazing concentrated fire at the bars. And somehow, the Monster Men still came at him. Once, he diverted its fire toward them—but he realized quickly he couldn't do it again. He had to get through.

The grating gave way, rushing forward on a jet of water. Batman shimmied through and surged ahead—

—into nothingness. There was nothing beyond that he could see. Just a black tunnel of water, heading ever downward. His body struck a wall, knocking his mini oxygen supply loose. If any Monster Men had made it through the hole he'd made, it wouldn't matter.

His last thought, before consciousness left him, was a peculiar one: that bats could swim, but they tried to avoid doing so at all costs. He had taken so much wisdom from them. But apparently not enough.

THURSDAY, 11:19 P.M.
....

RAISE ARMY √
DO PUBLICITY √
KILL BATMAN √
RANSOM WORLD

ACT V

TIME TO PAY THE CHECK

CHAPTER 47

"**B**ATSY, I'VE GOT TO hand it to you," The Joker said. "You don't quit."

In his watery grave, Batman opened his eyes and looked up. It was Jack Napier, above the surface and speaking down. Fish swam by in the water between them.

Batman didn't know if it was another dream—or the delirium of drowning. But if The Joker didn't let death silence him, Batman wasn't about to let being underwater stop him from responding. It was only fair. Without gurgling, he asked, "Are you really him this time?"

"Accept no substitutes! They say imitation is the sincerest form of flattery, but I don't buy it." The Joker frowned. "Do you know Strange didn't pay me a single dollar in licensing? The nerve!"

One-dollar bills with The Joker's face floated by on the water above.

Batman asked what he really wanted to know. "You *did* die, didn't you?"

"I didn't see the end. But they say my autograph has gone up in value, so maybe so."

Batman remembered his other questions. "The guys you had in the cathedral—"

"I sent 'em up there earlier to watch from above, for the Feds."

The Joker put his gloved finger to his head. "Not just a pretty face, pal."

"And what you said to me about my parents? Being a kid when you killed them?"

"Since when do you take anything I say seriously?" The Joker put his hand over his mouth in a yawn. "Are you going to finish dying now? I hear Vicki Vale is back in town. I may be dead, but I'm not old!"

Batman felt someone pick him up—starting to carry him away. "I think they're taking me away," he said.

"Ask for a coffin with cable. The reception in mine is the pits." The Joker waved. "So long, Bat-Breath. See you in the funny papers . . ."

BATMAN OPENED HIS EYES to blinding sun.

He was prone, lying in the dingy sand. He could hear water coursing nearby. The sun, he could see, was just off the horizon. Morning had come, and with it, the end of the foul weather.

Batman pushed against the ground—and collapsed before even getting to his knees. He felt as if his body had been hit by a steam-roller. With extreme effort, he forced himself onto his side. He be-held a dark opening, behind, that led into a hillside. It was where the storm drains fed into the river. But he was improbably far from the stream to have washed up on the silt.

His eyes narrowing, he saw heavy footprints leading back to the great culvert and down into the water. They weren't from his boots. Someone had carried him out. He strained to look around. The long levee overlooking the nasty beach was tall; it might have explained why no one had discovered him yet.

When he turned his head back to look into the sun, he realized that someone already had. A figure loomed over him, cast in shadow—and holding a piece of scrap iron like a bludgeon. When he saw the person's face—or lack of one—he knew who it was.

"Karlo," Batman coughed.

"Yes." Karlo hovered, not moving.

Batman tried to get up, but his muscles failed him. Breathing hard, he gestured behind to the footprints. "You . . . saved me."

"I didn't," Karlo said. "I wouldn't." He waved the heavy implement. "I mean—Strange says I have to kill you."

"Who says . . . you have . . . to listen?"

"He did something to me. Played sounds."

"Sounds?"

"Applause. Laughter. But not just that." Karlo took one hand off the bar and let it hang in his hand. His other hand rubbed the side of his head, leaving an imprint. "He said there was something in the sounds. Encoded—to make me listen."

"Hypnotic."

Karlo shook his head vigorously, and his cheeks rocked back and forth like a pendulum. "I think it's worn off. But that doesn't matter." He threw the bar to the ground and grabbed his face, trying to still it. "He's promised me a cure."

Batman sat fully up. "He's lying. He just wants to use you."

"But if there's even a chance—!" Karlo looked to the massive tunnel, still gushing water. "I saw what he did to those other people. Those were Last Laughs once. If he has a way to turn them back, maybe he can help me, too!"

Batman didn't think Strange was in the antidote business—or that he would ever give up his leverage over anyone. "Even if there is a cure, he'll never give it to you."

Karlo's head hung. It was clearly an idea he'd contended with, if not accepted. "That's not all," he said. "He's—he's got something on me."

"Beyond playing The Joker?"

Karlo nodded. "Before. It's something I did."

Batman formed a guess about what it was. "Kingston."

Karlo's eyes widened. "What do you know?"

"I didn't get to tell you earlier. I said Davis's body had been buried in the grounds outside the ruins of Axis Chemicals." Batman gestured around him. "In the runoff area, just like this. But when I checked out the location tonight, I found another body near there. Fresher. Just dumped, not buried. A couple of weeks ago, at most."

The news clearly took Karlo's breath away. "Kingston."

"On the night of *Pygmalion*, you traded places with him, didn't you? You tried to ruin him."

Karlo raised his arms to the sky. "I didn't intend to ruin him—not at first. But I didn't kill him!" He appealed to Batman. "I locked him in a trunk. I admit it. I'm a jerk. Then he died. A heart attack, or stroke—"

"Or poison. His skin color and fingernails suggested it. And there was an injection site near his neck."

Karlo stared. "What?"

"The coroner is checking into it now. The tox report will say for sure." Batman reached up—and Karlo took his hand and helped him stand. "Would Strange have had a chance to find him while he was in the trunk? Asleep or unconscious?"

Karlo stammered. "Yes. Yes, he could have. He was in the dressing room while I stepped out." His eyes narrowed. "Can that even be possible?"

"He had his medical bag," Batman said. "For a scientist of Strange's skills, it's a definite possibility. Strange saw a chance to control you—by framing you for killing Kingston. And he took it."

"Why?"

"Because he needed The Joker. He'd been trying to get into Armsgard for years. To get back what he lost when they fired him."

"What? Smylex?"

"And whatever he's used on these monsters of his. Smylex was only the start. There were a hundred variants. The Joker brought him to Axis Chemicals to mass-produce Smylex, but I'm willing to bet he used that opportunity to put the others on the market."

"The market. The black market?"

"Maybe. Hence all the other kinds of cases in the Smylex Ward."

Karlo slapped his chest. "Like me!"

"You were *all* his science projects. Your case gave him what he needed."

Karlo stalked around the beach, clearly dumbstruck by the news. Batman saw the man's facial muscles twist their way through a sequence of exaggerated expressions. From shock, to confusion, to white-hot seething rage.

At last, he started moving faster. Hurrying down the coastline, to where a steep path led up to a bridge.

Batman tried to follow—but couldn't yet summon the energy. "Karlo, wait."

"He made me a freak. And then he made me think I killed Kingston!" Karlo looked back in anger. "I'm going to find him—and then I'm going to kill somebody for real this time!"

ATOP THE LEVEE a significant distance from where the storm drain flowed out into the estuary, Norman Pinkus peeked over his newspaper. He was barely able to make out the figure of Basil Karlo charging away from where he already knew Batman had been deposited. The newspaper gofer sat back against the park bench, pleased. It had all transpired as he'd hoped.

Norman knew that he himself was the *true* hero in Gotham City, figuring out the mysteries that stymied the *Gotham Globe*'s reporters and sending anonymous tips. Nothing was a mystery if you had ready access to the greatest information resources of the world and a mind for instantly knowing what things were relevant. He just wasn't capable—or willing—to intervene himself. That took nerve he didn't have—and, in the present case, muscles.

And when there was no one to act for him, he got creative.

It was clear to anyone in the world that The Joker's threat to the water supply was a trap for Batman—and it had been just as clear to Norman that the vigilante would respond to it. He still wasn't sure what to make of Batman; he was flashy and violent, all the things

Norman was not. But he was certainly preferable to what the mad professor had in mind for Gotham City. What Norman needed to ensure Batman's survival was someone with muscle who knew the sewers—and whose cooperation could be bought.

He had them both.

The *Globe*'s reporters had occasionally teased a local urban legend about a monstrous being in the sewers; Norman knew it was piffle. Anyone with a microfilm reader could figure out that the Red Triangle Circus had sought refuge down there, with members emerging now and again for crimes—or groceries, in the curious case of the Strongman who emerged weekly from the sewer in the alley behind Norman's impoverished apartment on McSparren Street.

It had taken all Norman's courage to approach him the night before—but the prize the gofer offered was well within even his meager price range.

A trenchcoated behemoth sat down with him on the bench. "Did Batman survive?" Norman asked.

"Yeah, I got him just in time," the Strongman said. "He was right where you guessed he'd be. You got the goods?"

Norman put down the newspaper, looked both ways, and handed over the big bag at his feet. "Five large anchovy pizzas from Perluigi's—with extra anchovies in the sauce. I'm afraid they're cold."

"My boss likes it cold." The Strongman peeked inside the bag before picking it up. "These are his favorite."

Norman understood. Perluigi's was way up on Theatre Row; he doubted they delivered to the sewers downtown.

The Strongman stood. "The Bat Guy was heavy. You some kind of helper for him?"

Norman thought about how to respond before settling on the truth. "I'm nobody."

"Just as well. I'd like to take him on sometime when he's not drowning." With that, he made his way down the levee.

Norman let out a deep breath. He'd never taken such a risk before, but it had paid off. He folded his newspaper and hurried to the nearest bus stop. It wouldn't do to be late for work.

As he waited for the bus, he toyed with the idea of letting Batman know about his assistance somehow. A method came to mind, but he doubted the vigilante would get it. After all, *Batman* wasn't Gotham City's greatest detective. That job was taken.

I'm a legend in my own time, Norman Pinkus thought as the bus arrived. *A shame nobody knows who I am!*

CHAPTER 48

THE BATMOBILE WAS GONE.

Batman had left it shielded the night before—but he had also parked it in the presence of the Last Laughs. He'd traveled far underground since then, and the signal from his remote control wasn't able to reach the car. By the time he made his way on foot back to the site of the battle, he found little trace of the earlier confrontation. He could tell from the marks on the wet pavement that someone had hoisted the car, shields and all, onto a flatbed to haul away.

Worse, he found he wasn't able to raise Alfred on his waterlogged communicator. That had put him in an uncomfortable position. He didn't feel up to leaping onto passing vehicles to hitch surreptitious rides, and while he'd been able to reach the site of the car without drawing curious eyes, a pedestrian Batman at morning rush hour was a sight he didn't want anyone to see.

Fortunately, a payphone had saved him from one of the more ignominious moments in his short career. When Alfred and the limo arrived behind an abandoned storage facility to meet him, he found that Vicki was in the back seat—having selected a change of clothes for him.

"This feels familiar," she said, standing guard outside as he changed in the back.

"I've absolutely got to start stationing more rides in town," he replied, shimmying into slacks. "And more clothes."

"The Batmobile is in a warehouse in East Hollis," Alfred said from the front seat. "The shields have not been opened."

"That settles that," Bruce said. "No impound lot there. That's where the Last Laughs are."

"We can go there, Master Bruce. You can have the car drive itself right out."

Buttoning up, Bruce thought it over. "Maybe not. Strange thinks I'm dead. There's nothing they can do to the car right now."

He got out of the car to put on his jacket. Vicki started to help him—only to take a step back. She crinkled her nose. "You need a shower."

"Don't mention water." He spoke so Alfred could hear through his open window. "The Joker was Karlo—one of the patients from the Smylex Ward—working for Strange."

"I knew it," she said. "I knew it wasn't him."

"I think Karlo's quits with Strange." He looked to her. "You're no longer in danger from The Joker. You never were."

"So what?"

Her response startled him. "So you can go. Back to whatever it was you were doing."

"Wow," she said.

"Wow, what?"

She walked around to the back of the car.

Bruce asked Alfred to excuse him and went around to follow. Out of the butler's earshot, he asked again. "Wow, what?"

"You can solve every mystery in the world—but you still don't get me." She pointed at him. "I didn't just come back so I could bask in your protection. You were afraid the worst person in your life had risen from the dead. I wasn't going to let you go through that alone." She paused. "Not because we're a couple, or because we were. But we shared that trauma. I wasn't going to let you go through it again alone."

Bruce considered her words. "Yeah. But now—"

"It's still not done. And until it is, I'm not going anywhere. Except maybe to the theatre."

Bruce realized what she meant. "The benefit."

Vicki gestured to the car. "You'd better get in and hear this."

Once they were inside, Alfred started driving and informed Bruce about the messages that Julie Madison had been leaving. "She's delighted that you and Strange came to her with the idea of restaging the benefit Saturday night."

Vicki shook her head. "Woman's known you half her life and couldn't tell that wasn't you."

"Be that as it may," Alfred said, "she is looking forward to seeing him."

"Knox has been calling, too," Vicki said. "He didn't know what to make of you suddenly appearing with Strange on TV."

"Strange definitely has some kind of reason for wanting the benefit to be restaged," Bruce said. "I have a feeling I know what it is."

"Can't you call the performance off?" Alfred asked.

"He knows I can't. But I know what to do. Thing is, it'll require help. Both inside and outside the Imperial."

"Then we have a day and a half," Vicki said. "I'll be there. Whether you want me to or not."

"I'll attend as well, if you need me," Alfred said. "Perhaps this time the play will not end in tears."

IF YOU KILL BATMAN *and no one is there to see it, does anyone get the credit?*

Hugo Strange was certain Batman was dead. If one of the Monster Men didn't snap his costumed neck, he was almost certainly drowned, caught in the cage when the flood came through. This felt like an achievement, but only to a point. Batman was an eccentric, for sure—a kind of character no one had ever seen before. But he was a relatively new phenomenon. It wasn't as if he'd become some kind of folk hero. He'd never get that chance now.

Batman had died for two reasons: being outsmarted by Strange, and because he was a human. Strange's Monster Men were not, not anymore. They were superior. Many had survived the deluge; before dawn they'd crawled out of various storm drains like insects flooded out of a nest. Strange and Lawrence had kept trucks running all up and down the path of the drain, picking them up. They'd also laid claim to the Batmobile, before the police could get their hands on it.

A great and unexpected prize, but Strange hadn't even looked at the car. That chance would come later, when he'd have all the time in the world. By the end of the week, he'd never want for resources ever again, and would be able to operate openly without worry of arrest or interference. Alexander the Great didn't suffer enemies. He absorbed them, transformed them, made their strength his own.

And what strength Strange didn't have, his science had created.

There were still Last Laughs in his employ that had retained their humanity; his plans required a number of fully operating brains, such as they were. Lawrence had told them that Strange spoke for The Joker, and that the Monster Men were The Joker's creations; that had made them even more fervent followers, if that was possible. If someone truly believed The Joker was a god of chaos, there'd be little shock in finding out he had demons in his vanguard.

Strange had ruled out returning to Gotham General again; if Batman had been able to figure out his identity, there could be danger in returning. He had everything he needed from there, anyway. Everything else he required was at the secondary site—and at the Capra, which he visited later in the day.

With Lawrence in tow, he walked through the halls backstage. "We'll crack open the Batmobile later. You're certain your people understand the equipment for tomorrow night?" Strange asked.

"Yup."

Always there with a long-winded response. Strange realized he'd better go over the timetable again. "I'm famished," he said, opening the door to Kingston's former dressing room. It had the refrigerator, still stocked from when Karlo was staying there. "We'll run through the plan again while I—"

Karlo sprang from behind the door and punched Strange in the jaw so hard his glasses flew off. The older man stumbled backward, into the arms of a surprised Lawrence.

"You bastard!" Karlo yelled, his face a fright.

Strange held his jaw—and spat blood. He looked daggers at Karlo. *"How dare you!"*

"How dare *you*! You killed Kingston!" Karlo pointed to his melting face. "You did *this* to me!"

Karlo reached out. Grabbing Strange by the lapels, he yanked him forward—and around. Then he shoved him away, hard. Strange's fall was broken when he landed in the seat in front of the mirror.

"I'm going to kill you!" Karlo said.

"I'd think twice—if you can think at all." Strange saw what was about to happen. "Lawrence!"

The tough had his gun out. It was cocked and pointed inches from Karlo's head. "Should I?" Lawrence asked.

"I don't know," Strange replied, babying his jaw. "You tell me, Karlo. Should he?"

Seeing there was no way to resist, Karlo sagged.

Strange rose, stepped forward, and punched him in the gut. Lawrence followed up by striking the actor on the back of the head with his weapon. Karlo went to the floor.

The doctor knew he had little chance of harming Karlo, given his transformation. But he still took satisfaction in repeatedly kicking him, one polished dress shoe to the face after another. "You meaningless mote!" Strange shouted. "You were never anything before I gave you your gift."

Karlo curled up in agony. "My *gift*?"

"You have never appreciated it. You were a nothing. *Nothing!*" Seeing Karlo offering no further resistance, Strange stepped over to reclaim his fallen glasses. "You aspired to a life telling lies for the entertainment of others. Trying to please others is the lowest form of achievement!"

"What about all those speeches you give?"

"For me—*never* for them!" He loomed over Karlo. "But since we met, you have become something. You've played the greatest roles, for an actual purpose."

"Your purpose!"

"There *is* no other purpose. Nations. Religions. Races. All these distinctions without differences. You cannot divide by zero."

"I never know what you're talking about."

Strange stepped over and looked at his own reflection in the mirror. "Did a fool like you ever learn in school what solipsism is?"

"I read," Karlo said. "You think nobody else exists!"

"Not quite. I am a *contingent* solipsist. I am open to the idea that others may exist. But if they somehow do, I will not for one second accept that their agency should outrank mine. Those who oppose my will shall lose theirs."

Karlo had nothing to say to that.

Strange paused to clean himself up. "I may still have uses for you. Including a future role as a lab animal, if you don't cooperate. What is in your cells and veins has value, even if you don't recognize it." He glanced over to Lawrence. "Did you understand that?"

"No."

Strange rolled his eyes. He had to simplify. "I want him alive. But out of the way until after the performance tomorrow night."

"We're gonna be busy," Lawrence said. "Where should I put him?"

Strange looked around—and something he saw in a corner gave him an idea. He stepped over and found an old stage trunk with a hefty lock. He smiled. "We'll put him in there."

Karlo's eyes bugged. "In the trunk?"

"Irony. That's something you 'show people' prize, isn't it? In you go!"

CHAPTER 49

THE STARS WERE OUT above Theatre Row—and on the red carpet at the Imperial, just fifteen days after the calamitous end to its previous production. There was more security this time, in light of the reemergence of The Joker, but the police were trying to keep a low profile so as not to interfere with the benefit.

Vicki Vale hadn't been in town for the previous play, and she wasn't attending as a celebrity now. She wore a long-sleeved black knit dress, but also her ponytail and oversized glasses. A hefty bag was slung at her side. It was a working evening, in more ways than one. And if there was trouble, she sure as hell wasn't going to be in heels.

She'd snapped dozens of photos when she encountered her former work partner in the lobby. "Together again," Knox said. "A dynamic duet of words and pictures!"

"I see you still don't have an off-switch."

"Hey, we're a team, like Woodward and Bernstein. They called them Woodstein." He put his hands together. "Valeknox!" He blinked when she gave no response. "Knoxvale?"

She shook her head.

"You're right. Too Tennessee. I'll come up with something." He looked around. "Are you going to tell me what the hell was up with that TV interview? What are we even doing here?"

"We're solving a mystery. A lot of them, actually." She put down the bag. "Get ready to take notes."

She snapped pictures as the city fathers filtered in. Mayor Borg, Harvey Dent—and a whole lot of money. A lot of it was personified in the white-haired gentleman who'd just entered with a young man beside him.

"Mister Shreck," Vicki said.

"Vicki Vale. I didn't know you were back in town."

"Life of a journalist," she said. She'd known Shreck's Department Store in her role as a fashion photographer; she had never met Max Shreck when he didn't give her the willies. As now, when he reached over to kiss her hand. When Knox sidled up next to her and offered his hand to the mogul as well, Shreck recoiled. Vicki was happy to get her personal space back.

"I think I met your date outside," she said.

Shreck blanched. "Who?"

"Or was she your assistant? With the glasses?"

"Oh." He waved dismissively. "My secretary. She had to catch me for a signature."

"Well, she seemed nice enough. I hope you got her a ticket to the show."

Shreck chortled. "High culture for her is probably watching soap operas without the commercials." His actual companion for the evening joined him. "You know Chip?"

Vicki nodded—and snapped photos of father and son together. Chip Shreck was an expensive suit, a lot of dental work, and a blank stare: if there was a brain in there, she'd never seen any indication of it.

Knox pointed his tape recorder at Max. "You weren't here two weeks ago. Why tonight?"

"With everything this city has been through since then, I thought I'd offer my support—and strength. The Joker poses no threat to Max Shreck."

"You seem pretty sure. Why?"

Chip grabbed his father by the lapel. "Come on, Dad."

Max gave Knox a look that said he never wanted to see him again. Then he nodded to Vicki before heading into the crowd.

"Always something fishy with that guy," Knox said.

Vicki agreed. "Doesn't that guy have a wife?"

"A mystery for another day." He pointed. "Come on, Vale. Bruce just showed!"

BRUCE AND ALFRED ENTERED the Imperial lobby as they had two weeks earlier—but also not as they had. Then, he'd had no idea that Karlo would be impersonating Tolliver Kingston onstage. This event, he knew, was only happening because Karlo had impersonated Bruce Wayne—but he was willing to let it play out. He'd made preparations.

Alfred was also not exactly as he was at the previous event. He pulled alongside him an oxygen tank on wheels. He wasn't using it, but he had the line and mask at the ready.

Bruce found "Doctor Auslander" where he was before, smiling alongside Gotham City's wealthiest citizens. If anything, the event had brought out far more VIPs than the last one had, despite the recent chaos of the city—and it was all because of Bruce. Or rather, Karlo, who he'd learned had made personal calls to donors the day of the broadcast, posing as the billionaire.

No wonder Julie Madison was so happy. Bruce himself had never had time to do the same. *Maybe I should hire Karlo—if I can ever find him.*

Strange spied Bruce. For several moments, Bruce thought the doctor might bolt as he approached—but instead, he smiled wanly. Strange glanced at Alfred, who was taking a breath from his tank. "Is your man unwell?"

"It's been a rough month," Bruce said.

"So it has," Strange said. "Nice to see you in attendance."

He started to turn away, but Bruce took him by the arm and guided him into an alcove. Remembering the part he needed to play,

Bruce spoke confidentially. "What's the idea, having someone imper-sonate me on television?"

"The Smylex Ward has bills to pay," Strange said. "It was short notice. A busy man like yourself might not have been available—and you were essential to making certain the benefit happened."

"You could have just asked me."

"No, I couldn't have. You might have said no—and that, I could not allow." Strange straightened. "For the sake of the victims."

"Don't give me that." Bruce gritted his teeth. "When this is over, you're out. Do you understand? Takagi will see it my way. So will Commissioner Gordon!"

Strange raised an eyebrow. "You really think they'll believe a rich layabout with a mad theory over a distinguished scientist?"

"I think they will."

Strange held his gaze for several moments—and turned. "Yes, perhaps it's for the best. We should take up our differences then, after, in front of the proper authorities. It would be quite embarrass-ing to us both to cause a scene." He backed into the crowd, smiled, and drew his arms apart in a broad gesture. "For now, I have a presen-tation to make. Enjoy the program!"

Bruce watched him head off—as did Alfred, who put down the mask. "I can't say I'm delighted about what I'm going to have to do, Master Bruce. But it will be good to play a role in that popinjay's comeuppance."

"You get to apologize to Julie this time." Bruce heard the chimes. "Come on, let's head in!"

HEARTBREAK HOUSE WASN'T A MUSICAL, but an orchestra played be-forehand nonetheless—another part of the hastily arranged benefit. Bruce saw that the programs from the play were still dated from during the original Smylex panic; he imagined the Imperial company felt lucky not to have discarded them. It had two fewer acts than *Pyg-malion* and the production was abridged as well, so he wasn't surprised that no concerns had been raised by Strange's demand for time up front to present a video. It was a benefit, after all.

A screen descended from the rafters above center stage, part of the Imperial's modern setup. Strange crossed the stage to where a microphone stood. The audience applauded.

In his private box, Bruce looked to the door behind him. It was almost time.

"Ladies and gentlemen, as you may have heard, before our entertainment, I'd like you to see a video about my work." He smiled. "To be honest, it is more about me. But something about this setting brings out the ham in us all."

The audience laughed.

"You will find parts of it quite surprising. But I ask you to give it your full attention. I promise it will keep you in your seats."

The video started. *"Everything is reflex,"* boomed the professor's voice through the speaker system. *"Everything is reaction."*

Just as the picture of a young Hugo Strange appeared onscreen, Bruce got up and headed to the door. "It's showtime."

He walked into the hallway quickly. Hugo Strange's voice could be heard in the auditorium—as well as sounds of audience response. Most of it was coming from the sound system. It sounded as if some in the audience were joining in the laughter and applause, but not a lot; it probably seemed strange to people in the hall that the video had prerecorded responses.

By the time he found Vicki in the hall on one of the lower floors, it had become clear that what Strange was showing was not what the audience expected. His sad life story was not turning into a triumphant tale of scientific achievement culminating in his work at the hospital—but rather something else entirely.

He hurried toward Vicki, who stood by an exit door leading to the auditorium level. He found her shoulder bag on the floor before her and pulled out a portable stereo. Lawrence would turn up his nose at the size of the thing—but then he wouldn't like what it did anyway. It was the right size for what it was.

After checking his watch, he opened the door. The audience was quiet. *"Hugo Strange understood that subjugation was not enough,"* boomed Strange's voice over the loudspeakers.

Sounds like a real thriller, Bruce thought. *Hate to ruin it.*

He switched on his mini-boombox and opened the door to the hall. In a swift movement so he wouldn't be seen, he reached in and dropped the device into the garbage can just inside the exit.

He closed the door quickly. Vicki had her bag back and was holding an emergency exit open for him. "You look nice," she said. "The suit you want is in the limo."

"No, I'm using the one from my other ride here." He glanced up. "Alfred is about to move. Go bring him out."

"I will. Be careful!"

ALFRED PENNYWORTH FANCIED HIMSELF a Renaissance man, a fan of the arts. He had not partaken of many elements of popular culture, unlike his original employer, Thomas Wayne. Thomas, tragically, was much more likely to see something lacking in substance—like *Footlight Frenzy,* which he saw on the night of his and his wife's deaths. Alfred had never wondered if better taste would have saved the Waynes, but he had thought about whether his own snobbishness had kept him from being there as well that night.

Shaw at the Imperial was never something he was going to complain about, but what he was enduring was. A bizarre accounting of Hugo Strange's life flashed past onscreen, wandering through moments of espionage and criminality. Gotham City's finest, spread out below, were sitting, spellbound.

He didn't know what Strange was saying to cause that response, because the hearing aids he had in both ears were nothing of the sort. When Master Bruce had departed, he'd turned them on, and had heard nothing but white noise since. And now his watch said it was the proper time.

My apologies to George Bernard Shaw—and to you, Miss Madison.

He turned the knob on the oxygen tank. As he did, its doors opened, discharging what was within: a dozen bats. Two at a time, they flitted to the railing of the balcony box. They roosted there for just a moment before soaring outward.

Alfred turned the knob back to close the tank's doors and leaned forward, almost afraid to watch. The bats, driven mad by the ultrasonic sound projector Alfred's employer had just deposited on the auditorium level, raced around the Imperial, swooping all about. They did not harass the audience, but they did distract people's attention from the video.

He dialed back the white noise. Strange's video continued, but now a low murmur in the hall had added to the noise. No one had fled for the exits, but people stood up randomly, attempting to shoo the animals.

Vicki appeared in the door behind him. He could hear her whisper to him. "Is it working?"

"It seems so." Karlo had told Batman of a sonic waveform that made listeners more docile and receptive to suggestion; Alfred and Bruce had found just such a thing in the published research of Hugo Strange. "We had no idea what frequency, if any, would counteract the subliminal signal," Alfred whispered. "But we knew what frequency the bats would respond to."

Vicki looked out alongside him. Strange wasn't onstage, but as his video continued, people certainly weren't as rapt by it. Rather, the calls about the bats were now being supplemented by shouts of surprise and outrage at the story Strange was telling.

"Come along," Vicki said. "I don't think we want to be here when this ends."

"I am in total agreement, Miss Vale."

CHAPTER 50

KARLO HADN'T KILLED TOLLIVER KINGSTON, but he had locked him in a trunk for a few hours. Since then, he felt he'd more than paid his penance for it. He'd spent a full day trapped inside the chest at the back of Kingston's old dressing room, unable to do much more than roll over. He'd listened the night before through the trunk's lining as Strange had spelled out his plans for the Imperial to Lawrence—and then been forced to repeat them again and again for good measure. Comprehension wasn't the henchman's strong suit. *"Even I understand,"* Karlo had wanted to shout.

The room outside having been silent for hours, he had strained repeatedly to break free. It was futile. The lid was fastened by multiple locks on the outside. He'd heard them being clicked shut; so many it seemed like overkill. All that remained was to feel around his surroundings in the darkness. The only thing he found was a small metal plate screwed into the underside of the lid. He started trying to work it free.

Maybe I can use it to carve my way out—in a million years!

He'd been trying for a minute when he realized there were letters stamped into the plate. He traced them with his fingertips.

D-A-S-H. Karlo stopped working and thought, trying to remember the history of the Capra. It had spent years as a vaudeville house, playing host to a variety of singers and comedians—and not a few magicians.

"Of course!"

He stopped worrying about the lid and rolled over, his hands searching the back of the trunk. He finally found two small notches, feet apart—and with fingers in both, threw his weight against the trunk wall. The back fell open and he rolled out, free at last.

He got to his knees and examined the trunk, so long ignored. Nobody knew whether Harry Houdini had ever played the Capra. But he often worked with his escape artist brother, "Dash" Hardeen. And Dash had left without all his luggage!

Karlo's eyes took seconds to adjust to the light. The clock showed what he was afraid of. The performance at the Imperial was under way. Strange was going to make dire use of the knowledge he got from poisoning Karlo. But that theatre was around the corner and up the street—and the actor knew his way there in his sleep.

He hurried into the hallway. *Maybe there's time!*

"—*THOSE WHO STOLE FROM ME, ridiculed me, belittled me? They will learn my name. And nothing after that.*"

Strange had put on ear protectors so as not to be deafened by his own video—but he knew the timing of the speech by heart. He knew his cue was coming. He'd been busy behind the great screen while the video was showing—and his actions had started well before that.

During the orchestral prelude, Lawrence had led the Last Laughs and Monster Men in storming the back entrance. The noise hidden behind music, they'd corralled all the actors and backstage staff and locked them in the cellar. Strange had been in charge of everything in the Imperial thereafter, making sure people and equipment were in place.

And now, it was time. He stepped around the screen and walked back to the microphone. He removed his headphones just as the Imperial's sound system boomed, "*My quest is at an end. As are your lives as human beings.*" The screen went blank, and he opened his mouth to speak.

The noise came from the audience. Catcalls. Boos. Shouting. Hugo Strange's name called out—along with insults.

Liar. Crazy. Perverse.

Shaken, Strange looked across the hall. The waveform embedded in the sound effects in the video should have pacified the audience, just as it did Karlo and the Last Laughs. Yet they were acting as though they hadn't heard that part at all. Only his testament. Several people were on their feet, shaking their fists at him. Others were standing, preparing to walk out.

He shouted into the microphone. "Silence!"

He gave a hand signal to stage left, where Lawrence threw a switch. The screen lifted into the ceiling, revealing ten Monster Men, lined up in their tattered clothes. Some still covered in filth from their sojourn in the storm drain system. As one, the once-humans snarled, baring their teeth—prompting screams of horror from the audience.

"Ladies and gentlemen, stay where you are. If anyone attempts to leave, my Monster Men are quite prepared to tear them apart." For good measure, a pair of Last Laughs in gas masks painted to resemble The Joker's face appeared onstage, bearing machine guns. Strange pointed to the balconies. "You up there, as well. No one leaves this building!"

Behind him, several gas-masked Last Laughs wheeled out tanks on wheels. It was the fumigation equipment, stolen from Bug Me Not; the only thing Strange had really intended his would-be bank robbers to steal while he was busy ransacking Armsgard. Other minions headed up the aisles, rolling more tanks into the middle of the crowd. Others arrived on the upper deck. Once in position, everyone shot thumbs-up at Strange.

"As I was saying, these creatures surrounding me are the future— your future. You are the richest people in Gotham City. Its elite. I despise you, each and every one of you. But I presume your families will give anything—*everything*—for me to reverse what I'm about to do." He gritted his teeth. *"And those who won't will join you."*

He put his mask on, savoring the screams in the hall. No one would laugh at him again. He stepped over to one of the tanks onstage and grabbed the hose, turning the end toward the crowd. He turned the dial, releasing—

—*bubbles*. Countless bubbles, small and large, coursing into the crowd and rising. More came from every tanker on the floor, filling the air above the Imperial crowd with glistening orbs.

Then he saw something else. Bats came down from the rafters and cavorted amid the bubbles, flitting back and forth.

Strange stepped forward to the front of the stage, looking up at them in astonishment. At once, Strange understood why his sonic waveform had failed to do its job—and who had been the cause of it. And when a new voice came over the sound system, everyone in the hall understood, too.

"Ladies and gentlemen, this is Batman. Don't panic. I found where Strange was storing his chemical weapon—and made a switch. The contents are no threat to you."

Shock rumbled through the hall. Batman's voice was unknown to almost everyone in Gotham City; hearing it first here and now sparked confusion and surprise in the crowd.

And then, elation.

"The Joker isn't real, either. He died months ago. Help is coming—but for your safety, remain in your seats."

From amid the bubbles and bats, something black whizzed past Strange. He heard loud smacking sounds and turned. One of the two gun-toting Last Laughs and then the other collapsed, struck by something. Their guns fell, never fired.

Strange faced the Monster Men, still at attention onstage. "I want you to—"

More noise, this time from overhead. A cable shot down, its bolo wrapping around one of the beefier creatures. A second later, the hulking figure went soaring into the air. A second cable, and then another disappeared—and then a third and a fourth.

The Monster Men reacted with the very ignorance that Strange had intended for them to have: they stared at the ceiling, their mouths open like the foolish turkeys of folklore. Strange looked up, too, at the metal equipment framework in the rafters. Suspended on electrical pulleys, it gave the Imperial's stage crew a way to hoist the lights, scenery, and projector screen to the ceiling. It also now held something else: four dangling, spinning Monster Men, a grotesque nursery mobile of misanthropes.

Metallic bangs followed from even higher above. *One, two, three, four, five, six.* Strange craned his neck so he could get a better look— only to start backward in shock when he heard a gruesome crack. He stumbled backward as the entire assembly came crashing down, lights, monsters, and all toward the stage.

Everything went sideways, in more ways than one. Strange tumbled so he was half-hanging off the stage into the orchestra pit—and saw behind him the metal frame collapse on top of his remaining horrific creations. Monster Man collided with Monster Man, while huge lighting units struck others and smashed to bits. The big plastic tanks that should have held Hegemon burst into a shower of soapy suds that sloshed across the stage.

Strange looked back to see the Last Laughs who'd been in the aisle and along the sides charging down toward the stage. But it was no place to be. Tangled up in metal, sparking cable, and one another, the Monster Men who had remained conscious lashed out in any direction they could. Against one another.

They're not supposed to do that! Strange had been sure to make that suggestion to them during their conditioning, but the frenzy onstage had overcome what little reason he had afforded them. They brawled in the wreckage and slop comically—and when the Last Laughs reached the stage, they were met with a detonating smoke grenade. Soon they were swept up into the cloud of confused violence, as well.

For the audience, it was a spectacle that was equal parts amusing, incredible, and terrifying; for Strange, it was entirely the latter. And that was before the black cape blossomed from above.

Batman had made his Gotham City theatrical debut.

To the oohs and aahs of the crowd, he lit atop the smoky debris pile and immediately went to work, pummeling Monster Men and Last Laughs alike. He disappeared into the smoke—and a second later Strange saw one of his minions knocked sideways, crashing into an orchestra pit that the musicians had already fled. And then another henchman followed.

Strange watched the fight, spellbound, from the stage floor until he felt someone pick him up. He was carted away to the exit over someone's shoulder.

Once through the door and returned to his feet, Strange saw who his savior was.

"The cops are out front," Lawrence growled. He drew his gun. "What now?"

Putting his glasses back on correctly, Strange glanced back through the door at the melee. It had all been a trap—for *him*—but all was not lost. His life had been one contingency plan after another, and it would not end in a cellar, with a standoff and hostages who had no meaning to him. He had another play.

And as he saw who it was that was waiting just outside the fire exit, he realized his chances had just improved.

SECONDS AFTER THE POLICE entered to secure the main hall of the Imperial, Batman headed backstage, in search of the company. He found and freed them all, including a Julie Madison whose expression was so acidic it might have melted the door lock all on its own. But he did not find who he expected at the planned meeting point once that was over.

Instead, opening the fire exit door, he saw Knox, holding his recorder and looking frenetic. "Bats!"

The breathless reporter had been pounding at the door, unable to get back in. "What's wrong?" Batman asked.

"Vale's gone. And Bruce Wayne's butler too!"

Batman looked down the alley into the darkness. "What do you mean, gone?"

"I caught as much of Strange's story as I could—but when the fighting started, I went looking for Vicki. She was missing it. She had the camera!"

Always thinking of the story, Batman thought. He grabbed Knox by the shoulder. "Where is she?"

"I'm trying to tell you. Strange and Lawrence found them outside the auditorium. They had a couple of those glandular cases with them."

"The Monster Men?"

"Whatever. I followed them down the alley," he said, pointing. "Lawrence loaded them into the back of a pickup and left!"

Batman and Knox ran toward the corner. The lights of Theatre Row shone all around, but there was no sign of the truck—just an increasing number of police cars in front of the Imperial.

Knox looked to Batman. "They could have gone to the place where they were storing everything."

Batman doubted it. "I was at Jo Jo's garage earlier—that's when I drained the chemicals from the tanks. Strange would know I'd find him there."

They were looking back at the theatre when Batman saw Karlo running toward the Imperial at a breakneck pace. He had no face—and he didn't slow down, not even seeing the police. He didn't stop until Batman stepped in his way.

Karlo knelt over, panting. "Where's Strange?"

"He's left—with hostages," Batman said.

"Then I'm too late."

Knox looked at him. A light went on. "You're Clayface!"

"Am not!" Karlo said.

"Never mind." Batman interceded. "They took off in Lawrence's pickup—with those soldiers of Strange's."

"They didn't go to the Capra," Karlo said. "I just came from there."

Something jarred Knox's memory. "Wait," he said. Remembering his tape recorder, he started running it back. "I never turned this off. They were still talking when I walked up on them!"

Batman listened as Knox cued it forward. The last thing before Knox encountered Strange was the doctor speaking to Lawrence. *"Just as we discussed,"* he said. *"We head for high ground!"*

Knox shook his head. "Damn it. They didn't say."

Karlo put up his hands. "No. That's not just an expression!"

Batman looked to him. "What?"

"I heard him tell Lawrence when I was prisoner. He's got a fall-back position—in Gotham Cathedral!"

Batman and Knox looked to each other. Knox said what Batman was thinking. "Not again!"

Batman saw Gordon arriving in front of the Imperial. He directed Knox. "Go. Tell him!"

"Got it." Knox started running. "I still want an interview," he yelled over his shoulder. "With both of you!"

"Just go!"

Batman stood for several moments, calculating. In the meantime, Karlo saw all the police—and shook his head. "I guess I'd better go."

He had started to walk away when Batman stopped him. "Wait a second. I have an idea." He looked Karlo in the eyes. "I have something for you in my car."

"Your—?" Karlo gulped. "But wait. I heard Strange say his people had stolen the Batmobile."

"It's a different—" Batman started to say. "Never mind." He pointed to the shadows of the alley. "Stay there. I'll be right back!"

CHAPTER 51

WHAT GOOD IS THE WORLD *without my genius?*

Hugo Strange was always thinking. After reclaiming his property from Armsgard, he had been faced with a dilemma. Many of the vehicles the Last Laughs had stolen were stored in the spacious temporary building on the property of Jo Jo's tavern, and the fumigation equipment had wound up there, too. But there was much more material than would fit, and as secret bases went, the Capra was just a theatre with a parking problem.

But there existed a great piece of real estate. An abandoned location with a huge interior, right in the middle of Gotham City. And it was built like a medieval fortress, to boot. The Last Laughs had been able to bring loot from both Armsgard and The Joker's weapons trove into Gotham Cathedral by driving right into the wide rear doors in the middle of the night. The gargoyles had never complained.

Now, Strange had assembled the remaining Last Laughs and what remained of his dwindling number of Monster Men inside, prepared to activate a plan that was as ambitious as it was diabolical. It was sure to work, and that was only just and right.

The world without his genius was nothing.

He and Batman had gone tit-for-tat on failed traps. Somehow, the costumed lunatic had escaped drowning; Strange had slipped free from Batman's grasp at the Imperial. Strange had no doubt that the hero would find some way to track him across the city—maybe with a Bat-blimp, or something just as extravagantly silly. So it was only logical to make the cathedral a trap as well as a bastion—and to bait it properly.

Nobody was better made for that than Vicki Vale.

He'd been surprised to see her at the Imperial before the show-that-wasn't—and elated. Batman had gone to extreme lengths to save her before, and likely would again. The old manservant Alfred Pennyworth he'd taken as an afterthought, in case Bruce Wayne's money allowed him to escape what was coming for Gotham City. A sad man who was willing to take his butler everywhere was likely to pay for his survival.

Not his return, of course. Strange would never surrender leverage again.

Temporary stairs into the belfry had replaced the ones destroyed months earlier, and he had brought his hostages back onto the upper level. Vicki Vale, less than happy to return here, had never stopped straining against the hold of her monstrous captor.

"You won't get away with this."

"You don't even know what *this* is," Strange responded. Portable lights glowing, he readied the device that Napier had used to break into broadcasts. "The Joker made a critical error here. He failed to bring enough forces into the cathedral."

Alfred, similarly held, looked around. "I don't see so many."

"They're here—just otherwise occupied." Strange connected wires to a generator. "Again, The Joker entered here without any plan but escape. I have a plan, and escape is not my intention at all."

The photographer looked about at the cases of supplies. "What, are you going to live up here?"

"Of course not. I'm not a bat. But what will happen will take some time."

He checked his pocket watch. *Still no Batman.* He shrugged. So the hero would suffer the same fate as everyone else below.

Strange looked over to Lawrence, who stood with the video camera. "Ready," the henchman said.

"Watch and learn," the doctor said to his captives, then turned toward the camera. "I am Hugo Strange, with a message for the people of Gotham City. Or, rather, those of you fortunate to live, say, one hundred feet above the surface . . ."

BATMAN SAW THE MESSAGE from his vehicle.

"*I considered ransoming the rich and famous earlier tonight,*" Strange said. "*Instead, I will ransom the whole city. When I finish speaking, my forces will fire mortars from Gotham Cathedral. Rounds containing Hegemon, my miracle compound. The resulting cloud will be enormous, transforming every man, woman, and child into an atavistic imbecile.*"

Batman marveled at Strange's depravity. But he continued to listen.

"*Without pre-conditioning, I will not exercise control over them—but I can take care of that later. They have nowhere to go. Those unaffected wealthy, in high-rises, will be my prisoners. And will surely pay to be spared. For safe passage down through the cloud and out of the city.*

"*As for the United States government, which treated me so cavalierly, know this: Gotham City is now independent, and under my command. Any attempt to free the people of this city will be met with war conducted by the people of this city—for me.*"

Strange approached the camera, his glare appearing large on-screen. "*I am the new hegemon. Foreign powers who wish my friendship are welcome to apply. But for this nation—and Gotham City—evolution is backing up and turning around, down another path. Goodbye.*"

The image went to static. Batman switched off the screen—and just in time, because as promised, he saw tiny figures assembling higher on the ramparts of the Gotham Cathedral. He could see them because this time he was approaching from outside rather than within—and in a new vehicle he had been just starting to test before the current crisis.

The Alpha Bat.

The Alpha adapted one of the attack helicopters Wayne Industries had a hand in creating to fill a hole Batman had perceived in his vehicle fleet. It provided a way to cross longer distances through the air than the Roost was capable of, while also offering close-assault and evac capabilities that the Batwing would never have. He'd brought it into the city just in case and hidden it near the Imperial the night before; as it was capable of carrying two, it was roomy enough that changing into his costume inside it before the theatre melee was no problem at all.

Neither was the chopper challenged by what he was attempting now: spiraling up and around the cathedral, even as Last Laughs perched outside fired automatic weapons at him. Strange had said the ten-story level was where the cloud would reach, and indeed, Batman hadn't seen any mortar placements below that. So he had little compunction about firing at the Gothic structure near his attackers, dislodging them.

Gotham City's Historical Buildings Registry could take it up with him later.

As he ascended, he deployed his scope and saw Monster Men assisting Last Laughs in positioning mortars. One fired, and then another—from positions on the church's northern and eastern sides. Batman was certain the same was happening on the other side.

It was time for the Alpha to earn its name.

Alpha bats led others. In the present case, Batman toggled a switch—and watched via the rear camera as dozens of small bat-drones spilled from the cargo hatch. Each one, a Batarang without the sophisticated guidance; they partially relied upon the copter for that.

As Batman swung the chopper on a soaring ascent around the cathedral, the cloud followed behind him. When he reached two hundred feet, he leveled off—and the orbiting drones established a screen high above the ground. While each mortar round descended, one of the beta bat-drones peeled off and exploded nearby.

He continued the process—and watched with satisfaction as his countermeasures intercepted each chemical round. The detonations were large, resembling flak bursts—and he knew the poison's chemistry well enough to be certain that the energy would break the gas down into harmless particles, to be carried away by the wind.

The shots from above stopped. He had more drones, but he wasn't going to give Strange's minions any more chances to reload. "Target practice resumes," he mumbled.

STRANGE STEPPED BACK FROM looking over the ledge—and staggered around in shock. How on earth was he supposed to create plans accounting for a person with such resources? Darius III had scythed chariots in his arsenal; Alexander had prepared for them. Where were the king of Persia's attack helicopters?

"Mister Strange seems upset," he heard the imprisoned Vicki say.

"He prefers 'Professor,'" the butler responded. "But 'Inmate' is coming along fast on the outside."

Strange turned and thought to strike them—one or both. It would be satisfying. But it wasn't too late. He still had forces inside—and more chemicals. He could make more rounds. And, he thought as he patted his jacket, he was personally unassailable.

Lawrence approached him. "I'm out."

"What?"

The henchman looked around uncomfortably. "I don't like this building, and I ain't stayin'." He pointed his gun at Strange and began backing away.

Strange had calculated it might happen; Lawrence's exposure to the sonic waveform had been some time ago. Karlo had broken free from it, and his exposure had been more recent. He thought for a moment to use his ace in the hole against Lawrence—but it would be a waste of a valuable resource.

He tried reason. "If you go down there, you'll be at risk, just as everyone else is."

"Ciao."

So much for reasoning with a dolt. He watched as the man with the sunglasses disappeared.

"Getting a little lonely up here," Vicki said.

A voice came from the shadows. "Not so much."

Batman! Strange stepped back—and watched as the crusader came into view, stepping around a column. He'd found a place to land, Strange figured.

That was fine. Strange could always use a helicopter. "Now!" he called out.

Monster Men leapt out at Batman. Two from behind pillars; two more plunging down from above. Batman wrenched away from them, attempting to dodge.

It was a lighter suit of armor the hero was in, Strange saw; a little grayer. Perhaps his outfit had been damaged in the brawl at the Imperial—or perhaps Strange was just remembering it wrong. It had been so frenetic. But the lighter kit seemed to be working to the hero's advantage now. He rolled free from one punch, causing a Monster Man to break his fist against a stone column; another he wrestled with, only to break away.

Batman then hurled some kind of weapon at the brute. The Monster Man attempted to smack it away—only to find that the gummy projectile had adhered to his hand. The slow-witted creature's attempt to dislodge it resulted in his other hand getting stuck. Batman took advantage by delivering a high kick that slammed his opponent into a wall.

Strange moved closer to where Vicki and Alfred were being held as the fight continued. Batman still had fight in him but was clearly tired. When another sticky bomb trick caused Batman's two remaining opponents to get stuck to each other—and the floor—Strange decided to take no more chances.

"Batman!" he yelled. He pointed to the two remaining Monster Men on their feet: the ones holding his prisoners. "Surrender, or I will order them to tear these people apart!"

Panting, Batman looked at Strange—and sagged. He was the same man the doctor had encountered before, but he was clearly tired. Beaten. He shrugged. "What now?"

"This," Strange said, drawing a canister from his pocket. It operated on the same principal as the knockout gas projector he'd used on Karlo back at Armsgard, but this held something else: Hegemon.

"No!" Vicki cried out.

"Don't do it," Alfred pleaded. "For the love of mercy!"

Strange ignored them. "You are strong," he said, approaching Batman with confidence. "After this, you'll be stronger still. But you will also know your place. And I will decide whom you fight." He held the canister before the hero's exposed face and sprayed.

Batman grabbed his face and fell to his knees in agony. Strange took a step back and basked in the moment. Even without the sonic conditioning, Batman would be helpless after the transition. Strange could break him—or turn him—at his leisure.

The vigilante continued to writhe. Strange tapped his foot. "Oh, do get on with it."

"Okay," Batman responded. He parted his fingers and looked up, displaying a dripping wet—and misshapen—face. *"Boo!"*

Karlo! Strange took several steps back, startled. That's when he saw the Monster Men holding his captives let go—and slump to the stone floor. Another Batman, this one in the darker, bulkier uniform from the Imperial, stepped between them, sparking electrical shock weapons in each hand.

Still clutching the canister, Strange turned back to the gray-clad Karlo. "You didn't transform!"

"I already did—or don't you remember?" Karlo tore at his Batman mask, and it ripped off, revealing his melted face. Its metamorphosis began again, becoming a picture of rage.

Strange looked back at Batman—and then at Karlo. "You, working with *him?*"

Karlo quoted Caliban. *"I'll be wise hereafter, and seek for grace."* Then he added, "Maybe I'm immune now. But you're not!"

Karlo charged forward and grabbed at the canister, still half full in Strange's hand. It exploded in both their faces. Strange, old and over-matched, inhaled—and smelled lilacs. Then he doubled over in agony, forgetting what flowers were and what they smelled like.

His wonderful mind left him, a miracle a millisecond. The last thoughts in Hugo Strange's brain were how to do quadratic equations, and something about puppies. His parents never let him have one, and it was past time to let someone have it about that.

BATMAN HADN'T INTENDED TO arrive later than Karlo; putting the actor in the suit from the limo was meant as a distraction for Strange and his minions. Karlo had been game for it. But Batman hadn't found anywhere to land; the Alpha was still hovering over the cathedral, with a ladder reaching down.

Batman heard its blades now as Karlo wrestled with Strange in the same spot where he and The Joker had tangled months earlier. The transformed Strange had inhaled an enormous amount of the chemical; Batman had needed to hustle Alfred and Vicki away while it dissipated. But somehow the thing Strange had become wasn't in-capacitated. Rather, it was instantly alive with anger—and ready to respond as Karlo grappled with him.

Realizing the Monster Men posed no threat without Strange's guidance, Batman moved his attention to the fight. Delivering a final and powerful punch, Karlo knocked the Strange Thing back. Then he pounded the professor-monster's head against the outer retaining wall.

By the time Batman reached him, Karlo was standing on the ledge, holding Strange's limp, mutated body. He couldn't tell if the actor intended to drop Strange—or jump, himself, along with him. "Karlo, what are you doing?"

His Batman cape blowing in the breeze, Karlo looked back. Tears ran down his blistered face. "He made my life a nightmare!"

"I know," Batman said. Vicki and Alfred arrived at either side of him.

"Did you hear me?" Karlo sounded exhausted. "All my life, I've been overlooked. Ignored. Strange didn't even know who I was when he stole my face—and didn't care when he made me something worse. *My life is a nightmare!*"

"Nightmares end," Batman said. He reached out with his hand. "Yes, he used you. Made you his guinea pig. His puppet. His weapon. But you don't have to play the part he wrote for you." He paused. "Karlo, you're the one onstage. Make the part your own."

Karlo looked down at Strange's supine body in his arms—and shook his head. He turned and climbed back to safety, with their help.

Karlo put Strange down. *"What a thrice-double ass was I, to take this drunkard for a god, and worship this dull fool!"*

Batman and Vicki looked at each other.

"Those are Caliban's last lines," Alfred said.

Karlo nodded. "He doesn't have any more."

```
BLACKGATE INFIRMARY
TRANSCRIPTION OF WRITING BY
PRISONER HUGO STRANGE,
AS DISCOVERED BY OFFICER

A IS FOR APPLE
B IS FOR BAT
C IS FOR BAT
BAT BAT BAT BAT BAT BAT BAT
```

CHAPTER 52

THERE HAD BEEN MANY assemblies on the exercise yard behind Police Plaza before; officer graduation ceremonies had taken place there for years. But while it wasn't unusual in the least for Commissioner Gordon and Harvey Dent to be there—along with a couple of members of the media—the presence of a costumed superhero was unique.

And yet, few eyes were on Batman. Rather, they were on the sixty Monster Men—and Women—who stood in arm and leg irons in the middle of the field. All in well-organized ranks and files, all listening to the one person they'd obey.

"I have information you will want to hear," Hugo Strange said through a megaphone. "Your conditions can be reversed. Batman and the people at Gotham General found that fact was in Hugo's—I mean, in *my* notes all along."

A low rumble came from the assembled mutated Last Laughs. Apparently they had some understanding, Batman realized.

"But you will all need complete blood transfusions—all to take place in the hospital at Blackgate Prison." Their leader pointed to a row of police vans. "Board the vans. Once you have been restored to health, you will serve Hugo Strange no more. This is a fresh start. Take advantage of it."

The lines of Monster Men turned. They began boarding the vans.

Batman stepped beside the speaker and waited until the last one had driven away. Then Karlo removed the glasses, hairpieces, and beard that made him Hugo Strange.

"You finally got his accent right," Batman said.

"He kept changing it," Karlo said. "I swear I'm never playing that guy again."

"You won't have to. Strange is locked away at Blackgate Infirmary. But they'll hit him with the same treatment. Then it's off to a cell."

"If his lawyer doesn't get him into Arkham Asylum. He definitely qualifies." Karlo rolled his eyes. "He'll be a volunteer counselor there before you know it."

Batman gestured over at Dent and explained that the city wasn't planning on charging Karlo for his crimes committed before his association with Strange; the events on the bus were a clear case of diminished capacity. Charges had also not been sought for his imprisonment and impersonation of Kingston during *Pygmalion;* Karlo had come clean about those actions publicly, begging the forgiveness of the Imperial's players and staff.

Karlo had even apologized again at Tolliver Kingston's funeral— but as it happened, he was one of the only people who attended. In the weeks since Tolliver Kingston's disappearance, so many accurate horror stories about the actor's behavior had come out that the man had no reputation to rehabilitate.

"The legal situation involving your actions as The Joker is more complicated," Batman said, "especially where the depot is concerned. But your evidence against Strange has value."

"Thanks. I'll do anything anyone asks—" He stopped. "I mean, I'll stop doing what anyone asks." Flustered, he smiled. "You know what I mean."

Batman watched as Karlo's face changed shape—beginning to resemble the actor's own, before his exposure.

"Sorry there isn't a cure for you yet. They'll keep searching."

"I know. And it's not just Bruce Wayne anymore. Max Shreck opened his checkbook—he made a huge donation to the Smylex Ward."

Shreck. Batman had wondered if Shreck's sudden generosity had been connected to any of the Last Laughs' mayhem, and whether Karlo had been involved in any of it. The speed of his contribution suggested that he had a reason to want Karlo to remain quiet.

But neither Karlo nor anyone else had come forward with anything on Shreck, and Batman didn't expect them to. The Last Laughs weren't counted on to remember much after their transformations were reversed, and Lawrence had been last seen racing out of town in a stolen pickup with two huge speaker units in the truck bed. It was fine. Shreck was notoriously dirty; if he was operating outside the law, Batman would trip him up another time.

"I guess living with this condition is my punishment," Karlo said. He shrugged. "And at least they're letting me work while it's all sorted out."

Batman nodded. "You've opened the Capra again."

"Someone made a huge anonymous contribution to the Save the Capra fund. It came with an endowment for the Goat's Town Players."

Batman already knew about it—because Bruce Wayne had funded it. "What's the first production?"

"The Imperial did pretty good reviving George Bernard Shaw, earlier. So we're thinking *Man and Superman.*" His smile crinkled. "Er—no offense."

Batman didn't respond—but he did shake Karlo's hand when it was offered.

"Thank you, Batman. For everything." Seeing Dent approach, Karlo walked over to speak with him.

Meanwhile, Knox stepped over to Batman's side. He watched Karlo from afar. "There goes the Phantom of the Capra."

"You're big on names."

"Yeah, 'Clayface' seems kind of rude now."

Knox had finally been able to get his scoop, writing about Strange's transformation to Auslander, and how he'd duped everyone—even Bruce Wayne. He hadn't made the billionaire look too bad in the article; the Smylex Ward was still a good idea and was continuing, under Takagi's more watchful eye.

And Batman had been able to provide Knox with something else, in appreciation for his help in locating Davis. "Thanks for the interview," Knox said. "Although I don't think the print medium can properly convey the gripping variety between your sixteen different responses of 'No comment.'"

"Next time, go into broadcasting instead."

Knox laughed. "Batman tells jokes. I love it."

Seeing Gordon approaching, the reporter made himself scarce.

"You called it," the commissioner said to Batman. "We found The Joker's corpse, just where you said to look."

Batman nodded. Strange had said Lawrence and the Last Laughs had moved the body somewhere "appropriate." On learning that they'd been spending much of their time at Jo Jo's, a local tavern, Batman had made an educated guess. "So they buried him under the party deck out back."

"The Joker, dealing from the bottom of the deck, as usual. We'll keep what's left of him under lock and key from now on." Gordon offered his hand. "I don't know how you managed to handle everything again, Batman, but thank you."

"Not everything. I'm sorry we didn't catch on in time to stop what happened at the depot."

Gordon regarded him. "When I spoke to you on the roof a couple of weeks ago, it was to share something I'd learned from a lifetime doing this. Here's another. You can't save everyone."

"I can try."

"That's why you're Batman—and I'm a tired old beat cop." He patted the Caped Crusader on the back. "We'll talk again in forty years."

BRUCE HAD BEEN BACK in the Batcave poring over blueprints for a couple of hours when Vicki walked down the stairs.

"I'm packed up," she said, walking toward him.

"Back to the special assignment?"

"I took a leave of absence from my leave of absence," she said. "But I'm nothing without my camera. I have to go to work."

"Understood." He stood up from the table as she arrived beside it.

She looked down at the schematics. "Another crazy car?"

"Not quite," Bruce said. "I've got mobility in the city and over it. But not beneath."

"Beneath."

"Yeah, the sewers and storm drains of this city represent a huge network for criminals to operate in." He gestured to the prints. "This would be amphibious."

"Amphibious." Vicki looked over at Alfred, who had just descended behind her. "Can you believe this? He wants something amphibious."

"I suppose it worked for the Royal Navy," the butler replied.

She rolled her eyes at him. "You're just as bad as he is. I think you find this amusing."

Alfred clasped his hands behind his back. "People in my line have stood in service of all manner of men, Miss Vale. Great and small, honorable and venal. Compared to some, I am convinced that Master Bruce's interests are positively pedestrian."

"Incorrigible," Vicki said. Then she smiled, and he smiled back.

"I regret to say your car has arrived, Miss."

Vicki nodded. "I'll be a second."

While Alfred made himself busy out of sight, she turned to look at Bruce. "Are you going to be okay?"

"Now that I'm actually getting to sleep."

"You're not having the nightmares anymore?"

Bruce shook his head. "All the questions I had about Jack Napier's final night were resolved. Gordon found a prison snitch who said Lawrence confessed that The Joker had sent him and the two other guys up into the cathedral beforehand to stand lookout."

"And The Joker saying he was a kid when he killed your parents?"

"He didn't know I was Batman when he said it. It was just blather on his part. He babbled constantly. The fact that it was accurate was a coincidence."

"A stopped clock is right twice a day."

"Or a broken one. My mistake was taking any of it seriously."

"You do tend to do that." She watched him. "So it's back to work. And I guess to the Julie Madisons."

"No." Bruce shrugged. "I mean, not *that* Julie Madison. She called me once everything was sorted out. She got disgusted with the craziness and took off for the West Coast."

"I don't blame her."

"She always wanted to be a movie star, anyway." Bruce looked away. "I mean, maybe you're right. I need someone more like me."

"Too bad you're one of a kind."

Vicki offered an embrace, and he joined her in it. She held him tightly.

"I'm happy you're okay," she said, her chin over his shoulder. "And I'm glad that you saved the city. *Again.*"

She pulled back, and he looked at her. "And?"

"And my position hasn't changed."

"I understand," Bruce said. And he really did. He released her. "I mean, I'll never like it. But I understand."

His eyes followed her as she turned back toward the stairs. There would only be one Vicki Vale, he knew. Maybe someday she could find a way to be part of his life again.

Maybe.

Alfred stepped forward as she reached the steps. "Shall I—?"

She stopped him from following her. "I'll see myself out. I know the way." She kissed the butler's cheek. "Bye, Alfred."

After Vicki left the Batcave, Bruce went back to his blueprints. Alfred stepped over to the Batmobile with wax and a cloth—only to break the silence after a few moments. "Sir, there is something on your windshield."

"A flyer? Always nice to get a good price on a car wash."

"No, sir, a postcard." Alfred removed it carefully and brought it over.

Bruce switched on a light above a table. "It must have been put there when I was in town to see Karlo. I didn't activate the shields."

"It appears to depict the Rama Fountain from Gotham City's Hotel Internationale," Alfred said, placing the card under the light. "It has no postmark. But it does have a return address of Amonate, Virginia."

Bruce didn't know the town, but he had visited the hotel many times. It was as posh as it got. Small words cut from a newspaper were pasted in the message area. It was a couplet: "*Strange death I did foil, as The Victor pen'd. Some day we'll meet, our rivalry to end.*"

Alfred looked up. "Iambic pentameter! Karlo, perhaps?"

"I doubt it. He was never near the Batmobile. But I was away from it." Bruce read over the rhyme—and noticed the capitalization. "There are *two* Hugos in this," he said. "Strange and Victor."

"Victor Hugo wrote of a sewer rescue of a young hero in *Les Misérables*," Alfred said. "A rescue by Jean Valjean."

"Yeah, and look at the zip code," Bruce said.

Alfred read. "Two-four-six-oh-one—Valjean's prisoner number!" He smiled. "Master Bruce, I believe this person is claiming responsibility for saving you from drowning."

"Or sending someone to do it." Bruce turned away to a computer and ran a check. "The return address is Two Clarke Street—but there's no Clarke Street in Amonate." He typed another inquiry. "But get this: Arthur C. Clarke won two Hugo Awards—for *Rendezvous with Rama* and *The Fountains of Paradise*."

Alfred beamed. He flipped the card to its picture side. "Don't you see, Master Bruce? *The Rama Fountain!*"

Bruce took it from him. "So whoever saved me claims to be a rival. A villain? Another hero? Valjean acted heroically but was also a criminal."

Alfred thought. "I think we can only say one thing for sure. *Whoever this is seems to like riddles.*"

BATMAN

WILL RETURN IN

BATMAN: REVOLUTION

BY JOHN JACKSON MILLER

COMING FALL 2025

ACKNOWLEDGMENTS

IN THE SUMMER OF 1989, comic books were a serious business, thanks to many masterpieces—but the general public still saw them as campy, in part due to Batman's TV show in the 1960s. Comics fans looked toward the Caped Crusader's return to theatres with no little amount of dread—made worse by headlines screaming "Biff! Pow! Bam!" As a journalism student editing the University of Tennessee *Daily Beacon,* I felt it, too—but I assigned myself to review the film on opening night anyway. It wasn't like there was anything else to do in town that summer. How bad could it be?

What I found, instead, was a life-changing event. Theatregoers arrived in costume, long before "cosplay" was a word; all cheered as the credits rolled to Danny Elfman's score. And then we were transported somewhere else, with the first words spoken by Prince, telling us he'd seen the future—even as our eyes settled on Anton Furst's amazing Gotham City. By the time Michael Keaton and Jack Nicholson made the scene, we knew nothing would ever be the same. And as the camera and the music climbed to find Batman looking at the Bat-Signal in the final moments, I said it aloud: *This movie just redeemed comics in the popular culture.*

I ended up going twelve times.

Beyond changing the perception of comics, it altered my own path. Three years later, I got a job editing a magazine about comics;

ten years after that, I wrote my first professional comic book. Twenty years after *that*, I was looking forward to seeing Michael Keaton's Batman appear again in *The Flash* when editor Tom Hoeler offered me a chance to do something I never even considered possible: expanding the world seen in *Batman* and *Batman Returns* in prose form.

I'd say I was speechless after I got the offer, but I confess I was instead screaming "Yes!"

My thanks go to Tom, of course, as well as Benjamin Harper and our partners at Warner Bros. My appreciation also goes out to *Batman* co-screenwriter Sam Hamm, artist Joe Quinones, editor Andrew Marino, and the team behind the *Batman '89* comics at DC. Their post–*Batman Returns* setting for the comics partly moved me to explore the time in between the two Burton films instead. Definitely seek the comics out!

I looked as well at two works that I'd already committed to memory years before: the novelizations by Craig Shaw Gardner. As the only places some characters were named, you may have already found a fun reference or two to them. I also greatly appreciate the kind words I received during this project from Michael Uslan, the force behind bringing Batman back to the big screen.

My thanks to Bat-maniac Brent Frankenhoff, who provided not just proofreading, but a sounding board for ideas. My wife, lifetime DC fan Meredith Miller, also helped by proofreading in a year where she didn't have a lot of time to spare.

And as you might have guessed from the last chapter, we're just getting started. Look for my next effort, *Batman: Revolution*, coming soon!

ABOUT THE AUTHOR

JOHN JACKSON MILLER is the *New York Times* bestselling author of the Scribe Award–winning *Star Wars: Kenobi* as well as *Star Wars: The Living Force*, *Star Wars: A New Dawn*, *Star Wars: Lost Tribe of the Sith*, *Star Wars: Knight Errant*, and the *Star Wars Legends: The Old Republic* graphic novel collections from Marvel. He has written novels and comics for other franchises, including *Star Trek*, *Battlestar Galactica*, Halo, *Iron Man*, Mass Effect, *Planet of the Apes*, and *The Simpsons*. A comics industry historian, he lives in Wisconsin with his family, assorted wildlife, and far too many comic books.

ABOUT THE TYPE

This book was set in Dante, a typeface designed by Giovanni Mardersteig (1892–1977). Conceived as a private type for the Officina Bodoni in Verona, Italy, Dante was originally cut only for hand composition by Charles Malin, the famous Parisian punch cutter, between 1946 and 1952. Its first use was in an edition of Boccaccio's *Trattatello in laude di Dante* that appeared in 1954. The Monotype Corporation's version of Dante followed in 1957. Though modeled on the Aldine type used for Pietro Cardinal Bembo's treatise *De Aetna* in 1495, Dante is a thoroughly modern interpretation of that venerable face.